DESTINY'S BRIDE

"Why are you so reluctant to say what it is you want, Breda? Didn't your father bring you up to always tell the truth?"

"Of course he did—"

"Then why won't you admit that from the moment we met, you felt something between us?"

"I was also brought up to believe that a young lady should practice modesty at all times and not be forward."

"I apologize," Richard said. "Besides, it's hardly a father's place to teach a lovely daughter the rudiments of love that I intend to teach you."

Before she could stop him she was enveloped in a dark and passionate embrace, and his mouth was hot and sweet on hers. She made no attempt to struggle against him, for what was the use? He was her destiny, every bit as much as this enchanted place, where scents of bracken and clover and aromatic yarrow stunned the senses like a witch's love potion . . .

DREAM LOVER
JEAN INNES

ZEBRA BOOKS
KENSINGTON PUBLISHING CORP.

ZEBRA BOOKS

are published by

Kensington Publishing Corp.
475 Park Avenue South
New York, NY 10016

First printing: January, 1991

Printed in the United States of America

Chapter One

There was a special scent in the air that April morning, even in Cornwall, where for Breda Vivien every day was scented and special. April was her very favorite time, and unconsciously she tilted her head and breathed in the familiar fragrances of this bursting month, feeling the warm caress of her tumbling dark hair on her slender shoulders as she neared the rugged coastline.

She was never sure which she loved the best, the glittering sheet of ocean stretching away toward a far-distant and misty horizon, beyond which was the American continent and the New World; or this, the wild expanse of moorland, ablaze now with all the glorious colors of spring, the rich purple of heather and the sunshine yellow of gorse, the aromatic white blooms of yarrow . . .

She smiled at her own lyrical thoughts, relieved to find the guilt was lessening that she *could* still smile after the traumas of recent months. But life went on, and her brother Philip would have been the first one to say as much. It was three months now since he had died after doing his patriotic duty for two years in the Crimea for Queen and Country. Three months since she'd heard the news, and been forced at the early age of eighteen years into the role of mistress of the vast Vivien estate and all its assets.

She glanced back toward the direction of the house now, its chimneys just visible above the rise of moorland with its waving grasses and bracken, and felt a warm glow that at least its comforting solidity never changed. The house that was the center of the vast Vivien estate sat high and proud. It was far above the huddled rooftops of Falmouth town, with its jumble of little cobbled streets and enormous sweep of harbor, crowned by the hilltop on which the bastion of Pendennis Castle had stood for centuries.

The whole area was one of natural beauty and history, and Breda was now the rightful owner of the Vivien estate and its tin mines, although for a time there had been some anxiety about that fact. She remembered the family solicitor's dire words and the shock she had felt at learning that the estate was entailed.

"But why was I never told of this?" she had asked the man, appalled.

He had pitied her sad face then, young and straight-backed as she was, brave and slim in her mourning black. Her brother's death had come too soon, even more so after their father's. Then he'd seen the new resolve in Breda's green eyes, seen how they suddenly sparkled and come alive, not so much with the pain of distress but something more. He had known then that she would survive, come what may. Breda Vivien was made of far stronger stuff than most flibberty-gibberty young women of his acquaintance.

"No one thought it necessary, my dear. Philip was fully expected to have inherited the estate, and eventually to marry and produce children in the natural order of things."

"But what now? Just what does this entailment mean to *me*, Mr. Flowers?" She was in no mood to be put off by high-sounding statements or legal phrases. He was white-haired and elderly, and she seemed to have known him since the day she was born, and was in no way intimidated by his legal chambers in the heart of the town.

He looked thoughtful, admiring the ability in one so young to put aside her grief while she attended to practical matters. He spoke objectively.

"It means, my dear Breda, that the estate cannot pass to an unmarried woman."

She gasped.

"Well, if you think I'm marrying the first Tom, Dick or Harry who asks for me—and *especially* one who would have to be a fortune-hunter if he knew of the circumstances—"

Albert Flowers smiled faintly, well used to her outbursts. "I never entertained the thought for a single minute," he said dryly, his tone saying more than the words that he knew very well that the spirited Miss Breda Vivien was never likely to do any such thing. "And if you will just let me finish—"

She clamped her lips together. She had spoken half in jest, but she realized with a sinking feeling in the pit of her stomach that it might come to that after all. If she wanted to keep the home and land that she loved . . . she imagined for a moment the indignity of

7

advertising for a husband to fulfill the role, and pushed away the unpleasant images. Nobody had ever forced her to do anything she didn't want to do, and they wouldn't start now! Her father had frequently called her too willful for her own good, but it was always said with a softness for her that he couldn't deny. She had been his darling, his girl-child . . .

"Please finish, Mr. Flowers," she mumbled. "Tell me what I must do."

He allowed a half-smile. "Well, first off, you can stop this sudden little show of humility. I've known you too long, Breda!"

But not long enough, apparently, to recognize a moment of poignant remembering, she thought.

"What *you* do is nothing. I will do all that's necessary, which is to insert a notice in all the newspapers in the country to the effect that Philip Vivien of Vivien Hall in the County of Cornwall is dead, and asking any living male relatives to come forward, since they may hear of something to their advantage."

Breda felt a surge of anger at the stark words. Something to their advantage . . . She imagined briefly some down-and-out seeing the newspaper item and rushing here with all speed to claim what was hers, and had always been hers. She clung to that thought with a fierceness that sent the color flooding to her cheeks again. But before she could speak, Mr. Flowers had gone on.

"Perhaps I didn't make myself quite clear, Breda — or rather, you didn't give me the chance!" he mildly reprimanded her. "The claimant must be found within six months, or you inherit anyway. If you should marry within that given six months, it would in any case override anyone's claim. But I'm legally obliged to put the information in the public domain."

She put her own interpretation on it all.

"So it's just as I said. If I take any offer of marriage that's going, my home will remain my own even if some shady character turns up out of the blue. And I'll wager there'll be plenty of rogues claiming to be Viviens! It's monstrous, and I can't think how such an entailment was ever sanctioned!"

"I'm sorry, but it goes back well before your father's time," Flowers said with some sympathy. "As to your finding a husband, I hardly think that would be any difficulty! You're a very beautiful and desirable young woman, and if I was fifty years younger myself—"

She wasn't listening to his heavy attempt at flattery. Something else had entered her quicksilver mind.

"What of Wheal Breda? The mine belongs to me, and you know it does! My father named it for me on the day I was born. Am I to lose that too, if some unknown relative turns up out of nowhere?"

"I always thought you considered the name something of an embarrassment," he reminded her mildly.

She brushed that aside.

"You're not answering me, Mr. Flowers," she said insistently.

He sighed, seeing her direct gaze. Few people got the better of Breda Vivien when it came to verbal exchanges. He thought her brighter than many men, and in his world that was peopled principally by men, it was a rare compliment.

"Everything would belong to the claimant," he stated. "But since we've never heard of any relative, close or distant, I think you need hardly trouble yourself too much on that score, my dear. And no rogue would get away with a pretended claim. He would be investigated very thoroughly. You have my word on that."

There was nothing more to be learned, and the newspaper announcements had been duly inserted several months ago. So far there hadn't been a single response. Breda felt her heart lift, knowing that with each day that passed, everything around her became more securely hers.

She gazed down now on the Wheal Breda mine, and felt a stab of pride in its achievements. The mine went out deep under the sea, as did various other Cornish mines, but Wheal Breda had proved to be the richest of them all, producing quantities of the finest tin. The tall stone mine chimney and great engine-house were the only evidence that far beneath those glittering waves, in burrowing tunnels, men worked and sweated for the Vivien estate. In charge of them all was the man striding arrogantly toward her now, the Pit Captain, Sam Stone.

She didn't like him, and never would. He was as hard as his name, black of hair and eyes, and built like a bull. But he was a captain of vast experience in Cornish tin mining, and he extracted good work from the men, despite his uncouthness. Breda often thought it more likely that they worked their damnedest rather than risk his caustic tongue and lash.

"Is everything satisfactory here today, Sam?" she said, following an old custom of her father's by visiting the principal mine each morning for a daily report. Not that Sam Stone ever told her anything of significance, finding it amusing that a chit of a girl should interest herself in mens' doings, and invariably trying to take advantage of the situation.

"Everything's in good order," he said in his usual leering way. "You just leave everything to me, as I've told 'ee a hundred times, me dear. I'll see to the work, and you just pretty up the countryside wi' your pert little ways. We make a good team, you and me, and could make an even better one, given half a chance."

She felt her face flame at his gaze, knowing of his reputation with the village girls, and suppressing a shudder at the thought of those fleshy lips crushing hers.

"You just keep your place, Sam Stone, and remember that Wheal Breda belongs to me, not you! And mind your manners when you speak to me!"

The man chuckled coarsely. "You've as fine a pair of flashing eyes as a man's ever likely to see when you're good and mad, girl," he said, ignoring her words as if they'd never been spoken. "Any man 'ould be glad to tame 'em into softness—"

"Well, that's something you're never likely to see," she snapped, hating him for the insolent way he looked her over like some prize cow. She wished she had the nerve to send him packing, but she knew she lacked the know-how to find another Pit Captain of his worth.

"Just get back to your work, and don't bother me unless it's absolutely necessary."

" 'Twas you seeking me out, not t'other way 'round," he reminded her.

11

"Only because I'm following on my father's custom, you oaf," she flashed back.

"I'll see 'ee tonight then," he called, as she twisted on her heels and began marching away as best she could over the uneven turf. "I'll come and report the day's accounts to 'ee, as is the custom . . ."

His voice dwindled away as she toiled back over the moors, clenching her teeth. She felt the angry sting of tears in her eyes in a rare moment of self-pity. Thoughts milled about in her head. She had never been meant to deal with men such as Sam Stone, nor did she have the desire to do so. She wished briefly that she was taller, so that she'd appear more imposing when he taunted her. She wished her father was still here to deal with these business matters that were strange and unfamiliar to her. She wished desperately that it was Philip coming home from the sea today, instead of the man she was to meet at Falmouth harbor off the steamship *The White Princess* . . .

She paused to catch her breath. What was the use of wishing, anyway? Philip was dead, and Richard Delacey was the man coming home to Cornwall, bringing all of Philip's belongings with him to deposit with a grieving sister. Richard Delacey . . . she'd put off thinking about him for as long as possible, but she couldn't put it off much longer. Breda didn't know him, but she hated him with an irrational hatred, simply because he was alive and Philip was not. And that was just about as wicked as anything could be.

"What in pity's name is the matter with me?" Involuntarily, she spoke aloud in the loneliness of the moors, her soft voice carried away on the breeze.

She was normally known as a buoyant young

12

woman with a keen sense of fun, and here she was, in danger of letting recent events crush her very spirit. And no stranger by the name of Richard Delacey was going to make her depressed. She'd left the house today feeling cheerful in the warmth of the lovely April sunshine, if only because she'd been dreading today, but now it was here and would soon be over. This should have been the best day ever, of course, meeting a ship come home from the Crimea . . . Her own father had always said it was pointless to cry over things that couldn't be changed, and you couldn't ever bring people back, however much you loved them.

She squared her shoulders and went back to the house with her chin high. She'd soon deal with Richard Delacey, whoever he was. She'd give him short shrift, thank him for delivering Philip's things to her and send him on his way. She didn't owe him any more than that, despite the carefully worded letter he'd written her about his intentions. At least the man was a gentleman. Her own thoughts put her instantly into a more positive frame of mind.

She went swiftly up to her bedroom and peered at her heightened color in her dressing-table mirror. The gentle Cornish breezes were too soft and mild to coarsen her skin, and the morning had given her a dewey-fresh look. She examined herself critically, from the glorious fall of blue-black hair that was typically Cornish, to the extraordinarily large green eyes, and the womanly shape that seemed to be emerging more with every week that passed.

She had never lacked for suitors. Despite the new knowledge of the stupid old entailment, she steadfastly vowed that when she married, it would be for love or not at all. So far, no man had even come anywhere near to fulfilling the dreams of a young girl's heart.

"Don't you do it, Breda," her friend, Nan Greenwood, had said in her usual earnest way, on hearing of the outrageous condition. "You could have any man you wanted, so you just be content to wait for Mister Wonderful to come along, the same as I'm going to."

"I have every intention of doing so," Breda had grinned at her friend's round, indignant face. "When did you ever hear me letting a man dictate to me?"

"Well, yes, he'd need to be a pretty exceptional one," Nan agreed with a chuckle. She eyed her friend dispassionately. "Let's see what he requires—he'd have to be wealthy to be a match for you, of course, you couldn't be happy with a pauper—"

"Of course I could, if he was the right man!"

"And he'd have to be tall, dark and splendid," Nan went on relentlessly without pausing to take a breath. "You'd never settle for anything less than perfect, being such a child of nature and always finding perfection in plants and talking to them as if they had ears, and forever wanting to be out of doors as much as possible—"

"You make me sound so *odd*." Breda had giggled, knowing well enough it was true. And the phrase *a child of nature* had charmed her, especially from Nan's prosaic lips, who looked as if she never had a poetic word in her plain little head, and could sometimes come out with the most astounding truths.

"You're not dippy, just waiting for the right man."

"Aren't we all?" Breda countered. "Aren't you?"

Nan looked away, suddenly cross. "Well, you'll never have trouble in finding him anyway. You could charm the birds off the trees with those eyes of yours, though your sharp tongue might scare him off a bit at first."

"I might remember that when I come across this paragon of my dreams," Breda had laughed, hugely amused at this character analysis, and not even airily considering the fact that Mister Wonderful might be anywhere on the immediate horizon. With the blissfully natural assurance of a girl who'd always been able to have anything she wanted, she wasn't even looking for a husband.

The housekeeper was anxious for Yandle to take Breda to Falmouth in the trap to meet the ship.

"I don't need molly-coddling, Mrs. Yandle!" she said in exasperation.

"So you say, but there's many a hazard between here and the town, and the Lord knows what vagabonds are on the road these days," she said darkly.

"I'm perfectly able to take care of myself. I'm not a child any longer."

"Aye, that's certain sure for all to see," the woman muttered. "You're a lovely young woman, and there's plenty of dangers for the likes of you, Miss. I don't forget when you rode bareback over the moor a while back and stumbled over a rotten stump. A sore head and bruised ribs for more than a week wasn't exactly fun for you, I seem to remember."

Breda put her hand on the woman's arm, and spoke more softly, recognizing the concern of a woman who'd served her family well for many years. "Mrs. Yandle, I know you mean well, but I need to do this alone, don't you see? I would have been meeting Philip, instead of this other man, and I want to be alone with my thoughts."

The woman sniffed, not being one to show emotion, and gave up any further attempt to sway Breda's intentions. She merely muttered that Yandle would bring the trap to the front of the house and let Breda go.

And very soon she was climbing into the trap and flicking the horse's reins. She clicked her teeth to get the nag moving. She wasn't afraid of driving him down to Falmouth town by herself. She wasn't afraid of anything.

She kept resolutely telling herself as much, to keep herself strong and to will the rest of this day over. She thought of other occasions when she'd been unafraid, like the time she'd insisted on going into Wheal Breda, simply because it was named after her, and it was her right . . . it had been a chilling and sobering experience, and one that she had never repeated.

Naturally she didn't hold with all the nonsense about the spirits in the mines that even the hard-headed miners believed, or the mysterious knockings the little demons made, wanting their dinners . . . but all the same, she was Cornish to the core, and such tales could never *quite* be disregarded. One visit into the dank dark tunnels shored up by pit props beneath the sea had been quite enough.

But today, brilliant sunlight was dancing over the distant water, and the moors were as familiar as the granite stone of Vivien Hall that had seen generations of her family. So was the great engine-house and towering chimney of Wheal Breda on the slopes of the sea cliffs she was passing now. All of it helped to create a feeling of safety and continuity in her mind, one that gradually lessened the nearer she came to Falmouth town.

The town seemed full to bursting. The arrival of any ship drew the crowds of sightseers like a magnet. One that was newly home from the Crimean war had womenfolk from far and wide flocking to the quay to greet their men with hugs and tears of joy or sadness, according to each returning hero's condition.

Breda swallowed momentarily, and concentrated on the precarious business of controlling the horse and trap through the narrow streets that were milling with people and vehicles. The town had too many crowded buildings for its size, and was frequently rank with smells that were both cloying and nauseous.

She finally neared the quayside, where several large ships and dozens of smaller ones jostled and creaked against one another. She quickly scanned the notices that announced today's arrivals of ships. *The Mallie* from New York . . . *Queen of Sheba* from Tenerife . . . how glamorous and exciting it sounded . . . and *The White Princess* from the Crimea, already spilling its passengers onto the quayside so that she stood still for a moment, wondering what she should do next.

All around her, the sea breezes wafted in a pungent mixture of salt and oil and fish. It was so strong it almost took her breath away. It made her wish even more that she was back in the genteel drawing room of Vivien Hall, with its fragrant bowls of potpouris and floral arrangements, diligently changed by Mrs.

17

Yandle at the first drooping of leaves or petals.

But she wasn't at Vivien Hall. She was here, doing the last thing she could do for her brother, collecting his belongings from the friend to whom Philip had entrusted them. Her brother, Captain Philip Vivien . . . how proud she would have been if he had been one of the regimental officers alighting from *The White Princess* today. And how upset, if he had been one of these other poor wretches she could hardly bear to look at, some having great difficulty because of missing limbs or bandaged eyes, and needing help from willing hands.

She turned away, ashamed of herself for being unable to look at them any longer . . . and realized just as quickly that someone was studying her from the other side of the quay. A tall dark man with broad shoulders and a rich deep tan to his skin most probably gained from spending long hours beneath an eastern sun. Even from this distance, she saw that his eyes were dark as coals, his mouth quite forbidding until he smiled.

He didn't smile at *her* at that moment, but at a lady whose arm he accidentally brushed. Breda saw the lady look up into his face, and saw how her expression changed into that of a coquette at the speed of that masculine smile.

They were a couple who probably deserved each other, Breda thought with brief cynicism. It was entertaining to assess people from a distance and wonder about them, and she and Philip had done it many times in those lovely far-off days of childhood. If she had to assess this tall stranger now, she'd say he was most likely an adventurer, but while the thought spun

18

into her mind, her eyes began searching again for the unknown man she was here to meet.

Even as a sudden unwelcome intuition came into her mind, the dark-haired stranger was standing directly in front of her, blocking her view so that she couldn't see past him. Close beside her, he was even more powerfully built than she had realized. He towered above her so that she was obliged to look up into his face, and it wasn't a feeling Breda Vivien enjoyed.

"Would you excuse me, please?" she said, in a voice that would have frozen a lesser man. The corners of the stranger's mouth quirked upward as if she had said something terribly amusing.

"I'm not sure that I will, if you're the lady I believe you to be," he said.

His voice was almost drowned in the excitement of a group of people suddenly spotting their own returning kin. Breda stared at the man resentfully, wondering if she'd heard aright. She was half willing him not to be Richard Delacey, and half hoping that he was, because she already disliked him on sight!

"I'm sure we've never met before," she said shortly, a little apprehensive at the way the crowds seemed to be closing in around her. She was sure that if she *had* met this man before, she would definitely have remembered him. She was angered for even acknowledging the fact, even to herself.

To her sudden alarm he caught hold of her arm, his grip sure and firm. She remembered Mrs. Yandle's warning in a shiver of fear, as if she were about to be abducted. It would be so easy for an unscrupulous rogue to bundle a girl into a waiting vehicle, and no one would be any the wiser. Breda told herself not to be so feebleminded, and tried to shake herself free as the man's grip tightened.

"Would you please let go of me!"

"Not until I've got you safely to the other side of the quay. Or do you want to be squashed to a pulp by the stretcher cases?"

Breda stood mutely as a small group of wounded men was carried past them by medical orderlies whose only consideration was for their charges, and the devil take the civilians who hampered their progress. The sight of them brought the Crimean War very close, even though it was now thankfully over. For these poor casualties it lingered painfully on, and for the first time Breda was glad her brother hadn't lived to face the life that some of these poor wretches now did.

"Thank you for assisting me," she said as calmly as possible to the stranger. "Please let go of me now."

Her arm was pinched tight by the man's strong fingers, and she would probably bear the bruises of his attentions. If only he'd go away . . .

"Miss Vivien, isn't it?" he said. "Miss Breda Vivien, Philip's sister?"

She couldn't identify his accent. It wasn't softly Cornish, like hers, but it wasn't entirely dissimilar. But she was less concerned with that right now than the realization that he was the one man she didn't want to see and had been obliged to meet.

"How did you know me? You *are* Richard Delacey, I take it?" she added.

"You were described to me very thoroughly by your brother, and besides that, I had your likeness to help me."

As he spoke, a brief smile touched his mouth again and just as quickly vanished, as if he must surely know how painful were these first moments when his very presence reminded her so much of Philip.

"My likeness? Philip gave that to you?" He was the only one who had it, and it was no more than a faded charcoal sketch of herself that Nan had once done. Philip had carried it with him to bring him luck, he'd said jokingly, since he had no lady-love for a talisman.

Her eyes moved slowly from the man's expensive attire, which was that of a gentleman and not the bright scarlet of an officer's uniform, to the light piece of baggage at his feet. Presumably, it contained all the belongings that had once been her brother's, as well as his own effects. In that moment, the thought overwhelmed her.

Because of all the painful memories he would evoke, the day that had begun with such determined cheerfulness on her part, and the ease with which she would dismiss this messenger, dissolved into grayness. The clear blue sky merged into an inky blackness. It was as if someone had turned out the sun as a chill struck through to her bones, and there was no substance in her limbs to hold her up.

Without realizing it, she leaned heavily against the bulk of the man beside her, and his arms reached out immediately to steady her, but it was too late. Somehow she clung to the supporting arms of Richard Delacey and simply let the world swirl away.

She was dimly aware of a jolting movement and of

21

a strange drumbeat close to her ear. For a few moments Breda felt completely disembodied, and then she realized she was being carried in someone's arms, and that the drumbeat came from someone else's heart. Richard Delacey! She glowered up at him through a haze of embarrassment as he strode away from the quayside with her as if she was feather-light, his baggage easily slung over his arm.

"Where are you taking me? Put me down at once!" She said through dry lips, feeling no end of a fool.

"Certainly." He dumped her on the ground, and even while she registered that here was a man who would waste no time with the vagaries of women, dizziness washed over her for a second. She was so cold that she knew she must be ashen. She had never fainted before, and it hadn't been a pleasant feeling.

She heard his voice soften a mite.

"Look, I'm told there's a tearoom in the next street. We'll go there and talk, shall we? I can spare half an hour or so before I check that my trunk is off the ship."

She looked at him speechlessly, red spots of color staining her cheeks now. He could spare her half an hour or so indeed! Her natural reactions bubbled up inside her.

"I thought you'd come to bring me Philip's things. Is this how you treat his bereaved sister, by sparing her half an hour or so?"

She hardly knew why she was so angry with him. He was nothing to her, and she certainly didn't want to spend any more time with him than she had to! But perversely, she didn't see why he should dismiss her quite so abruptly. She didn't see that at all.

"You don't look particularly bereaved to me," he said.

Her mouth dropped open. She quickly reversed her opinion of him. No gentleman would speak to a lady in such an ungallant way. She glared at him.

"I think you've been too long in the company of men, Sir, to know how to speak with a lady," she said caustically, in a way meant to quell him.

It did nothing of the sort, and unexpectedly his face relaxed into a sensual smile that lit his face and made her draw in her breath. When he smiled like that, he was the most handsome man she had ever met, probably no more than thirty years old, with the kind of arrogant self-assurance that could easily make him a rogue or a confidence trickster, or a lover . . .

"You're quite right, of course, and it's something I've every intention of putting right in the future. War makes a man forget the finer things in life, like the smooth touch of a woman's skin and the softness of her hair."

For one wild moment she really thought he was going to reach out and wind a tendril of it around his fingers. And she had the uncanny feeling that if he once did that, she would be entwined with him forever. She shook off the feeling at once. She had only just met him, for pity's sake! How could she be having such strong and powerful feelings about the man?

"It's all due to being a child of nature," she seemed to hear Nan's fanciful voice droning. "When you meet your Mister Wonderful, you'll know it, sure as the sea ebbs and flows, and there'll be no stopping you from losing your heart to him, whether he's good or bad."

"That's stupid talk," Breda said out loud before she

23

could stop herself, just as if Nan had been talking beside her. She saw Richard Delacey's face harden, and realized he thought she'd spoken in answer to his own words.

"I'm sorry you think so. From the way Philip talked about you so much, I expected to meet someone as bright and charming as himself. I didn't know my words would offend you so much, and I apologize for them. Let me buy you some tea and hand over Philip's things to you, and since it would clearly be your wish, you and I need never meet again."

She stared ahead numbly as he steered her toward the nearby tearoom, with its welcoming smells of hot spicy buns and fragrant brews. And while they were being seated and Richard was ordering tea for them both, she was asking herself just why his last words should have sent her spirits spiraling downward.

"Philip wrote a letter for you shortly before he died," he said abruptly a little while later. "I think you should read it now if you can bear it. Perhaps then my presence won't be quite so unpalatable to you."

"I'm sorry if I seem so—so—"

"Unfriendly? Yes, you do." He was relentless. "You obviously have no consideration for the fact that I lost a good friend in Philip, and meeting you was also something of an ordeal for me."

She hadn't even considered this aspect of it, she thought guiltily.

"I'm so sorry," she mumbled again, and then she felt his hand close over hers, completely covering it as it lay on the table.

24

"Will you please stop saying that you're sorry! I think I prefer it when you're angry. It's more your usual style, I suspect, although I'd like us to part friends if that is possible."

He didn't wait for an answer, but handed her a long envelope. She opened it silently, and the ghost of her brother was speaking the written words in her ear.

"My dear Breda," it began,

"If you're reading this letter it will mean that I'm dead and I want you to promise not to be sad for me, love. I've always had the strongest feeling that I'll never see Cornwall again, so this is my good-bye to you.

"I'm entrusting this letter to Richard Delacey, a good friend. You can trust him implicitly, and let him advise you in matters concerning Wheal Breda. He's a first-class engineer and it's long past time attention was given to the old workings, so don't neglect them.

"I know you've a will of your own, but you could do far worse than marrying Richard, Breda. He'd be my choice for you, so give it serious thought. God bless you."

Chapter Two

Richard Delacey silently handed her a clean handkerchief. She took it blindly, wiping her eyes and then blowing her nose hard.

"Keep it," he said dryly, when it was obvious she didn't quite know what to do with the piece of linen. "You'll probably be needing it again before the day's out."

"I doubt that. I rarely cry," she said, on the defensive at once.

He looked at her as if she were an idiot child. Come to think of it, it was the way he made her feel, Breda fumed.

"Then you should. Tears are healing and help to release the tension inside you. Without them, you're like a volcano ready to erupt at any minute."

"You fancy yourself an amateur philosopher as well as an engineer, I suppose?"

"No, just an observer of human nature."

How had she ever thought him charismatic! He was insufferable, thinking he knew everything about her. The fact that he was right only made his analysis the more irritating.

She remembered Philip's letter. This man would be his choice for her indeed! Much as she had loved her brother, she knew he had been more gullible than she was, and more easily taken in by a clever man. Besides, Breda was perfectly capable of finding her own husband, and would do so in her own good time.

"It can't have been easy for you to read Philip's letter in the company of a stranger. I should have suggested that you do it at home. It was my mistake, and I apologize for it." Richard said.

It was obviously meant to reassure her, but it had the opposite effect. She wondered suspiciously if he always tried to find the right words to say. Carefully *studied* words, perhaps?

She pushed all that aside as her thoughts went to something else Philip had written. The man was an engineer, and Wheal Breda's old workings needed urgent attention. The tinners had been muttering such things for years, but her father had always rejected the possibility of the mine flooding, the constant fear of the owners whose mines went far out beneath the sea.

Of course there was seepage. The tinners themselves accepted it, but Breda's father had always asserted that it was perfectly natural, and there was no call for panic. Breda, who knew nothing at all about it, was confident that her father had been right. And if technicians were needed, there were Cornish engineers who knew the land and its substance far better than a stranger.

"Where do you come from?" she asked Richard, the question taking him by surprise.

"From the south of Ireland, although I've lived and worked in England and abroad for many years now. I've gone wherever my work has taken me."

She still sensed that he spoke as if he indulged her, as if she'd had a shock that was scattering her thoughts so that she would discuss anything but the thing uppermost in her mind, which would naturally be her brother. He was wrong, but she didn't enlighten him.

In fact, if the truth were told, it was a relief to have got today's errand over and done with, and she'd had three months to get used to the idea that Philip was never coming home again.

"That explains it then. You're a grockle." She was suddenly crisp, amused, her emerald eyes gleaming in the soft lamplight of the tearoom. Because now she understood the origin of his richly rounded and undeniably attractive accent.

"A what?" He began to laugh, wondering if she was slightly deranged after all.

"A grockle. Foreigner. Somebody from upcountry England, or even worse, from across the Irish sea! We don't take kindly to strangers, Mr. Delacey. We're a very insular race, we Cornish."

She spoke teasingly, but with a steely warning in her voice. She couldn't stop the words tumbling out, but she was secretly annoyed at her own rudeness. Her father would have washed his hands of her, saying that such talk was for the lower orders, not for the more educated, like themselves, and certainly not for the daughter of the Squire of Vivien Hall!

"It's the same in the isolated area of Ireland where I was born." Infuriatingly, he took the sting out of her

28

words by agreeing with them. "It's odd to think it takes something like a war on the other side of the world, where islanders of the same race are thrown together in a common cause, to make friends of us all."

She saw that he was refusing to be angry with her. Or perhaps she just didn't matter to him. She was simply the young sister of a friend he'd once known, and he'd be as anxious to part company from her as she was from him. The realization of it piqued her far more than it should. But his next words told her she was wrong again.

"I'd best go and see that my trunk has been put ashore. Will you be all right while I go back?"

"Of course I will! Just give me Philip's things and I'll go on home when I've finished my tea."

"You'll do no such thing. I shall escort you there personally. I know something about the lonely Cornish roads, and I understand that Vivien Hall is across a considerable expanse of moorland. Wait here for me. In the meantime, you might like to look through the bag at your feet. Everything in there belonged to your brother."

She stared after him. He was taking control of her life in a maddeningly authoritative manner. She had no intention of waiting here for him, nor of allowing him to escort her home. She didn't need escorting anywhere!

When he had gone, his tall frame exciting considerable interest from several young women seated near the entrance, Breda looked down at the expensive leather holdall. She couldn't look inside it for a long time, and finally she opened it carefully and slowly. There was a folded regimental uniform inside. On top of it was a leather wallet that she recognized at once. There were the usual personal effects, hair toiletries, a bundle of letters from home, her own charcoal likeness . . . her eyes blurred as she bundled the lot back into the leather bag.

However stoical she was, she wasn't ready for this yet. Not here, in this anonymous place. She needed the seclusion of her own room to weep a little over Philip's things, and then to put them away and be strong, the way their father would want her to be. She'd been a tomboy child, and her father always said she should have been a man . . . but she didn't have a man's strength, nor did she want it. Sometimes it was simpler just to be the woman that she was and give in to her emotions, just the way Richard Delacey had suggested.

"Drat the man," she stormed inside, but the words came out loud. "I've only just met him, and already he's getting under my skin."

"Do you always talk to yourself, or is it a Cornish peculiarity?" his voice said beside her, making her jerk up her head, startled.

"How long have you been standing there?" she said accusingly.

"A minute or two. My trunk had already been put ashore with an urchin looking after it, so if you're ready, we'll go."

Breda stared resentfully.

"You don't have to feel responsible for me, you know. I'm quite capable of looking after myself. I'm not a child!"

"I can see that perfectly well for myself," he answered, and for the first time she realized the way his gaze was running over her in a slow and sensual manner that told her exactly how he was seeing her. It was a look that made her pulses suddenly race and her cheeks burn.

"I choose to make you my concern," he went on. "It was Philip's wish that I should do anything I could for you. He had another hope for us too, although I realize this is neither the time nor the place to discuss it."

So he was aware of Philip's suggestion that she should marry him! Or had he perhaps put the idea into her brother's mind while he lay dying, knowing that Breda would now be a wealthy woman? How could she tell? Her fertile imagination ran away with her, and nothing about this man came out well.

"I would prefer it if we parted now," she said coolly. "I take it you have somewhere to stay in Cornwall, and people to visit?"

She knew she'd said the wrong thing as soon as he answered.

"I hoped you'd ask me to stay at Vivien Hall for a few days. I'd like to see the place that Philip told me so much about, and I think he expected it. He was also anxious for me to make a detailed study of the Wheal Breda mine, and naturally my professional services are at your disposal, free of charge, Breda."

"We do have engineers in Cornwall," she said, bristling, and deciding he was just too smooth to be true.

"Is there one working for you now? From Philip's remarks I gathered there was some urgency to make a full inspection."

"You probably already know that there's no one. I imagine you know all that was in my brother's letter, so if you're really anxious to take a look at the mine, you can stay at the Hall for a couple of days."

It was as ungracious an invitation as was possible to make, and she hardly knew why she tried to anger him with every sentence. He didn't take the bait, but merely said gravely that it would be his pleasure to visit her home. His impeccable good manners made her feel very gauche and young and very much less than the young lady she haughtily tried to be as she swept out of the tearoom with her head held high.

He insisted on first-name terms. Breda's father had brought her up to know her place and to insist that others knew theirs. There were two types of Cornish people, the free and easy workers, and the gentry. With the insularity of the well-bred Cornish, the Viviens weren't given to informality on short acquaintance, but Breda knew instinctively that this man would cut right through the conventions.

She hardly knew what to make of him, nor why he should be so concerned about her. Unless he really was a fortune hunter who had wormed his way into Philip's confidence.

And then she felt her heart thud as they went to the waiting horse and trap . . . had *she* been his target all the time? She was acknowledged to be the young and lovely daughter of Vivien Hall, and now its heir. The inheritance was a rich one, including the stately house and vast tracts of land, and the rich undersea tin mine and all its assets, as well as several smaller ones along the coast.

Breda Vivien was now a woman of some substance, and she could obviously fire a man's interest in other ways than the mere sexual. She wasn't sure that the knowledge pleased her overmuch.

"Have you been to Cornwall before?" she asked abruptly, as Richard helped her into the trap. Without asking her permission, he took up the reins himself.

"Oh yes. I've always worked farther afield than this though, around St. Austell and the china clay country. But the engineering problems of miners are much the same, whether they mine for tin or clay or gold—"

"Gold!" She was startled out of her suspicions for a moment.

"I was in America when gold fever struck in the far west. It didn't concern me at the time, but I well recall the madness among those who lusted after it."

She stared, never having met anyone who had traveled across the Atlantic Ocean before.

"You seem to have traveled extensively . . . Richard." She forced herself to say his name. "Is America an exciting place?"

He gave a short laugh. "If by exciting you mean civilized, then no! At least, not in the gold fields. Of course, it was all newly discovered then, and there was a frenzy for the first prospectors to make money and stake their claims. It was more often hell on earth, with the heat and the steaming downpours and ruthless men that were drawn there like moths to a flame."

She was surprised by the bitterness in his voice. She spoke in her usual frank way, words first, thoughts later. "Why did you stay then? Why did you even go there in the first place? You say it didn't concern you, but weren't you greedy for some of this gold as well?"

He looked at her, and she was caught off guard by the intensity of his dark eyes. They were strained now,

33

as if with the pain of remembering something he'd far rather forget. For a wild sweet instant, she felt an urge to put her arms around him and kiss away that pain . . . and then remembered that it was hardly the way a well brought-up girl reacted toward a stranger.

"I had my reasons," Richard said.

She turned away and the moment was gone. She lifted her head a fraction, with what her father always used to call her horse's mane reaction. She was annoyingly intrigued by Delacey, and it always infuriated her when people became enigmatic just when she was dying to know more.

Then she decided that she didn't really care what his reasons for leaving America were, because although she'd felt obliged to offer him hospitality, he'd soon be on his way and they need never meet again.

"Well, whatever your reasons, and whatever kind of folk you met in America, you'll find us a different breed, even from those farther upcountry in Cornwall."

Richard laughed, urging the horse into a healthier action after his lengthy wait at the quay.

"That's the second time you've referred to this mysterious 'upcountry'. If you're trying to frighten me away, I must warn you that I don't scare easily, Breda. When you get to know me better, you'll know that when I see something I want, I dig my heels in."

She looked at him again, her eyes flashing. Whether or not a double meaning was intended, she took it that way. She admitted that at any other time, she may well have been charmed by the thought. He was looking straight ahead now, and in profile he was a very handsome man, with a long straight nose and a very strong chin. He had a well-shaped head that sat proudly on his shoulders, adding to that undeniable air of arrogance. His hair was as rich and black as that of the true Cornish men.

She could see at once how her more gentle brother would have been overwhelmed by the character of the man. Philip had never wanted to go to war, and it had only been their father's insistence and family pride that had made him enlist and play soldier. And with what dire results, she thought with a twist in her heart.

Young as she was, Breda knew she had always been made of stronger stuff than her brother—as certain potential suitors had found out, she thought, knowing how her own refusal to play the simpering miss had thwarted their attentions. Wayward, strong-willed, obstinate . . . all had been applied to the head-strong Miss Vivien at various times, and not always in a complimentary way.

"I hope your remark doesn't apply to acquaintances as well," she said, deciding that sarcasm was the best way to deal with this. "You'll find that even in the wilds of Cornwall, ladies expect to be treated properly and that we also prefer *gentlemen* to rogues."

She felt a little shiver of excitement as she spoke, because most gentlemen of her acquaintance were deadly dull, and this one promised to be anything but that. He'd traveled the world, for one thing, and not of necessity nor at the Queen's expense . . . oh yes, he definitely intrigued her. She no longer bothered to deny it.

"You're including me in the latter category, I presume," he said calmly.

Breda felt that she may have met her match. He met statement with statement. There was no arch flirtatiousness in his manner. He spoke his mind, and she realized she was beginning to enjoy the sparks that crackled between them.

At least he was more interesting than some of the overly genteel men she was obliged to meet at county balls and the midsummer festivals and gatherings of which the Cornish were so fond. She was working on something scintillating to say at that moment, when she heard a sudden thundering of horses' hooves.

"Hold on to me!" Richard snapped. "Link both arms in mine and hold tight."

A pair of horses pulling another vehicle was running out of control down the steep hill that they were climbing. The horses narrowly missed a group of people screaming and cowering near a doorway.

Without thinking, Breda did exactly as her companion ordered, clutching his arm with both hands locked together, and felt real fear as their trap rocked crazily when one of the runaway horses brushed their own.

She wanted to scream, but she seemed incapable of making any sound. Terror had dried her mouth and prickled her skin. She didn't want to be crushed against a wall by some beast of a horse. She wanted to live, to get to know this man who had come into her life . . .

Fleeting, inconsequential thoughts flashed into her mind during the moments of danger, and she could no more stop them than stop the foaming, lathered horses charging past them, their eyes rolling, their driver desperately trying to stop their hurtling descent.

Breda was conscious of the brute strength in the man by her side as he fought to gain control of their own terrified nag despite the hampering of her embrace. That he was skilled as a horseman was undeniable. He was the type who would be skilled in everything, she thought numbly, in the eternity it took before they were free of the steep hill, and at last the horse was trotting more calmly onto the open moorland above the town of Falmouth.

By now she was shaking all over. In the last few minutes they might both have been killed. A sob was torn from her throat, and she realized she was still clinging to the arm of the stranger. But his soft words were all for the horse, gentling him, as her father used to say. And then at last he turned to her.

"My poor sweet love," he said, in a soft voice that was more usually reserved for animals and children — or for more intimate tete-a-tetes between a man and a woman. "This has been quite a day for you, hasn't it?"

Somehow his arm was around her shoulders, and he was pulling her into him, and it was much simpler just to lean there until the trembling stopped. Except that it didn't stop, and slowly it dawned on her that this was a different kind of trembling now, because it was the first time she had been so close to a man who wasn't a relative. A man like this — powerful and dominant — and still something of an enigma.

She was aware that she could feel the warmth of his thigh against hers, the wool cloth of his trousers and the thin fabric of her saffron yellow gown doing little to stop the heat generated by their limbs where they

37

touched.

In those still unnerving yet heady moments, she was aware of something more—it was as though all her senses were coming alive for the first time in her life. She breathed in the scent of the man, his clothes, his skin, and wondered wildly if she was in the grip of some kind of madness.

Her voice seemed to stick in her throat as she first tried to speak normally, and then resorted to a more frivolous tone.

"There's no need for you to concern yourself about me at all, I assure you! I'm nothing to you, and you were merely being kind and acting as delivery boy. And, well, if I've been exceptionally contrary at times, then I apologize, and assure you I'm grateful for your kindness—"

"For God's sake, don't you think I know all that?" Richard was suddenly rough-voiced. "And don't say that you're nothing to me. Your brother was my friend, and through knowing him, I know you."

"Please—I don't want to talk about Philip," she said, her mood changing swiftly once more. "It's not that I don't feel emotion, but I prefer to control it—"

She heard his explosive oath. It didn't shock her, hearing plenty of such words from the tinners.

"There's always more trouble in this world because people are damn fool enough to control their emotions instead of letting them out!"

Breda gasped, fury overcoming every other emotion at that moment.

"I'd thank you not call me a damn fool, Mr. Delacey—and I promise you I feel the sting of that very sharply."

He grinned down into her flushed, outraged face, glad she wasn't so much a lady that she couldn't say exactly what she thought. He was even more glad to know that she was the woman he had expected to see.

"Then perhaps it's time you felt this," he said, his voice suddenly soft.

And before she could protest or guess at his intentions he had pulled her closer into him, trapping her with both arms. His head was against the light and she couldn't read the expression in his eyes. But she could feel his breath on her face, warm and seductive. He held her captive by his powerful embrace, and then his mouth was pressing hers.

It was no more than a touch at first, his firm male flesh meeting her pliant softness, and then it deepened and held her breathless, his mouth moving hungrily against hers with all the passion of a virile man who had been without a woman for a long time. And for all the ferocity of it, Breda knew now that there was all the difference in the world in a man's kiss that was not that of a father or a brother.

She knew she was being manhandled in a captive manner, and that she should kick out . . . but the sweet abandonment of desire overcame all reason, all other thoughts. Her eyes closed involuntarily, but the dazzle of sunlight was still there behind her closed lids, and pleasure washed over her like a warm rippling breeze. She was pressed as tight to him as if they shared the same skin and she lay against him and let it all happen, glorying in the sensations that were new and spectacular.

Vaguely she became aware of another vehicle rattling by, and she pushed him away from her, remembering her position, and just as swiftly as she'd felt the sweet surge of desire for this man, she felt a burning anger toward him.

He had been able to make her forget, wantonly and disgracefully, the very reason for his being here—to return her brother's belongings.

"How dare you do that," she whispered raggedly, pressing her hand to her mouth where his own had been.

She heard his heavy breathing, and knew that the kiss had not affected only her.

"You're quite right, of course," he replied in a slow, enigmatic voice. "This was neither the time nor the place, and would be far better kept for another day."

She felt her face burn once more. "I think you misunderstand me! I've no wish for your attentions at all, and I'd thank you to remember it."

His eyes were gleaming in a way that she found disconcerting. Was he laughing at her now?

"*You* may believe that, but no man who had just held you in his arms would be as ready to do so," he said, in a maddeningly rational way. "I'd say that you're a woman very much in need of a man."

"Good God!" She said, forgetting all about propriety now in the face of this outrageous man. "You've no right to speak to me in that way, nor to suggest such things. It's no more than the way animals behave toward one another!"

Now he was definitely laughing at her. She saw the curve of that handsome mouth and the dancing lights in his fine dark eyes. "We all procreate in the same way."

"Well, I've no intention of procreating with you or

40

anyone else!" she said hotly, deciding he was just impossible. "And I'd thank you to show proper respect to your friend's bereaved sister."

She clung to her dignity as best she could, deciding that Richard Delacey was indeed an adventurer, and the sooner she got rid of him the better. A few days hospitality, that was all . . .

She stared directly ahead, shrugging his arm away from her shoulders. Her stomach churned as much as her emotions, and the heat in her cheeks was echoed in every part of her. She was even more incensed by the fact that he seemed uncannily aware of the way she was feeling. For those few moments in his arms, she had forgotten everything but the insistent needs of her own body—and he had known it.

Those needs had been totally dormant until now. As the pampered and beautiful daughter of the indulgent Sir Charles Vivien, she had been well-cushioned against outsiders, for the Vivien estate was isolated and they had few real acquaintances. But once her blood was stirred, it was like the momentous release of a volcano . . .

"I don't apologize for my actions or my words." He said, to her further disbelief, as he flicked the horse's reins to get it moving again. "I find it hard to forget that I'm a stranger to you, because I feel I've known you for a very long time."

"If that remark is intended to get you into my good graces, it's a little late."

"Not at all. In fact I've heard Philip sing your praises so often I began to wonder if this paragon of beauty could really exist."

Breda gasped at his nerve. But she approved of one

thing about him. He could speak of Philip quite naturally, which was far more refreshing than the hushed tones of the servants and mine workers when they'd heard the dire news. And even worse, their avoidance of Philip's name altogether as if to wipe him out of memory.

"I probably know more about your childhood than you've forgotten," Richard went on as the trap rattled on toward Vivien Hall. "I know the secret hiding place you and Philip found near the entrance to Wheal Breda where you used to drive your governess mad when she couldn't find you. I know that you once sprained your ankle and had to be carried home through the rain and caught a chill that nearly killed you when you were five years old. And I have your likeness. I knew how you looked, even though nothing could have prepared me for the color of your eyes. You've grown up since the sketch was made, but you see now, Miss Breda Vivien, why you and I could never be strangers. Could we?"

After all that, he turned and gave her that long direct look again, aware that her mouth had dropped open as she stared back at him. Once again her senses flashed a message through every nerve end in her body, loud and powerful and strong. It was just as if she could hear a small insistent voice inside her head telling her the inevitable. That this was the one man out of all the world who was destined to belong to her. Fate had sent him, and there was no denying fate . . .

Or so everybody said. But Miss Breda Vivien, contrary to the tips of her toes, had become accustomed to reversing what the world expected of her, just for the hell of it all. Even to what fate had prepared . . .

"I'll decide when I want to call you my friend," she told him haughtily. "You've got to earn the right to friendship before it's given lightly."

She stared pointedly ahead, but not before she'd seen his swift, charismatic smile. She felt his hand close over hers for a moment and heard his low laugh.

"Did I mention friendship?" She shivered, hearing the seductiveness of his voice. "You and I were meant for far greater things, love. Together we could conquer mountains."

Prosaically, because she was becoming alarmed at the depth of her own emotions, and the unbidden sensations he could arouse in her so unexpectedly, she said, "We don't have mountains in Cornwall."

"Then you and I will invent them. Or find our own."

This conversation was getting beyond her. The Cornish were supposed to be the fey ones, the mysterious, clever ones . . . but this man was oceans ahead of her when it came to wit and repartee. That he was educated she had no doubt—an engineer, she remembered.

They had engineers in plenty in Cornwall, a collective term for those who assayed the veins of ore from the tin and copper mines, examining the precarious wooden structures that went right out under the land or the sea, giving their yea or nay to safety precautions in court cases regarding owners' negligence, often open to bribery and growing fat on the proceeds . . . but she knew instinctively that there was more, much more, to Richard Delacey.

They lapsed into an uneasy silence, until with something like relief, Breda saw the tall mine chimneys of her own tin mines come into view.

Standing like sentinels on the high moors, surrounded by whispering bracken and golden furze and the white blooms of yarrow, they epitomized Cornwall for her like nothing else. She knew this country and was as much a part of it as it was a part of her. Unconsciously, she took long deep breaths, intoxicated as always by the invigorating, sweet-scented air.

"You're very beautiful," Richard made it a simple statement of fact. "I'm amazed that no man has snapped you up already."

"What an inelegant thing to say," she flashed back, somehow feeling that momentarily she had the better of him without knowing why. "I've no wish to be snapped up, as you so charmingly put it."

"Don't you want to be married and have children, and start your own dynasty? I thought it was what every woman wanted."

"Perhaps—when the right man comes along, but I'm in no hurry. I'm only eighteen years old."

"A mere child." She could hear the smile in his voice again, but it didn't have the same power to nettle her in these moments when she was surrounded by all that she loved best, the moors and the sea and the mines, and with the gaunt old granite-built house that was Vivien Hall coming into view on the skyline.

"Anyway, from now on, you can stop looking," Richard said matter-of-factly.

"*What* did you say?" Breda stared, hardly able to believe that anyone could be so arrogant—if he meant what she thought he meant.

Apparently he did.

"I mean that now that I've arrived in your life you

can stop looking for a husband."

God, but he was so insufferable! All Breda's finer feelings scattered like the dust of a dandelion clock in a moorland breeze.

"You surely aren't suggesting that I marry *you,* Mr. Delacey!" She put all the withering scorn she could muster into her voice. Far from being crushed, she saw the dancing lights in his eyes again as he ran one long sensitive finger beneath her chin and his face came very close to hers.

He didn't kiss her again, although she fully expected him to. And she was furious at the sharpening of her senses and the beating of her heart, and even more by her frisson of disappointment when it failed to happen.

"We'll see, my sweet one," he said in that soft sensual voice she was beginning to know. "We'll see."

Chapter Three

Breda discovered that introducing Richard Delacey to the Viviens' housekeeper was surprisingly difficult. In the end she made only a small announcement of the man who had accompanied her home.

It was obvious that Mrs. Yandle was still troubled by the reason Breda had gone to Falmouth to meet him that day, nor had the woman expected him to be with her when Breda returned to Vivien Hall. Especially when the girl was looking suspiciously bright-eyed, but not with any visible distress . . . Mrs. Yandle didn't like strangers.

"Mr. Delacey will be staying for a few days," Breda told her, almost in defiance. "You'll see that a guest room is prepared for him, won't you, Yandie?"

Without realizing it, she used the old childhood name for the woman, used whenever she had wanted to wheedle anything out of her. Mrs. Yandle's sniff was audible as she said that she would, with a dark look at the handsome newcomer. Without any telling, Breda guessed that their two rooms would be as far apart as possible.

Quickly, Breda asked for some tea to be served to them in the parlor and took him along to the pretty room whose windows overlooked a sweeping expanse of sea. He wandered around it for a few moments, with the air of a man who liked to get his bearings as soon as possible, and made a room very much his own by his presence.

"How long have you been ruled by the dragon lady?" Richard asked quizzically at last.

"She's not as fearsome as she likes to appear," Breda said, bridling in defense. "She's known me all my life and she's naturally protective toward me. She's been my nurse and confidante and friend as well as a family servant and deserves my respect."

"Your loyalty is touching."

"And in reply to your other comment," she rushed on, uncertain whether he was sarcastic or not, *"nobody rules me!"*

His tone was frequently half-mocking, and she didn't yet know what to make of him. Sometimes the things he said roused her total mistrust. She told herself that she didn't need this. She didn't have to have him here. He was Philip's friend, not hers. But she didn't want to think too deeply of Philip right now, nor how different this homecoming might have been. A different man at her side, a joyous greeting from the staff, instead of the sad little bundle of her brother's belongings — and Richard Delacey.

"Do you have some antipathy toward servants?" She said, her sarcasm as biting as his.

To her surprise he swore softly. She was well used to the fact that men often took refuge in expletives, but she hadn't expected such an artless question to produce one.

"Only those who prove themselves to be bastards of the first order," he retorted, making her gasp at the venom in his voice.

She was intrigued at once, and immediately wanted to know more, had Mrs. Yandle not come into the room at that moment with a tray of tea and seed cake. The door had been left ajar and it was obvious to Breda that the woman had heard both their remarks. Breda could see that she was bristling with rage at such language in front of her young lady. She banged the tray down on a table, forgot her place and spoke her piece.

"I don't know who you are yet, Sir, but I'd remind you that this is Miss Vivien of Vivien Hall, and even a servant knows that 'tis not respectful to speak so in front of an innocent young lady—"

"Good Lord, Mrs. Yandle, I've heard plenty worse!" Breda stopped her in mid-speech. She knew the woman meant well, but was mortified at being treated like a child, especially in front of this man.

"That's as may be, but you're without a man's protection now, since both your menfolk have passed on, and I dare say there'll be plenty to take advantage, given half a chance." She sniffed hard, and Breda forgot to stay up on her high horse and went to her at once, putting an arm around the ample shoulders.

The bizarre incongruity of it all completely went over her head, knowing how the woman had doted on both herself and her gentle brother.

"Mrs. Yandle, I was forgetting my manners. I should have told you a little more about Mr. Delacey. He's a most respectable gentleman, an engineer in

48

fact. You know that he was Philip's friend, and now he's mine."

Dear God, now she was defending the man! And that last phrase—she hoped very much that Richard Delacey wouldn't see any significance in her choice of words!

"Well, 'tis not for me to say who's to stay in the house, Miss Breda, and I'm sure I never meant to give offense," the woman said stiffly. She glanced sideways at Richard as he spoke gravely to her.

"I promise I won't be a nuisance to you, Mrs. Yandle. And I understand that your man is in charge of the stables here. Perhaps he'll show me some of the horses later on, for sure and I've a great fondness for them."

Breda registered the newly exaggerated accent in his voice, and Mrs. Yandle's eyes were shrewd now.

"An Irishman, are you?" From her tone, it didn't necessarily bode approval.

"That I am, and with as keen an eye for a thoroughbred as any man on this earth. My family breeds them for racing in the south of Ireland."

True or not, this was news to Breda, but it clearly impressed Mrs. Yandle. And Breda was still amazed at the way he had deduced that the one way to get through Mrs. Yandle's prickly hide was by an affinity with her own man in a love they presumably both shared!

If it *was* true, of course, it would explain the way Richard had handled their terrified horse so expertly when they'd been threatened by the runaways on the road out of Falmouth. And if he had a family that bred racehorses in the south of Ireland, it put a different complexion on his background. It spoke of money, and labelled him as something different from the roguish adventurer Breda had suspected him of being.

"Well, if that's settled, can we please have this tea now?" she said, unreasonably put out that her first instincts would seem so clearly wrong. "My mouth is parched, and Cook's seed cake is always delicious. I'll see to it myself, Mrs. Yandle, thank you."

"Very well, Miss Breda." She hesitated. "About the guest room for the gentleman. Would it be one of the ones overlooking the sea in the west wing?"

Unknown to the gentleman in question, this was a moderate acceptance, and Breda gave a slight smile.

"Yes please. I'm sure Mr. Delacey would appreciate a view of the mines and the Atlantic Ocean."

Particularly as he himself had been across that seemingly limitless expanse of water to the continent beyond she thought—a sea voyage that Breda simply couldn't envisage no matter how hard she tried. When the housekeeper had left them, pointedly leaving the door ajar, she poured two cups of tea from the silver teapot and handed a cup to Richard.

"Why are you smiling?" he queried. "I must say it's a pleasant, if not very frequent sight."

She decided to leave the exploration of his intriguing background until later. She laughed, her eyes mischievous and teasing, feeling more relaxed at that moment than at any time that day so far.

"You wouldn't know the significance, but if Mrs. Yandle had continued disapproving of you, you'd find your belongings in a room overlooking the stables, where you'd probably have been disturbed all night by restless horses."

And he probably wouldn't have minded that, given his own background . . .

"So this means she approves of me, does it?"

"For the moment," Breda grinned. "She's always been protective of me, and will be even more so now."

"Why do I sense a warning in those words? And added to that, should I take them as a compliment?" Richard said, the sensuous smile playing about his mouth.

"You must take them as you please," Breda said airily.

"Will my room be next to yours?" he pursued.

She felt the flush deepening in her cheeks. "I doubt that very much! We'll be on the same corridor, which is quite a different thing! The west wing has the most spectacular views of the ocean and enjoys the most beautiful sunsets. And of course, the mine chimneys have a strange beauty of their own. Sometimes they're lit by sunlight so that the granite glints with all the minerals it contains, or in stark silhouette against the night sky—"

"Why are you so nervous with me?" Richard said.

"I'm not!"

Of course not—her palms were always as clammy as this when a charismatic man stared at her fixedly with dark and impassioned eyes that seemed to have the power to mesmerize her . . .

"Then why are you babbling so much? I only asked if my room would be next to yours. It was an innocent enough question."

Oh, but that was a gross understatement! As far as she was concerned, nothing about him was innocent!

51

She ran her tongue over her dry lips. The tea was doing little to quench her thirst, but perhaps it wasn't only liquid refreshment that she craved. She hadn't even realized that she missed something until today. It was all making her feel slightly lightheaded, knowing that his very presence was turning her orderly world upside down.

"I trust that you'll remember you're a gentleman, and that this is a gentleman's house," she said in a voice that was meant to be cold enough to freeze a summer's day, but came out more as a croak.

"But with no gentleman holding the reins now," he stated. "Doesn't that trouble you mightily?"

Breda caught her breath between her teeth, hating him again at that moment. Why did he have to remind her? He wouldn't know about the entailment, of course. He wouldn't know that she would be obliged to marry within six months if a claimant turned up — which so far, thank God, he hadn't!

"That's an unfair remark Mr. — Richard. I lost both my father and brother within the last year, and I consider I'm handling both situations fairly well. Please don't disturb me with any more emotions than I can handle."

He drained his cup and placed it on the table beside him, wiping his mouth deliberately with his napkin. Despite herself, Breda couldn't help watching the trail of the white damask, remembering how that mouth had taken hers and awakened her to a passion more stunning than anything in her life before.

"There's only one way in which I wish to disturb you, my dearest girl," he spoke with a frankness that could have been sincere or insulting. "I only want what I've wanted for a long time now, ever since I first saw your likeness and began to learn all about you from your brother. From that day on I knew there was only one woman in the world for me, and that I must have her—"

"Stop this—please—" she whispered, beads of dampness beginning to stud her forehead.

He didn't touch her, and they were half the width of a room apart, but his sensuality was reaching out to her and making her weak. She was totally unable to stem the tide of desire rushing through her at his look, and it was shameful to be feeling so wanton toward a man she had known for barely half a day, and for such a reason. He bewitched her, she thought desperately.

"I want you to be under no illusions about me, Breda," he went on relentlessly. "I've had you marked as my woman for a very long time, and nothing will change that. I never meant to speak so soon, but I mean to have you. You know that your brother wished it too, and when I want something badly, I never let anything stand in my way."

He'd referred to himself as a husband earlier, but even through her bemused senses, she realized he wasn't speaking about marriage now. He spoke with the primitive simplicity of a man's lust for a woman, and the words were heavily charged because of it. She strove to be outraged, but because something stronger than the mere conventions of the day were taking control of her, it was almost impossible. In the end she sought refuge in the only weapon she had, in a voice edged with sarcasm.

"Has it never occurred to you that I might already

have ideas on the man I want to marry? You're not the only man in the world, you know—"

One minute he was sprawled out in her father's favorite chair. The next, he was across the room and pulling her to her feet as if she was made of thistledown. In an extraordinary, spine-tingling way, it was exactly how he made her feel.

His voice was low, full of that rich timbre that she was beginning to find so dangerously attractive. The mellow Irish accent was more pronounced, and she realized it could be turned on at will, or just deepened naturally when he was aroused. She didn't need to be a clairvoyant to know which state he was in right now. It was blatantly obvious in the most arrogant masculine way.

"I have every intention of making you realize that's exactly what I am, as far as you're concerned. The only man in the world for you, just as you're the only woman in the world for me. We're a matched pair, Breda, and it will be my pleasure to teach you the delights of love. So don't play me up against any imaginary beau. I know from Philip that there's no one else. Your letters were too full of the doings of the estate and the tin mines and the frivolities of a young woman on the brink of life, and never included the remotest hint of an attachment."

He stopped speaking. He'd done all the talking, but it was she who was breathless. The easy way he referred to her brother was emotional enough, but it also sobered her. She struggled to release herself, but his grip was too strong, his face moving down toward hers and his mouth claiming hers in the warm darkness of his kiss once more.

Almost without knowing it, her arms were holding him in return, her mouth responding. Her body was pressed close to his, their heartbeats merging into one throbbing sensation. And there was more . . . she was still innocent of men in the biblical sense, but she felt the way his body hardened against hers, and knew its significance.

After a timeless moment when she seemed to be quite boneless in his embrace, she pushed against him. A lesser man might have staggered and fallen, but he merely stood looking down at her, towering above her.

"You forget yourself, Sir!" she gasped. "I offered you hospitality, not a game played with servants. I'm no whore, to be used whenever you think it amusing. I'd ask you to remember that you're under my roof, and only because of your relationship with my brother. Your attentions are far from welcome at this time."

She bit her lip, knowing it was trembling. She never normally spoke so frankly, nor had any need, and she was shamed by her own words. Besides that . . . what on earth had possessed her to utter that final sentence? It could so clearly be taken to mean the all-clear to court her at a more propitious time. If he noticed it, he didn't comment. Instead, he had a cold hard look about his mouth now that took her by surprise.

"I assure you, love, I'm not in the habit of consorting with servants, still less with whores. And never in this world would I compare you with either. I see that I have my work cut out to convince you of my good intentions, and that this is not the time. If you will

55

excuse me, I would like to see my room and take a bath. I understand that Vivien Hall has all the amenities."

Her chin lifted, her thoughts shifting immediately. "Oh yes. My father had bathrooms installed a year ago. We may live in the wilds of Cornwall, but we're not barbarians. We offer every civility to our guests and expect the same in return."

She spoke with all the haughtiness that had made many a prospective suitor change his mind about courting the lovely Breda Vivien. She saw the small smile chase over his features for a second, and then it was gone as he gave a small bow. She pulled on the bell-rope and the housekeeper appeared in a moment, as if she had been hovering outside. The thought that she might have overheard all that had been said in the parlor annoyed Breda intensely, and she spoke more sharply than usual.

"Mrs. Yandle, please show Mr. Delacey to his room, and then send Yandle to inform Sam Stone that I'll see him in the study at the usual time."

She plunged on, wanting Richard to hear her imperious tones, wanting him to know that she had a status here and that he had better respect it. She said it despite Mrs. Yandle's raised eyebrows, because both of them knew there was no earthly need to remind Sam Stone of his daily appointment in the book-lined study . . . but it also served to remind Richard Delacey that whoever *he* was, *she* was Miss Breda Vivien of Vivien Hall.

She wilted when she was finally alone for the first

time since meeting him. She knew she should be mourning Philip all over again, on this day when she had reclaimed all that was his. She was even guilty that the tears wouldn't come. She felt more bedevilled than bewitched now, feeling it was wrong to be unable to mourn.

It was far too early for Sam Stone to come to the house, but shortly after Richard had left her, she had another visitor. Her friend Nan Greenwood walked straight across the room to take Breda's cold hands in her own. The girl was clearly upset and held Breda's hands tightly.

"Are you all right, Breda? Was it too much of an ordeal for you to go to Falmouth to meet the stranger?"

Breda swallowed, hardly knowing how to answer, but before she could say anything, Nan went on talking.

"I should have insisted on going with you, I knew it! You look so pale. Was the man as horrid as you expected from his letter?"

Her words jolted Breda. She knew there had been something bothering her all this time, and she hadn't been able to put her finger on it. Letters . . . there had been letters from Philip of course, as many as a fighting soldier could manage to write, but never a mention of a close companion by the name of Richard Delacey. Yet there had been so much of her that Richard apparently knew. And so keen a desire on Philip's part that she should marry him.

She wondered now, if Richard Delacey himself had put the idea into Philip's head, and her brother had been too weak or too gullible to recognize a fortune hunter when he saw one. One of the things that still worried her about the man came more sharply into focus.

"Breda, is something wrong?" Nan said, when the girl didn't reply. "If you need a shoulder to cry on, you know mine's broad enough, God knows, and I can guess how your imagination's been working, with this man to remind you all over again."

Breda took a deep breath. Without knowing why, she had to get it all out into the open.

"I've invited him to stay for a few days." She said it quite stoically, not asking for sympathy. "By the way, you'll never guess what Philip said, Nan! He thinks this Richard Delacey would make me an ideal husband. Did you ever hear of anything so outrageous?"

Nan's rather vacantly wide blue eyes widened. She was not the most beautiful of girls, even though just occasionally she sparkled into a simple prettiness. Right now she looked positively pudding-faced, Breda thought uncharitably, feeling she had every right to feel uncharitable in the circumstances.

"I think you're sun-touched," Nan said positively. "Have you started imagining that Philip's sending you messages?"

Breda laughed shortly. "No, I haven't, you ninny. Richard brought a letter with him, and Philip made no secret of the fact that he thought we'd be right for each other."

"And what do you think?" Nan said, staring.

Breda felt her heart lurch. Richard Delacey had come into her life so recently, and yet already he seemed to fill it. It was almost a surprise to think that Nan didn't know him yet. That until now she hadn't

58

known that he was here in this house, upstairs at this very minute, probably lying indolently in one of the new bathtubs, his naked body glistening with soap-suds, the little bubbles bursting on the virile dark hairs of his chest.

"Breda! I'm sure there's something wrong with you! You look so odd, and even your eyes seem to be burning."

But not with any normal pain, Breda thought acutely. They burned with the dawning of a different kind of emotion, one that she was only just beginning to know, and shouldn't even be entertaining on so short an acquaintance, about a man she wasn't entirely sure she could trust.

She became aware that her mouth was dry, and she willed away these erotic images of a man who was a stranger, yet someone whom she felt she had always known. His own words came back to haunt her, and the feyness of her Cornish heritage mocked her determination to remain aloof at all costs. In the heart and soul of her, she knew she could never do it, not as far as he was concerned.

"I'm all right," she said huskily. "The shock of Philip's death was obviously revived when I met Richard Delacey, but I'm all right now."

"So what's he like, this man?" Nan said cautiously. Like Mrs. Yandle, Nan didn't like strangers. She didn't trust them. Sometimes, Breda thought, Nan could be so irritating, needing everything spelled out for her in words of one syllable. It was the inbreeding, Breda's father had once said sagely.

The Greenwoods were an insular lot who had produced children in and out of wedlock within the family for generations in a way that would never be tolerated in more conventional society, and which resulted in a certain simplicity of nature, however wide-eyed and innocent their young women. Nan was a perfect example.

"Well, is he an old dodderer, or someone not half bad? Are you going to tell me anything about him or not!" Nan said, becoming cross now.

Richard's own voice suddenly drawled at them from the doorway, amused, lazy, oozing with unconscious — or conscious — seduction.

"Perhaps you'd care to make a judgement on that for yourself."

As Nan spun round to look at him, Breda saw her eyes widen still more. For a few seconds she tried to see the man as Nan was seeing him, for the first time. Tall, dark, his coal dark eyes were laughing, his clothes fresh, his skin glowing from the recent bath. The aura surrounding him was vital, charismatic, and totally male. He was at once the hunter, the knight in shining armor, the rogue, and Breda could sense Nan's instant infatuation. In fact, she could read it as clearly as if it had been mile high letters written against the cloudless April sky.

The realization infuriated Breda in a way that was completely incomprehensible. She didn't want him, so why should she care that Richard Delacey was smiling so charmingly at her friend, and that Nan was cycing him as if he was God's gift to Victorian womanhood!

"Nan, this is Richard Delacey. My friend, Nan Greenwood." She made the introductions ungraciously, uncaring if they thought her curt. She wasn't

60

here to make cozy alliances between acquaintances. The very thought of it was like a burr beneath her skin.

"I'm very happy to know you, Miss Greenwood," Richard said. "It's a relief to me to know that Breda has had another friend during these last months."

"Another? Oh, I see, you mean yourself," Nan said in some confusion, without seeing anything at all except the sight of this beautiful man.

But she managed to grasp something of the fact that Breda was scowling, and her affections were just as swiftly withdrawn as given. She looked somewhat doubtful now as Richard walked toward Breda and put an arm loosely about her shoulders. His effrontery took Breda's breath away, so much so that she didn't even move, as if the embrace meant less than nothing to her. But she was more affected by the circle of his arm around her than she admitted.

"I hope Breda counts me as her good friend, and that eventually we may be more than friends, just as Philip had wished, but naturally we have to get to know each other properly first."

He took his arm away and moved from her side, with just the right amount of sincerity in his voice to make Nan approve of him, while freely releasing any hope of obtaining this lovely man for herself in the enchantment of realizing that Philip's death had inadvertently brought him and Breda together.

Nan was totally naive, assuming that although they'd been strangers until today, such a fact was cast aside in their instant attraction. Breda could see how the thoughts were chasing around Nan's fertile if somewhat stultified brain. To her it was perfectly clear that the two other people in this room were made for each other, despite Breda's furiously flashing eyes that boded the onset of her usual quick temper.

"Mr. Delacey presumes too much," she said stormily. "But since he was Philip's friend and has brought his effects home, the least I could do was to offer him some *brief* hospitality."

She managed to imply that the man was probably in dire straits, and that it was no more than she would do to help an animal in distress. She was aware of Nan's astonished eyes on her and averted her own.

"Where is your home, Mr. Delacey?" Nan said, attempting to cover what she saw as Breda's lapse.

"In the south of Ireland, Miss Greenwood."

"Oh, please call me Nan! Everybody does."

Richard smiled. "Of course. Well, I live in the south of Ireland in a little place called Kilmenna. My family has always bred horses there."

"And will you return there?"

"I'm not sure yet. I'd planned to do so, but circumstances have a habit of changing plans. I'm a free agent, so it depends on how I feel in the near future."

She might not have been there at all, Breda thought, fuming, still unwilling to admit that Richard Delacey was the most disturbing man she had ever met . . . and that she wanted his total, undivided attention.

Through the window Breda could see the large, swarthy figure of Sam Stone striding toward the house, and guessed that Yandle had taken her words at face value and now Sam would be mad that it wasn't yet his proper time for meeting his employer.

True to form, he approached the front of the house as if he had a right to be there, filling her with the same old resentment against him. She hated his leering eyes and suggestive talk, but her father had sworn by his good sense and management over the tinners in his charge.

"I'm terribly sorry, but I must speak with my Pit Captain about various things," she said swiftly. The daily routine had to go on.

"Then perhaps Nan would care to show me the grounds, while you're occupied?" Richard said. "I dare say you know the place well enough to point out various items of interest."

"Oh, of course," Nan's voice was joyful at the thought. "It will be my pleasure."

Fuming again, she watched them go, wishing their places could be reversed.

Mrs. Yandle announced him, and the man almost pushed past her, stomping into the room and standing with feet apart, and rough hands on hips like some Goliath.

"Is it true we've a stranger among us claiming to be an engineer, Miss?"

Heaven knew how he'd heard the news already. Whether it was through Yandle or the swift grapevine heralding any kind of news, Breda neither knew nor cared. It was none of his business, but she nodded curtly.

"Mr. Delacey is a first-class engineer, and a friend of my brother's. He's visiting for a few days. Now, was there anything else of my personal business you cared to know, or can we get along to the study and get down to our own affairs?"

He followed her along the passage in silence and sprawled opposite her in the panelled study. Across the desk from him, Breda felt less threatened by his presence than she sometimes did. After a small silence, he spoke calculatingly.

"So I dare say there's compensations for you, even after bad times, ain't there, Miss? Not that I'll be that pleased to see a stranger about the place."

She glared at him. The man was so uncouth, he couldn't even see that his words were in appalling taste. She couldn't speak for a minute, and he blundered on, his small eyes gleaming. She realized at once that he'd had more than a fair share to drink, or he'd never have been this bold.

"I mean, you're a right tasty boss, and we don't want no strangers coming in and taking over, do we? You and me both want the best out of the tinners, Miss, and I aim to be the best Pit Captain you ever had. Mind you, there might be certain conditions attached to that, and if you ever wanted to make more of our acquaintanceship than there is now, I'd be ready for it any time you say the word. It wouldn't be no bad thing, an alliance between we two—"

"Get out of here! We'll forget about today's meeting until you come to your senses and sober up, and can speak to me with more respect!" She found her voice at last, and instead of screaming at him, she spoke with venomous control. "You'll do your work the same as you've always done, and if I find that there's any trouble from you, or any hint of making the men go slow, you'll find that a woman's skirts make me no less of a boss than my father was, or my brother would have been."

He stood up, his large hands flat on the desk, the veins in his bull-like neck taut and corded as he leered in a way she always found particularly hateful. "Your woman's skirts ain't going to be a hindrance to me, girlie," he said meaningfully. "One sniff of 'em and I'm your man—"

"Never in a hundred years!" She stood up too, despite the fact that she was head and shoulders shorter than he. She didn't even pretend to misunderstand him. "Now get out before I have you thrown out. You're not the only Pit Captain in the County."

She stood her ground without flinching. Her shoulders were stiff with rage, and then she felt real fear as he came around the desk and put his huge hands on them. She could smell him, dank from the mine and rancid with his own sweat, and it was a great effort for her not to shudder.

"But I'm the best, and we both know it," he sneered. "Don't get too all-fired high-and-mighty with me, Miss Vivien. You might be needing me more than you think yet."

She tore out of his grasp, but she didn't have to scream at him to get out again. He was already moving away from her with his long strides, insolently slamming the door of the study.

Breda's head throbbed. She'd never had to deal with the business side of the estate before now, and she'd made a complete mess of it today. Nothing had even been mentioned of the usual day's assessments.

She wondered now why she ever bothered, hating the daily meetings with Sam Stone. Monetary dealings she could safely leave in the solicitor's hands. It had been her wish to take on the same rituals as her father, as if to pretend that he was still alive, that things continued the same. But they didn't, nor would Philip ever take up the reins.

She could be cheated and she'd never know . . . but the tin mines themselves ran smoothly enough under Sam Stone's dictatorship, and the solicitor saw to everything else. It wasn't a woman's work, but it had never occurred to her until now that Sam Stone could make trouble if he chose. He had absolute control over the men. Breda had never before felt so keenly the loss of a strong man in her life, nor longed for one more . . .

On instinct her gaze went to the window, where Nan Greenwood and the tall handsome figure of Richard Delacey were just coming into view through the shrubbery. Her pulses quickened at the questions spinning around in her head. And the answers she didn't want to acknowledge were already there, in her head and in her heart.

Chapter Four

"I've been telling Richard about the annual spring ball you always have here at Vivien Håll," Nan said the moment they entered the house. Her eyes shone like pale gems, her whole manner more alive than usual—until she recognized the fury in Breda's face.

"Of course," she added hastily, "I realize you wouldn't dream of holding such a frivolous occasion this year, Breda—"

"Oh? And why should you think that?"

Breda hadn't given the ball a single thought until that moment, but feeling contrary and unreasonably annoyed at the way the other girl seemed to be holding the dashing Richard Delacey's attention, she spoke tartly.

"Well, under the circumstances, I suppose I just assumed you wouldn't want to have all those people around," Nan began to flounder. "I mean, it's the first spring since your father died, and then there's poor Philip—"

"Your sensitivity does you credit, Nan," Richard said before Breda could utter a word. "But knowing

Philip as well as I did, I'm perfectly sure he wouldn't want an annual custom denied to all those who enjoy it. My opinion, for what it's worth, is that good traditions should be continued. Life goes on, after all, and Philip would have been the first to say so. What's your feeling on it, Breda?"

She took a deep breath, hardly realizing how she'd been holding it in all this time. "Oh, you think to ask my opinion, do you? I was beginning to think the two of you had it all arranged between you already!"

Nan looked alarmed now.

"Breda, you know I didn't mean to interfere in your affairs with my thoughtless remarks!"

"Oh, all right, I know you didn't. For pity's sake, don't look so sheepish," Breda said peevishly, seeing the ready shine of tears in Nan's blue eyes. "And I suppose you're right at that. I shall have to give the ball some thought. That's not to say I shall definitely go ahead though! If our usual guests were to think it in very bad taste, it would just be a total flop, because none of them would come."

"*I'd* come," Nan said stoutly.

"Good. That's one dancing partner for Richard then."

For the life of her, she couldn't seem to stop the veiled sarcasm, and it didn't help to know very well that Richard Delacey was silently laughing at her. She knew it as sure as she breathed. Nor did she have any idea just why she was being so prickly with Nan, or why she was suddenly consumed with the feeling that she wanted to hit out at somebody.

"Perhaps it's time I went home," Nan said in a

small voice. "I can tell this has been a strange day for you, Breda, and you'll want to be on your own for a while. Will I see you tomorrow?"

Taking in the sight of her crestfallen face, Breda immediately forgot all about being high-handed and gave her friend a quick hug. She spoke quickly.

"Of course you will, goose. Come to tea—and, oh blazes, just ignore my scratchiness, will you? You're quite right. Today has been—well, odd, to say the least."

"I know," Nan said generously. "And I don't blame you for feeling strange—especially about the other matter we discussed. And you can't deny that he'd fit the requirements handsomely! If I were in your shoes I'd stop looking a gift horse in the mouth and take what's offered!"

She mixed her metaphors glibly, evidently taking Breda's words to refer to the marriage proposal, but her response was in such a loud stage whisper that Richard couldn't fail to hear it. He was smiling broadly as Nan left the house. Breda tensed her hands at her sides, silently counting to twenty, since ten would never be enough to calm her fractured nerves, especially with Nan's oblique reference to the fact that Breda might need a husband pretty smartly if ever some remote claimant to the property appeared in answer to Mr. Flowers' advertisement. She prayed that Richard wasn't going to be overly curious about Nan's words.

He'd stayed where he was while she showed Nan out with fierce instructions not to be so free with her words, but when she returned to the room she found herself holding up her hands, palms toward him, as if to ward him off.

"Please don't say it — I know I goad Nan unnecessarily at times, but we've been friends far too long for her to take offense, and our relationship probably takes a bit of understanding."

"I think I understand it perfectly," he said.

She glared at him. "Of course you don't. How can you? You're a stranger here." She stopped abruptly, because in an infuriating way she knew that somehow they had never been strangers, nor were destined to be.

Her own brother had stated that he'd choose Richard for her husband, a wish echoed by the man himself. And she was honest enough to admit grudgingly that out of all the world, he was definitely the most *interesting* man she'd ever met . . . and the most virile, intelligent, and yes, handsome.

Damn Philip, she thought, shamed and appalled at even letting such a thought into her head about her beloved brother . . . but she couldn't think what had possessed him to do this to her. Dictating his wishes, even from the grave . . . she shivered, wishing such a ghoulish thought hadn't entered her head.

And against the two of them, she wasn't sure how long her own desires were going to hold out. She wasn't even sure why she was so insistent on keeping Richard Dclaccy at arms' length, but it probably had a lot to do with the fact that the man she married had to be *her* choice and not someone chosen for her, or forced upon her.

Such customs were well relegated to the past, even

here in the depths of Cornwall, where life stood blissfully still compared to the fashions and foibles of upcountry England.

Richard didn't even comment on what she'd said, but sprawled out in one of the best armchairs, already looking as if he owned the place.

"Why don't you tell me more about this annual spring ball? You and I both know Philip would have said go ahead with it. And I'd say it was the best thing that could happen for you."

"Oh? And why is that?" she said, sparkling at once, and wondering what gave him the right to decide what was best for her!

"You need something to clear away the gloom of the past and have something to look forward to. Besides that, it would be a good night to announce our engagement."

She gasped. "I haven't said there's going to *be* any engagement."

"You haven't said there isn't," he said calmly. "And incidentally, just what are these requirements that Nan thinks I might fit?"

So he *had* heard it, and bided his time to ask her about it. She ignored it totally. In any case, she thought she'd made it plain enough that there wasn't going to be any engagement. Richard Delacey wasn't a fool, and he'd have guessed easily enough what Nan meant, though please God, not the real reason for it . . . He was obviously trying to goad her into a discussion about their so-called relationship, and as far as she was concerned, nothing of the kind existed.

71

"I hope that by suggesting I should continue with the annual ball you don't imply that I should forget my father and brother," she said icily instead.

"Of course I don't. God knows I'd never want that. I'd remind you that Philip was my friend too. But you can't mourn forever. You're a lovely young woman, and you must look to the future."

The compliment went over her head. Her eyes were bright with anger, drawn into whichever way he turned the conversation, despite herself.

"And I suppose you see yourself as part of that future?"

A lesser man might have replied humbly that he wished it only if it was what she wanted. Richard Delacey's slow sensuous smile made her catch her breath. His voice was rich with meaning, the Irish brogue exaggerated for effect.

"I was part of your future from the day you were born, me darling."

He was outrageous. She lifted her chin and felt it tremble at the way his gaze rested on her soft mouth and then go lower, moving slowly and lingeringly past the fast-beating pulse in her throat, to where the soft swell of her breasts felt suddenly naked at that hot look. It was just as though his look stripped her of all her garments, and she felt a rushing need to cover her body with her hands and keep what little control she had over herself. She'd always considered herself a strong woman, able to control her own destiny, but she'd never faced an equally strong personality before, one whose destiny he clearly saw as inextricably bound up with hers.

"I insist that you stop saying these things to me," she intended to speak imperiously, but the words came out as a mere husk of sound.

"Why do you insist on such an impossible thing?" Richard spoke gently now, in a voice that oozed seduction, as if he no longer had to put pressure on her. He still didn't touch her or move closer, yet she felt that with every glance, every word, every breath he took, he held her captive.

"Is it so very distasteful to you to consider being my wife, Breda?"

Her eyes closed briefly, and immediately she wished they hadn't. In that instant, the imagery of being Richard Delacey's wife was too vivid, too glorious, and far too wanton to be comfortable. Her eyes flashed open again, and in that moment he had moved across the room, his movements sure and graceful for so large a man; and before she could say anything more, she was in his arms.

"In case I've been clumsy with my intentions, I'll be more formal. Will you be my wife, Breda?"

She looked up into those dark, intense eyes, willing the response he wanted from her, and felt the male hardness in his body as it pulled her close to him. Desire seared through her like a flame, awakening all the hidden fires within her. It would be so easy, perilously easy, to give in to those desires, and go where all her senses were leading her. But just as instantly, she knew that desire wasn't enough on which to build a marriage. There had to be something more. There had to be love.

"No," she whispered. "I won't marry you."

His embrace tightened until she felt as if her bones were about to be crushed. Far from being incensed by her reply, his dark head bent toward hers, and she was enveloped in his dark kisses. And dear God, but she couldn't deny the primitive need that he aroused in her . . . she felt almost shamed by the power of her own desires, but hardly knowing how it happened, she was holding him close to her, and kissing him back.

"Why won't you marry me?" he said aggressively, when his mouth was a mere breath away from hers. "Everything about you tells me that you feel the same way I do."

"And how is that?" she whispered back, unable to free herself from his embrace.

"Don't you know?" As he looked down at her, the flame of passion ran through her again, making her weak, drying her mouth, heating her skin.

She could hear sounds of life in other parts of the house, and imagined Mrs. Yandle's horror and outrage if she came to the room and found her mistress and the stranger locked in a compromising embrace. She wrenched herself out of his arms. She backed against the wall, and knew at once that it was a mistake, because he followed her, his dark shape almost enveloping her.

"I know that you forget yourself, Mr. Delacey," she said as freezingly as she could. "You knew that my brother was a gentleman, and it's not the practice for a stranger to enter a gentleman's house and try to sweep his sister off her feet."

"You would prefer a slower courtship, then?"

It wasn't what she had meant at all, but it seemed as if there was no way she could rebuff the man.

"I prefer no courtship at all!"

In answer, he ran one finger sensuously around her cheek until it touched her full bottom lip. Before she knew what he intended, the tip of his finger moved, feather-light, over her chin and down, until it reached the fast-beating pulse in her throat . . . and then lower. Somehow she was finding it hard to breathe as that one finger was joined by two more, sensitively moving across the deep valley of her breasts, tantalizing, teasing . . .

Breda knew she should stop this at once, but she seemed totally unable to move. Her skin tingled with awareness of his touch, and he was sending her into a kind of trance. Then his hand slid across the outside of her gown to cup her breast, and she felt its treachery as her nipple yearned against his palm.

"You see, my Breda?" he said softly. "Your voice tells me one thing, but your body tells me another. Have you never heard of the language of the body?" His hand exerted a firmer pressure for a moment. "This is part of it. So is your fast breathing, and the darkening of your pupils."

She jerked her head up to look into his eyes.

"Is that why yours are so much darker too? Can it be that the dashing Richard Delacey is also affected by the mere chemistry of a woman's attraction?"

She heard the way he breathed more quickly too, and he was standing so close to her that she could still feel the hard evidence of his desire.

He gave a short laugh and moved away.

"Any man who isn't affected by a woman's attraction isn't worthy of being called a man," he said. "But never call what we feel mere chemistry. Chemistry doesn't take account of two peoples' emotions."

She'd had enough of this character analysis, and more than enough of the way he was turning her ordered life upside down. She spoke deliberately, her own mistress once more, at least for the present.

"I don't feel anything for you, Sir, except a polite regard for a friend of my brother and gratitude to you for bringing me his belongings today. Apart from that, I've no intention of feeling anything more."

She swept out of the room, not caring what he was going to do with himself. As his hostess, she knew she should be seeing to his comfort, but it seemed to her that his main source of comfort was in seducing Miss Breda Vivien!

Before she could try to stop the thought, it was sending an unexpectedly wicked thrill coursing through her veins. Until today she had never thought of herself as a sensual woman, but until today she had never met a man who could awaken all the dormant feelings inside her. She had never met Richard Delacey.

"How long is your visitor going to stay, Miss Breda?" Mrs. Yandle said primly, disapproval written all over her face as Breda strode through the house.

She might have felt a brief empathy with the Irishman, but by now her normal mistrust of anyone outside the county had returned, and the evidence of it was suddenly like a burr beneath Breda's skin.

"As long as he wants to stay, and as long as I invite him, Mrs. Yandle," she snapped. "Do you have any objections to that?"

The woman sniffed loudly. "Oh, 'tis not for me to say who stays here."

"That's quite right, so I'd be obliged if you'll show as much hospitality to my brother's friend as if he was a Cornishman." She emphasized the reason Richard Delacey was here at all.

"You just watch these charmers, that's all. I'd be failing in my duty as a longtime servant not to warn you, and I'm old enough not to take offense at the way you try to ride roughshod over me, Miss Breda."

They were a match when it came to verbal fisticuffs, and servant or not, the old boss-boots was more likely to ride roughshod over Breda whenever she got the chance, and they both knew it! Breda began to laugh.

"I can take care of myself, Yandie." She paused, and then said teasingly, "Just as a matter of interest, what would you think of him as a husband for me? I'm only jesting, mind, but you're always so clever in these things. Do you think he'd be suitable for me?"

She was annoyed to realize she was suddenly holding her breath. It didn't matter what Mrs. Yandle thought. It would make no difference in her life or to her choice of husband. Except that there were some who said that Yandie had the second sight, and it didn't do to tamper with what such folks saw.

"You can do your own choosing, Miss," she said with another sniff, refusing to be drawn. "All I'll say is, it'll have to be a real man to tame you. None of your chinless lords and sons of landowners with an eye to your wealth, but somebody who's got plenty of spirit. You'd know better than me if your visitor fits any o' that."

Breda watched her go back to her kitchen, a wry smile on her face. Did Richard Delacey fit that description any more than the so-called chinless lords and sons of landowners Mrs. Yandle had decried? Breda didn't need any time to consider the answer. He was all that, and more.

She went to her room to bathe and get ready for dinner. She felt a small thrill of excitement, knowing she would take dinner with Richard, a tete-a-tete nonetheless intimate despite being surrounded by servants. She allowed herself to revel in the soapsuds dreaming for a moment. Why not . . . why not? The treacherous needs of her own body as she pictured a permanent life with Richard Delacey were almost impossible to resist. He would be a demanding lover. She knew it as surely as she knew the moon waxed and waned. One that would be worthy of the spirited Breda Vivien . . . one destined to be her husband.

She sat up abruptly in the fragrant aura of the bath, refusing to let her wayward thoughts go further. She had to know him better before she allowed any such considerations to take root in her mind. Anyway, she didn't need a husband yet, unless a claimant for the Vivien estate appeared. So far her fears were unjustified.

Perhaps she didn't need a husband at all, but that was a future that was totally beyond Breda's thinking. Of course she would marry when the time was ripe. It was what every young woman wanted, to be loved and cherished by the one man who would fulfill her every dream.

Richard Delacey sat at the far end of the gleaming mahogany dining table, while the maids served them a dinner of oxtail soup followed by a delicious partridge and vegetable pie, which was one of Mrs. Yandle's delicacies. He was as far from Breda as it was possible to be in the long dining room, and yet she was conscious of every movement he made in his elegant attire.

"I've decided we'll hold the annual spring ball as usual this year," she said abruptly.

"Good. I think you're very wise. May I ask what's made you come to this momentous decision?"

She looked at him through the candelabra, his face made hazy by the flickering candlelight, and she was filled with exasperation.

"I should think it's obvious enough. I can't hold out against you *and* Nan telling me it's for my own good."

He laughed. "I didn't think you were a woman to take too much notice of what other people wanted. It's always got to be your decision in the end, hasn't it?"

"Do I seem so dogmatic to you?"

He leaned back in his chair, the glass of wine sparkling in his hand as he raised it to his lips.

"Let's just say I prefer a woman to behave like a woman and not a harridan."

She gasped. "And are you implying that I—"

She stopped as the maid appeared with the serving-dish of dessert, a delicious-looking mixture of custard and fresh fruit topped with rich cream. For a second, Breda had the strongest urge to throw it at him. When the maid had served them and gone silently away, Breda glared at him.

"I wasn't meaning that at all," he said patiently, not pretending to misunderstand her. "And God forbid that I'd tie myself for life to a wilting violet of a female! I much prefer one with whom the sparks fly occasionally."

"I didn't realize we were discussing your marital prospects, but please don't include me in them." Breda said, knowing she was on dangerous ground, but seemingly unable to avoid the issue.

"Why not? You're the woman most closely involved."

She put down her spoon and fork with a clatter.

"Look, how many times do I have to tell you? I've no intention of marrying you!"

"And how many times do I have to tell you that I've every intention of making you change your mind?"

If it was possible to believe that the air could crackle with their clash of personalities, Breda could believe it now. But through it all, she accepted that she felt alive again as she hadn't felt alive since her two bereavements. She gave Richard Delacey credit for that.

"So you're going to hold the annual spring ball as usual," he said, as if none of the last exchanges had happened. "When will it take place?"

She pulled her thoughts together, suddenly glad of something to occupy her mind.

"It's usually less than a month from now, the first Saturday in May when the weather's really warm. But I'm not sure I can be ready in time."

"Why not? What is there to do? You don't have to do anything yourself, do you? Presumably you just wave a magic wand and your minions will rush to do your bidding. You obviously hire musicians, and servants will provide the refreshments, so all you have to do is appear calm and lovely on the night."

When he had finished she let out her breath in a loud huff. Clearly he had no idea what entertaining on a large style involved.

"Are you deliberately trying to make me angry, or does it just come naturally to you? Of course I have things to do! I have to make out the guest lists and get them printed. Then I have to get them sent out, and arrange the bedrooms for guests who'll want to stay overnight. I have to decide what food and drink will be served and decide on the decorations to be set up in the gardens. We usually have Chinese lanterns around the lawns and a puppet show, and a game of charades as well as the dancing."

She paused for breath, realizing that her enthusiasm had quickened her voice as she spoke, and that Richard Delacey was smiling at her from the far end of the table.

81

"You see? It sounds wonderful, and I'm sure your usual guests would be very upset if the tradition didn't continue. As for getting all these things ready, I don't doubt that if anyone can manage to get things organized, Breda Vivien can."

"You seem to have great have faith in my ability!"

He raised his glass to her. "Then take it as the compliment it's meant to be, and stop looking for hidden meanings in everything I say."

Mrs. Yandle appeared in the room, and Breda composed her face quickly.

"Was everything to your satisfaction, Miss Breda?"

"It was a delicious meal, Mrs. Yandle. We'll take our coffee in the drawing-room. Oh, and Yandie—do you think we could possibly be ready to hold the annual spring ball at the usual time this year?"

The woman's face broke into a rare smile.

" 'Course we can, lovey," she forgot to stay up on her high horse and spoke as she thought. " 'Tis a good decision to make, and 'twill be the best thing yet for bringing life back into the house."

As Richard moved swiftly to hold her chair for her, Breda thought unerringly that it wasn't only the thought of the spring ball that was bringing life back to the house. At least, not to its mistress.

They moved to the drawing-room and sat together, leaving the windows undraped to watch the glorious pink and gold panorama of the Cornish sunset. The aroma of freshly brewed coffee and tiny sweetmeats on a side table added to the ambiance that was undeniably soft and companionable.

"I always loved this room," Breda said unexpectedly. "When we were children, Philip and I used to come here in the evenings to watch the sun go down, and try to imagine what it would be like on the other side of the world."

She bit her lip, because it conjured up such lovely images of days that would never return. She expected Richard to make the most of her sudden poignancy, but when she glanced at him she saw that he too was looking out of the windows as if seeing something beyond the present. Remembering the times he and Philip had shared, perhaps, in the camaraderie of military men that excluded women.

"We had a view similar to this at home, except that we didn't have the sea close at hand. But the hills all around the grounds rose up so majestically that Maureen always called it the nearest place to heaven."

Breda was startled at the warm huskiness in his voice, accentuating the rich timbre that somehow held all the charm of Ireland in its sound.

"Is Maureen your sister?" She had to ask, but she was hesitant, since momentarily he seemed to be caught up in a world of his own.

"Was," he said, the emphasis on the word betraying his bitterness.

"Do you want to tell me about her?" Breda asked tentatively.

"Not now," he said. "Perhaps at some other time."

There was a sudden awkwardness between them that didn't exist while they were fighting. There were things about him she didn't know that he didn't care to tell her. And while it made her so damnably curious, Breda realized it was probably going to be a harder bridge to cross than any she had encountered before. She turned abruptly and rang the bell for a maid to come and pull the drapes to shut out the April night.

"That doesn't change anything," he commented, with only the slightest smile lifting the corners of his mouth.

"Since I don't know what happened to your sister, you can hardly expect me to be clairvoyant and offer you any sympathy," she said, pithy again.

"I wasn't asking for any. Do you want more coffee, or do we have to ring a bell for that as well?" He lifted up the silver coffee pot impatiently as Breda glowered at him.

"You think I'm nothing but a—a—*drone*, don't you? Isn't that the word for it?" she said at last.

"I only know what I see," he said, not waiting for any further invitation, but pouring out more coffee for them both.

"And just what do you see, Mr. Delacey?" She knew she was provoking him, wanting to be flattered and complimented. And knowing just as instantly that she didn't, not from him, not if it meant nothing more than the artless flirtations of the kind of men who were known as chinless wonders.

"Oh, don't bother to answer," she said quickly. "I'm really not interested in your opinion of me."

"But that's not so, is it?" He was not flirting now, but being brutally honest. "And if you want the truth, what I see is a very spoiled young woman, used to snapping her fingers and getting everything she wants—"

"Really!" She leapt to hear feet, furious that the angry, smarting tears were filling her eyes. "Well that just shows that you don't know me at all! If I could have everything I want, don't you think I'd have my father back—and Philip too?"

She hardly knew the moment when his arms closed around her and the coffee was forgotten. Her thoughts were as blurred as her eyes, and she didn't want his comfort. She was too upset to know what she wanted at that moment, but it certainly wasn't any more of his snide remarks.

"My poor sweet darling," his voice said, seductively soft in her ear. "I've upset you again, when it was the very last thing I intended to do, and if you'd only let me finish what I started to say—"

"And what is that?" She jerked up her head so sharply to glare at him that it cricked her neck. "Do you have a whole selection of unpleasant things to tell me about myself, Mr. Delacey?"

"No," he said softly. "I was about to add that despite the fact of this very spoiled, but very lovely young lady who's so used to getting everything she wants, she has another conquest. Whatever your forthright manner may do to other suitors, Miss Vivien, it doesn't make the slightest difference to my intentions."

"Indeed!" She said, knowing her eyes would be flashing brilliantly enough by now to make most others back off. But not Richard Delacey. He still held her captive, and she furiously tried to ignore the ripples of excitement the nearness of his body was sending through her being.

"Indeed," he challenged her.

For a few seconds Breda said nothing. She could hardly breathe anyway, what with the changing emotions running through her, and the way she was imprisoned so firmly in that hard male embrace.

"I think you've overlooked one thing," she said finally, trying not to let her voice shake. "You said I'm used to getting everything I want. But I think I've told you repeatedly enough that I don't want *you!*"

He gave that low throaty laugh that could make her toes curl, and she bit the bottom lip that was suddenly trembling as his gaze went over it.

"I told you once before that your words may say it, but your eyes deny it as much as your body, my darling. Make no mistake, Breda, I mean to make you mine, and there's nothing in this world you can do to stop it."

His mouth closed over hers then, his hand sliding upward to comb through her hair with his fingers to caress the back of her neck and prevent her from wrenching away from him. But for the life of her she couldn't. The sweet shivering seductiveness of that kiss was simply too much for her to resist.

And why bother? a small voice inside her whispered. This moment of surrender he might think he felt in her meant nothing. It may not be seemly for a young woman to enjoy the pleasures of a man for pleasure's own sake, but why should it be so wrong—for as long as it suited her?

Besides, his last words had condemned him. *Nothing she could do to stop it* indeed. Mr. Richard Delacey had yet to learn that nobody controlled the will of Breda Vivien except Breda Vivien herself. And she had yet to learn that that was the most foolish delusion of all.

Chapter Five

Breda spent a restless night. It was easy to tell herself she could deal with whatever Richard Delacey had to offer. It wasn't so easy to forget that just along the passage in the best guest room was the most virile man she had ever met, and that at any moment she might hear the creak of floorboards outside her door, or the soft turning of her door handle. She was in a fever of heightened nerves, attuned to every night sound, every whisper of the breeze in the trees.

Once, when she heard a soft tapping sound, her heart leapt in wicked anticipation only to discover it was the brushing of leaves on the casement from the tree outside her window. She knew it was wrong to feel so let down. It wasn't the way any well-bred lady behaved, but the feelings Richard Delacey were awakening in her had nothing to do with propriety.

By the time she awoke the next morning, her head throbbed, and she was far from ready to face Richard's alertness and good humor, which she discovered was his normal morning demeanor.

"Did you sleep well?" he asked over the kippers and

marmalade toast.

"I did not," she muttered, knowing she was glaring at such cheerfulness and unable to prevent it.

"I'm sorry. I'm sure it would help if you came to a definite decision, instead of weighing up all the pros and cons and getting nowhere."

For a second she stared at him and then put down her knife and fork with a clatter.

"You surely don't imagine I spent half the night debating whether or not I should accept your ridiculous proposal of marriage! I find you a very arrogant man, Mr. Delacey, and I do have other things to think about beside yourself! Nor would I dream of marrying a man I had known for so short a time!" She finished witheringly.

"Then I hope you'll give me the opportunity to remain at Vivien Hall so we can get to know each other better," he said.

"That's not what I meant."

"If you wish me to make an extensive inspection of the mine, I shall need to stay on a while anyway." He went on as if she hadn't spoken. "Besides that, the thought of your annual ball has interested me greatly. It's a long while since I've had the pleasure of dancing with a beautiful woman."

She couldn't deny that his words flattered her, and took her attention away from anything else for the moment.

"Actually, it was the ball that kept me awake last night," she lied. "I've been working out my guest list."

"Good," he was brisk at once. "I suspect that's the first positive step you've taken for some time."

"I suppose it is," she had to agree with that, and

also with the fact that he was the catalyst pushing her toward more positive thinking. Somehow she had been goaded into thinking of the annual ball, even to thinking about marriage, when she'd been perfectly content to live her daily life without the need for such complications just yet.

"I very much hope my name was to be included on the guest list," he said in a surprisingly gentle voice now. "Could you bear to have me stay on until then, Breda? You only have to tell me if you think I would outstay my welcome, but I would truly welcome the chance to get to know you better."

She was very aware of her heated cheeks as the thought swept into her mind that it only took the right man to come along for even the strongest-willed young lady's resolutions to crumble . . . and whether he spoke in that soft seductive tone or the resolute way that made her toes tingle, she knew she was crumbling very fast.

She tried to be cool. "Of course you're included in the guest list, and if you really want to stay on until then, you'll be welcome—as long as you promise to keep your distance!"

She paused as he threw back his head and laughed.

"Sweetheart, I shall make no such promise! Would you have me promise to stop the moon from rising every evening? I could no more promise not to touch you than to do such an impossibility. You've already set all my senses on fire and my purpose will be to court you. I've made no secret of it, have I?"

She looked at him helplessly. They were the width of the dining-table apart, but she could feel the magnetism of the man, and was drawn to him irresistibly.

And if she was tempted for a moment to throw him out right now, she knew it was simply more than she could do. She was becoming bewitched, she thought in no small fright, and took refuge in speaking to him in a no-nonsense voice instead.

"I would prefer it if you were to cool your ardor a little and come down to the mine with me this morning. I make it a practice to visit Wheal Breda each morning, and if you're going to make an inspection of the mine you might as well meet my Pit Captain as soon as possible."

"Very well," he agreed, his tone changing at once to match hers. "Though I suggest we approach him cautiously about my inspecting the mine. Philip told me something about the man, and I gather he's aggressive toward intruders into his domain."

"So he might be, but Wheal Breda belongs to me and not to Sam Stone," she said, bridling at once. His mere name was enough to make her shudder, and she didn't need Richard reminding her that the Pit Captain was an oaf. Evidently his reputation had preceded him, thanks to Philip, and she wished for a moment that her brother hadn't told this man quite so much about their affairs.

As soon as they had finished breakfast Breda fetched her shawl, and since the day was quite balmy they set out on foot for the mine. The bracken over the moors crackled beneath their feet, heralding a fine hot summer, and the scent of wild flowers was fragrant and enticing. Once, when she stumbled, Richard's hand was quickly there beneath her elbow, and somehow she found her arm linked with his for the remainder of the walk.

Sam Stone watched them approach from the engine-house of the mine, the habitual dark scowl on his face.

"So we're having visitors today, are we?" he greeted Breda coarsely. "You should have warned me, and I'd have instructed the men to mind their language in front of your gentleman friend, Miss."

"This is Mr. Richard Delacey, a friend of my brother's," Breda said, keeping her voice even with some difficulty. "He's an engineer—"

"Oh ah, an engineer, is it?" Stone said sharply. "Come to see if we're doing our job properly, I suppose? From upcountry London, are we?"

"If it's anything to you, I'm not from London," Richard said coldly, clearly resenting being quizzed like this. "And I'd ask you to keep a civil tongue in your head when you speak to Miss Vivien, man. I'd remind you that she pays your wages."

"But perhaps you're thinking of moving in and taking over, by the way you're clinging on to the maid," Stone sneered.

"Sam, will you please stop this!" Breda snapped, furious at the uncouthness of the man. She hadn't realized quite how used she had become to it over the years. Usually, she could either deal with it or ignore it, but today she was seeing his familiarity through Richard's eyes, and felt doubly humiliated by the suggestive remarks.

Sam Stone shrugged. He gave an elaborate low bow that was more insulting than an apology and stepped back for Breda and the visitor to pass, but she stood her ground.

"You will please show Mr. Delacey the engine-house and the workings of the mine," Breda said coldly. "He'll merely be taking a quick look today, but sometime soon he'll be making a full inspection and make a full report to me and the Stannary Court on Wheal Breda's safety."

She felt Richard's fingers digging into her arm, and remembered too late that he'd wanted her to keep the purpose of his visit to the mine secret a while longer. She saw the flash of Sam Stone's eyes.

"I've told 'ee often enough there ain't nothing wrong with the mine," he growled. "A bit of seepage never hurt anybody, and there's none of my men who'll say otherwise."

"You have engineers working down there to verify this statement, do you?" Richard said sarcastically, at which Stone's face went an ever darker hue.

"My men do real mens' work, not ponce about in offices wi' drawing materials and wrecking other folks' livelihoods wi' their findings! We don't need none o' your sort to tell us Wheal Breda's perfectly safe—"

"Philip Vivien didn't think so," Richard retorted. "It was he who asked me to inspect the mine, and I intend to do so fully when the time suits me."

Breda intervened, seeing how the brittle atmosphere between the two men was in danger of changing to something far uglier.

"But not today, Richard. This is merely a social visit, Sam, and we want to get back to the house quite soon, so will you please do as I ask and show Mr. Delacey around!"

For a moment she thought he was going to refuse, but he knew it was more than his job was worth, and he stumped inside the engine-house with the two of them following. He explained the finer points of the constantly throbbing pumping-machine, and then took them to the adit of the mine itself, near the shore.

"I wouldn't advise 'ee to go down too far in them fine clothes," he said shortly to Richard. " 'Tis slippery underfoot, and mighty clammy to the skin."

"It's not the first time I've been into a mine, man, but I'll just venture a short way today," Richard said, and Breda waited at the opening they called the adit for the ten minutes he and Sam Stone were gone.

She never liked being here alone. The mine stretched far beneath the sea, and for Breda that fact alone could conjure up all kinds of unpleasant pictures of earth falls and being buried alive beneath tons of sea water. The thought was a horrifying one that had frequently caused her childhood nightmares when her father had first explained all that the mine entailed.

"Is tin so important to us then?" she had asked naively. Her father had laughed, and rocked her on his knees.

"Bless you, my honeypot, of course 'tis important. Cornwall's prosperity comes from tin, and we have ourselves a goodly share of it. Don't ever underestimate the importance of tin to a Cornishman, Breda."

"But couldn't the miners die if one of the props fell down?" she had asked with her new sketchy knowledge of the way the tunnels were constructed.

"They know the risks, and they're willing to take 'em," he'd said briskly. "And you're not to worry your pretty head about things that don't concern you, my love. You just leave all that to me."

But now he was gone, and so was her brother Philip, who had been intended to carry on the family business, and now Breda was the only one left . . .

She gave a sudden shiver as a small breeze blew like a sigh across the moorland above, and was mightily relieved to hear the sound of mens' voices again as Richard reappeared at the adit with the Pit Captain.

She couldn't read the expression on Richard's face right then, but Sam Stone looked as arrogant as ever.

"You let me know when you and your gentleman friend be coming here again, Miss, and I'll get the tunnels all swept out and tidy-like," he said, oozing sarcasm.

"There's no need for that kind of talk, Sam," she snapped. "Mr. Delacey will make the inspection when he's ready, and you'll give him every assistance, do you hear?"

"Deafness ain't one o' my afflictions," the man snapped back, and turned on his heel to disappear into the darkness of Wheal Breda once more.

Breda hardly dared looked at Richard. It certainly wasn't the way an employee should speak to the woman who held the purse-strings, and she was afraid Richard would think less of her for letting him get away with it. To her surprise, she felt his hand cover hers and squeeze it tightly.

"I take it he's got some qualities that make up for the rest?" he said quietly.

"He's acknowledged to be the best Pit Captain around here," she muttered. "But sometimes I wonder if it's all worth it. For the little I know about tin mining, I'm very tempted to sell up and let some other owner deal with the man."

"What stops you?" Richard said, as they began the long slow climb back to the top of the moors.

Breda shrugged. "Loyalty to my father, I suppose. Certainly nothing more! He named Wheal Breda for me, so I feel I should let it continue its run until it's worked out, and it's far from that yet."

"Its run would come to a very abrupt end if the walls were to collapse."

"Did you see anything to make you suspect that there's real danger?" she said, appalled, stopping so quickly that she almost pulled him over.

"I didn't get the chance to see much. Sam Stone was in no mood for visitors, and I need no overseer breathing down my neck while I make a full inspection. From a quick look, it seemed no worse than any other undersea mine, but as I said, I didn't go very far inside."

She let out her breath in a long sigh. "Thank goodness. For a minute I thought you were going to tell me the tinners were in imminent danger."

"No—probably not," he said cautiously. "But how long is it since any repair work was done on the props and roof-stays and ladders?"

"I don't know. It will all be in the records in my father's study, I suppose."

"Then I think I should take a look at them—if you've no objection?"

"Of course not. It's what I want—I mean, it's what Philip wanted."

She avoided his eyes, but he wouldn't let it go at that, and he pulled her slowly round to face him. They had completed the long climb now, and the wide

96

sparkling bay lay far below them, silvered in the morning sunlight. Far out to sea in the blue-white haze, small boats plied back and forth, and the sails of an occasional ship voyaging between Cornwall and America billowed majestically toward the horizon.

"Why are you so reluctant to say what it is you want, Breda? Didn't your father bring you up to always tell the truth?"

"Of course he did."

"Then why won't you admit that from the moment we met, you felt something between us?"

"I was also brought up to believe that a young lady should practice modesty at all times and not be forward—"

"And did this noble father of yours never teach you about love? Was there no love at all in that great mausoleum of a house of yours?"

"Of course there was," Breda said. "My childhood was a very loving one. My mother died when I was young—but I dare say you know that already, since you seem to know so much about me! My father lavished all his attention on Philip and me, and we wanted for nothing. How dare you say he never taught me about love!"

She took refuge in anger, because this conversation was becoming far too personal again, and she didn't want to remember the loneliness of being a young girl growing up in a household that catered mainly to male pursuits and interests, nor how she had missed a mother's loving care in her formative years.

"I apologize," Richard said gravely. "Besides, it's hardly a father's place to teach a lovely daughter the rudiments of love that I'm speaking about. The kind

97

that only a lover can bring to her."

Before she could stop him she was enveloped in a dark and passionate embrace, and his mouth was hot and sweet on hers. After the dankness of the mine, his lips tasted warm and inviting. The fire of his passion sent a searing excitement running fast through her veins. She made no attempt to struggle against him, for what was the use? He was her destiny, every bit as much as this enchanted place where they stood locked in a lovers' embrace, with the scents of bracken and clover and aromatic yarrow stunning the senses like a witch's love potion.

The sound of horses' hooves clattering over the track was the only thing to make them break apart, and just as before, Breda felt shaken at the intensity of her feelings toward Richard Delacey. She hardly knew him, yet she felt as if she had always known him, and would know him always. It was a strange and mystical sensation, but one to which a true Cornishwoman would always give credence.

They walked on more sedately over the springy turf as the mail coach clattered away into the distance, scattering a fine dust in its wake. And Richard spoke so softly she had to lean her head to one side to hear him.

"So, Miss Vivien. When are you going to give me the answer I want more than anything in the world?"

"Not yet," she whispered back. "I can't let myself be ruled so completely by my emotions. Marriage is for always, Richard—"

"Do you think I'd want you for anything less than always? An eternity together wouldn't be too long for me."

He was so smooth, so adept at always finding the right thing to say. He took her breath away . . . but her feet were still on the ground, and she wouldn't let herself be persuaded so easily.

"I want you to stay here as my guest until after the spring ball," she said steadily. "You must give me that much time at least to make up my mind, Richard. After that, we'll see. You might decide by then that you couldn't put up with me anyway!" She said, trying to make a joke of it. But one look at his face and she knew he was taking her seriously.

"Haven't you been listening to a thing I've been saying to you, Breda? I mean to marry you, and there's nothing you could say or do to change my mind on that."

"Not even if I had another suitor tucked away somewhere?"

She had to tease him, because this intensity was beginning to unnerve her. He stopped as abruptly as she had, and gripped her arm.

"Is there someone else? Philip never mentioned another man to me," he said sharply.

"Would I tell my brother everything? Oh, for goodness sake, Richard, I do know a few other men! I haven't lived like a recluse, despite the fact that Vivien Hall is so remote. My father had friends who have sons, and a few of them have made overtures toward me in the past. I'd think there was something wrong with me if I was totally ignored!"

"There's certainly nothing wrong with you!"

"Then will you please let go of my arm before I'm black and blue! And stop being so jealous. There's absolutely no need."

He looked at her suspiciously. "I'm not jealous. I'd fight any man who came within a mile of you, and I'd win!"

She laughed. "You're very sure of yourself, aren't you? I bet it would really annoy you to hear the occasional lewd suggestion that I hear from Sam Stone."

She was taken aback by the sudden aggression in his eyes and voice.

"I promise you that if the bastard does it in my hearing, I'll break his head!"

Clearly, he saw no reason to apologize for the oath, and despite his proprietorial attitude, Breda felt a small thrill of admiration. Sam Stone would make the strongest man quail, but not Richard Delacey . . .

"I've decided to go ahead with the spring ball," she told Nan that afternoon. "And I've also been thinking it's time I came out of the doldrums and started to get involved in things again. What do you say to our going to Helston on May 8th for the Furry Dance celebrations? Father has friends there who will give us hospitality for several nights, and I thought perhaps Richard might be interested in seeing one of our quaint old customs too."

She paused for breath, knowing that Nan was grinning knowingly. "So you expect him to still be here in a months' time, do you?"

"Not necessarily, but he doesn't seem all that anxious to leave," Breda said coolly, and determined not to let Nan know it was exactly what she expected . . .

It had been an inspiration to think about going to Helston for the ancient Furry Dance. It was a time-honored Cornish custom that would never die out, with the garlanded dancers weaving their way in and out of the houses from the middle of the day until long into the early hours of the following morning, or just as long as their stamina held out. It was all to do with ancient fertility rites, and that mystical oneness with the earth and sea and sky that all true Cornishmen held dear.

Richard joined them for afternoon tea while they were still discussing the new arrangements.

"We're definitely having the spring ball, and Breda's suggesting we go to Helston for their annual celebrations on May 8th," she announced in her usual headlong way.

Breda clattered the cup into Richard's saucer before handing it to him in some annoyance.

"Thank you, Nan! Perhaps you'll leave it to me to ask Richard if he wants to join us. He may not! He does have a home of his own to go to, you know, and I hardly think he intends to stay in Cornwall forever."

Without warning their glances met and held. And she knew in an instant how dearly she wanted him to stay; how fervently she longed for his declarations to be genuine and not fuelled by any sense of greed. She still didn't know him well enough to judge, and her brother Philip had been known to be gullible, his judgement sometimes clouded by liking a person without ever seeing anything devious in them. Philip was so ingenuous himself, and he expected everyone else to be the same . . .

Quickly, she averted her eyes from Richard Delacey's as the usual pang assailed her, realizing she was thinking of her brother in present terms.

"You're quite right," he agreed, to her surprise. "I don't intend to stay in Cornwall forever. I have a home in Ireland and I must go back there in due course. But I'm intrigued by these celebrations Nan speaks about, and I've heard something of them. I've also got a rough idea of where the town is that you mention, and surely you ladies don't normally travel there on your own?"

"We do not," Breda said shortly. "My father has taken us to Helston in the past, and we've stayed several nights with old friends. It's all quite respectable."

"Will you allow me to chaperone you both?" Richard said. "You'll be quite safe with me, I assure you."

This was what she had intended too, but she didn't want him to realize it that easily! "I'm not sure—"

"Oh, Breda, you said just now that Richard would be interested in our quaint old customs! Do say yes! I know my father will agree to it if Richard escorts us."

Breda glared at her. Since Nan's father hardly seemed to care when she came and went as long as she brought no trouble home, her comment seemed ludicrous. But the idea of travelling with Richard and staying with family friends at Helston was suddenly exhilarating, even though her secret thought was who was going to chaperone the chaperone . . .

"Are you afraid to spend time with me?" he asked softly now, as if there were only the two of them in the room.

"Of course not," she replied at once. "And if Nan's father agrees to it, I don't see why we shouldn't go."

Her eyes dared him to query whether she thought there would be safety in numbers. Where he was concerned, being in the midst of a whole host of people

102

wouldn't diminish the sparks between them whenever their eyes met or their fingers touched.

She ran her tongue around lips that were suddenly dry. Fate had a strange way of deciding things for you, and there was little anyone could do to fight against it. It was a maxim she had always believed, and she sometimes wished it wasn't so.

"Have you drawn up the guest list for the ball yet, Breda?" Nan asked, forcing her to drag her thoughts back to more urgent things.

"It rarely changes from year to year, so it was simply a matter of going through last year's list. I'm writing the invitations by hand, both to make it more personal in the circumstances and to get them sent out quicker. Yandle will organize their delivery in a day or two. I see no reason why it can't all be ready in time."

Nan looked at her enviously. "I do admire you. You see a situation and you act on it. If there's something you can't avoid, you always make the best of it."

Breda thought dryly that she was trying hard to avoid the fact that destiny, and her brother Philip, were throwing her into a stranger's arms! But she knew Nan meant it seriously and she gave the girl a swift smile.

"I only wish I lived up to your opinion of me! Now if we've finished our tea, how about helping me to decide on the decorations for the ball? They're all stored in the attic, and you know how I hate going up there alone." She knew how Nan adored being involved in anything to do with what she thought as the glamorous life of the Viviens.

"Well, I'll leave you two to get on with it," Richard

said, getting to his feet. "I'm going into Penzance to send some letters and packets home. Is there anything I can do for you while I'm there, Breda?"

"I don't think so, thank you."

She didn't know why it should be something of a shock to hear him mention home. Ever since meeting him, she had thought him something of a maverick, and somehow rootless. He was always so cagey about telling her anything about his past life, that she sometimes suspected the home in Ireland was no more than a myth to make him seem respectable and give him some stability.

She was being utterly foolish, of course. Everyone had to live somewhere, and there was no reason on earth why she should feel such doubts about him — none but the fact that she couldn't be sure whether Philip had ever mentioned the entailment to him. That was the whole crux of it. He had burst into her life and tried to overwhelm her with a proposal of marriage without ever mentioning love. He had preyed on her vulnerability, using his considerable charisma and giving her no time to think. He wanted to marry her quickly, and in Breda's mind there could be only one reason for it. He wanted Vivien Hall and all that it stood for. He wanted it more than he wanted *her* . . .

"Are you all right, Breda? You've been standing as still as a marble statue for a good five minutes. You're not really scared of going up in that old attic, are you? We could always ask Mrs. Yandle to come up there with us —"

"Of course I'm not scared! I've got a lot on my mind, that's all."

Nan spoke matter-of-factly. "Oh well, my father says too much thinking softens the brain, especially in females."

Breda began to laugh. "As far as you're concerned, your father's probably right! Come on, let's get started."

She put an affectionate arm around Nan's shoulders, and Breda pushed everything else out of her mind as they ascended the step-ladder to the extensive attic that ran the length of Vivien Hall. Once there, they spent an agreeable couple of hours, sorting through the Chinese lanterns and paper decorations that would shortly transform the lawns and gardens into a fairyland.

It was amazing how quickly you could get things done when you really tried, Breda thought a few days later. It was easier still when you could delegate most of the tasks to other people, she reminded herself, when all the invitations were on their way, and she and Richard were going into Penzance themselves to hire the musicians who normally played for the Vivien spring ball.

It was an opposite journey to the one they had shared so recently. They had been strangers then, and now she wasn't sure just what they were. More than strangers, less than lovers, not quite friends, perhaps . . . friends trusted each other, and she still wasn't sure whether she could trust him or not.

"Laying ghosts?" he asked her as the carriage took them toward the southern coast of the peninsula.

"Not really, though I was remembering the last time

we took this road," she admitted.

"Do you think you know me any better now?"

She looked at him resentfully. There was no avoiding contact in the swaying carriage, and as ever, she was aware of his thigh pressed close to hers, and the warmth of his body wherever it touched her.

"You're not the easiest of men to know, are you?"

"Why do you say that?"

"Because you tell me so little about yourself. I'm at a disadvantage, since Philip told you so much about me, but you've chosen to tell me so little."

He shrugged. "That's because there's so little to tell. You know most of it. I come from Ireland from a respectable family, and I believe your brother vouched for my honesty."

And you once had a sister . . . Breda would have asked him about her there and then, had not another vehicle come flying past them at a fair rate of knots. The driver was so intent on controlling his horses he didn't even notice them, but Breda twisted round in her seat at once, her heart pounding.

"We must turn back, Richard. The musicians can wait until another day. I'm sure that was Mr. Flowers! He always drives like a maniac—"

"Calm down, me darling," he lapsed into his Irish brogue as if to bring a smile to her face, but she was in no mood for teasing. "Now tell me why this Mr. Flowers, whoever he is, should make us turn back on this fine and dandy morning?"

"He's my family solicitor," Breda said, knowing her voice shook a little.

"Well, that's no reason to suppose he's going to see you, is it? He must have other clients—"

106

"Not around here! There's no other house for miles in this direction. Turn around, please!"

They'd come barely a mile from Vivien Hall, and he knew she must be right. After a minute when he registered her sudden pallor, he did as he was asked without further question. Breda prayed that he'd assume she thought Mr. Flowers wanted to see her on some family matter concerning Philip, and that the very thought was upsetting her.

He would never suspect what she most dreaded hearing, that the solicitor had received some news of a claimant to the Vivien estate, and was rushing with all speed to inform Breda Vivien of the fact.

Her mind raced ahead with the speed of quicksilver. If that were the case, and the claim was proved to be true, then Breda had two choices. There were always choices, but in this case each was every bit as unpalatable as the other.

One was to hand over her home and all that she loved with as good a grace as possible—and she'd see hell freeze before she did that! The other was to marry within six months of Philip's death, and three of those months had already gone . . .

Chapter Six

The small carriage was outside the house when they arrived, the horses snorting and complaining at their rough handling. The driver had obviously been admitted inside the house.

"It *is* Mr. Flowers," Breda said, her voice catching.

"Do you want me to see him with you?"

"No! No, thank you." She tried to breathe slowly and not to show him how distressed she was feeling.

"Then if you care to give me the address in Penzance, I'll go there myself and arrange with the musicians to play at the ball. I presume it's only a matter of reminding them of the date?"

"That's all. They'll be expecting to hear from me, since they come here each year."

She told him the address quickly, and went inside the house, too agitated to say anything more. Let him think what he liked, just as long as he got away from the house and didn't overhear what the solicitor had to tell her. She couldn't bear it, not yet. She felt like a sick animal about to hear a death sentence, and needing privacy to lick its wounds.

"Oh, Miss Breda, that Mr. Flowers is here." Mrs. Yandle came bustling out to the doorway as soon as she saw her. "In a right state he is too, the old fool, driving as if he's a two year old, and having to take a drink of brandy now to settle him down. It's just as well he did have to sit awhile though, or he'd have missed you. I told him you were gone to Penzance —" she stopped, her hands on her hips. "But you're not in Penzance, are you!"

"It's a long story, Yandie. Tell Mr. Flowers I'll be in Father's study, and send him in as soon as he feels able."

She always felt more composed in the leather-lined study, where her father's spirit seemed to lend her strength. And a sixth sense told her she was going to need all that strength in the next few minutes. She seated herself at her father's desk and clasped her hands together, her nerves jumping as she heard the tap on the door and called a cracked instruction to come in.

"Mr. Flowers, have you got some news for me?" she said at once, motioning him to a seat.

"If you'll give a body time to sit down, then I'll tell you, my dear," he said mildly.

She bit her lip, knowing it wouldn't be good news. All the inheritances had been settled after her father's death, and then after Philip's. All that Mr. Flowers could want to see her for now was the worst of news.

"You'll have guessed," he said abruptly, and Breda's heart sank.

"Someone has written to you with a claim to the estate?" she stammered.

He inclined his head a fraction and shuffled some papers out of a battered briefcase. He cleared his throat and waved a letter in front of her.

"I've had a communication in reply to the notices I placed in the national newspapers, my dear," he said more kindly, seeing the unhappiness in her expressive eyes. "I did warn you that it might happen."

"But it has to be proved. Who is it, and how do you know that the man is genuine?"

"If you will allow me to read the letter to you, I think you'll agree that we must give him the benefit of the doubt. His name is Amos Keighley—"

"What kind of a name is that!"

"It's a Yorkshire name, Breda, and if you'll allow me to continue—"

She bit her lip. However much she protested or ridiculed, she knew in her heart that this claim would be genuine. Why would anyone from the north of England claim an inheritance in the far southwest, unless it were so?

"The letter reads as follows," Mr. Flowers went on. " 'Dear Sir, I write in answer to your advertisement. I believe I may be the person you are looking for. My grandmother's name was Frances Vivien and she came from Cornwall. She married a Yorkshireman, my grandfather, and they settled here in the Dales. I have documents to prove this. I am willing to travel south to validate my claim and to show you the appropriate documents. I await your reply. Yours faithfully, Amos Keighley.' "

He handed the letter to Breda and she scanned it quickly, the letters running into one another as the angry tears blurred her eyes. The person she was looking for indeed! This Amos person was the last one in the world she ever wanted to see!

"He's obviously an articulate man," Mr. Flowers said

110

at last. "We have no choice but to see these documents."

"I won't have him here, not yet! Tell him to send them."

The solicitor looked at her awkwardly. "My dear Breda, have you forgotten how the time is running on? The estate must be claimed within six months of your brother's death."

"I know that." She stopped, her mouth twisting. "Oh, I see. You think I'm playing for time, is that it?"

"I think you have to face up to facts. This man may well be genuine, and if so, there's nothing at all I can do to prevent the terms of the entailment being carried out. But I need to know some facts from you. Can you verify if there was ever a Frances Vivien in your family? She's obviously dead now, or the man would have discussed all this with her."

"I don't know. I'd need to look in my father's records. I know he had some aunts, but whether any of them married or went away from Cornwall, I've no idea."

"Then shall we find out?" Flowers said gently.

She took down the huge family bible, but the faded names in the front of it related only to their own Vivien line, going back several hundred years.

"There's an old box that Father used to keep family things in," she said reluctantly. "I could never bear to look inside it, but there may be some reference in there."

She didn't want to look in it now. Still less, did she want to know. There were many of her father's private letters that she had still not opened since his death, feeling that if he hadn't wanted to share them with her in life, he still had a right to his privacy. But this was different. This was something that affected her whole future. She reached down the box from a high shelf and blew the dust from it.

"He never let Yandie come in here to dust, for fear she would disrupt his papers," she said with a vague apology.

She untied the strings around the box and opened the lid. She felt her heart contract as she did so. There were childish things in here. There was a poem she had laboriously copied from a book. There were drawings she had done as a child, although she was hopeless at drawing, and it was Philip who had been the artistic one. There was an excellent sketch of her father, clearly done by Philip, and with the proud words, My Father, flamboyantly scrawled beneath. There were notes from the children to their father and a birthday card from her mother to her father.

Breda wanted to weep as all the forgotten things were revealed. At the bottom of the box there was a large sheet of crackling paper that she unfolded with trembling fingers. She stared, not understanding what it was for a moment.

"It looks as if your brother attempted to construct a family tree," Flowers said. "I dare say he intended making it for your father as a gift and then gave up when it got too complicated."

"But Father kept it all the same," Breda said bitterly. "How I wish he hadn't."

For there, near the top of the family tree, written among the names in Philip's large handwriting was the name of Frances Vivien, married to one Thomas Keighley. They had a son, also named Thomas, and there was no more information about them on the family tree, but who was to say that they too didn't have a son, whose name was Amos Keighley?

Breda slumped back in the leather chair, suddenly faint.

"It's true," she whispered. "I hardly need to see the documents to know it's all true—"

"But I do," Flowers said crisply. "Solicitors don't work on the evidence of a mere letter, my dear. I shall need to see whatever documentation this Keighley has in his possession."

"After this?" Breda threw down the incriminating family tree, feeling almost as if Philip had betrayed her. It had probably been intended as a loving record for their father, but instead, it had damned all her chances of holding on to their family home.

"I shall write back to Mr. Keighley immediately, and he will no doubt want to see us both as soon as possible," the man tried to be as impartial as he could, but even he grieved for the girl he had known since babyhood. "My dear, you must see that I have to do my duty."

"Of course. I'm not blaming you, Mr. Flowers—but I'm planning on having our usual spring ball at the usual time, and I'd rather the interloper didn't arrive before then!"

She couldn't think of him as anything else. She could hardly think at all. She just held on to inconsequential things as a kind of lifeline. This Amos fellow wasn't going to spoil her spring ball . . .

"I hardly think my letter will reach him in time for him to make arrangements in so short a time. But you must be prepared for the interview eventually, Breda."

"Mr. Flowers—what if I burn this family tree, and pretend I had never seen it?" she said wildly.

113

He looked at her reproachfully. "You forget that I have seen it too. Would you have me lie, Breda? You also seem to forget that if proven, this distant cousin has every right to the property. We can't dispute that, nor can we fight the entailment."

Guiltily, she hardly noticed him leave, mortified at his censure that she had suggested burning the document. She wished desperately she had never found it, nor that Philip had been so diligent in wanting to record everything. Philip was too good at arranging other peoples' lives, she thought in a sudden burst of anger, whether deliberately or not. He had even tried to organize her choice of husband . . . her eyes blurred again as she stared at the sketchily constructed family tree. If he only knew what he had done for her now . . .

How long she remained sitting rigidly in her father's chair with her eyes tightly closed she didn't know. She wanted to shut out the world and pretend that none of this was happening. She tried to concentrate on the forthcoming spring ball that usually brought such joy to Vivien Hall. Unbeknown to everyone else, it would almost certainly be the last time a true Cornish Vivien would be its hostess . . .

Just as surely, Breda knew she couldn't let it happen. It wouldn't have been her father's wish, and certainly not Philip's. And she was a Vivien to her fingertips, with the fierce pride of her family and the need to hold on to what was rightfully theirs. No unknown Yorkshireman was going to usurp all that if she could help it. If she had to sacrifice herself for Vivien Hall, then she would do it. There was still one way . . .

She took a deep breath, even more glad now that she had decided on having the spring ball. It would help her

114

cause. It would be the ideal time for making a certain announcement . . . she felt her mouth tremble, knowing that she dared not let Richard know the truth of it now. In her heart, she felt that Philip hadn't revealed anything about the entailment. If he had, she was sure Richard would have taunted her with it, however teasingly. He was honest enough for that.

She gave a wry smile. She had mistrusted his motives all this time, yet now she was certain that he was an innately honest man. While what she intended to do was far from honest.

She left the study, waiting in a fever of impatience for him to return from Penzance. She spent the hours racing her horse across the moors, as if the wind in her face and hair could help to wipe out all the anxieties of the confrontation with Mr. Flowers. When she returned to the house, it was to find that Richard had come back and was in the drawing-room, gazing out of the long window at the sunlit gardens outside. Her heart churned for a moment, watching him. In profile he was a very handsome man, one that any young woman would be charmed to have courting her. She moved forward, and he turned as he heard her footsteps.

"Is everything all right, Breda? You looked so alarmed when you saw the solicitor fellow that I nearly didn't go to Penzance after all, in case you needed me."

"But you went? You organized the musicians for the ball?"

"It's all arranged," he said impatiently. "But what about you? Is something wrong?"

For a second she nearly blurted out everything, and then she ran across the room to him, holding out both hands. He took them at once, a mite startled at this unexpected show of friendship.

"Nothing's wrong, and I was just having a fit of silly womanly intuition that doesn't always prove correct. But I just wanted to say how glad I am that you're here, Richard. I was stupidly disorientated when I saw Mr. Flowers, and after he'd gone I started to get quite gloomy, thinking how sad it was that I no longer have my father or Philip to lean on in a crisis. For now, at least, I have you."

His fingers tightened on her own, and his first startled glance softened into something far more loving.

"You have me for always if you want me, and you know that. You only have to say the word."

"Give me a little more time," she murmured, lowering her eyelashes, more because she knew she was leading him on for her own ends than through any intention of flirting. It would seem highly suspicious if she were to throw herself into his arms at once.

She felt him pull him to her, and this time she didn't push him away. She let her head rest against his chest, and she was well aware of the beating of his heart. It matched the way her own was suddenly racing.

She looked up into his dark eyes, and a surge of emotion she hadn't expected flowed over her. She didn't know if what she felt was love. She only knew that in some extraordinary way, she suddenly felt very safe with Richard Delacey.

"Will you wait until after the spring ball to make a thorough inspection of Wheal Breda?" she said, her voice husky. "During the next few weeks, I'd like us to get to know each other better, without any thought of business interfering."

"Of course, if that's what you want. A few more

weeks can hardly make any difference, especially as the seas are fairly calm at this time of year. But why this change of heart? I thought you couldn't wait to get me out of your life."

She gave a forced laugh. "Are you going to embarrass a lady, Richard? Surely you know the old adage of allowing her to change her mind about certain things?"

He laughed back. "If it means you're changing your mind about marrying me, I don't care how long it takes."

He folded her into him, and she gave a small shiver. He may not care, but she did. If she were to make Vivien Hall completely safe, she had to be married within the next three months. There could be no lengthy engagement, no year-long planning of the kind that many other young ladies in the County enjoyed with Mamas indulging their every whim. There could be none of that. It was probably going to seem like a very hasty affair, and certain thoughts might well enter other peoples' minds as to the unnecessary haste, but all that would have to be overlooked. No one must know the truth, least of all Richard.

For Breda the next few weeks were alternately idyllic and filled with guilt. She knew very well what she was doing. She had never flirted so outrageously before, nor held a man at arms'-length, while giving every intimation that all this was only a delightful interlude. When the time came, she had every intention of submitting — as long as the outcome was marriage, and she was quite sure that Richard's intentions were completely honorable. He had said so often enough.

117

But until now, she had never even realized how deeply she was entrenched in her own family heritage. It was that which made her determined to cling on so desperately to what was rightfully hers. Her ancestors had built this house, and under her father and grandfather the mines had prospered and grown. She couldn't relinquish all that to a greedy Yorkshireman who wouldn't know the first thing about tin or the Cornish way of life. She'd do anything to stop that from happening . . .

And Richard Delacey was hardly the worst of choices for a husband. Breda acknowledged that freely, if only to herself. There was strength in his character, and an endearing vulnerability too. She discovered it one night, when they were sitting companionably together on the big sofa in the drawing-room, and he had finally told her of the great sadness in his life. She had been complaining about Sam Stone's snide remarks that day. Sam was ridiculously jealous of Richard, and made no bones about it.

"Your new man's been hanging around long enough, ain't he?" Stone had sneered. "When you going to send him packing?"

"It's no business of yours," Breda had snapped. "But if you must know, he'll probably be around for a very long time."

"Not thinking of getting wed to him, are you? They Irishmen are nothing but charmers wi' words, and you want a Cornishmen for a real man, girlie, one of your own. I'd give 'ee a taste of it if you'd just say the word —"

"I'd see hell freeze before I'd give you more than the time of day, Sam Stone! And I'd thank you not to keep pestering me like this. Do your work and mind your business."

"You do right to put him in his place," Richard said bluntly when she told him. "Men like that are the scum of the earth, no matter what their worth at their jobs."

She twisted round in his arms.

"You seem to have an unnatural aversion to the man, apart from the way he speaks to me. Or am I imagining things?"

"It's the man, and his work, and everything about him."

"His work?" she echoed, not understanding. Surely if Richard was a mining engineer, he'd come across plenty of such men.

"Mining," he said abruptly. "It's a twist of fate that my business was mining engineering. A cross I have to bear."

"Your cross? I don't understand, Richard. Don't you want to examine Wheal Breda for me? If it's a problem—"

He spoke tersely. "I'm making too much of it as always. Usually if the men are agreeable I take no notice, but when I come up against a rogue like Sam Stone my blood boils. In any case, I agreed readily to testing Wheal Breda because Philip asked me to. I made a promise. Then I met you, and the promise became a duty I wouldn't shirk."

When he didn't continue she spoke quietly. "Don't you think it's time you told me why? Ever since you came here you've hinted at some great tragedy in your life. Is it connected with mining—and is it something to do with your sister?"

"Is this your Cornish intuition at work again?" he

119

gave a wry smile, and then nodded. "But you're right this time. It's to do with Maureen."

"Tell me," Breda said softly. She leaned her head against him, warmed by the wood fire that Mrs. Yandle had lit since the evening was cooler of late, and feeling a heartache already for the story she was about to learn, sensing with certainty that it was this that had clouded Richard's life.

"My sister was about your age," he said slowly. "She was just as beautiful too, though her eyes were blue instead of green. Cornflower eyes, our father used to call them. He adored her. But then, everybody did. She had the sunniest nature of anyone I ever met."

Although Maureen was his sister, Breda felt a shaft of jealousy for this unknown girl who could put such poignancy into Richard's voice, but she stayed silent as he lapsed into a world of his own for a few minutes.

"There was a drifter who came into town looking for work, a charming enough fellow, and we gave him some work with the horses for a spell. He said he was a miner, which interested me, and I encouraged him to talk about his work. He had grand ideas all right. He was going to the gold fields in California to make his fortune. Well, you'll have heard enough of such tales in Cornwall, I daresay."

"Oh yes. We've had our share of miners doing the same thing. Whether they ever got what they wanted is another matter, since I never heard of any of them again."

Richard's voice hardened. "And did any of them entice an innocent young girl to go across the ocean with them?"

She put her hand to her throat. "You don't mean that

120

he and Maureen —?"

"That's exactly what I mean. By the time we discovered they'd gone, it was too late to stop them. He'd made his plans well, you see, and the boat had sailed for America before we realized anything was amiss. Maureen left a note, begging us to forgive her, but swearing that she couldn't live without this Denzil fellow, and that she'd write again as soon as they were settled."

"How terrible," Breda said softly, her brief jealousy vanishing instantly now that she understood his pain. "And did you ever hear from her again? Did she and her — her Denzil make good?"

He looked at her. "Her lover, you mean," he stated brutally. "Our family is as respected and old-established in Ireland as yours is here, Breda, and the scandal almost killed my father. My mother had died some years previously, so at least she was spared the shame."

"But it wasn't your shame!"

"Haven't you heard the old saying that mud sticks? Father wouldn't rest until something was done about the situation, so I did the only thing I could. I went after them."

She stared in astonishment. "You went to America on a—"

"If you're going to call it a wild goose chase, then perhaps you and I aren't as compatible as I believed," he said in a clipped voice, and Breda felt the stirrings of alarm. He was so remote, so far away from her, when she so desperately needed to be close to him. And she'd brought all this on herself, by worming the truth out of him, she thought furiously.

She put her hand on his arm and felt how tense he was. She spoke humbly. "Richard, I apologize. I spoke without thinking. Of course you had to go after them. I know only too well how anxious you must have been. I know all about bereavement, and losing Maureen that way must have felt just as bad."

"It was."

"But did you find them? America is such a vast country. Did you have the faintest idea where to begin?"

"Naturally. If you'd studied your geography and history lessons diligently, you'd know that the gold fields are in California in a certain area, so of course that was where I went. In any case, some of the hired hands at home remembered hearing Denzil boasting about the fortune he was going to make at Sonora. It meant crossing the whole damn country to reach the place, and when I did it was nothing short of a hell-hole."

Breda listened with troubled eyes as he ranted on, seemingly oblivious to her presence. She wondered if he had ever told anyone else this story so minutely. She wondered briefly if Philip had known about it.

"How do you mean, a hell-hole?" she whispered as he paused for a moment, not wanting to break the spell.

"It was filled with the worst kind of scum, immigrants from Europe, Chinese, Mexicans, all fighting to stake their claims on whatever gold they could lay their hands on. And the Americans fighting to keep them off, claiming that all the gold was rightfully theirs. The entire place had sunk to the level of an outlaw town, with murder, rapes and robbing being commonplace."

Breda licked her dry lips. "And did you find Maureen?" she asked, knowing in her soul what the answer must be.

"I found her," he said grimly. "By the time I got there her lover had deserted her and there was no trace of

122

him. Maureen was working in the gambling den of a saloon. She wanted to get away from the gold fields as quickly as possible and make for the coast where the respectable folk lived. But the only way she could make a little extra money was by giving her favors to men, if such animals could be called men."

He stopped, and she could see how painful it was for him to continue. In his imagination he was no longer here in the comfortable drawing-room at Vivien Hall, but somewhere in that terrible place where his sister was reduced to living the life of a strumpet. Breda's heart went out to him, and to the young Maureen too, who must have been completely terrified at being deserted in an alien country. No wonder Richard mistrusted men of Sam Stone's ilk . . .

"So what happened next? Did you bring her home?" she asked tentatively, still not knowing whether Maureen had survived her ordeal or not, since he'd been so mysterious about her.

"She never came home. She caught a fever while I was trying to persuade her that we wanted her back, no matter what she'd done. She died alone in her miserable room above the saloon while I was desperately trying to get a doctor to come to her. The only one in the town didn't pay much attention to the troubles of saloon girls."

There was silence in the room for a minute, broken only by the sudden crackling of wood in the fireplace and a small bursting of sparks.

"Richard, I'm so sorry, and I'm privileged that you told me about Maureen. It makes a kind of bond between us doesn't it?"

She said it without any devious intention, but he

looked at her blankly.

"You lost Maureen, and I lost Philip. We both know how it feels to lose a loved one, but life has to go on. You've said it often enough to me! They wouldn't want us to mourn forever." She sought for something to say to bring a small smile to his face. "I gave in about the spring ball, didn't I?"

"You did," he said slowly. "But I'm thinking that the only thing to bring my father any comfort is to see me again. I'm all he's got left now, and talking about Maureen has made me long to see him again too. We don't cling to each other's coat-tails, but he's growing old, and needs to know he still has a son."

Breda felt sudden alarm. He mustn't go home yet, not until their future was settled. But she couldn't even hint at such things now, when he was still wrapped up in his private world. She was plunged into a depression so swift it sent the ready tears to her eyes. He saw them, and misinterpreted them, pulling her into his arms.

"Don't be sad for me, Breda. I'm sorry if I upset you, and it's probably done me a lot of good to get it out in the open. I can't say it feels like it just now, but they say that sharing your troubles is good for the soul, don't they? And you're right. The past is gone forever, and we should look to the future."

He was so close to her that she could almost taste the scent of his skin, and involuntarily she closed her eyes, knowing that he was about to kiss her. And she wasn't going to resist . . . she was never going to resist again. There was love and compassion in this man, and even if it wasn't all directed at her, it drew him to her as much as anything else about him. He was the one man in all the world she could love for eternity.

"I'm not sure I know you any more, Breda," Nan said to her a week later. "You were a real cold fish when Richard first arrived, and now you're practically throwing yourself at him. It's hardly decent!"

Breda felt herself flush. They were sitting together on the garden hammock and Richard had gone inside to organize cool lemon drinks for them all.

"Perhaps I saw what I was missing," she said dreamily. "You've never been slow at telling me about some of the young men you've dallied with, and I decided it was time I stopped acting the lady, or I shall end up an old maid!"

Nan looked at her in astonishment.

"You're not telling me you've given in to him, are you?"

Breda laughed. "You're so quaint, Nan! Given in to him indeed! No, I haven't, not in the way you mean, and nor has he tried to force me. Did you think he was that kind of man?"

Secretly, she wasn't quite sure if she was pleased or sorry on that score! She was in no doubt that he was a very passionate man, and would be a demanding lover. Marriage to Richard Delacey would be a union in every sense of the word, and if she thought for a moment that he would settle for anything less, she was sadly mistaken. But it certainly wasn't what she would want. Now that she had forgotten her inhibitions and allowed him to court her, she had discovered an unexpected rapport with him. She glowed whenever he came into a room. She missed him the minute he was gone. She was falling in love with him, and she no longer bothered to

125

deny it to herself.

"I always said he was the man for you, but I thought that *you* thought he was an adventurer," Nan said flatly, answering her question a moment later. "What's happened to make you change your mind? Or is it just the thought of that silly entailment? Nothing will ever come of that, I'm sure."

She had been careful to avoid telling Nan about Mr. Flowers' visit. Nan was a darling, but she was also a blabbermouth, and the less she knew about the claimant to the Vivien estate the better.

Breda gave a sudden shiver. She herself tried not to think about it, nor of her about-face with regard to Richard Delacey. She tried not to remember that she was allowing him into her life because of less than honorable motives. If he ever found out, he'd despise her, and it was the very last thing she wanted.

"You're not to say anything to Richard about that, do you hear, Nan?" she said sharply. "He doesn't know about the terms of the will, and I wouldn't want him to think—"

"Then you *are* planning on marrying him!" Nan exclaimed, her blue eyes sparkling with mischief. "You sly old thing. Does Richard know it yet?"

"Does Richard know what yet?" The man in question appeared beside them with a tray of fruit drinks, unable to guess why two young ladies who had been looking rather serious until that moment suddenly convulsed with laughter.

Chapter Seven

The day of the spring ball promised to be one of those blissfully warm days with which Cornwall was so often blessed. The sky was a cloudless blue, more reminiscent of high summer than the remnants of spring, and Breda Vivien felt a special tingle of anticipation as she admired her new ball gown on its hanger, showing it off to Mrs. Yandle, and waiting for the housekeeper to tell her how fine she would look.

Because she was officially still newly out of mourning for her brother, she had chosen a beautiful bronze water silk that rustled sensuously whenever she moved, and caressed her shape with all the finesse of a lover's embrace. With her dramatic green eyes and dark hair, the gown only emphasized the flawless dewy English complexion that many of the older Mamas would envy. In her hair she would wear two glittering bronze pins, and around her neck the beautiful emerald necklace that had been left to her by her mother.

"You know what they say about peacocks," Mrs. Yandle said tartly. "All their finery's in their feathers, but it's what's inside their heads that counts, and that's

127

precious little from the size of them!"

Breda laughed, determined that nothing was going to annoy her today, especially not the waspish tones of the woman who'd known her since she'd been born. By now, Breda knew that the more Mrs. Yandle thought of her, the less compliments she'd be given.

"Oh, Yandie, you're surely not implying that I've got nothing between my ears either!" She pouted in mock dismay.

"I'd say you've got plenty, if all that I've been observing these last few weeks is anything to go by. Are you sure you know what you're up to?"

Breda felt her face redden. She turned to the dressing-table mirror and pretended to fuss with the kiss curls she was coaxing around her cheeks for tonight.

"I don't know what you mean—"

"And I'm just as sure that you know very well what I mean," the woman said bluntly. " 'Tis a dangerous game you're playing, lovey, and I don't want you to get hurt, that's all. There's plenty of fish in the sea, and I never thought you'd be throwing yourself at the first one to come out of it."

"Yandie, you do talk stuff and nonsense at times. Mr. Delacey didn't come out of the sea!"

There was no point in pretending not to know what the older woman was talking about. She'd spent just about every waking moment with Richard these last weeks. They'd as good as prepared the spring ball together, as close companions as it was possible to be without being lovers or kin.

"He came here from the sea, didn't he? Whether 'twas on a ship or not, the end was the same," she said with her own brand of logic. "Just you go cautiously,

Miss Breda. He's a charmer all right, but go slowly, there's a love. There's no need to go rushing into things before you're out of the cradle."

"I'm past eighteen, for heaven's sake! I'm old enough to be married, and if I wait much longer I shall be on the shelf." She caught sight of the woman's pursed lips, and gave her a quick hug "But you needn't worry, Yandie, I've no intention of marrying a man I can't love. So if anything *did* come of me and Richard Delacey, you can be sure it's not because I'm being pushed into it against my will!"

She wouldn't go farther than that. She wouldn't admit that she was already falling head over heels in love with the man, charmer or not. She had weighed everything up carefully. Perhaps Richard didn't love her yet. He'd certainly never said so. He wanted her . . . but that wasn't the same thing as loving her. It could even be that some of his ardor came from a deathbed promise to her brother . . . Breda shivered. She didn't want him to be beholden to her out of a sense of duty. She wanted him to love her, *love* her . . .

Whatever Richard's reasons, she knew now that she wanted him with a fever inside her that she wouldn't have believed herself capable of feeling until now. And Mrs. Yandle had been right in one thing.

In these last few weeks, she had made no secret of the lowering of her defenses toward him. She had given him every encouragement, and he had responded just as she had expected him to. By now she had persuaded herself that it wasn't wrong. Richard had made no secret of his wish to marry her, so there was no reason why he should suspect an ulterior motive in her apparent change of heart toward him.

129

And tonight . . . she closed her eyes for a moment. What better night could there be for announcing their engagement? There was only one small snag. Presumably because of her constant rebuffs, he hadn't mentioned marriage recently, but she was quite sure that it was still his intention. The only thing was that now it had to be hurried up a little, and it was up to her to persuade him . . . somehow . . . it wasn't the kind of thing a lady did, but when it was a matter of necessity, a lady had to put such considerations behind her.

"Whatever you decide, me and Yandle will be right behind you," the housekeeper said gruffly. "Only since you ain't got your dear Mama here to advise you, I wouldn't be doing my duty if I didn't give you the benefit of my thoughts, would I?"

"Of course you wouldn't, Yandie, and I love you for it!" Breda threw her arms around the older woman again. "Now go away and see what those workmen are up to, for heaven's sake! You know you hate to have them in the house for too long, and the kitchen maids will be telling them to do all the wrong things."

There was nothing more guaranteed to send the woman marching from the room and down to her domain. And Breda could sit at her dressing-table a while longer, dreaming of tonight and its outcome. By the end of the ball, she was fully determined to be the betrothed of Mr. Richard Delacey . . . and besides that, she thought more prosaically, it would make the forthcoming visit to Helston that much more respectable. Miss Vivien and Miss Greenwood would be accompanied by Miss Vivien's fiance . . . a little thrill of pleasure washed over her at the thought.

By the time she walked sedately down the curving

staircase that evening, she knew she was looking her radiant best. The soft tendrils of hair had been teased and pulled by a none too careful maid, and finally arranged by Breda herself. The bronze ball gown looked fabulous, and the emeralds rested against her creamy throat in a blaze of color. At the foot of the stairs, Richard watched her descend, and she thought he could hardly be aware of how her heart was thudding at the look in his eyes. She put her hand in his, and he raised it at once to his lips with all the gallantry she could wish for.

"You look ethereal," he said huskily. "You'll outshine every other woman in the room, my darling."

The simple words made tears prick her eyes. For an agonizing moment she wished desperately that she had the courage to tell him of the entailment, to throw herself on his understanding . . . but she didn't dare. She couldn't be sure that his pride would allow him to marry her under those conditions. And by now she wanted to marry him so much that the longing was almost a physical pain, and had nothing to do with holding on to property or material gain.

"I think we make a very elegant couple," she said in a voice just as thick as his. "A lady is never more complemented than when she has a handsome man by her side, and I'm proud to have you beside me tonight, Richard."

He gave her hand a squeeze. "Perhaps we'd best stop this mutual admiration and go and greet your guests. The first of them have already arrived, and it wouldn't do for their hostess to be seen philandering with her visitor."

"I hardly call it philandering, Richard."

"Then what do you call it?" he asked.

The foot of the stairs was suddenly a magical place,

and Breda could feel her heart pumping very fast. She spoke very softly.

"I thought you were very definitely courting me."

"And I had begun to think you were no longer objecting to my seriousness," he responded, "but I'd also decided to let you call the tune for the time being. Our future is in your hands, Breda, whenever you say the word."

Whatever she might have said then was not to be, because the door from the drawing-room suddenly opened, and a group of people came toward them, the women butterfly-bright in their silks and satins, the gentlemen perfect escorts in dark evening attire. They were all old family friends, and they crowded around Breda with cries of pleasure at seeing her look so well, and eyeing the stranger beside her with undisguised curiosity.

"Everyone, I want you to meet Mr. Richard Delacey, a very good friend of Philip's and also of mine."

She couldn't say more. She couldn't blatantly announce that he was the man she was going to marry — and quickly! Not until it had been formally discussed between the two of them. And in the midst of all the guests flocking to the annual spring ball at Vivien Hall that night, she somehow had to engineer it so that they were alone together long enough for her to make it quite clear to him that she welcomed his proposal.

By midnight Breda had almost despaired of finding a moment alone with Richard. The Mamas claimed him for their daughters in every dance they could; Nan clung to his arm like a limpet and persuaded him to escort her around the buffet supper tables, and to fetch her drinks, until Breda could have screamed. It was as if the whole world was conspiring to keep them apart.

"What do you think you're playing at?" she hissed at Nan under cover of a game of charades when everyone was laughing loudly at the antics of some of the mimers.

"I don't know what you mean," Nan said innocently.

"Yes you do! You've monopolized Richard for the last hour, and I need to talk to him!"

"Well, now's your chance then. I saw him go into the garden a few minutes ago, and I don't *think* he took a lady with him," she said with mischievous bad grace. "He told me he wanted a breath of air."

Breda didn't wait any longer. She turned swiftly and slipped out through the long open French windows, glimpsing a dark-clad figure lounging against one of the balustrades. Her heart began to beat unevenly as she moved toward him. He had no idea how he could control her destiny. It was a weird feeling, and one that she wished hadn't come into her mind just then.

"Why are you out here all alone?" she said tremulously, linking her arm naturally through his. He smiled down at her, making her catch her breath. God, but she loved him, she thought wildly. She loved him so much . . .

"I was just standing back and watching you in your world," he said. "It's sometimes a good thing to do."

"Is it? It sounds a little final to me, rather like the words of a man who's planning to leave it all. You're not, are you, Richard?" She felt a sudden panic.

"Would it worry you so much if I did? I thought you couldn't wait to be rid of me at one time!" He teased

133

her.

"And now I don't want you to go." She breathed the words, knowing she was throwing herself at him, but knowing that she mustn't allow him to leave! And she realized it was no longer the thought of the entailment that was causing her panic now—it was the thought of losing him.

He drew her slowly into his arms. The shadows secluded them from the main house, where the sounds of merriment and gaiety were muted.

"Are you saying you want me around for ever?"

"I suppose I am," she said in a weak voice.

She fully expected him to kiss her then and declare his undying love for her. Instead, his hands became hard on her shoulders and he held her a small distance away from him.

"But I'll not be your puppet, nor your substitute brother, Breda. There's only one place for me in your life, and that's as your husband."

Wasn't that all that she wanted . . . "I could never think of you as a brother, Richard. And you'll never be anyone's puppet," she said, her mouth dry.

She heard him begin to laugh softly.

"Then I suppose I shall have to settle for husband, if you'll have me. Will you, Breda?"

With his last words, all the teasing went out of his voice, and the air between them was suddenly charged with tension. Vaguely she heard the swell of music begin inside the house again, and it echoed the sudden swell of emotion she felt toward this man.

"Yes, Richard, I will marry you."

His arms enveloped her then, and his kiss blotted out everything else. It was a deep, passionate kiss, the possessive kiss of a man who knew what he wanted and had finally got it. When they broke away, she leaned against him once more, hardly able to believe it had happened. In the midst of her confusion, she managed to drag one important item from her scattered thoughts. She made her voice teasing, but she was unable to look up at him, since his answer would mean so much to her.

"Do you think we should marry quite soon, in case I change my mind again?"

She felt the deep resonance of his laughter against her breasts. "Oh, I was thinking something of the same, my darling. I'm not letting you go now that you've promised yourself to me. Do we say a month from now? The First of June would seem a good date, since it's also my birthday."

"That would be wonderful! And Richard — why don't we announce our engagement here tonight? All our friends are here, and it will crown the ball."

"Of course. And since it's your affair, I shall allow you to call for silence, and then hand the announcement over to me. I've no wish for a woman to be making my wedding announcement." He spoke with male arrogance, and she laughed.

"Let's go back inside and do it now then. Oh Richard, I'm so happy. If I forget to tell you, always remember that I was so happy tonight."

He kissed the tip of her nose. "You're a funny girl at times, but I suppose I have to expect these odd comments if I'm to marry a Cornishwoman!"

She was glad he couldn't see her blush, but even if he could, he'd put it down to excitement. So would everyone else in the company when they went inside and made their announcement. Breda found that she was

135

very nervous as they made their way to the musicians' corner, and she asked them to stop playing for a few moments. The dancers broke apart, looking around curiously as the drummer gave a short drum roll for silence, and Breda began to speak in a somewhat shaky voice.

"My dear friends, you probably know how difficult it was for me to decide whether to carry on with our annual spring ball this year. But on the advice of my brother's good friend, Richard Delacey, I knew it was the right thing to do. Life has to go on, and I'm so glad to welcome you all to Vivien Hall. By now, you've all met Richard, and will understand why Philip thought so highly of him. If you will indulge us a little longer before resuming your dancing, Richard has something special to say to you."

They exchanged an intimate glance that probably alerted some of the guests to what was to come. To underline it, Richard put his arm around Breda's slender shoulders. Across the crowded room, she caught a glimpse of Nan Greenwood's incredulous look, and smiled faintly.

"Ladies and gentlemen, I knew Philip Vivien for some long time, and was proud to call him my friend. I'm even more honored and privileged to tell you that this evening Miss Breda Vivien has agreed to become my wife."

He had to pause a moment while various sounds of approval and surprise and finally applause broke out. Smilingly, he held up a hand for silence.

"Neither of us wants a lengthy engagement, and the wedding will take place on June First. Because of Breda's recent bereavements, we've also decided on a very quiet wedding, with just one or two witnesses. I'm sure you'll all understand our reasons for this, and will want to give us your blessings."

There was no need to say any more. They spent the next hour shaking hands and receiving congratulations, and by the time the last guest had gone home or retired to one of the guest rooms, and the musicians been despatched back to Penzance, Breda leaned back against the soft cushions on one of the sofas in the drawing-room, utterly spent. Richard was beside her. Everyone else had gone, and no servants would disturb them in these last much-needed quiet moments together.

"Well, I don't know what previous occasions were like, but I'd say tonight was very successful, and of course the news about our engagement lightened any hint of gloom considerably." Richard commented.

Breda turned her head to look at him. He had loosened his neck-tie and looked very much at home, very much the Master of the house. She was aware of a darting thrill at the thought.

There was also a new shyness at being alone with her betrothed for the first time since it had all become official, and realizing that their status had imperceptibly shifted. She wasn't quite sure how to deal with it yet. When they had been silent for several minutes, and the shyness had changed to a strange nervousness, she sought for something to say.

"Why did you say it was going to be a very quiet wedding, Richard?" she finally asked the question that had been simmering in her mind ever since he'd made his announcement.

He didn't answer straight away, and when he did, he

sounded unusually cool.

"I assumed it would be what you wanted," he said. "I don't know why you've decided to marry me, Breda, but I hardly think it can be for love. Security, perhaps?"

She was aware of the new steely note in his voice, and it coincided with an unpleasant sinking feeling in her stomach.

"What an odd thing to say," she hedged. "But I suppose everyone hopes for security in marriage."

"But not everyone has the advantage of holding on to an estate like Vivien Hall and all its mineral assets just by saying "yes" to the first available suitor who comes along, do they?"

Long before he had finished speaking, Breda's blood had run cold. She had never believed in such fanciful expressions before, but now she knew it described exactly the way she was feeling. There was nothing but ice in her veins, and she hardly knew how to look at him. But she didn't need to. One minute they were sitting side by side, and the next he had grasped her chin in his hand, twisting her face to look at him, and making her gasp with fright. There was no tenderness in his eyes. Nothing at all but cold accusation.

"Well, my sweet betrothed? Are you going to tell me more lies? Look at me with those treacherously beautiful emerald eyes without blinking, and tell me you haven't decided on playing safe by marrying me before someone else steps in and claims your inheritance!"

"Richard, it's not like that!" she whispered through cracked lips. He couldn't possibly know about Amos Keighley, she thought crazily. She knew he hadn't been in contact with Mr. Flowers, and why should he? There was only one person who could have blabbed about the entailment, thinking it was all right now to do so. She was always such a blind simpleton.

"I suppose Nan told you some cock-and-bull story —" she said shakily.

She remembered now how Richard had gallantly danced with Nan after the announcement of the engagement, as he had danced with all the ladies to avoid showing any preference.

"Nan told me about the entailment," he said brutally. "And I'm not fool enough not to see that it's the reason for your change of heart toward me. You made it clear enough in the beginning that you found my attentions as offensive as Sam Stone's, so what else is there to think?"

"I might have changed in other ways. It doesn't have to be the only reason," she said faintly, and stopped as he gave a harsh laugh.

"My dear sweet Breda, don't play the innocent with me. You want to keep your hands on this pile of Cornish granite, and you'll go to any lengths to do so. Admit it!"

He gripped her chin so hard that she cried out, trying to pry his fingers away from her tender skin. She could scarcely believe that he could be so hard. It was a side of him that he hadn't shown her until now. His pride was obviously as great as hers, and there was no way she was going to let him know that she loved him now. Loved him! She would as soon love a scorpion!

"All right, I admit it! Vivien Hall means everything to me," she gasped. "I'm only doing what my father would expect me to do, and Philip too. He was the one who wanted me to marry you, didn't he?"

"But not for the same reasons." He let go of her chin

at last, but one arm was still around her shoulders like an iron band. She felt real fear at the rigid anger in his face.

Angry tears sprang to her eyes before she could stop them. "You don't understand. How could you? This is my home. Where would I go if someone else claimed it!"

"If no one has done so yet, I doubt that a claimant will come galloping over the hill at the last moment!"

She swallowed convulsively. He knew so much now that she should probably tell him everything and throw herself on his mercy . . . but one look at his face, and she knew she had no right to expect any mercy! And anyway, what good would it do?

He was obviously intending to leave her to face the shame and ignominy of being jilted. He must have planned this evening just as carefully as she had, only in his case it had been with motives of spite at her deceitfulness. She closed her eyes at the thought of how some of the less charitable Mamas and their daughters would titter at the idea of the lovely Breda Vivien being virtually left at the altar.

"All right, so I agreed to marry you for all the wrong reasons," she said with as much bravado as she could manage. "But you'll get your revenge by my humiliation when I have to tell everyone that there won't be any wedding after all."

"So you're going back on a promise as well, are you?"

She stared at him. For a minute she couldn't think properly. And then her heart gave a giant leap, because if he meant what she thought he meant . . .

"You mean you're still willing to go through with it?" she said huskily.

To her utter amazement he pulled her more seductively into his arms, his mouth a whisper away from hers.

"You promised to marry me, Breda, and haven't I been telling you ever since we met that I'm determined to have you? I've no intention of allowing you to back out of that promise now."

"Even though you know I — I —."

He gave a short laugh. "I don't flatter myself that you love me or ever could, my dear," he said with barely-concealed sarcasm. "I know this pile of granite means far more to you than any man ever could. But that doesn't mean that my desire has lessened. If anything, it's heightened it to some degree. And one day you'll be begging me to love you. I promise you that."

She closed her eyes again. If he only knew that she'd beg him now if it wasn't for her pride. She'd tell him that he was so very wrong, and that she was already headlong in love with him. But the little demon inside her head told her that Richard Delacey deserved no such declarations, and certainly wasn't going to get them. Begging him to love her, indeed!

She became aware that his one hand had slipped around her slender waist now, holding her so close that she could feel the angry beat of his heart. All this would still be a blow to his male ego, she realized, however much he arrogantly tried to hide it. And the other hand had slid upwards, caressing the full curve of her breast beneath the soft fabric of the bronze ball gown.

Her mouth dried. No man had ever touched her there before, and she knew she should protest. But no man had ever been her betrothed before, and she was totally unsure of how much intimacy he was to be permitted.

141

"I mean to extract everything a husband has a right to expect from a wife, Breda," he said softly. "Be under no illusion about that. This will be no marriage of convenience, if that was what you were thinking."

The hard ball of his hand was slowly circling over her breast now, and she felt the sudden sharp quickening of her nipple. The sensation filled her with a new and exquisite pleasure that permeated into her loins with such swiftness that she gasped out loud. She felt the heat in her cheeks and then the ripple of another pleasure as Richard's mouth came over hers and parted it gently with his tongue. She felt its tip inside the softness of her cheek, exploring and teasing, and finally filling her in a way that left her in no doubt of its meaning.

She should protest, she thought weakly, but everything he did was igniting a fire inside her too powerful to resist. She yielded into his body, discovering the sensuality of her own nature with a primitive hunger. She wanted him so badly . . . she hadn't even known that a woman could hunger so for a man, but as his hands continued to caress her, she gave up all pretense and wound her arms around his neck in total surrender.

"So." He murmured finally, removing her hands from their grip. "It seems there's a passionate woman hiding inside that calculating little body after all."

She could have wept at the unemotional words, though if she had been more experienced she might have realized by his labored breathing that he was moved as she.

"Is it calculating to want what's rightfully mine?"

"Not at all. It's only the means you use to get it that are questionable."

In an instant he seemed to have reverted to the condemnation of minutes ago.

If she could have read his mind, Richard thought, she would have known how shaken he had been by her ready response to his passion. She would have guessed that if he held her so pliant and receptive in his arms for very much longer, he would have been unable to resist declaring that his feelings for her went far deeper than mere lust. That he had loved her for a very long time, ever since he'd first seen her brother's sketchy likeness of her. But he wouldn't tell her that, and be at such a disadvantage, when all she wanted from him was his name and the security that marriage brought.

"I think I would like to go to bed now," Breda said in a small voice, since there seemed nothing else to be said between them. They each knew where they stood now. They were both prepared to go through with this farce of a marriage, even if it broke her heart to think of it in that way.

"A good idea," he said briskly. "And I think that before we go to Helston to stay with your family friends, we should make some of the wedding arrangements. I doubt that my father would want to be here, since he dislikes travelling intensely, but I shall inform him of the event, of course. Is there a particular church you'd like to be married in?"

She looked at him blindly. Suddenly he was so businesslike, as if all this meant no more to him than a job of work to be done. And just as suddenly it made her angry.

"You're sure you don't want a hole-and-corner affair so that people will really think there's a shotgun being held to your head!"

"I'll ignore that remark, but perhaps you'll give it

143

some thought in the next day or so. Even a small wedding needs to have certain arrangements made."

"Are you sure you wouldn't like me to make my will at the same time, so that if I died of shock on my honeymoon everything would go to you?" Appalled, the words were out before she could stop them. She had no idea why she said them, but she cried out as she felt him gripping her shoulders.

"If you think I'm marrying you for the sake of your property, then you don't know me at all," he said harshly.

"I *don't* know you. I'm not even sure that I want to know you," she snapped.

"It's a bit late for that, my darling," he said, the words insulting her. "In a month's time you'll be my wife, and you'll have promised to love, honor and obey me. Love will be a mockery in our case, but you will honor my wishes, and you will certainly obey them. You won't find it difficult, for I shall take the greatest care in knowing every bit of you as pleasurably as you will know me."

"You—you arrogant pig!"

He laughed and pulled her into his arms again, so fast that it nearly knocked the breath out of her. His kiss was brutally hard this time, bruising her lips, and she felt trapped by him in far more than the physical sense. What had she done? she thought in stunned panic. She had been pushed into accepting his proposal of marriage when all her instincts had been against it from the very beginning. But destiny had decided otherwise. Destiny, and her brother Philip, the unknown Amos Keighley, and Richard Delacey himself.

She pushed against him and rubbed her sore mouth.

144

"Have you forgotten that you're a gentleman?" she whipped at him. "Or was all that a masquerade too? Did you trick my brother into thinking you were of equal status to him, when all the time you were nothing but a charlatan?"

He leaned back on the sofa, his arms linked behind his head now, indolently watching the way her breasts rose and fell in her furious temper.

"If that's what you think, why did you agree to marry me?" When she didn't answer, he went on softly. "I'll make you one last promise, Breda. I shall never back out of our arrangement, despite knowing the reason for your apparent desire for me. If anyone calls off the wedding, it will be you. Is that what you want?"

She bit her trembling lips. *Damn* him, she thought. He knew very well she had no choice . . .

"It's not what I want," she said stonily.

"Then I suggest you go to bed and get a good night's sleep. We don't want our overnight guests to suspect that we've been making too merry in our newly-engaged state, do we?"

He made no further attempt to touch her, and she stood up, her legs almost giving way beneath her where they had been so tense for so long. She didn't understand him. He could be so tender, so much the perfect lover in every way . . . and at other times he could be so hateful.

"Good night," she said with a sob in her voice, and rushed out of the room with eyes blinded by tears. So much so that she never even saw the sudden pain in his.

Chapter Eight

Richard's examination of Wheal Breda was put off until their return from Helston. The overnight guests who had remained after the ball finally left, but the forthcoming visit to Helston was only a few days away. In the meantime Breda had had words with Nan and told her just what damage she had done.

"I didn't mean anything by it! I thought you must have told him yourself. You kept saying he wanted to marry you and you were holding him off. I thought you'd come to some sort of arrangement," Nan said heatedly.

"Well, we have now, and I don't want to hear another word about it, do you hear? It's our private business, and I'll thank you to keep out of it." Breda was as upset as Nan at the sudden flare-up of temper between them.

"I will! I'll keep out of your way from now on!" said Nan in a huff. She went flouncing off home, only to return a couple of hours later with pots of honey from her father's bees, abjectly apologizing and asking for forgiveness.

"Oh, of course I forgive you, you goose. I only wish you wouldn't let your tongue run away with you quite so

146

much!" Breda said at her crestfallen face.

"I'll never, ever talk out of turn again," Nan declared, which set them both laughing, knowing it was an impossible task.

The following day, Breda and Richard went into Penzance to make the church arrangements for their wedding. Breda had readily agreed to Richard's suggestion that only a few witnesses were to be there, and that it was to be conducted as quickly and privately as possible.

Now, perversely, while they were actually on their way to see the Vicar, she rebelled. She spoke out mutinously.

"Richard, I don't want a small wedding. I won't have it said that Breda Vivien was married as secretly as if she was a thief in the night! My father would be scandalized if he knew of it. He always said I was to have a splendid send-off, and that I was to wear my mother's wedding dress and veil. It's of the very best Honiton lace, and is a family heirloom," she added for good measure.

"So you see no reason why you should be done out of showing yourself off, despite the fact that we'll be marrying for reasons other than love," Richard stated bluntly.

"I do not," she answered, ignoring both the jibe and the little stab of pain in her heart. "Why should I deprive half the County's gentry of attending a big wedding, and why should I deny myself the pleasure of the most important day in any woman's life!"

He glanced at her in the swaying carriage, but she refused to look at him and gazed steadily ahead.

"And it will obviously be the most important day in your life, since marriage will secure your hold on Vivien Hall."

She turned her face to him then, and saw that his was

as granite-hard as Cornish stone. She spoke in a brittle voice, hating the thought of humbling herself to him, but hating the animosity between them too.

"You know I'm not totally averse to you, Richard. Why do you persist in trying to humiliate me all the time? If we're to live together as man and wife, surely we should try to get along harmoniously?"

If she thought he was going to make some seductive comment on her deliberate choice of words she was mistaken. He sounded as remote from her as if they were oceans apart.

"Perhaps this is a good time to tell you of my own plans, Breda, since you seem to be so wrapped up in yours. One week after the wedding, I intend going home to Ireland. I haven't seen my father in a long while, and before you ask, I prefer to go alone. He's getting old, and news of my marriage will be enough of a shock to him without my bringing my new bride to meet him. Besides, I'm quite sure you'll be happier to stay at Vivien Hall and glory in your restored possessions. Does that answer your question?"

"It does not! It sounds as if you'll want to get as far away from me as possible, which seems very strange after you practically hounded me to marry you!" She was incensed and bewildered by his coldness, and more distressed than she intended letting him see.

"You forget that I've a life and family of my own," he went on, apparently simply refusing to be goaded by her accusations. "As I said, my father is growing old, and I've a need to see him soon."

"But why can't I go with you? Won't your father think it very odd that you leave your bride after one week of marriage? Everyone else most certainly will!" She paused. "Or is that your plan? To humiliate me still further by making everyone wonder what has gone wrong between us so soon?"

"I care very little what other people think," he said with a shrug. "But to get back to this business of the wedding. If a big affair is what you want, then so be it."

"It is," she said recklessly. "The bigger and costlier, the better! No one is going to say that this was an unromantic union, and since all this was your idea originally, you will oblige me by being every bit as attentive as a bride has a right to expect—at least in public!"

She was trembling now, wondering how this conversation was getting so out of hand, and very near to tears. He made no secret of the way he thought about her in private now, but in public she couldn't bear it if everyone were to guess at his furious feelings. He may not call it a marriage of convenience, but to Breda it was very obviously going to be no more than that.

"I assure you I shall be everything a bride requires of a husband, and even more so in private than in public," he said in a suddenly seductive voice. "I've already promised you that, my darling, and you'll have no complaints."

Miserably, she almost wished that he hadn't promised anything. She almost wished that after the wedding, they should simply part, and that she would never hear from him again. It would solve everything, if only she hadn't fallen in love with him. She certainly didn't wish to share his bed, if he despised her so much . . . but she knew to her shame that she could never agree to that cold state of affairs, however much she should. A deeper, more passionate part of her told her that despite all, she still wanted him, still had to possess him and be possessed by

149

him.

"We shall need to send out invitations," she said quickly, pushing the sensual images out of her mind and deliberately thinking ahead to more immediate matters. "And there must be a reception at Vivien Hall. Everything must be seen to be done properly.

"Of course. If you give me the list of guests who were present at the ball, I'll personally see that they get their invitations, with the help of Yandle to give me directions. I presume you'll want the same people to attend?"

She nodded. "As well as the old friends we shall see in Helston. They rarely travel out of the town, but they always promised my father they would come to my wedding."

She lifted her chin high as she spoke, trying to hold back the tears, and desperately to think of this as the kind of ordinary yet infinitely exciting wedding plans every young girl had a right to anticipate. Instead of which, this particular wedding was a shameful and hasty union for mercenary reasons, where all the love was on one side only.

She felt Richard's hand cover hers for a moment, warm and protective, his voice moderating a little from the terseness of moments before.

"Everything will be all right. Successful marriages have been built on far less than this."

She took it as a crumb of comfort. If he spoke of it as a successful marriage, it hardly sounded as if he meant to leave her forever when he went to Ireland. For once, she held her tongue and didn't try to force him into saying any more about it. And gradually, her inborn optimism returned. Once they were married, she could make him forget her deceit. In time, love might grow between them. She already had enough for them both, and although she might still be innocent of men in the biblical sense, she was woman enough to know how she aroused him whenever he held her close. He certainly wasn't immune to her, and life wouldn't be all bad . . .

By the time they left for Helston with Nan Greenwood and all their baggage, the wedding invitations had been sent out, the church was booked, and the serving men would be returning to Vivien Hall for another happy occasion on June First. Weddings in Cornwall were taken seriously, with speeches and celebrations getting wilder and wilder among the guests and revellers long after the bride and groom had retired for the night, Nan told Richard on their journey.

"Is that so?" He gave Breda a sly smile, his good mood having seemingly returned to him, much to her relief. "And will you come and sing a serenade beneath the bridal window, Nan?"

She looked startled for a moment and then grinned.

"If you'd ever heard my frog's croak, you'd know better than to ask that of me!"

"It's no matter," Richard said easily. "My bride and I will have far better things to do on our wedding night than to listen to serenaders."

Breda saw Nan blush a fiery red, and chided Richard laughingly.

"Stop it, for pity's sake. You'll have her expiring with embarrassment next!"

"No he won't," Nan protested at once. "I'm not such a ninny that I don't know what — what — "

"What happens between lovers?" Richard suggested.

Nan immediately looked prim. "I was going to say what happens between married couples! But I don't think it's something we should be discussing. You should keep that kind of talk for yourselves."

"You're quite right, Nan," Breda said, quite unable to stop herself smiling. Richard could be outrageous when he wanted to be, and Nan's pretended worldliness soon fizzled out when matched with his. But she didn't particularly want Yandle overhearing this conversation as he drove them to Helston, for he'd surely be reporting it back to his wife that evening. And Breda would be in for a piece of tongue pie from her self-appointed guardian housekeeper when she got back, whether she was old enough to be married or not!

The old family friends, Charles and Edwina Pollard, welcomed Breda and Nan rapturously, and drew Richard into their home with added pleasure when Breda told them her news. It was a small manor house compared with Vivien Hall, but was comfortable and roomy enough to accommodate guests.

"You will come to my wedding, won't you, Aunt Eddy?" she said persuasively, giving her the childhood name she'd always used. "It wouldn't be the same without you both there, and it's going to be a simply splendid affair!"

Edwina Pollard laughed indulgently, her old eyes twinkling.

"I'd be surprised if anything you managed was anything but simply splendid, Breda dear," she teased. "You always got your own way, no matter what you wanted. And of course Uncle Charles and I will come, just as we always promised your dear father. The only sadness will be that he and Philip won't see their dear girl married to the man of her choice."

Breda avoided Richard's eyes as her adopted aunt hugged her. It wasn't only Richard she had deceived, she thought. The deceit went on, involving everyone else she loved, all the friends who would be so happy to see Breda Vivien come out of the dark tunnel of grief . . . she swallowed hard, knowing it certainly wouldn't do to appear melancholy since her future was apparently going to be sunny from now on.

"As Breda has told you, I knew Philip Vivien well," Richard put in, covering Breda's awkward little silence. "And I know he'd have been delighted that we're going ahead with the wedding. I hope you don't think its too soon? Breda and I haven't known one another long, although I feel as if I've known her forever."

"I think it's the very best thing that could happen to her," Edwina said warmly, clearly charmed by the tall handsome stranger who seemed so enchanted with his betrothed. "We all love her so much, and it's bad for a young girl to be alone, especially in that great barn of a house!"

"And it would have been terrible if—" Nan began.

"Nan!" Breda snapped. "Weren't you going to get your things unpacked? Nan can never travel without twice as much baggage as anybody else," she said in explanation to Aunt Eddy.

"That's because I rarely go anywhere!" Nan said in a small voice, well aware that she had been about to give the game away about the entailment.

"Oh, why can't I learn to keep my mouth shut?" She wailed to Breda later, when they were both sitting on Nan's bed. Breda sat with folded arms and pursed lips, gently shaking her head.

"Short of fastening it with tape, I don't know! Do be more discreet, Nan! I don't want the whole world to know that Richard's only marrying me to keep my head above water!"

Who was being indiscreet now! She bit her lips as the words slipped out before she had time to think. She saw Nan's pale eyes widen as she stopped sorting through her clothes and sat down heavily beside her.

"You must be mad if that's what you think. Anybody with half an eye could see that he's crazy for you, Breda. He must have told you he loves you a hundred times by now!"

Breda avoided a direct answer.

"You're right, I must be mad," she said, seeming to capitulate. "I must be having pre-wedding nerves, I suppose. They say every bride suffers from them, and it has happened pretty suddenly, hasn't it? A few weeks ago I didn't even know Richard Delacey existed, and very soon now I shall be his wife."

"For better or worse," Nan breathed romantically. "Oh Breda, you must be the happiest girl in the world. I know I would be if I had a man like Richard in love with me."

"Would you, darling?" Breda said softly, her eyes ridiculously damp at the outspoken honesty of the other girl. "Well, I'm sure your turn will come. It's just a matter of waiting for the right man."

She got up from the bed and said she was going to do her own unpacking. She moved quickly away from those trusting eyes, wondering for a moment just how her own life had become such a tangled web of lies and deceit. She had always hated deceit, yet circumstances had somehow carried her along with it . . . she turned the door handle of her room and went inside, still troubled as she closed the door behind her.

"This is a very welcome surprise," she heard Richard say.

Breda started. Without thinking, she had entered the room she had always used in this house, forgetting that Aunt Eddy had told her she would be in the larger one opposite. This was now Richard's room for the next three nights, and he was in the act of removing his travelling clothes for fresh ones. His shirt was pulled out of his trousers and unfastened to the waist.

After her startled reaction, Breda seemed to take in everything at once. It was the first time she had been aware of the virile abundance of hair on Richard's broad chest or the continuing tan of his skin. She felt the wild pulsebeats behind her ears, and the hot surge of color that swept into her cheeks as she backed toward the door at once.

"I'm sorry! I always had this room before, and I came in here without thinking — " she said in confusion.

He crossed the room quickly, his hand closing over hers as she reached the door handle. She was captured there, unable to move forward or back, and his eyes were dark with sudden passion as she felt the warmth of his body against hers.

"There's no need to be sorry, sweetheart. In three weeks' time you and I will be sharing every intimacy, and you surely haven't forgotten that."

"I haven't forgotten it," she whispered. "But that's

three weeks away, and I hardly think — "

"What? That our host and hostess would be pleased to know you had come to my room uninvited?" he said softly.

Her eyes flashed. "You know it was a mistake! I just told you so — "

His mouth was on hers before she could say another word. It moved sensuously, and she was helpless to do anything but respond. It was what she wanted so much. *He* was what she wanted so much . . . her eyes closed in ecstasy, and her arms were around his neck, her fingers pushing through the dark hair at his nape and caressing the back of his neck as his arms encircled her waist. The thin fabric of her afternoon gown did little to separate them, and she felt a sudden darting thrill at the unexpected roughness of his chest. She felt an almost unbearable longing to press her hands against it and to feel for the first time the way that a man's virility showed itself.

"I see no reason why you and I should not have a successful marriage, do you, my love?" he said softly against her mouth. "We have one very important thing in common."

"Do we?" she whispered back, her senses swimming from the way he was pressing her so seductively against the door. She felt a wantonness she had never known before, and sensed instinctively that if he were to carry her to his bed right now, she would be powerless to protest, all her sense of propriety abandoned . . .

"You're a very passionate woman, Breda, and for as long as the marriage lasts, it will be my pleasure, and yours, to see that you have all the passion you desire from me. We're two of a kind, my darling, however much you may try to deny it."

He might as well have thrown cold water in her face. She heard nothing else but that one death-knell of a phrase . . . *for as long as the marriage lasts* . . .

She couldn't look at him, for fear she would see the mockery in his face. She leaned against him, and because he was so much taller than she, her cheek was pressed to that tantalizingly dark hair on his chest, but the realization of it no longer had the power to give her pleasure.

"You don't intend it to last forever then?" she choked out the words.

She held her breath, and then he was tipping up her chin, and forcing her to look at him. He was against the light and she couldn't read the expression in his eyes.

"I never go back on a promise," he said deliberately. "If the marriage is to survive, it will be because you want it to. At least you'll have saved Vivien Hall from outsiders, and that's your main concern, isn't it?"

"You think that once I've got what I wanted, I'll never want to see you again?" she said huskily.

"You tell me," he stated.

She wriggled free of his hand on her chin. She didn't want the tell-tale expression on her face to give her secret away. She turned her face sideways, and without thinking she put her hands on his chest, as if to push him away from her. And realized in an instant how difficult it was to keep them still, when all she wanted to do was let them roam over that virile expanse.

"I consider that a vow made in church is the most solemn made on this earth," she said quietly. "Whatever our reasons for it, I don't take marriage lightly, Richard."

He took her hands away from his skin with a sudden-

157

ness that surprised her, and moved slightly away from her.

"Good," he said briskly. "Now that we've got that settled, you can do your first wifely duty for me, and then I suggest you go back to your own room and freshen your face. I thought you could show me something of the town of Helston before it gets too late in the day."

"What wifely duty?" she stammered, and heard him laugh as she clasped her hands together.

"Don't look so suspicious, my dear girl!" He said, in a surprisingly gentle voice. "Do I frighten you so much?"

"Of course not —"

"Then come over to the bed," he said, and laughed again at the alarm that showed in her eyes. "No, you ninny, I'm not about to seduce you here and now, delightful though the prospect would be. I merely want you to pull off my boots for me."

Stupidly, she looked down at the gleaming knee-high leather boots he wore, and blushed furiously at her naivety. He must think he was marrying a simpleton, she thought furiously, and moved across to do his bidding. He sat easily on top of the bed while she knelt on the carpet to get sufficient leverage on the soft leather, pulling and tugging while he leaned back, hands squarely on the bed, his gaze never leaving her face.

Finally the job was done, and she saw how he flexed his stockinged feet, and resisted the impulse to massage them for him. She must really be going mad, she thought faintly, echoing Nan's earlier sentiments, if everything about the man could send her into such a rapturous servile mood! Breda Vivien, who had never needed to do a servile thing in her life!

She scrambled to her feet.

158

"Will that be all — *Sir?*" she said in diffident mockery.

He stood up and pulled her into him once more with a teasing laugh.

"For now — *wench*. But I'll deal with you later!" He said, picking up her mood at once, twirling an imaginary moustache and then playfully whacked her backside. Breda gasped, but they were both suddenly laughing too much for her to take offense. And the tingling sensation of his hand on her rear, and of her own fingers on his skin, stayed with her as she hurriedly went back to her own room and leaned against her own door.

"I love him so much," she whispered to herself, closing her eyes. "And all he wants from me is —"

She caught sight of herself in the dressing-table mirror. She had seen herself before after Richard's kisses, but never like this. Never with her cheeks so fevered, nor her eyes so wide and darkened, nor her breasts so proudly peaked . . . there was a voluptuousness about her now, that would tell anyone who saw her that she had come straight from the arms of a lover.

She turned away from her own image, quickly pouring water from her washing-jug into her bowl, slopping it over the rim in her haste. She splashed the cool water over her face, wondering for the first time how she was ever going to deceive Richard Delacey on her wedding night into thinking she didn't love him, when his every touch ignited a flame of desire inside her that must surely be a match for his . . .

They strolled about the town of Helston along with the mass of humanity that had come to witness the annual Furry Dance on the following day. Nan and the Pollards had accompanied them, so at least Breda was spared the anxiety of being alone with Richard.

It was an odd thing to come into her mind, she thought, when she knew she would shortly be spending entire nights and days alone with him, but right now she was filled with nervousness, and welcomed the presence of other people. It was no more than wedding nerves, she told herself stoically, avoiding the knowledge that it went far deeper than that.

"Helston is a very old town, Richard," Charles Pollard told him, already on familiar terms with the young man who was to marry his beloved Breda. "King John gave it a charter in the eleventh century, and Edward the First made it a coinage town for tin. There used to be a Coinage Hall here where all the weighing was done, but it's long gone now, and other towns have taken over in importance for the tin trade. Anyway, that's enough of history for one day, I'm sure."

"But the Furry Dance goes back into ancient times, I'm told," Richard encouraged him to talk, as they strolled among the milling crowds in the steep narrow main street. As his affianced, Breda now had her arm firmly tucked into his, while Nan and Aunt Eddy walked on either side of Charles.

"Oh my word, yes! There have been many explanations for it, but we believe the name comes from the Cornish *feur*, meaning a holiday. Some will say that it comes from the Roman festival of Floralia, and that may well be true as well. No one really knows, but the dance has gone on for centuries. The town band leads the dancers, and you'll be awakened early by the sounds of drums and fiddlers, even from our house on the outskirts of town, since it all begins at seven o'clock in the morning."

"Really! Then Breda has been teasing me. She told me it begins at mid-day," Richard commented.

"That's when the chief dance begins," he nodded. "But the youngsters do their stuff in the morning. You'll enjoy it all, but especially the spectacle of the mid-day dancers, my boy. The town notables perform then, dressed in full morning dress, top hats and all."

Breda glanced up at Richard as the weird tale went on. Even she thought it sounded garbled and countrified, and wondered just how it must sound to a stranger's ears.

"You'll be thinking us a very quaint lot of people by the end of this visit, Richard. Perhaps you'll be changing your mind about marrying into Cornish society!"

She heard Charles Pollard chuckle.

"I hardly think you need have any fear of that, my dear. Any fool can see that the boy's head over apex in love with you!"

"Charles, really!" Aunt Eddy chided him, but it gave Breda the chance to avoid looking at Richard again. In love with her indeed. He was as much in love with Nan Greenwood as with Breda Vivien, and that was not at all.

"Haven't we done enough walking for one day?" Aunt Eddy complained presently. By then they had visited the church and various other points of interest, and been shown where the road to the Lizard led out of the town, that ancient and mysterious gorse and heath-covered promontory where the Land's End plunged to the sea in magnificent and rugged sea-pounded cliffs, in England's most southerly point.

"A cup of tea would be welcome," Charles agreed. "We'll be doing plenty of standing and walking tomorrow, so we don't want to wear out the old feet today, do we?"

"Thank goodness." Breda murmured to Richard. "I'm beginning to feel terribly dry. Uncle Charles always did have the stamina of an ox."

She realized how natural it was to talk to him in these little asides, and that she had been doing so all the time they had been walking about the town. As long as the antagonism about the entailment didn't flare up between them, they had an easy camaraderie that boded well for the future, she thought hopefully. It would be disastrous if they were to be at loggerheads all the time.

"You're not suggesting that we should all be up at seven o'clock tomorrow morning, Uncle Charles?" she asked him when they were all seated in a tea-room with steaming cups of tea in front of them.

Charles laughed. "It depends how much you want to see of the Furry Dance, my dear."

"All of it!" Nan said eagerly, and Breda groaned.

"But not at seven o'clock in the morning," she repeated. "You know it will go on all day long, Nan—"

"And by midday people from miles around will be crushing into the town, so that no one will be able to see anything" Charles went on relentlessly. "You saw what it's like today, Breda. No, I think we must plan to get here by ten o'clock at the latest. We'll have a late breakfast to sustain us for the day, and bring some drinks with us, since it will be hopeless to try to get into the tea-rooms."

She should have remembered how enthusiastic her adoptive uncle could be when he entered into the spirit of anything . . .

But after all, the day couldn't have been better. They arrived without too much trouble by ten in the morning, leaving the Pollards' man to take the carriage back home, and instructing him to return for them at five o'clock in the afternoon.

"I'm sure that will be long enough, and the warmth of the day will be gone by then," Aunt Eddy said.

They found a good vantage point in the main street, where the noise was already deafening from the children and the band, and the clapping from the onlookers. Everyone was in a party mood, and its effect was catching. The Pollard group was soon clapping in unison with all the rest, and it didn't matter if they were jostled on all sides, because it all added to the excitement of the proceedings. The air was fragrant and sweet with blossoms as the garlanded children skipped in and out of the houses, and many of the visitors were tempted into following them so that the entire town seemed to consist of a giant chain of dancing people.

There was one moment when Breda felt a sense of panic. She was swept along the street by a group of young men and girls who urged her to join them, and without wanting to, she had broken away from her own party. The revellers had laughingly let her go after a few minutes, but when she looked back she couldn't see Richard and the others.

It was as if they had been swallowed up by the gigantic crowd surging forward and pushing her along with them. There was no longer any street separated from the more sedate watchers lining it. It was just one heaving mass of singing and dancing people, and Breda felt suddenly crushed and frightened.

It seemed an eternity before she saw Richard struggling to reach her. Even then, there were moments when he disappeared among the excited crowd and herself. Time and again, Breda held out a frantic hand to him, almost screaming out his name above the din, and at last he reached her, grasping her hand and hauling her backward away from the dancers.

"It's all right, darling, I'm here," he said, keeping both arms tightly around her as he maneuvered them both back toward the side of the street. "Don't be scared."

Although she still shook from her experience, she knew she wasn't scared any more. She felt reassured and safe within the circle of his arms. It was an extraordinary feeling, considering that she had mistrusted him from the first moment. And yet she recognized that the more she came to know him, the feeling had been steadily growing. She would trust him with her life — which was literally what she was about to do in a very short space of time.

Chapter Nine

Mrs. Yandle came running out to meet Breda and Richard as soon as the carriage clattered up to the front door the following evening, having deposited Nan at her own home on the way.

"Oh, Miss Breda, I'm that glad to see you back! There's visitors here for you, and I'm sure I don't know what to make of 'em. Rough-speaking man he is too, or would be if I could understand half of what he's saying. All I know is he's lording it about the place as if he owns it. If it wasn't for that nice little wife of his and the children dropping with sleep, I'd have shown him the door and no mistake, but he insists that you've been expecting him, so I've put them all in the drawing room, knowing you'd be back from Helston soon."

Mrs. Yandle gulped for breath after her long tirade, and Breda stared at her with her heart thumping fast and her nerves jumping all over the place, knowing at once who the visitors would be.

"Were you expecting visitors?" Richard said. "You didn't mention it."

She ran her tongue around her lips, completely

thrown off-balance. "I never expected them to just turn up," she gasped, hardly able to think about what she was saying. "I thought the exchange of letters with Mr. Flowers would go on for a while, and then it would be too late—"

She saw Richard's eyes narrow, and knew he was quick-witted enough to be putting two and two together. She dragged her thoughts together and spoke quickly to the affronted housekeeper.

"I'll speak to them at once, Mrs. Yandle. Perhaps you'd see to the baggage, Richard—"

"I will not. Yandle can do that," he said coldly. "I believe these visitors will be of interest to me as well as to you, or am I misreading the situation?"

Mrs. Yandle looked from one to the other with a frown between her eyes. The expression in her eyes was clear. Sometimes this pair behaved less like lovers than like prize-fighting partners . . .

Why now! Breda thought in agony. *Why couldn't this Amos Keighley person have waited another few weeks until she was safely married and it wouldn't have mattered if a dozen claimants had turned up wanting to get their greedy hands on Vivien Hall!*

For of course it would be Amos Keighley in the drawing-room right now. Complete with a wife and children too . . . she closed her eyes in panic for a moment. It was all too much . . . it was just too much . . .

"Well, Breda?" She heard Richard's voice, still as cold as charity and twice as uncompromising. "Shall we go inside and see what your visitors have to say for themselves?"

She put her hand on his arm. Hers trembled, but his

was rigid with anger.

"Richard, will you just wait and let me explain—" she whispered.

"I hardly think any explanation is necessary. And from the look on your face, I think you know very well who your visitors are and why they're here. As your *fiance*, I think we should confront them together, don't you?"

And then I suppose you can have the sadistic pleasure of denying that you ever meant to marry me, Breda thought sickly, *or if not, then certainly saying that the wedding is now off!* The emphasis he put on their relationship told her so.

For of course he wouldn't want her now. She had deceived him once by not telling him of the entailment. He would never forgive a second deception when he discovered she had known about this hated distant Yorkshire cousin ever since Mr. Flowers had come puffing up to Vivien Hall.

In seconds her safe world seemed to be crumbling, and she had difficulty in subduing a great cry of anguish. It was in her soul, and she couldn't let it out. She loved Richard so much, and he looked at her now as if she was less than nothing. She just couldn't bear it . . .

He moved ahead of her, and she followed him numbly, feeling as though her legs would no longer hold her up. Somehow they did, and when Richard opened the drawing-room door and stood back to allow her to enter first, she held her head high and prepared to face the group of people inside.

A thin, pretty woman and three young children were seated near the window, an anxious-looking cluster of people. The man stood in front of the fireplace, legs firmly apart in the way of a squire of the manor. Breda hated him on sight, with his red farmer's face and bull-like neck. She forced herself to speak.

"Good evening. I'm sorry I wasn't here to receive you when you arrived, but I trust that my housekeeper has given you all some refreshment."

"We're all right on that score," the man interrupted. "Now then, you'll be my cousin Breda, I take it, and I'm Amos Keighley. I gather you've been away gallivanting somewhere."

He didn't even bother introducing his family, Breda fumed, feeling a brief pity for them. But it seemed obvious that Mrs. Yandle hadn't given anything away about Richard's presence here. Breda could imagine her taking an instant huff at this oaf. His wife put out a hand to restrain him, to which he took not the slightest notice.

"I am Breda Vivien," she said steadily. "And this is Mr. Richard Delacey —"

She had been going to say 'my fiance', but she stopped just in time. It would be humiliating if Richard were to deny it at once, and anyway, before she gave anything away, she needed to know what the Keighleys' plans were. Perhaps they wouldn't even want to remove to Cornwall, away from everything they knew in the north, and would be content to be absentee landowners.

A shiver of hope ran through her, and she moved to sit in a chair near the family, giving a faint smile to the small fair-haired girl with the thumb in her mouth. Richard remained standing, arms folded as the two men implacably eyed one another. Amos Keighley

168

shifted his gaze to Breda.

"Now then, you'll know why we're here, young Breda. I'm a blunt man and I believe in speaking my mind, so there's no point in putting off what's to be done."

She looked at him, and her hopes faded. Even though he glowered, he hadn't been able to resist letting his eyes dart about the room from time to time, sizing up the value of paintings and carpets, the costly glassware her mother had collected over the years, and the general ambiance of a well-to-do estate.

"And just what is to be done, Mr. Keighley?" she said shakily.

"Before you answer that, Sir, I think it's time I made something quite clear," Richard put in pleasantly.

Keighley glared at him. "I really don't see that there's owt here to do wi' you, *Sir*. This is family business between my cousin and myself, and I'd thank you not to interfere." He paused suddenly, his eyes glinting. "You're not the lawyer feller who put the notice in the newspaper, are you, and tried to tangle me up wi' fancy long words in your letters?"

"No, I'm not the lawyer fellow," Richard said coolly. "I'm Miss Vivien's fiance. In case you're not *au fait* with the meaning of the word—"

"I know well enough what it means! So the lass will have somebody to take care of her when we move in here. 'Tis all to the good, to save me the trouble of offering her a home—"

"Amos, for pity's sake have some consideration for Miss Vivien's feelings! All this will have been a shock to her," the wife said in some distress. She looked at Breda, her pale face flushing slightly. "I'm sorry, lass, but none of this is of my doing. If it hadn't been for young Harry's chest, I'd have pressed yon lad to do nowt about the claim at all."

Breda managed to translate roughly. The elder of the boys was presumably young Harry, since he hacked obligingly at her words; and she inferred that 'yon lad' was apparently Amos himself.

"Be quiet, Mary. This is my affair, not yours," Amos said, but with a mite less harshness in his voice as he waited for the child's breathing to steady. There was some softness in the man then, Breda thought, if only for his children.

"I don't think you fully understood my words, Sir," Richard went on. "The fact is that under the terms of the entailment, a genuine claimant to the estate must be found within six months of the demise of Mr. Philip Vivien—"

"Good God, man, I can read! I know all that, and I don't need it spelled out for me. I'm the claimant, and there's no man on earth who'll say I'm not genuine." He was all aggression now, his face redder and more bloated than ever. "I've worked in mines and on the land, and I'll see this place don't languish under my care, not that 'tis any business of yours—"

"And if Miss Vivien marries within those six months, she retains her inheritance," Richard went on relentlessly while Breda held her breath. He glanced at her, and she knew that her eyes were huge and pleading. He looked directly at Amos Keighley then, who had become suddenly silent and suspicious.

"Miss Vivien and myself are to be wed on the first of June. All the arrangements are made, and we marry in Penzance, well within the six months required. If you'd

170

waited a week or two, you would have been informed, and could have saved yourself a wasted journey south."

It was hard to say which of Breda's feelings came uppermost then. Joy and gratitude toward Richard, whose face was still so granite-hard she dared not move to his side; a weird kind of fear for Amos who looked as though he was in the grip of a seizure; sympathy for the gentle Mary, weeping silently as she gathered her clutch of children around her. It was Mary who spoke first, her voice thick and somehow defeated.

"I wouldn't care for myself, Miss Vivien, but 'tis Harry here that I fret over so much. The doctor says he must have a warmer climate for his chest, and the news about Vivien Hall was like a gift from heaven. Yon lad 'ould never move away from Yorkshire wi'out this to pull him, you see."

"And by God, you'll not do me out of it so fast, lad!" Amos suddenly roared. "How do I know this wedding's no spur of the moment idea, and the minute's my back's turned, you'll have no more intention of marrying the lass?"

"I can show you the invitations!" Breda said, incensed at the uncouth manners of the man. "Everything's already arranged, and you can check the facts yourself."

"I've every intention of doing so," the man growled. "Nobody makes a fool of Amos Keighley and gets away wi' it. I've traveled hundreds of miles for what was to be rightfully mine, and I'm not satisfied wi' what's happening here. It smells like bad fish to me."

"Perhaps you'd care to attend the wedding to satisfy yourself," Breda said sarcastically. To her horror she

171

saw him vigorously nod his head.

"Aye, I'm thinking mebbe I would."

"But not here! There are several good hotels in Penzance, and you don't look like paupers." She had already noted the good cloth in the clothes they all wore, and the sturdy boots on their feet.

"I'd ask you not to insult me, lass. I can pay for my lodgings, whether 'tis here or in Penzance—"

"Oh Amos, I think a hotel would be best for all concerned," Mary put in quickly. "Besides, I dare say you'll want words wi' the lawyer feller, and the address was in Penzance, as I recall."

"I shall certainly want words wi' the lawyer feller," he agreed grimly. He looked at Breda. "Can you arrange for us to be taken to Penzance tonight then, or do we have to stay here until morning?"

"Yandle can drive you. I'll arrange it at once. And—if you would like a proper invitation to the wedding—you are my family after all." She looked at the woman as she spoke, almost choking on the words. She had no liking for her cousin, but the soft-spoken woman wasn't to blame for her husband's failings, and the children were well-behaved and cherubic enough.

"It's very kind of you, Miss Vivien."

"My name is Breda, and you'd be very welcome, if you intend staying in the district that long."

"We intend staying to see justice done," Amos snapped.

Richard took a small step forward, his hands clenched at his sides, and this time Breda moved toward him, both presenting a solid front.

"I promise you that justice is being done. Miss Vivien will become my wife on the first of June, and the

172

estate will still belong irrevocably to her. There's nothing you or anyone can do to stop it."

Breda turned away to pull on the bell rope, and one of the maids appeared too suddenly for her to have been anywhere else but behind the door. She undoubtedly had been listening agog to everything, and from the avid look in her eyes she'd be well aware of the reasons for the hasty marriage between her young mistress and the handsome stranger.

It would be all around the servants quarters in no time. And among the tinners too . . . Sam Stone dallied with the maids whenever he could, and they all vied for his attentions, he being an important Pit Captain. This one would soon be racing off to Wheal Breda to give him her snippet of gossip. Breda groaned, knowing there was nothing to be done about it now. She gave the orders for Yandle to take the visitors into Penzance and see them comfortably settled in a hotel, and the group sat in uneasy silence for a few moments.

"What are the children called?" Breda said finally to Mary Keighley as the silence stretched on.

"Harry's the eldest, and the others are Alice and Billy," the woman said. "Say hello to Miss Vivien, all of you."

"Hello, Miss Vivien," they chorused in embarrassed voices.

"You can call me cousin Breda if you like," she heard herself say, immediately wondering why she'd done so. "I've never had small cousins before."

"They're good children," Mary said, as if she needed to defend them. "They just don't get on wi' the hard winters we get up north, especially not Harry here."

Breda didn't want to feel guilty on account of Harry, who looked at her with great brown eyes and a thin, sensitive face. He was about ten years old, she guessed, and nothing like his father. All the children resembled their mother in features and bearing, which was their very good fortune, Breda thought.

It was a relief to them all when Yandle arrived with the carriage, and the family departed with their wedding invitation, and a dire promise from Amos that he'd see her in church if not before. At the last minute the tiny girl, Alice, ran back to Breda and threw her arms around her waist.

"I like you," she lisped, and ran back to her mother.

When the carriage had gone with a rumble of wheels and a cloud of dust, she went back inside the house to face Richard again. Her heart sank at the set look on his face.

"You've really taken me for a fool, haven't you?"

"I never meant to! You knew about the entailment—"

"But not that someone had put in his claim. How long have you known? Was it before you accepted my proposal, or do I really need to ask? You'd never have accepted it otherwise, would you? It's exactly as I said. This pile of stone means more to you than anything living—or dead!"

She flinched. "How dare you! It's because of what this estate meant to my parents and my brother that I have to preserve our heritage. I'd do *anything*—"

"Even marry a man you don't love," he finished for her.

The denial hovered on her lips. *Oh, but I do love you . . . I love you so much . . .* but even if she'd dared to say the words, she could see he was in no mood for listening to them. He wouldn't believe her anyway. He'd never believe her now. If only she'd been open and honest about the wretched entailment from the beginning, and told him the reason for Mr. Flowers' flying visit that fateful day . . . but there was no turning back the days, and her only consolation was that at least it appeared he still intended going through with the marriage.

She suddenly dissolved in tears. She didn't want to have to cope with all this. Life had suddenly become an intolerable burden, and even saving Vivien Hall was too much to expect a young girl to have to deal with. Richard made no move to go to her. He was as immovable as the Sphinx.

"Did you mean what you said?" she said huskily, unable to stop the tears running down her face and into her mouth. "Is there still going to be a wedding?"

"Why not? Why shouldn't I get my hands on this stately pile as well as the next man?" he said crudely. "You're not the only one to benefit by it, and I still mean to have my pound of delicious flesh, my darling."

There was no tenderness in the words, and then he pulled her into his arms so fast she felt the breath knocked out of her. His mouth ground against hers in a kiss that held less passion than fury, and she trembled at the thought of what was in store for her. Whether he acted out of hatred or blind hurt she couldn't tell, but for the first time she felt real fear at what she had deliberately set out to do in marrying

175

Richard Delacey.

Thankfully, the feeling didn't last. After a sleepless night of worry and weeping, she awoke with new resolution in her mind. She saw everything she had to do with new clarity. Before any of this had turned their world upside down, Richard had made no secret of his wish to marry her.

For whatever reason, he had pursued her, and she had finally agreed. The marriage was clearly advantageous to them both. Breda swallowed, knowing that what it entailed for her would be nights of joy mingled with pain, submitting to a lover who didn't love her, but who had every intention of possessing her. She was entering into this contract willingly.

It was an affront to God, she thought with a sudden acute shame, but it was all for the sake of her ancestors and for Vivien Hall, and that was the one redeeming feature in her eyes. It would save what was rightfully hers from these Yorkshire interlopers.

And after a suitable interval, she would go to Richard and offer him his freedom. He could go back to Ireland and she would never try to claim anything from him. They would each be as they were before. She closed her eyes for a moment, wondering how any woman who had known the seductiveness of Richard Delacey could ever be as before . . .

She was nervous of seeing him the following morning, but he had apparently been giving as much serious thought to their future as she had. They walked around the gardens together, heads bent, not looking at one another.

"There's no point in our fighting over this situation, Breda," he said at last. "Either we stop it right now and go our separate ways, or we go on. It's up to you."

"Is it?" she murmured. "But I have no right to ask it of you. I've deceived you, and it's more than I expected that you would still agree to the wedding."

"I told you once I never go back on a promise. I gave Philip my promise a long time ago that I would make you my wife."

It wasn't what she had expected to hear and she looked at him oddly now.

"Why?"

"Someday I may tell you," he said briefly. "In the meantime I suggest you take the next few weeks to do all the things a prospective bride needs to do before her wedding, and I shall make it my business to go to Wheal Breda during this week."

"Another promise you mean to keep," she stated.

"That's right."

On the surface they were talking reasonably normally. But deep down Breda knew that nothing was ever going to be the same between them again. They had met through less than normal circumstances, and the marriage had almost been forced upon her, but there had always been more than a spark of magnetism between them. Now, all that seemed dulled to oblivion, and the marriage was no more than a duty, and she wondered if that spark would ever be revived again.

A few days later she watched as Richard strode out for Wheal Breda after breakfast. She would have liked to go with him, but he went on business, he told her, and it was best that he went alone, since he had no idea how long it would take.

She had neglected her own visits to the mine lately, and relied on Sam Stone to call on her with the daily details. She was especially annoyed to discover he had met Amos Keighley at one of the taverns in Penzance, and he made no secret of the fact that he knew as much about her business as she did.

It was some hours later when Richard returned to the house. He was grim-faced, with Sam Stone storming at his heels like an angry bulldog. She was in the garden lazing on the garden swing, but she sat bolt upright as she heard them arguing.

"I tell you the mine's in serious danger of total collapse if you don't get those props seen to immediately. And I don't mean next month or next week, but tomorrow, man!"

"And I tell 'ee they props are good for ten years or more yet," Sam Stone bellowed back. "I've shook 'em and rattled 'em, and they stand as firm as a rock, and no poncey Irish engineer is going to tell me a bit of seepage means we got trouble up above."

"You'll have plenty of trouble if the roof comes crashing down with tons of seawater following it. Do you want the deaths of all your miners on your conscience, Stone? Or do you just have a death wish for yourself?" Richard was shouting back just as loudly, and Breda jerked the swing to a stop and jumped down.

"Stop it, both of you!" she yelled at them. "I don't know what's been happening, but the safety of the men in my employ is the most important thing, and you're to take Richard's advice, Sam, no matter what it costs. Do you understand me?"

178

"Oh ah, I understand plenty, missy," the man sneered. "Now that your fancy-man's become your intended, I suppose you'd better heed what he says.'Tis only right and proper, since he's the means for you to hang on to your big house, ain't it?"

He didn't get a chance to say any more before Richard's fist connected with his chin. He was a big man, but the blow took him by surprise and he staggered and tripped, sprawling on the ground, and leaping up again at once. He lunged forward to strike Richard, but Breda leapt between them, pushing them apart and screaming at them.

"Stop it, do you hear? I won't have you fighting. And Sam, you'd better just watch what you say. You may be a good Pit Captain, but you're not the only one in the County, and I'll be rid of you in a minute if you insult me or Mr. Delacey again."

The man twisted away from her, his dark face ugly, his chin split and bleeding from Richard's punch.

"You'd better watch what you say as well, missy. There's plenty of folk who'd wonder if Mr. Delacey's more interested in closing down the pits than the bother of keeping 'em working. An incompetent engineer could say what he liked for his own ends."

"You bastard! What possible reason could I have for closing down the pits? They don't belong to me!"

"They would when you marry the boss, wouldn't they? Leastways, that's what I've been told, and there's plenty of stories going around in Penzance about it since a certain gent and his family came south," Sam crowed. "Anyway, I reckon the tin in Wheal Breda's pretty near worked out."

"You never said anything of the sort before," Breda

said, stunned for a moment by the words. She knew the current yield was nothing like it used to be, and was compensated by the moorland pits, but she could hardly believe that Wheal Breda was nearly worked out!

"Mebbe I didn't want to worry you."

"And maybe you didn't want to lose your cushy job," Richard said keenly. He moved threateningly toward Stone, and the man backed away.

"You mind your own work and leave me to mind mine," he shouted. "But take a warning, and leave well alone, Delacey. There's no reports needed on Wheal Breda, nor no call for new props or reinforcements. The men are perfectly safe."

"That's for me to decide, not you," Richard said coldly.

"Richard, please come inside the house and let me attend to your hand," Breda pulled him away as the argument looked set to go on and on. He looked down briefly, automatically flexing his knuckles and wincing as the bruised and swollen skin cracked, and a trickle of blood oozed out from each one.

"I'd gladly spill more blood than this on that one," he muttered. "I don't trust him, Breda."

"No more do I, but standing here glowering after him will do no good, and you need some witch-hazel on those knuckles to stop them swelling still more, or they'll be very painful tomorrow. My father always kept an apothecary box in his study."

He gave a brief smile. "You fancy yourself as a bit of healer, do you?"

"I know enough to tend simple wounds," she said tartly. "And to scold grown men from brawling in public!"

His smile faded and he looked thoughtful as they went indoors to the study together. He sat on one of the leather chairs while she brought out her father's box and found witch-hazel and lint.

"I didn't like the threat behind your Pit Captain's words," he said. "Nor the fact that he's been talking with that odious cousin of yours."

"Neither did I, but what can he do?" she said.

"I don't know, but I mean to make out my report and hand it in to the Stannary Court as soon as possible. As for not being a competent engineer—"

"I didn't believe that for one moment!"

He smiled faintly. "Thank you for your support, my love, but I have credentials to uphold my words. If anything should happen at Wheal Breda because of that fool's neglect, I want it put on record that he was told about the dangers."

"Good. Now just hold still, and try to be a model patient, will you?"

She took his right hand and placed it on her father's desk. The knuckles were already blue-black and skinned, and he winced again as she spread them out and dabbed them with witch-hazel. The fingers were strong and broad, and she felt a great tenderness for him as she gently tended each one. He was a strong man in every way, and no matter how he taunted her, she still loved him. Nothing had changed that, nor ever would.

She bent her head over her task, and only when she had finished and glanced up at him, did she see how his own eyes had softened toward her. For a long and breathless moment their glances locked and held, and she wished desperately that he'd tell her he loved her too. Even if it was a white lie, she wouldn't care.

"I guess I shan't be writing any report for a few days," he said gruffly, as he studied his stiffened fingers. "It will have to wait, but no harm will be done. I don't expect the mine to collapse immediately, but it didn't hurt to put the fear of God into Sam Stone that it would."

"But you meant it seriously, didn't you? The repair work must be done?"

"Oh yes, and it must be done soon," he said.

"But you'll keep out of his way and not get into a fight again? A fine sight you'll look in church with a hand in bandages and your eyes blackened," she said, in an attempt to lighten the suddenly tense atmosphere between them.

"Yes, nurse," he said, putting his good arm around her waist. "Everything will be functioning properly for my wedding-day, I promise you."

She felt the blush run up her cheeks and down her throat. Everything was going to be all right, she thought desperately. And in a spontaneous movement she leaned forward and kissed his lips, realizing just as instantly that it was the first time she had done so voluntarily. It was no more than a feather-soft touch of warm flesh on warm flesh, but as she felt his ready response, it still had the power to stir her senses, just as everything about him did.

The first day of June shimmered with summer heat, so that the entire expanse of moorland around Vivien Hall resembled a hazy mirage. Breda stood in front of her dressing-table mirror, gazing at the vision that was herself. For once, Nan was too awed to say anything, and Mrs. Yandle continually cleared her throat, fussing over the long train of the wedding-dress and arranging the Honiton lace veil with loving and reverent hands.

"You're a princess, lovey, and I'd dare anybody to say different," she declared sternly to hide her emotion. "If only your dear father and brother were here to see this day. And your Mama too," she remembered hastily.

"I'm sure they know," Breda said softly. The face that stared back at her was paler than usual, her eyes a brilliant emerald.

Did they know? she wondered. Were her father and brother looking down at her now from their heaven and approving her choice? And was her mother a little sorrowful, because this wedding had been so hastily arranged, and her beloved daughter was marrying for a one-sided love?

She shook off the images quickly. It was too late now. And in the end, it *was* her choice. Today she was marrying Richard Delacey, whom she loved beyond all reason.

She swallowed. "Yandie, hadn't you better be setting off for the church?" she said huskily.

The team of servants would be seeing to the wedding-feast, and Mrs. Yandle had handed everything over to them with better grace than usual, since she wouldn't miss her young lady's wedding for the world. She and Yandle were driving some of the older and more trusted servants to Penzance to sit in the back of the church and witness the grand occasion.

183

"I'll send your aunt into you then, if you're sure you're quite ready."

"I'm ready," Breda said steadily. She and Nan would be escorted to Penzance by the Pollards who had arrived yesterday and would be leaving the following morning. She had begged Charles Pollard to give her away, and his answer had been a proud and happy one. And Nan was to be her one attendant, a flower girl bedecked with summer rosebuds that echoed the posy of sweet-smelling flowers Breda herself carried.

It still seemed like an unbelievable dream, she thought, as the carriages turned out of Vivien Hall and into the sunlight. The driver sitting in front with Aunt Eddy and Nan; herself in her finery, with Uncle Charles in the back. And all roads leading her to her destiny, to being Richard Delacey's bride . . . destiny's bride, she thought. Was it all really happening? Or would she wake up very soon and find it was all a beautiful fantasy?

Chapter Ten

The interior of the church was cool and dim after the brightness of the sunlight outside. Breda felt a strange sense of breathlessness as she stepped inside, leaning heavily on Charles Pollard's arm. From somewhere in the church the music swelled, heralding the arrival of the bride. Charles whispered to her to move forward, through the sea of admiring faces of guests in their splendid wedding attire, to where Richard stood waiting for her at the altar. She caught her breath.

Was this day really happening? Was she really about to plight her troth to a man she barely knew? As she met his eyes and his faint smile, she knew that this day had always been inevitable, that in some mystic way she had always known him. And that whatever circumstances had brought them to this moment, it was meant to be. There was comfort in that. There was Cornish logic . . .

As the service went on, the preacher said the words that were to bind her to Richard Delacey forever, and she sensed that if her father and brother were watching they would surely be approving. And then all the mystic sensations faded away, and there was only herself and the man who was sliding the gold band onto the third finger of her left hand, and telling the world of their intentions.

". . . with my body I thee worship, and with all my worldly goods I thee endow . . ."

Was there the smallest hint of mockery as he said the last? She couldn't bear it if there was. Not today, not now. She looked into his eyes, and couldn't fathom the darkness there. To the onlookers, it would probably be described as a look of intense emotion. To Breda, it was inscrutable.

And then the formalities were over, save for the signing of the register in the vestry. But they were now officially man and wife, and she belonged, body and soul, to Richard Delacey. She was his . . . and he was hers. A surge of pleasure filled her veins at the thought, and she had never realized until now how cold and tense she had been throughout the whole proceeding.

"A kiss for the bride, I think," she heard him murmur, as they stood in the tiny vestry and received congratulations from the intimate little gathering of witnesses there. "We must be seen to be happy, my love."

Again, she had no idea if he was mocking her or not, but she gave up worrying as his arms enfolded her and she surrendered to the magic of his kiss. Nothing could take this away, she thought. Even if he didn't love her now, there were emotional and physical ties between them that he certainly couldn't deny, and in time, who knew . . . ? Successful marriages had been born of far less. Hadn't Richard himself said something of the same?

It seemed no time at all that they were forming into a small procession and moving back through the long aisle of the church to the triumphant strains of the Wedding March, smiling to the left and right at their guests. Breda wished briefly that they could do it all again, to recapture and savor every moment, so that it didn't all seem like a hazy dream.

All except one moment when she looked straight into the brooding eyes of Amos Keighley, seated at the very back of the church with his family. He'd have come especially to see that she was truly wed, of course, and she was then startled to see an unlikely companion leaning forward to speak to him. Sam Stone!

Those tinners who wished to come to the church and were not on shift that day had been given free transport to and from Penzance from the Vivien stables, but she had hardly expected Sam Stone to appear so freely conversant with her Yorkshire cousin.

And then she forgot them all as she and Richard led the procession out into the brilliant June sunshine, to the applause of the townsfolk who habitually turned out to see a wedding.

For Breda, the rest of the day was still cloaked in a delicious haze. It was all somehow like a delightful interlude, a mere passing of time among people who loved her and were pleased for her; some who envied her her attentive and handsome husband; others who hid a tear at the fact that her own menfolk couldn't see this day, and that she had no mother to advise her on the more delicate matters concerning marriage.

Had they but known it, those delicate matters concerning marriage had Breda in a fever of impatience. The wedding feast was magnificent, the guests noisy and happy, and everyone was making it a marvelous day to remember . . . but all she wanted was to be alone with Richard. They hadn't been alone all day. Even their vows, said before God, had also been said before the preacher and an entire listening congregation. A man and wife needed to be alone to seal their marriage . . .

Did he think the same, or was she being terribly immodest in having these feelings? Breda wondered. She watched him now, as the day moved on into evening, and the shadows grew longer. He was, as always in company, the gallant gentleman, sharing time with the unmarried ladies and their Mamas, raising glasses with the gentlemen. She watched him, loving him so much that it physically hurt. And how was she ever going to go through the intimacies of their new life together and never let him know . . . ?

As if aware of her gaze on him, Richard slowly turned and looked across the room toward her. There were probably fifty people between them, but for Breda there was no one, only him. A wild pulsebeat throbbed in her throat, and she felt her lips part a little. It was as if she was suddenly unable to breathe properly, and the tight constrictions of the beautiful wedding gown were holding her in a vice. She had a wild desire to rip it away from her skin, to be free of everything but the desire in her husband's eyes.

"Are you all right, Breda? You do look flushed!" Nan said beside her. "I think you've had a little too much champagne. They say it helps to give a bride Dutch courage on her wedding night."

Nan, who knew nothing about the searing sensuality

that could flare in a moment between a man and a woman, spoke in an encouragingly confidential way. Breda tore her gaze away from Richard, staring at Nan unseeingly for a few seconds.

What would she say, this so-innocent friend, if she knew how Breda had momentarily experienced a fever of longing for nakedness between herself and her husband, and an urgency to know a man more intimately than she knew herself? Men were supposed to be the lustful creatures, but who was to say it was wrong for a woman in love to have longings too?

She blinked at Nan, and threw her arms around her old friend. "You're probably right, love," she said huskily. "The champagne's going to my head."

"And to Richard's too, I think," Nan teased. "From the way he keeps looking at you, I'd say he can't wait for the celebrations to end."

"Well, you can all stay as long as you like, but we shall probably retire quite soon," Breda said as evenly as she could, considering the way her heart was jumping.

Richard was slowly working his way around the room to her now, and her mouth was beginning to feel dry. It was funny, but the more champagne she sipped, the dryer it seemed to get.

"Shall we have one last dance together before we say goodnight to our guests?" he said as he reached her side.

He held out his arms, and she heard the musicians start up a waltz. Without a word, Breda drifted into his embrace, and the guests seemed to melt away from the main body of the room as the newlyweds held each other as close as convention would allow, looking into one another's eyes as they floated in time to the melodic

189

tune.

"Have you any idea how I'm aching to get you out of here and into our bedroom?" he murmured next to her ear as he swung her around.

"I think I've a notion of it," she whispered back. "Even Nan didn't fail to notice those watchful eyes of yours. Anyone would think you were afraid someone was going to snatch your bride away."

"Not a chance, my darling girl," he said, in a voice that had the power to set her senses on fire. "You're mine now, my beautiful Breda, no matter why or how. And I mean to keep you."

He laughed teasingly, holding her so close for a moment that she thought her back might break. She vaguely heard cheers in the background, and as she laughingly protested he released his possessive hold on her to dance with more decorum.

But if he had to be a little drunk on champagne to be saying all these heady things to her, she no longer cared. If his tongue was loosened, and he didn't mean half of what he was saying, she didn't care about that either. All she cared about was that he said them, caressing her with his eyes and his voice and the seductive touch of his hands . . .

"Richard, I think we had better not dance any more once this tune ends," she whispered, suddenly conscious that he was becoming rather too free with his endearments, and aware that their guests might be embarrassed by too reckless a show of public affection.

"I couldn't agree more. I suggest we make our departure and let them get on with their revelry, while we attend to more important matters of our own," he said, still oozing seduction in every word.

By now, she knew that her senses were so heightened she would have agreed to anything. The music ended, and the applause for the bride and groom led them quite naturally to wave goodnight to everyone and slip quickly out of the ball room. They encountered Mrs. Yandle at the foot of the curving staircase.

"You look a real picture, Miss Breda — I mean Mrs. Delacey, and this has been a wonderful day for us all," she said, dabbing at her eyes. "Now then, I've had hot and cold water jugs and towels put ready in your bathroom, lovey. Shall I send one of the maids to attend you?"

"That won't be necessary, Yandie," Breda said quickly, feeling the pressure of Richard's fingers around her waist.

"Goodnight then — Madam and Sir."

The woman turned quickly away, a tinge of red in her cheeks, and Breda felt a wild girlish giggle starting in her throat. It was obvious that Mrs. Yandle was feeling the weight of Breda's new status and didn't quite know how to handle it yet. Which was so foolish, because she was still the same Breda.

Some hours later, Breda knew how wrong her fleeting thought had been, because she would never be the same Breda again. She was Richard Delacey's wife, his woman, now and for all time. And while she lay, still sleepless, reliving everything so as not to forget one single exquisite moment, she listened to her beloved breathing in sleep beside her.

191

"You did right in not wanting a maid to attend you in the bathtub," Richard said as they reached the room they were now to share. "Why shouldn't a husband be given such a delightful privilege?"

Breda's heart leaped. "I'm not sure that was why I said it," she said in some confusion. "I just thought you'd had enough of company —"

He closed the door behind them and pulled her into his arms without letting her take another step into the room.

"Quite right," he said against her mouth. "Who wants a third person sharing their wedding night? And now, my love, since the hot water and towels are ready, I think we should take advantage of them, don't you?"

She realized that all the time he had been talking he had been gently unfastening the buttons at the back of the shimmering silk wedding gown. The precious veil had already been safely put away, and the pins had somehow slipped from her dark hair so that it tumbled down her back like a wanton.

She felt Richard's hands pushing the smooth silk fabric away from her shoulders, and then he bent to kiss each one, savoring each caress and bringing her quickly to the peak of desire. But she sensed instinctively that there was a long way to go yet before they reached the ultimate intimacy, and her senses shivered with each new sensation his touch aroused.

The slippery material of the gown slid still further, followed by her petticoats, until finally the full, satiny curves of her breasts were exposed to a man's gaze for the first time. Breda felt the sting of tears in her eyes, wanting to be perfect for him, and knowing from his indrawn breath and the expression in his eyes that he was not disappointed.

"You're so beautiful . . . you're like an unfinished painting of a Madonna and temptress all rolled up in one—"

"Unfinished?" she said huskily, unsure if this was a criticism or not.

"No woman is truly finished without a man," he said. "Why else would God give a woman her mystery and a man his seed for perpetuity?"

She had never heard him talk so seriously and yet so seductively at the same time. He was everything she had ever wanted, her husband, her lover . . .

His head bent lower, his tongue slowly circling her nipples one by one, its delicate coolness sending waves of desire rippling through her. Involuntarily she arched her back, throwing back her head so that even the caress of her own hair on her skin was an added aphrodisiac. Then she heard him groan softly.

"Dear God, but the need in me is too great to wait any longer," he said in a voice made urgent with desperation. "I want you here and now, Breda, and I must have you."

He was tearing at his own clothes now, and to her enraptured senses there was nothing abhorrent in his actions. Her passion soared to meet him, and his needs were her needs.

She slipped out of the wedding gown and undergarments and was swept up in his arms as he pressed her down on the thick fur rug at the foot of the bed. He looked deep in her eyes for one last moment. She felt the rough tangle of hair that covered his chest, a tantalizing friction against her delicate skin. She moved her hands freely against it for a few seconds, before he gathered her close, and then there was nothing at all between his flesh and hers.

The sweet pain of surrender was over in a moment. Breda hardly noticed the pain in the slow sensual movements that followed it. And his kisses distracted her so much, his mouth continuing to murmur her name against her lips as if he could no more control his words than his actions. Apart from her name and the endearments, what he said was completely incomprehensible to her. It was as though he was compelled to speak in that deep ragged tone, but couldn't bear to let her understand the words. They were Gaelic, perhaps, she thought vaguely . . .

There was a great deal of Richard Delacey he still wished to keep private. She was only able to think coherently for seconds at a time now, because her spirit was soaring in an ecstasy of loving. And this was no longer the time for conscious thought, only for sensation, and the essential knowledge that whatever the reasons or circumstances for their union, they were truly one, and neither God nor man could change it now.

"Oh Richard, I do—I do—" she whispered, as the rhythm of his love-making became more urgent and she could no longer fight her feelings for him.

Incredulously, she thought she heard him give a low delighted laugh against her throat, as if he was about to welcome her declaration of love. And then his grip on her tightened and she felt the rush of his seed spilling into her. At the same time his voice was caught in a ragged gasp as he twisted against her, holding her in a vice.

"Please don't profess to love me right now, my darling wife! Tell me tomorrow, when our ardor has cooled, if you dare!"

"What do you mean?" she stammered, feeling him already moving away from her, if not physically, then in every other way. As if he was afraid that he too had given away too much, his fingers trailed around her breasts, the tips darkened now with a passion she knew she would never be able to hide from him again.

"I confess that you are the most exquisite woman I've ever made love to, Breda, but I would prefer that you tell me you love me in the cold light of day and not when we're caught up in a love-spell! Perhaps then I'll believe it."

She stared at him, feeling at a distinct disadvantage as she lay pinned beneath him. He was so very much the arrogant male, the hunter, the conqueror . . . and all her pleasure in what had just happened vanished like will-o'-the-wisp, and she felt as though she had just been ravished. Feeling furious and betrayed too, at his reference to the fact that she was not the first for him. A man expected his bride to be virginal and untouched, while he was at liberty to gain experience where he may.

History had always decreed it so, but the injustice of it all made her push him away from her with an indignant shove. It took him off balance, so that he sprawled onto his side, but he merely laughed at her fury.

"Did anyone ever tell you that you look more like a gypsy than a lady with your eyes spitting green fire and your hair all unkempt, my sweet? Though I would hope that no one else but myself has seen you in quite this delectable state," he said, his eyes gazing at her body with lazy insolence. "I swear that I am going to enjoy my gypsy as much as my lady, no matter which side of you you show me."

"Oh, you—you contemptible—"

She made to slap his face but he caught her wrist easily and held it high above her head. He trapped her other hand in his, and pushed her back onto the rug. Her eyes blazed at him, but even while she raged at him, there was another, darker side of her that exalted in his mastery. She had always been a fiery woman, but it had taken Richard Delacey to set light to that fire, and fill her with a wild and answering desire.

While he still held her captive, he leaned forward and began a slow trail of kisses that began with her eyes and over her nose, to the soft curves of her mouth where he lingered awhile. His mouth went lower, around those rosy peaks that were so instantly aroused by his merest touch. Down and down, over the soft firm swell of her belly, to the dark triangle that parted almost involuntarily as he neared it.

She realized that she had stopped resisting. Her breathing had become shallow, as if she could hardly bear to draw breath and miss a single sensation that he was evoking in her. And then came the moment she had unconsciously been anticipating, as the warm tip of his tongue invaded her. Her fingers tightened in the hair at the back of his neck and she raised herself slightly, going to meet him and opening up for him.

She was drowning in new and ragingly exquisite sensations now, and time and space were merging. She felt as if she were in the grip of some mystical potion that opened up new horizons to her that were explosive and beautiful. Then she felt Richard gently cover her body with his once more. Her dazed senses awaited his lovemaking once more, but he merely lay, heavy and dormant over her, as protective as a warm blanket.

"Not yet, my love. Even a stallion needs time to recover, and I promise you that the next time we make love it will not need to be in such a rush. Now that we've savored what we each have to give, we will learn to take more time."

"Yes," Breda whispered, hardly caring what he said and agreeing to everything. She had promised to love, honor and obey him, and only she knew how deeply the first of those promises applied to her.

"So while my strength recovers, I suggest we take that bath before the pails of water lose their heat," Richard said more briskly, rolling away from her once more. "Do you suppose there's room in the tub for two?"

Breda looked at him to see if he was serious, but there was a teasing look on his face together with a gleam of determination. He meant what he said, and although the idea was one she would never have dreamed of doing yesterday, she was suddenly tingling with excitement at the thought of sharing the tub with her husband.

"I think we could manage to squeeze in," she grinned, and he hauled her to her feet.

She swayed in his arms for a moment, wondering if every woman's wedding night was as wonderful and extraordinary as this. And in one small way, sad, because despite Richard's undisguised delight in her, she knew he didn't love her. He had married her out of respect for her brother, and an integrity that never let him go back on a promise.

But she wouldn't even think of that now, when they played such delightful games together, and ran as naked as two children into the adjoining bathroom. The bathtub was narrow but much longer than the old style hipbaths, and had been installed by her father to modernize Vivien Hall. Richard poured the still steaming water into the tub, and topped it up with just enough cold to make it a comfortable temperature.

"There are bath essences too," Breda said. "Do you object to having them sprinkled in the water? I warn you they will make us both smell like a summer garden—"

"Since I expect our smells to mingle for the rest of the night, I can see no reason not to smell like a summer garden," Richard said dryly. She turned away, sprinkling the essences with trembling hands. He *must* grow to love her, she thought. At first it hadn't mattered. Now, it did. It mattered desperately.

He held her hand while she stepped carefully into the blissful water, and climbed in at the other end. The scented water rose in their nostrils, as Breda swished it about to scatter the fragrant bubbles. She picked up a washcloth from the little side-table, and Richard immediately took it from her.

"This is my task, I believe," he said softly, and the next half-hour passed in unbelievable pleasure, as Richard first soaped every part of her body and rinsed it off with his fingers running playfully over her skin. The sensations were both erotic and tender as he did this for her. Then it was her turn.

Under his instruction and guidance she too performed the most intimate ablutions for him, kneeling in front of him to reach around and run the water over his strong muscled back and down his spine. And feeling herself caught into him, her soapy breasts pressed against his chest and his mouth wet on hers.

"I think bath time has come to an end," he murmured. She had already become aware that his strength had returned, and that his need for her was proudly obvious once more. The shivering sensations ran through her like a flame, knowing she had the power to arouse him like this. No matter what, she had that woman's power, and it was something to remember if things should ever go badly between them . . .

But on this magical night, Breda believed blissfully that nothing ever could. No man could hold a woman so tenderly and not love her. She knew nothing of the ways of harlots or of the men who paid them for their services. She believed, in her innocence, that only love could produce this ecstasy . . .

And what she considered to be love flowed between them at a more leisurely and sensual pace when they had returned to the bedroom. They had patted each other dry on warmed towels, and lay between the sheets now on the bed they shared.

Long after the lingering sounds of revelry from their wedding guests had died down and they all slept exhaustedly in their beds, Richard Delacey continued to make love to his wife. He loved her slowly and sensuously, until her responses could no longer make him resist the wild thrusts that made her cry out with joy, and finally melt against him in sleep with her arms wrapped tightly around him.

Breda awoke slowly, stretching her arms above her head luxuriously, and thinking that life had never been so good. It was a week after her wedding day, and the love-making hadn't abated. He had never yet said that he loved her, and stubbornly, after that first awkward moment when he had stopped her, she had resisted making her feelings plain to him. It would be humiliating to let him know how much she cared . . . it was the one small cloud in what she saw as a perfect union.

Quite deliberately, she blotted everything else out of her mind. They belonged to one another irrevocably now. And despite any small scratchiness during the daytime, here in this room when night fell, there was only bliss.

Without opening her eyes, she let her arm stray to where Richard's head would be lying on the pillow next to hers. She loved these early-morning moments when they were both still sleepy, and unguarded enough to do nothing other than smile and hold and kiss . . . her eyes opened abruptly.

The bed was cold, although the pillow was still dented where Richard's head had lain on it. She ran her hand down the bed inside the sheets, but that was cold too. He must have gotten up very early, and she felt a shiver of unease run through her. She sat up too quickly, and felt her head spin.

Snippets of a previous conversation between them snapped into her head, as if a gleeful demon was shouting the words at her, paying her back for believing her happiness could last.

". . . One week after the wedding, I intend going home to Ireland . . . I'm quite sure you'll be happier to stay at Vivien Hall and glory in your restored possessions . . ."

". . . Won't your father think it very odd that you leave your bride after one week of marriage? Everyone else most certainly will! . . ."

". . . I care very little what other people think . . ."

But he couldn't be gone without saying a word, she thought in panic now, throwing off the bedcovers. She quickly wrapped a dressing-robe around her nakedness, as if the very sight of herself humiliated her as much as his desertion.

But he wouldn't have considered he had deserted her, she thought, feverishly rushing to the bathroom and giving her face and hands the tersest of wipes, and carefully avoiding looking at the bathtub that had been the scene of so many delicious romps this past week . . . he had told her most definitely of his plans . . . but surely he *couldn't* have gone without even a word.

She dressed hurriedly, hopping about on one foot while she tried to push her other one into a stocking that went every way but the way she wanted. She was totally distracted, and she knew she had better compose herself before she encountered any of the staff. She finished dressing and took several long deep breaths before she opened her bedroom door and walked more composedly than she felt down the long staircase.

"Oh, Miss Breda—I mean Mrs. Delacey—" Mrs. Yandle came hurrying out of the drawing room when she heard her footsteps.

"For pity's sake, Yandie, I'm still Miss Breda, so don't start getting all flustered about what to call me!" Breda said, irritated in a minute.

It was going to be a bad day, she just knew it, and she was ready to fly off the handle at everyone. She bit her lip, dying to ask about Richard, but knowing she'd give everything away if she had to inquire as to his whereabouts. But she didn't need to. She heard Mrs. Yandle give a loud sniff.

"I expected you to be out of sorts this morning, so I won't take the huff at that, then." She held out a long envelope. "Mr. Delacey said it seemed a crime to disturb

201

you when you were sleeping so peacefully, so he asked me to give you this before he went. Your breakfast's in the dining room whenever you're ready for it."

She walked off, stiff-backed with resentment, but Breda didn't even notice her go. She stared at the envelope in her trembling hands, hardly able to see it for her brimming eyes. She hadn't really believed he would still leave her after all that they had been to one another this past week, but he had obviously meant everything he said. He'd fully intended to go home to Ireland to see his father, and she had no idea how long he was going to stay there — or if he would ever come back. Was this his final revenge for her deceit?

She rushed out into the garden to the sanctuary of the small gazebo and ripped the envelope open. She was desperately afraid to read what he had written, and just as desperate to know if there was any crumb of hope left for them. She had never humbled herself to anyone, but she would have gladly done it now, if only he would say he loved her and was coming back to her.

"My dear Breda," she read, and her heart sank, for it was hardly the warmest of greetings.

"By now you will realize that I am on my way to Ireland. I thought it best to leave without disturbing you. We have already discussed my plans, and my arrangements have been made for some time. I am sure you will appreciate this time alone to think about the future.

"I have delivered my report on Wheal Breda to the Stannary Court and trust that you will ensure that the work is carried out. It is very necessary, Breda, so ignore any arguments that Sam Stone may make to the contrary. I gather the man is acquainted with one or two members of the committee, and may well have tried to discredit my claim for repair work, so I leave the final decision in your hands.

"There seems little more to say for the present. I will enclose my address in Ireland should you need to contact me for any reason. Take all care of yourself. Richard."

Not a word of love. Not a hint of the joys they had shared this past week. A slow burning anger made her tear the letter to shreds, wishing she had his throat between her hands as she did so! How dare he treat her this way! As if she were no more than a—a plaything, and now that he'd had his fill of her, he was off and away. He had always meant to have her, she remembered, and she had fallen straight into his hands. Or rather, fate had led her there.

She looked with blazing eyes through the long windows to the fragrant gardens beyond, and without warning her bones seemed to melt, the fury disintegrating. To her own disbelief, she found herself suddenly hating every stone of Vivien Hall. If it wasn't for this, she thought passionately, she might still have a husband. And there was no pile of granite on earth that could compensate for losing him.

Chapter Eleven

"Miss Breda, are you ill?"

Mrs. Yandle came searching for her some while later, after finding the breakfast in the dining room untouched and the tea cold. She spoke with some alarm.

Breda sat crouched in an armchair, small and vulnerable and shivering as if she were suffering from some dreadful malaise. She dragged her senses together and spoke in a muffled voice without raising her head from her arms.

"No, I'm not ill, Yandie. Just upset that my husband has had to go away—"

"Well, I never expected anything different," the housekeeper said in a relieved voice. "Such a thing for a man to have to do after only one week of wedded bliss. But dearie, if his father's ill, there's little else he could do in all conscience, is there?"

So that was the story Richard had put about. At least he had spared her the disgrace of hearing whispers that the man had left his bride after only one week with no apparent explanation! She sat up a little straighter, sniffing back the tears.

"I know, but I shall miss him so, Yandie, and I've no idea when he'll be back, you see."

Mrs. Yandle looked at her more generously.

"You'd be an odd bride if you didn't miss your man," she said dryly. "But I'm thinking you should do what a young lady always does when she's out of sorts."

"And what's that, since you know so much about it? I'm certainly not in the mood for entertaining or idle chatter," she said in irritation at the arch comment.

"Well then, go into town by yourself and buy yourself some fripperies, or go and visit that nice Nan Greenwood and take her off to Penzance for the day and have some lunch and a gossip in one o' those posh hotels wi' her. She never takes offense when your tongue sharpens."

The impulse to snap at her quickly died as Breda looked mutely into her knowing old eyes. "Am I so bad?"

"I've seen you worse, and lately of course, it's been all sweetness and light, thanks to Mr. Delacey's influence. Still, I'll admit you've got good cause to be scratchy now. 'Tis a pity Mr. Delacey didn't take you with him, but he knew how you still grieved for your Pa and for Master Philip, and he was afraid you'd be upset at seeing another old gentleman confined to his bed by illness."

"Did he tell you that?"

"Well, of course he did. How else would I know it? Now then, am I going to make you some fresh breakfast and hot tea while you think about what I've said? 'Tis a fine day for a lady to be going to town."

"All right," Breda said. "But you can tell Yandle to

205

saddle my horse and I'll take a ride — then I can return when I please. Some fresh air is probably what I need."

Yes, she would go to Penzance and mingle anonymously with the crowds. And if she wanted to linger aimlessly by the quayside, staring out at the endless sea where a ship had taken Richard Delacey to Ireland, it was nobody's business but her own.

Her gaze was caught by the shreds of paper she had pushed into the base of an expensive jardiniere. It was hardly the place to leave them, where some sharp-eyed maid might piece them together for a bit of kitchen prattle!

She gathered them up quickly, and thrust them into the pocket of her morning-gown. She would dispose of them in her own room, but not before she had put them back into order and memorized Richard's father's address. She might have need of it. She might even write to him, she thought wanly, if she could ever think of suitable words to say.

She studied the address intently for a few minutes. Grensham, Grannaby. She frowned at the simple couplet. It was easy to remember but it told her nothing. It sounded like a house in a small village where no other description was needed. She tried to imagine it, but he had told her so little about his past, except for the tragedy of his sister, and she couldn't be thinking of another sadness right now, so she gave up trying.

An hour or so later, Mrs. Richard Delacey rode serenely out of Vivien Hall on her piebald mare. She had forced herself to eat a little breakfast to please Mrs. Yandle, and she was dressed now in her favorite green velvet riding habit and a perky little hat of matching velvet with dyed peacocks' feathers on her head. She looked every inch the happy and beautiful young bride, and no one would have guessed that her heart was breaking.

She lifted her head, riding proudly along the track, and automatically passing the time of day with people she met on the road to Penzance without really seeing them. She had decided against calling on her friend Nan, being simply unable to face her good natured chatter and sympathy because Richard had been unexpectedly called away . . . Even Richard was being forced to add to the lies, she thought, but what was the use in dwelling on any of that now?

Long before she reached the town she realized the velvet riding habit was far too hot for the day. It was too late to go back and change, and at least while she was riding, the sea breeze was cooling enough. But once she reached the town she knew she was going to regret it, and made herself walk slowly and not be in a rush. She had nowhere particular to go, anyway, so there was no need for hurry.

Penzance was a bustling town with a long sea front and harbour, and her deflated spirits rose a little as she saw the weekly open-air market. Breda tied up her mare in the courtyard of an hotel, having decided to stay in town for lunch despite the warm day. She wandered around the inviting market stalls, browsing over ribbons and laces and plaster models of the town painted in the gaudiest colors imaginable, and smilingly ignoring entreaties to buy.

The market was complete with street entertainers hoping for a few pennies to be thrown their way. There was a hurdy-gurdy man with a monkey on a long rope and a ruff around its neck who clapped at the laughing children in its audience. There was a hot-potato man and someone selling toffee apples on sticks, around which there were always eager groups of children with parents. There was . . .

"Mrs. Keighley! Mary! It is you, isn't it?"

Her heart leaped for a moment, and she asked the question unnecessarily, since the small Alice clung to the woman's skirts, and young Harry and Billy were appearing at her side with three sticky toffee apples in their hands. Breda saw the woman's face flush in hot embarrassment.

"Yes it is, Miss — Mrs. — "

"I told you, my name's Breda," she said in quick irritation at Mary's fluster. "But what are you all doing here? I thought you'd have gone back to Yorkshire after — "

She fell silent. She'd been going to say *after the wedding,* but that would only point to the fact that her own plans had ruined all of this woman's hopes. She had no reason to feel guilty, Breda thought angrily, except that Harry's hacking cough was there to remind her . . .

"Our Harry took ill again, Mrs. — Breda," Mary Keighley said at last. "We took him to a doctor and he said the lad should stay in the south if he was ever to get well. Since we'd expected to be here for some time anyway, I persuaded Amos to rent a cottage for the summer, and see how the lad fared."

"So that's what you've done?"

"Aye, it is," she said defiantly. "Whatever you might think of Amos, he wouldn't see his lad come to harm. We're staying a short walk out of the town in an old fisherman's cottage. The man died a while back and it lay empty, so his son's rented it to us at a fair price."

"Well, I hope the sun does Harry some good," Breda said, filled with embarrassment herself now. "Though I don't think it will be such a good idea to be going back north when the winter comes! Surely that will be the worst time for Harry?"

Mary shrugged. "I dare say we'll have no choice."

The small girl tugged at her mother's hand. "Can we show the lady the cottage, Mammie?"

"Oh, I don't think so. I have somewhere to go —" Breda said quickly. Mary looked at her steadily.

"He'll not be there, if that's what you're thinking. He's going round the inns to find work to keep his family in victuals, though I dare say most of his wages will go into a pint pot afore he comes back," she couldn't resist saying bitterly. "But you're welcome to come and share dinner wi' us if you've a mind to it."

"Yes! Yes!"

The two younger children jumped up and down, shouting delightedly, and after a few minutes of indecision, Breda gave in. Why not? What else did she have to do but wander around aimlessly? The mare would be safe enough at the hotel, and against her will she was beginning to warm to this little family. Though her opinion of Amos Keighley hadn't changed, and she guessed that Mary had had to beg hard to let them stay south for the summer.

She walked through the busy market with the group now, finding Alice's small sticky hand tucked in hers. She had never had anything to do with children before, and she found the trusting grip oddly endearing.

"You mind you don't mess up cousin Breda's fine

209

clothes now, Alice," Mary called back as she led the way toward the sandy shore and the haphazard collection of fishermens' cottages.

"To be honest, it will be a relief to take off this jacket once we reach the cottage. But the child's all right," Breda said. "We're friends, aren't we, Alice?"

She realized she was quite enjoying herself, and the gloom of the morning was lifting. It would return, of course, she was quite sure of that. Tonight, when she reached out for Richard and he wasn't there. . . .

"This is it then," Mary said as they reached one of the cottages. "Not exactly what you're used to, of course. But it's homely enough and the little 'uns love being near the sea. They've never seen it before."

She made the comparison without rancor and Breda was sure she didn't mean anything by the remark. But just for a minute she tried to put herself in Mary Keighley's position. None of this was any of her doing. Her husband would have seen the notice in the newspaper and gone rushing to his wife, full of greed and high expectation at his good fortune. And Mary would have seen the new home as a way of salvation for young Harry's troubles.

"Mary, I am sorry — about the way everything's turned out for you — "

"Don't go feeling sorry on our account! What's meant to be will be, and there ain't much we can do about it. Besides, we had nothing before, so where's the difference? We're not paupers, mind, and we've never owed a penny to a soul."

But the forced cheerfulness in her flat northern tones told Breda more than words what a disappointment it all was.

"Amos will have been to see Mr. Flowers, of course?" she asked Mary carefully.

"Oh yes," the woman sighed. " 'Tis all as watertight as you said, and it didn't take much imagination to see that your lawyer fellow was clearly delighted the estate was to remain in the same hands. He told Amos that you and your husband had been into town to settle things legally wi' him. You're to be congratulated on that score as well."

Breda wasn't sure whether there was a hint of sarcasm in her voice now or not. Certainly no one could have guessed on the wedding day that she and Richard were marrying for anything less than love. And in their idyllic privacy ever since, if anyone had witnessed their love-making they would never have dreamed of anything less. She had to swallow hard to be rid of the lump that suddenly rose in her throat.

"We can walk right down to the sea from our cottage," Billy informed her. "Though Mam won't let us go on our own."

"I should think not," Breda said as they went inside the cottage, glad to have her thoughts diverted. "The sea can be very dangerous."

"Where's the man?" Alice piped up. "The man who was with you in the church?"

"He's had to go away. His father's ill." She stopped abruptly as a wave of misery shot through her. At the lies, at the innocence in the small girl's blue eyes, at Mary's sudden look of sympathy.

"That's a shame, so soon after you were wed. You'll be missing him."

"Yes," Breda said thickly.

"Take off your jacket and make yourself feel at

211

home then, and I dare say these little 'uns will amuse you while I put it safely upstairs," Mary said briskly.

She did as she was told, glad for a moment to hide the shadows in her eyes at Mary's words.

"I'll show you my shells if you like," Billy offered. "We've been collecting 'em, and I'm taking 'em to school to show my teacher when I get home."

"And while you're showing 'em to cousin Breda, I'll see to the dinner." Mary paused on the stairs, her fingers unconsciously smoothing the soft green velvet of the riding jacket. "I hope you like mutton stew, Breda. 'Tis the children's favorite."

It wasn't Breda's, but the hot meaty smell coming from the tiny kitchen was making her mouth water all the same. She'd only picked at her breakfast and the ride to Penzance and the walk in the sea air had made her extraordinarily hungry.

She was in a different world here, she realized, one that she hadn't known existed. Two worlds, really. The close confines of a small intimate cottage, and the far more exhilarating world that was peopled by small replicas of Mary Keighley, who were a delight to know.

The older boy, Harry, was more reticent than his uninhibited brother and sister, and clearly knew more about why the family was here than they did. But eventually he joined in the examination of the shells and held them between his fingers as delicately as if they were made of crystal.

"I'm going to paint some of the bigger ones," he said suddenly. "There's hundreds of 'em all ready for picking up on the beach. I'll paint pictures and such like, I mean, not just babies' scratchings. I brought my paints and brushes wi' me."

"How clever you are!" Breda said in surprise.

"Oh, he's a bright lad, our Harry," Mary said proudly from the kitchen. "His teacher says he could be an artist one of these days."

"And what does Amos think about that?"

Mary shrugged. "As you'd expect. He has no truck wi' it, and calls it poncey nonsense. But I say that if God's given us certain talents, then 'tis an insult to His name not to use 'em."

Breda was sorry for the wife who would obviously encourage her son, and for the boy, whose artistic talents were sneered at by a rough mannered father. In some annoyance, she realized she was starting to feel too much sympathy for Mary and her children. It was a mistake to have come here. She should have left well alone, and not gotten entangled with this family. She should make her escape before she got even more enmeshed in their everyday lives.

"We'll eat now," Mary declared, bringing a huge pot of stew to the table.

Breda saw how dramatically the other woman's role had shifted here in her own domain. At Vivien Hall she had been upset, diffident and embarrassed, and for very good reasons. Breda had assumed it was her usual docile manner. But here and now, without the presence of Amos Keighley, she was mistress, serene and capable, and a loving mother to her children. How strange that both of them should be so unsettled in their marriages, yet for such different reasons.

"When will Mr. Delacey be returning?" Mary said, echoing the thoughts in Breda's head as she ladled out the stew.

"I'm not sure. I hope he won't be away for too long.

But his father's health has been giving some concern, and Richard hasn't seen him for some time. He'll want to be sure he's well before he leaves Ireland again."

"And you didn't want to go with him?"

Breda flushed. "We thought it best — at this time — for me to remain behind."

"Oh. Yes, of course."

At the slight cooling in her voice, Breda realized that Mary thought she was referring obliquely to the cousin who had appeared out of nowhere to try and claim her estate. She hadn't meant anything of the kind, but to try and clarify it now would only have made matters worse, so she said nothing.

Later, when she had collected her mare from the hotel and was retracing her way to Vivien Hall, she pondered on the unexpected meeting and the family's situation. There was no doubt that it would always be beneficial to young Harry to stay south. Perhaps if Amos got a decent job here, they could stay on for good. Not at that meager little cottage, of course. There were far larger cottages on the Vivien estate that could be offered.

Ideas flew in and out of her head, to be as instantly dismissed. Of course she couldn't have Amos Keighley living on the Vivien estate. She didn't even want him in the district at all for any length of time.

She remembered seeing him at the back of the church at her wedding, black-faced and furious. He made her shudder. He was like a vulture, waiting to pounce, but the estate was safe in her hands now. Unless she and Richard both met with unfortunate accidents, when Amos would automatically inherit. . . .

The whirling thoughts made her head ache, and she

was thankful when the first sight of Vivien Hall came into view. It was late in the afternoon and she had stayed away far longer than she had intended. The sea sparkled far below, and the sun was blazingly hot on the back of her neck. The velvet riding habit was far too uncomfortable now that the day had got progressively hotter, and she looked forward longingly to a warm bath in which to relax.

"Mrs. Delacey."

She looked up, startled, as a voice called out to her. Sam Stone was making his way up the tortuous moorland climb from the direction of Wheal Breda. She reined in the mare and waited until he approached, bringing an unpleasant whiff of body odor and the dankness of the undersea mine with him.

"You've been neglecting us lately," he sneered. "You and that man o' yours. Had more interesting things to do, I presume?"

"I'd be obliged if you'd stop this coarseness, Sam," she said coldly. "I'm a married lady now, and my husband will have something to say to you if you continue like this."

"Oh — where is he then? I'm wanting words wi' him, as it happens."

"Well, you can't because he's not here. He's been called to his father's bedside in Ireland."

Dear God, but it was perilously easy for the lies to slip out until you almost believed them yourself . . .

"Is that so?" Sam spoke aggressively. Feet apart, he stood in front of her mare, his hands on the bridle so that she couldn't have urged the animal on without pushing him aside.

"If there's something you wish to say, you can say it

to me," Breda said. "Wheal Breda still belongs to me, so if it's something to do with the mine—"

"Oh ah, 'tis summat to do wi' the mine all right. 'Tis summat your fancy man wouldn't be too keen to know."

"Well, what is it?" she snapped, impatient with this goading, and realizing from the way he swayed slightly that he'd been drinking. After a shift, it was well known that he spent some time alone in the engine-house with his ale jug, boasting that he could hold his liquor better than any man in the County.

"I know a feller or two on the Stannary committee, see, and they're just as doubtful as me about your so-called engineer. So if you're about to make a big to-do about it and stop the men working wi' no money coming in for weeks on end while the repairs be done, you can think again, Missus."

"Is that a threat?" she said, hoping he couldn't guess how her pulse was racing uneasily at his words.

He shrugged his huge shoulders. His eyes glittered, and she knew he was just spoiling for a fight of any kind, physical or verbal. He was that sort of man. She felt suddenly sick.

"I never said so, but if you choose to think of it that way, then 'tis up to you, girlie—"

"You bastard!"

She was too incensed to mind her words, or even to think properly. She raised her riding crop and crashed it down on Sam Stone's unsuspecting head. The cord whipped around his neck, instantly producing an angry red welt. He bellowed with pain, and the mare reared up in fright, pawing him to the ground.

Breda tried desperately to control her, having no

216

wish to be thrown off and landing at Sam Stone's feet to be at his mercy. She sensed that right now he'd show none, and she knew real fear of the ugly black temper showing in the man's face. But she was a competent horsewoman, and her soothing words quickly calmed the beast while the man was still collecting his senses. Just as quickly, she dug her heels in the mare's flanks and was off like the wind while he was still shouting abuse after her.

"You'll not be rid of me that easily, bitch! You owe me plenty for all the blood and sweat I've put into your bloody pits to swell your coffers!"

Upset and unnerved by the incident, Breda leaned low over the mare's back, urging her into a gallop back to Vivien Hall. Once they reached the stables she slid off the animal, and realized how she was shaking. Every encounter with Sam Stone lately was unpleasant, and she knew she should take courage and dismiss him before he could create any real trouble.

If it wasn't for the fact that she had no real cause, other than the abuse that was part of his nature, and that he would undoubtedly incite the tinners to a strike for unfair dismissal, she would do so without a second thought. She wished desperately for her father's wisdom or her brother's strength to deal with the matter.

It wasn't a woman's place. Richard should be here to act as go-between whenever Sam Stone threatened her, she seethed. She wanted him and needed him, in every aspect of her life. She bit back a sob, knowing she was in danger of letting her anger turn maudlin again, and she quickly handed over the mare's reins to one of the stable boys.

"See that she gets a good rubdown, will you?" she

said. "She's had a fair gallop this morning."

"Right Missus," the boy answered cheerfully, and led the now docile mare away.

There was the remainder of the day to waste, and an even duller evening. *How on earth did I fill my days and nights before Richard?* she wondered. And what kind of a feeble creature had she become now, if her every waking moment depended on him so much!

She went inside the house, breathing deeply. Mrs. Yandle came to meet her, and Breda forced a smile to her lips.

"You were quite right, Yandie, the ride did me good. There was a street market in Penzance, and I found it quite interesting to browse around the stalls."

"I hope you had your friend with you then. There's all kinds of rogues hanging about them places."

Breda looked at her in exasperation, the words taking her mind off Sam Stone for a minute. "I don't need wet-nursing, Yandie. I'm a married woman now, in case you've forgotten! And anyway, I met — some people."

She hadn't intended mentioning Mary Keighley and the children, sensing that the mere mention of them would get Mrs. Yandle's back up at once.

"What people? Your father would never have approved of you talking to strangers, Miss Breda."

"Will you please stop *lecturing* me! Besides, they weren't strangers. I do know some people outside this house, you know!"

She paused at the foot of the stairs, untieing the ribbons of her hat and shaking her hair free.

"I'd love a bath, Yandie. Ask one of the maids to bring me some hot water, will you?" she wheedled, knowing how the skivvies always grumbled at being asked to do such tasks in the middle of the day. Just as if they had any right to complain when Mrs. Breda Delacey paid their wages, she thought.

"I'll see to it. Are you going to tell me who these people were that you spoke to then, or is it a secret?"

"Sometimes you treat me like a child," Breda said crossly, wondering why she put up with it, and knowing all too well. Despite her annoyance, it was still good to be cossetted by a motherly woman with her best interests at heart.

"All right then, it was my Yorkshire cousin's wife and children, if you must know. They haven't left Cornwall as I expected. The oldest child's not well, and they've rented a cottage for the summer in the hope that the good weather will help his breathing. There, now you know, and I suppose you're going to scold me for visiting them for my midday meal and not ignoring them completely!"

Mrs. Yandle's face softened at her defiance.

"That I'm not, lovey. Those little mites can't help the ways of their nasty father, and I'm glad you had a soft enough heart to be pleasant to his poor soul of a wife. And I'll not beg your pardon for my opinion, even though the man's your distant relative."

For once, Breda couldn't argue with her.

Some while later she lay back in the bathtub, eyes closed. It was quite a time since she had been riding, and she was surprised to find how her muscles ached, especially from the last struggle to hold the mare still when it reared at Sam Stone. But she wasn't going to think of that man now. The water was relaxing her jangled nerves, and she leaned back in the luxurious warmth, and thought of Richard.

She clung to the fact that for whatever reason he had left her, and for however long he was going to be away, nothing could take away the memories of the times they had shared together.

On the other side of the bathroom door the haven of their warm bedroom was a constant reminder of his kisses and the sweet fulfillment of lovers, and here in this steamy little room was where he had taken the washcloth and attended her so very thoroughly, revelling in her perfect proportions and saying with his eyes the words he never spoke.

She leaned back against the shaped headrest of the tub and closed her eyes, breathing his name.

"Oh Richard, I love you so. Why couldn't you have loved me a little in return?"

A creak of a floorboard somewhere in the house made her turn her head sharply, a joyous cry trembling on her lips, as if by some magic means she had conjured him up from out of nowhere. But the door remained closed, and the life of the house continued without him. And Breda could no longer restrain the tears that flooded into her eyes and down her cheeks.

"What a fool I am to waste love on a man who doesn't love me!" she said bitterly. "What kind of spirit is that for a woman to admit to? When he comes back, I shall offer him his freedom if that's what he wants. Indeed, I shall *insist* on it. I won't be humiliated by him any longer," she thought, despite the fact that she would be losing everything she had ever wanted. Despite the fact that he had married her for her sake, to save Vivien Hall. All of it meant nothing, if he didn't love her. And if he required it, she would be very generous to him for giving her back her freedom. She would give him anything he wanted if he wished to go.

The decision was made, and she rose from the bathtub like Aphrodite from the waves, wrapping herself in a towel, her eyes stony now. She couldn't live this lie any longer, even while she admitted and mourned the fact that their marriage had been idyllic for that one perfect week.

If he'd stayed, or taken her with him, everything would have been different, and in time he might have learned that love was stronger than mere lust. But he had chosen to go alone, leaving her that cold little note that told her nothing, except to emphasize his contempt of her. And in some strange way, seeing the close-knit little family at the fisherman's cottage today had only underlined all that was wrong in her life.

"Why didn't you come and see me before?" Nan complained a week later. "I've deliberately kept away from you two lovebirds, thinking you wouldn't want me around, and all the time you've been moping because Richard's gone to Ireland!"

"I'm not moping," Breda said.

They walked along the cliff edge together as they had done a thousand times before, but this time was different. They were no longer the same two people. The carefree days of old seemed to have slipped away from them, and each was recognizing it. There were secret places in Breda's life where Nan couldn't intrude. Even more secret than she could ever have guessed,

Breda thought sorrowfully.

Nan stopped walking, her voice full of resentment.

"Well, for a new bride who's got everything, you certainly give the impression that you've got the weight of the world on your shoulders!"

"I've got everything except my husband, haven't I, you ninny!" she snapped.

"I know that, but I'm sure he'll be back soon, and they do say that the making up is almost better than the fight. Not that you've had a fight, but I suppose it's the same thing," she added hastily.

"What on earth are you talking about?" Breda said in exasperation. "You talk in the daftest riddles at times, Nan Greenwood."

"I know," she said contritely. "It's one of my failings."

They stared at one another, and then they both began laughing at the idiotic way they both stood so aggressively with their hands on hips on the top of the whispering moor.

In a moment they had their arms around one another instead, and Breda was the one to apologize.

"I'm sorry, I'm in such a foul mood these days. It's too soon to hear from Richard, of course, and I do miss him so."

"You'd be a funny sort of bride if you didn't — " Nan began, and then she paused as they both heard the same noise at the same time. A deep rumbling sound that swelled and spread and seemed to come from the very bowels of the earth, or the mysterious ground beneath the sea . . .

"Wheal Breda! My God!" Breda said in a cracked voice. "Quickly, Nan—"

And then they were running and gasping, snatching up their skirts, flying over the soft moorland turf to where the cliff dipped toward the shore and the mine workings.

Chapter Twelve

Long before they reached Wheal Breda, they knew the worst had happened. The rumbling sound became a roar, and there was a great surge in the sea as giant waves were thrown up into the air and were sucked down into its surface again. The central core looked as though a giant hand had savagely pulled the sea inward. Outwardly, it was as though a tornado had struck the coast, concentrated in all its fury on that one specific area, while farther away from the area of the mine the sea was still calm and sparkling. Only inside its depths did it rage and envelop and drown.

"Dear God, we must help the men!" Breda was sobbing as they scrambled down the cliff-side, heedless of how their clothes and skin were torn and scratched in the process.

"There's nothing we can do, Breda," Nan was screeching at her. "They'll all be drowned—"

The piercing shrill of the disaster siren suddenly soared out from the engine-house, and Breda's blood went cold. She had only heard the mournful sound of a mine siren once before in her life, and then it was from a pit belonging to another owner. Because of their mine's continuing prosperity and well-being, every tinner in the Vivien employ had come to believe that theirs were charmed mines. Breda should have known how foolish it was to play with fate, because fate had a way of catching up with you, and there was always a day of reckoning.

By the time they reached the entrance to the mine there was an enormous cloud of black choking smoke emerging from the adit. Men who were not on that particular shift were already streaming down the cliff side ahead of the two scrambling women to see what could be done. Fancifully, she wondered if the earth had suddenly spewed men up from nowhere.

But they were the lucky ones. It was those caught beneath the weight of those crushing beams and the hungry sea below whose fate was in everyone's mind. *How many?* The words were hoarse in every throat. How many were drowned? How many women had lost their men. . . ? Which of the women running out of cottages and down to the sea with terror in their eyes were now widows?

As Breda and Nan reached the engine-house, Sam Stone came staggering out of it like a man demented. Breda's eyes were wild as she raged into him.

"You wouldn't listen to Richard, would you?" Breda found herself screaming, furiously banging her fists against his massive chest. "He made his report to the Stannary Court and you undermined it with your tittle-tattling. You've killed them all by your arrogance—"

"I've killed nobody!" He gathered his senses and roared back at her. His eyes glittered with a hideous savage delight. "Anyway, your man never put in any report that the danger was so near, and I'll swear it in a court of law if I have to."

"What!" She was sickened at his triumph when his men were dying in the drowned mine, her senses stunned by what he was telling her.

Nan pulled at her arm. "Breda, it's unimportant now. We've got to see if we can help any of those that got out!"

Breda couldn't think sensibly for a moment. She *knew* Richard had written out his report for the Stannary Court, and took it there himself, so how could it not have been registered? She had been waiting for advice from them to shut down the mine for repair work, and now she felt an enormous sense of guilt that she hadn't got the work started already. If anyone was to blame for this accident, perhaps it was Breda Vivien.

As she stood with horrified, dilated eyes, staring at nothing, she felt Sam Stone lift her bodily aside as if she were weightless, shouting at her to get out of his way as he went storming down to the adit. And she realized how hard Nan was shaking her.

"Come *on,* Breda. Don't you want to see for yourself?"

No, she didn't. She was terrified of going down that steep cliff-side where the tinners had gathered now, their womenfolk wailing and weeping. She expected them all to look at her with accusing eyes . . . Where in God's name had all these people come from so quickly! It was as though the endless lament of the disaster siren had drawn them all like a magnet.

"Do you know if 'twas my man down there, Missus?" a woman close by sobbed appealingly to Breda. "He were due to go on the change of shift, but I'm sorry to say he were late leaving the fireside today on account of one of the babies having the measles and crying for 'im—"

Breda stared at her uncomprehendingly for a moment, wondering how these people could defer to her even now, in such a time of crisis, but before she could summon up an answer she saw a young tinner come staggering up the cliff to swing the woman round and round in his arms, and her cries of anguish changed to tears of joy. This one at least was safe because he'd stayed with his sick child and reported late for work.

But the woman's words had given her a glimmer of hope. The disaster had happened during a change of shift, and it had long been a rule at the Vivien mines that one shift should be safely out before another went in, with only a skeleton number of workers below while the change-over occurred. It could be that the number of men drowned was far less than at first feared.

She smothered her swift feeling of relief, knowing that even one man drowned while in Vivien employ was a sorrow they must all share. All the same, one man was less than ten, and ten would be less than a hundred. . . .

She grabbed the arm of the tinner still being wildly embraced by his wife. "Is it true that the change-over was going on?" she gasped out.

The man made to brush her aside, and then gulped as he saw who she was. He touched his forelock briefly, stammering out his excuses for not being at work, and Breda felt sickened to anger again, needing less humility than hard facts right now.

"Never mind all that! Just thank your lucky stars that you weren't down there. But please *tell* me if it was change-over time, man," she said as he continued to mumble.

" 'Tis true enough, missus. Sam Stone will have the records of every man due to be on shift, and of the men coming out. There would have been far less than a score of 'em inside, by my reckoning."

Twenty men. Twenty wives without husbands. At least twice that many children without fathers. Breda shut her eyes for a brief moment, wishing she didn't have to face all this alone.

"They're bringing somebody out, Breda," Nan said in a suddenly hushed voice, and the vast crowd fell silent as the apparently crushed body of a man was carried out by those who had ventured in as far as they dared. Then the victim raised a feeble hand to the onlookers to show that he was alive, and a great cheer went up from the crowd.

"I'm going nearer," Breda said. "I have to be there to give what comfort I can."

"I'm coming with you," Nan said at once.

"Miss Breda, you're not to go down there!" She heard Mrs. Yandle's voice say from behind her. She turned to see the housekeeper and her husband, the stable boys and half the indoor staff of Vivien Hall hurrying down to join the rest. A disaster siren brought out everyone within hearing distance.

"It's my place to go, Yandie," she said, and then she slipped and slid down the rest of the way, helped by willing hands who appreciated that the young lady from the big house wasn't afraid to dirty her hands or face the grieving widows, to say nothing of the certain ruin of her own special mine.

Sam Stone was toiling with those helpers nearest to the adit. They could only venture inside a short way, be-

228

cause of the huge fall of earth and rock. Farther in, the earth would be seeped in water, and yet farther inside, the sea would have encroached totally. Only those who had been near the top of the ladders could get out. Most of them had injuries, some more serious than others. But the rest had been doomed from the moment the ladders and beams caved in and gave entry to the tons of rushing sea.

"There's mebbe a dozen dead, girlie," Sam bellowed at her. "There's nothing you can do until we get these fellers up the cliff. You'd do better to get away and see to the womenfolk. There's plenty will be needing comfort and a few coppers to put food in their bellies."

"Is there a list, Sam?" she shouted above the noise, her antagonism forgotten for the moment. "We have to be sure of the names."

He gave her an evil smile then that chilled her bones.

"That we will, Mrs. Delacey, for reading out in court." He said harshly, until his attention was pulled back to the wretch being brought out on a makeshift stretcher, and his expression changed a fraction as they both saw a young boy not thirteen years old, who'd recently been so proud to be taken on at Wheal Breda. Then she saw Sam shrug as he leaned over the dead boy, and glower up at Breda as others carried the boy away to his mother.

"You'll find the lists pinned up in the engine-house. One for the upcoming shift, and another for the fresh one. You can bring 'em here to me, if you've still a mind to be useful."

She turned away with stinging eyes, to be grasped by Yandle's strong hand.

"You're to go back up the cliff with my missus, my

229

dear, and I'll see to this. 'Tis no place for a young woman. Stay on the cliff-top if you must, but there'll be time enough to be making amends later."

"He's right, love," Nan whispered, her arm tight about Breda's waist. "Come away and let the men see to things."

And where was *her* man! Breda thought bitterly. Where was Richard when she needed him most!

But she allowed herself to be led back to the top of the cliff, to let Yandle find the lists and call out the names of men present who hadn't yet begun their shift. Those who had already started down the ladders to begin the new shift could be accounted for and mourned, and those brought out could be wept over with tears of relief. But there was so much chaos and noise that it was many hours before everything was certain, and the final number of drowned men was ascertained as twelve.

"Twelve men on my conscience," Breda muttered to Mrs. Yandle as the housekeeper pressed a glass of brandy into her hands at the end of a long and horrendous day.

She clutched at the glass without attempting to drink the burning liquid, wishing so hard that she could get the images of those weeping women out of her mind.

It had been the worst day of her life, even worse than the day her own father died, or she had heard the news about Philip. On those occasions, she had only had to deal with her own grief. This time, it felt as if she was dealing with the whole world's, and it was a heavy burden for one of her years.

She had been to every house where a man had died,

refusing to rest until she had spoken with every family, and promising that they would receive compensation. It was little enough that she could do, and with the loss of Wheal Breda it would make her look to the finances of Vivien Hall, but she knew her father would have done the same. It didn't bring back any of their men, but it gave their dependents a little dignity that they would appreciate later. Right now they were too numb with shock to do anything but thank her awkwardly and humbly, which to Breda just made the giving worse.

She was white with shock herself by the time she returned to Vivien Hall in the early evening, and Mrs. Yandle insisted at once that she lay down on a sofa and take some more reviving brandy. Breda looked at the liquid as if it were poison, unable to force it past her lips.

"You have nothing on your conscience, lovey," Mrs. Yandle said fiercely. "Mr. Delacey put in his report, and it was up to the Stannary committee to approve it. If the work hadn't yet begun, it was not your fault. How can any of us know when a mine will collapse? The tinners live with that knowledge every day of their lives, and such a thing is always in the hands of the gods. You're not to go blaming yourself, or you'll go mad with the worry of it." She went on relentlessly, trying to cheer Breda, but to no avail.

"Can't you see I'm already mad with the worry of it!"

She jumped up, unable to sit or lie down, and prowling about the room like a hunted animal.

"You don't know the half of it, Yandie. Sam Stone told me some terrible things —"

"That man!" The housekeeper snorted. "You don't want to give him the time of day!"

231

"But he said Richard hadn't given his report to the Stannary committee. If that's so, and he starts putting about the story that Richard was negligent in his findings—"

She stopped, bemoaning the vivid imagination that was soaring ahead of her. If what Sam Stone said was true, Richard would be blamed for not passing on the information, and it would be his neck in a noose . . . she had no illusions about that. Sam Stone would swear to the end that in his opinion the mine had been safe, and that if Richard Delacey thought otherwise he had been negligent in not making the danger clear. The courts were harsh and quick to condemn when deaths had occurred, their treatment swift and brutal. It was a hanging offense. . . .

Without thinking, she reached for the glass of brandy and swallowed it in one gulp, slopping it over her stained dress as she did so. It didn't matter. Nor did it matter that her head spun. Nothing mattered but the fact that she must warn Richard not to come back. She was quite sure he wouldn't have considered it for at least a month, but now she must write to him at once, urging him to stay away until she could see the way things were going here.

For a moment she put herself in his position, knowing he would be devastated by the news of the mine's collapse. It was part of Philip's trust that he should examine Wheal Breda and see that it was made safe. He too would blame himself for tarrying too long since arriving in Cornwall. Deep sobs were welling up in her throat at all that had happened between them, and Mrs. Yandle was putting her comforting arms around her and insisting that she go to bed at once and try to sleep.

"There's nothing more to be done tonight, lovey, and mebbe things will seem a little brighter in the morning."

Breda looked at her with dulled eyes. Things wouldn't be brighter for those twelve bereaved wives, but Yandie knew that too, and was doing her best to help. Breda patted her hand as if she was the one who needed comforting.

"Yes, I'll go to bed now," she said huskily, even though it was barely dusk. Never had a day seemed so long, nor the night in front of her so bitter and lonely.

"And I'll bring you up some hot milk in a little while, shall I?"

"All right." She gave in to being pampered, blown in the wind like a fragile leaf, and totally unable to bear any more thinking about tomorrow.

Except that the letter to Richard mustn't be put off. She must do it tonight, and Yandle must take it to Penzance first thing in the morning to catch the first boat leaving for Ireland. She found a sudden determination, but when it came to the point she hardly knew how to begin. In the end there was only one way and that was to tell the stark facts as succinctly as possible.

"My dear Richard," she started,

"I write with terrible news. Wheal Breda has collapsed and twelve men have been drowned. Sam Stone says that your report was never submitted to the Stannary Court, though I can't believe it, unless there was some treachery going on. Did you not deliver it yourself? Sam Stone has friends on the committee, and I'm so afraid they may have destroyed your report for reasons of their own. I know Sam didn't want the mine to stop working while repair work went on because of the loss of earnings, but that all seems so tragically ironic now.

"I'm writing to urge you to stay away for the time being, Richard. I'll find out all I can, but Sam Stone is going to make trouble, I'm sure, and I fear for you if the court finds you guilty of negligence. I beg you to do as I say and not to come rushing back until you hear from me again. I will write as soon as possible."

She longed to end with love and some tender message, but after his cold little note to her, she simply couldn't.

"May God be with you, Richard. Breda."

She seemed to crumble when she had finished, feeling that God had deserted her lately, knowing it was blasphemous to think so, but unable to help herself. And anyway, if he was the caring God He was meant to be, He'd surely forgive her in the circumstances . . .

She realized she was feeling extraordinarily lightheaded. She remembered she had eaten nothing all day, and the brandy was beginning to do all kinds of weird things to her. Perhaps it was better so, because then she wouldn't have to think . . .

Someone must have undressed her and put her to bed, because she remembered nothing else until the morning sunlight was streaming in through her window, and the memories of yesterday came rushing painfully back. As always she reached out for Richard, and as always she encountered only an empty bed. She swallowed back the tears and put one foot to the floor. Her head still felt heavy, and the next minute there was a tap on her door and one of the maids came inside with a tray.

"Mrs. Yandle said you were to stay there, Madam, until you've eaten something. She said you'd be in danger of falling down the stairs otherwise, begging your pardon, Madam."

"All right, Daisy, I'll do as she says," Breda said wearily, knowing Mrs. Yandle was almost certainly right.

Daisy bobbed obediently and went out of the room to tell the other servants that poor Mrs. Delacey looked awful, with great purple shadows beneath her eyes and looking as if she'd been crying all night long.

Breda looked at the nourishing food and felt repulsed by the very sight of it. How could she eat, knowing what she did? Her gaze wandered restlessly around the room and came to the letter she had written last night. Her letter warning Richard to stay away . . . and just as certainly she knew she must never send it. Because of course he would come rushing back to be by her side, and to deny everything Sam Stone was saying. He'd come straight back into a noose.

She swallowed back a sob. She wanted him so much, but she dare not let him know what had happened yet. It was crystal clear to her now. She leapt out of bed and tore the letter to pieces.

She jumped as she heard another tap on her door, and Daisy came in again.

"There's someone downstairs to see you, Madam."

She handed Breda a card from a salver and to her relief Breda saw the name of Mr. Flowers. She could trust him. He would tell her what to do.

"Tell him I'll be downstairs in fifteen minutes, Daisy," she said quickly. "And take this tray away."

"Oh, but Mrs. Yandle said—" the girl took one look at Breda's face and removed the tray from the room without another word. And fifteen minutes later, Breda was holding out her cold hands to those of the family solicitor.

"A bad business, my dear," he said at once. "And your husband's not here, I understand."

"Mr. Flowers, have you heard what Sam Stone's saying?" she burst out. "He says Richard never made his report to the Stannery committee about the condition of Wheal Breda. But I *saw* the report, and I know he delivered it himself—"

The man stopped her flow of words. "The story's everywhere, Breda, and it's a pity your husband's not here to answer it for himself."

"Is it?" she said bitterly. "You and I both know that he's safer in Ireland until we can get to the bottom of it."

"I'm afraid he'll have to answer to the court in the end. But that's not my main purpose in coming to see you today."

He opened his briefcase and drew out two packets.

"One of these packets contains a letter written a long time ago by your father, Breda. It was entrusted to me, to give you should the occasion for it ever arise."

"What occasion?" she whispered, aware from the coldness in her face that it must be ashen at this news.

"If ever Wheal Breda or one of the smaller mines collapsed, my dear. I don't think your father had any presentiment about such a thing, it was just that he was a far-seeing man who wanted to take every precaution for your future. Naturally, this letter was to go to either your brother or yourself."

She ran her tongue around her dry lips. "And the other packet?"

"They were intended to be opened in order," Mr.

Flowers said. "The letter first, and then the second packet. Would you like to be alone to open them?"

"No, I think I would rather you stayed," she said quickly. "There may be things I need clarified."

As it happened, there were none. It was all beautifully, poignantly simple. She looked at the words her father had written in his oddly old-fashioned handwriting, and wanted to weep. She gazed at them for a long time, and then looked up with brimming eyes at the solicitor.

"No matter what you say, I believe my father did have a presentiment about Wheal Breda," she whispered. "And he gives me clear instructions about what I should do." She smiled slightly. "In fact, I've already done it, Mr. Flowers. That is, I assured the families I'd arrange decent burials for the men, and give them compensation, but just *how —*" she looked at the end of the letter again, and slowly read it aloud.

"I pray that you will never read this letter, Philip and Breda. If you do, then I hope that the other packet I have entrusted to Mr. Flowers will relieve you of certain worries. God bless you both."

"May I open the second packet now, Mr. Flowers?"

He handed it to her and she broke the seal. It was bulkier than the letter and inside there were various documents. Breda stared at them and then at the solicitor.

"They seem to be shares," she said at last. "You don't look surprised. Did you know about this?"

"Your father told me of his plan many years ago, my dear. It was his insurance for his children. The shares were bought from many different sources, and my instruction was that if the scale of any disaster warranted it, to sell them immediately. They will give you financial

237

security, at least for the present."

"And will that be necessary?" she asked in alarm at his grave face.

"It depends on the outcome of all this," he said cautiously. "But your husband should be here to face whatever charges may be brought against him. He will *have* to be here—"

"No. Not yet! Not until tempers have cooled. I know the miners, Mr. Flowers. They'll want revenge, but it must be placed in the right quarters."

"And meanwhile you have all of Wheal Breda's miners idle, which is not a good state when resentment is simmering."

"They'll all be given jobs in the other mines," she said at once. "I'm seeing Sam Stone and a small deputation of miners this morning, and I'll make that quite clear. None of them will be out of work. And—these shares? You'll do what's necessary right away?"

"Today," he said, which underlined to her the importance of it all. She felt physically sick. She had never wanted for anything. The thought of needing money was completely outside her experience.

"There's to be a preliminary hearing at the Stannary Court next week," he went on. "I'll attend and report back to you, but I fear there's little doubt it will mean criminal proceedings against Mr. Delacey."

It was a nightmare, Breda thought after he had gone. She wanted desperately to run to Richard, but she couldn't, not yet. She had to be quite clear about what was happening before she warned him. And what then? If criminal proceedings were begun, he would be brought back ignominiously, and she knew he wouldn't want that. He'd choose to come of his own accord rather than be brought back like a hunted man. She shivered.

But first there were the twelve funerals to be got through, and she had vowed to attend them all, white-faced and with her jaw clamped tight as the names were solemnly read out by the preacher. It was too soon since her own bereavements, and the uncontrolled weeping of the women and children tore at her heart.

But at least those who survived were still in employment, however stretched it made the other mines. Once a miner always a miner, it seemed. They were a special breed of men who chose to live and work with constant danger in those dark dank holes, gouging the tin from the earth, to stack it in the little trundling carts to be hauled up the winding gear to the surface for the prosperity of their owners.

Breda shivered again. But at least she had temporarily placated Sam Stone. If she hadn't absorbed the men, he would have called a strike among the other tinners, and it could easily have spread to the entire county. And more hardship and fury would have been heaped on Breda Vivien's head.

"Oh Richard, why didn't I listen to you when you first arrived!" she thought silently. "Why did I delay, when Philip had urged you to move quickly!"

But no amount of wishing changed anything, and she could only thank God for her father's farsightedness in providing finances for just such a predicament.

Mr. Flowers duly informed her that there would be a court case in two months' time, when all the facts had been collected, and witnesses advised.

"I gave my word that you would see to it that Mr. Delacey was here," he told her. "I vouched for his integrity, and for your fervent need to see justice done, Breda, so I leave it in your hands now."

The words were quiet enough, but there was also a warning in them. If Richard didn't come back of his own will, he would be forcibly brought back. All the same, she wished the solicitor hadn't made it sound as if her need to see justice done didn't sound as if she wanted Richard punished!

"He'll be here," she said steadily. "You have my word."

"Good. And you're to consult me at any time, my dear. I'm always at your disposal."

"Thank you, Mr. Flowers," she said woodenly.

She was exhausted after he'd gone. She had to get Richard back, but she still didn't have any real evidence against Sam Stone. He'd said the report hadn't been seen by the Stannary Court, but it was only his word, and she'd no more trust him than trust a rat. She closed her eyes, remembering that meeting with the deputation of miners last week. Angry, still mourning their fellows, it had been a traumatic time in the drawing room of Vivien Hall, where most of the men stood awkwardly twisting their caps in the strange environment. Sam Stone had turned this to his advantage.

"You see how the gentry live, boys, while we sweat underground and live in hovels—"

"That's not the issue here, Sam," Breda said at once. "I'm here to tell you that none of you need worry about your jobs. You'll all be employed in other mines, and if you prefer, I'll leave it to Sam to make out the lists for each group."

"We do prefer it, missus," one of them growled. "A managing job's no job for a slip of a girl, begging your pardon."

She felt the painful color in her cheeks. "I didn't ask for this position, Penrose. If my father were still alive—"

Her voice broke, remembering that gruff, fair-minded man who would have sorted all this out far easier than she could.

"Well, since he's not," Sam Stone said crudely, "let's be having a show of hands to see if we're willing to continue in the Vivien employ."

She gasped, not having expected there to be any doubt. And there was not—it was only Stone's way of making her squirm still more, she saw immediately from the show of hands.

"I win my wager then," she heard Sam slur, and realized that he'd still found time for his habitual drinking, despite his rabble-rousing.

"What wager?" she didn't want to ask, but rose to the bait at the glittering challenge in his eyes.

"Wi' your cousin, girlie. He wagered that you'd take fright and leave the tinning to they that understand it, but I thought you'd dig your heels in. You were allus a stubborn woman, but still a mighty tempting one—"

"For God's sake, Sam, leave the girl alone. She's had enough to put up with without your clowning," the man Penrose snapped, to the muttering agreement of the rest, but Breda was alerted by his words.

"Have you been seeing my cousin?" she demanded.

"What if I have? A man's got a right to choose his companions," he crowed. "Oh ah, Amos an' me have been getting our heads together most nights down at the

241

Duck and Whistle. There ain't a lot else for a tinner to do when his mine's done for, but drown his sorrows, see?"

"And plot and scheme," she finished.

She heard him give a raucous laugh, and several of the other miners glanced at each other uneasily. The man Penrose looked more unhappy than most, but none of them spoke up. She knew then that she was right. There was scheming going on, and her cousin Amos was very much involved in it. And that could only be for one reason. To discredit Richard and herself, and get his hands on Vivien Hall. And she didn't need to be a genius to guess that there would be a fat bonus in it for Sam Stone for his part in the wickedness.

Somehow she managed not to say any more as she dismissed the meeting. Let him think she was a feeble woman who wouldn't know how to handle this situation. She wasn't sure that she did, but she was going to try! First of all she went into Penzance and made another visit to Mary Keighley and the children, ostensibly to ask how things were for them all, but to glean whatever information she could.

"He's worse than he ever was," Mary finally burst out when the children had gone down to the beach. "He's at that Duck and Whistle day and night, drinking himself silly, and bragging about when the day comes that he lords it at Vivien Hall. He's as tight as a clam with that Sam Stone too, and I wouldn't trust that one an inch. I've no more love for Amos, only disgust at the way he carries on, and the children are sore afraid of his moods. I'm sorry to complain and to tell you such things, Breda, but I'm that worried. If it weren't for Harry and the little 'uns, I swear I'd leave Amos tomorrow. Excepting that I'd have nowhere to go, o' course, and no brass."

She began to cry silently, and Breda held her in her arms and let her cry it out.

"You'd have somewhere to go, Mary. I'd look after you."

She jerked up her head. "But I can't do that! Don't you see? He'd think he'd won if you gave us a home, and I won't let him win. I'd throw myself into the sea before that."

"Don't talk so silly. A fat lot of good you'd be to your children then! Come on now, where's this Yorkshire grit I've heard about? Whatever that is," she added.

Mary gave a shaky laugh. "You're right. I've a lot to be thankful for, but I'll stay put in this cottage and he'll not beat me into the ground."

He wouldn't beat Breda either, she thought grimly as she rode home to Vivien Hall, her suspicions about Amos and Sam's association confirmed, and prepared herself for the next part of her plan.

Chapter Thirteen

The Duck and Whistle was a waterfront inn frequented by tinners and fishermen, and occasionally
foreign seamen from any ships in port. By ten o'clock
of an evening, its inmates were in their usual state of
intoxication, the place filled with dense choking
smoke and steaming humanity, its walls vibrating to
the sounds of bawdy laughter as the men whacked the
backsides of the serving-girls carrying their ale pots
high above their heads in an effort to move about the
tap-room.

In the chimney corner a young boy sat crouched
over his drink, his cap low on his forehead, a scarf
roughly covering the lower part of his face, not speaking to anyone. It was gleaned from one of the serving-
girls that he appeared to be French and didn't
understand any English. From then on, he was ignored
by the rest who saw no point in jawing with a lad who
kept to himself and couldn't make sense of their jokes.

If they only knew it, he followed them only too well,
his face becoming redder and redder as they became
more and more risqué. But he dare not show his em-

barrassment, nor the fact that the heavy cap and sweltering scarf hid the delicate features of Breda Vivien, dressed in a stable boy's garb borrowed from the laundry room at Vivien Hall.

She knew only too well the risks she took. If it was suspected that there was a woman in the inn, she would be hounded out — or far worse. It wasn't unknown for a woman spying on a husband to be raped for her insolence in intruding into a man's world, thinking this a deserved sport. If they discovered the identity of this particular woman, and knew how intently she listened to the huddled conversation between her cousin Amos Keighley and Sam Stone, interspersed by a couple of Sam's mining cronies, she didn't care to think about her fate.

They were well into their drinking by now, their words slurred. She doubted that anyone but herself could hear them, hidden as she was behind a pillar. And in this seedy little inn, it was rumored that a man's words could be guaranteed to go no further, since most of those who frequented it had a kind of dubious honor among themselves. If her father or Philip knew where she was and what she was doing, they would have washed their hands of her.

But they didn't know, and it was for the honor of Vivien Hall that she did it, even though she was terrified at being here, and even more so at the thought of discovery. And it didn't seem to be getting her anywhere. She'd been here nearly an hour now, and she still hadn't heard anything of real importance. She began to think it was hopeless when she heard Amos's bragging laugh and saw him slap Sam Stone on the back.

"Just wait till I'm in my ancestral seat, lad, and then

we'll be drinking fine French brandy instead of this evil muck!"

"You ain't there yet, Amos." Breda heard Penrose say.

She'd been surprised to see him in this company, since he'd always seemed more sympathetic to her than most. But she supposed he was under Sam's thumb like all the rest.

"I will be soon though, when we get my fine and fancy cousin out," Amos slurred. "She'll be discredited along with her man, and I'll see to it that Vivien Hall comes to me!"

"You're a cunning fox, all right," Sam leered. "But don't you go forgetting that we're partners!"

Amos gave his wheezing laugh. "Oh aye, I'll not forget. There's plenty would raise hell if they knew you slashed at the pit props to weaken 'em a bit, though I didn't expect it to bring the bloody lot down. And who persuaded you to get at your committee fellers to stop that engineer's report going through, eh, so the two of 'em would be in it up to their necks! Give credit where 'tis due, lad!"

Breda found it hard to breathe as she listened in mounting horror. Dear God, but he was more evil than she had thought. It was these two who had been responsible for the death of those twelve tinners. It wasn't an accident. It was murder . . . and no doubt Sam Stone expected to come out of it handsomely rewarded when Amos became master of Vivien Hall, as he so fancifully expected!

" 'Twas a bad business for the men to drown though," she heard Penrose growl uneasily.

"Well, we know that, lad," Amos snapped, a warning in his voice. "But just you keep remembering that it was an *accident*. We know Sam should have got 'em out in plenty of time and delayed the new shift like we arranged, and if he hadn't been so busy drinking himself stupid at the time—"

"Talking about drinking, where's that serving-girl!"

Sam was clearly not prepared to listen to any censure of his achievement, and roared out his order. As he did so, the whole group began shouting the same thing and banging their pint pots on the wooden tables. Under cover of the noise and disturbance Breda slid off the bench as smoothly as her shaking legs would allow. She scuttled out of the back door of the inn, taking in great gulps of fresh salt air before she disgraced herself and vomited out of total shock and disgust.

After a night that was a mixture of sleepless turmoil and haunted dreams, the next step was easy. Amid futile entreaties from Mrs. Yandle to let someone accompany her, she prepared to leave for Ireland the following morning.

"I'll be quite all right," she said, hugging the housekeeper. "There will be other passengers on the ship, and when I arrive I'll be with Richard, and he'll bring me home."

"But home to what?" Mrs. Yandle said sorrowfully, having every faith now in her young lady's husband, and refusing to believe anything scandalous about him.

"He'll come home to anything he has to face, Yandie," Breda said. "Now, no more arguments, and don't let me go with that gloomy face of yours to remember!"

There had been little to smile about of late, but the two of them pretended a false cheerfulness for the other's sake.

"Yandie," Breda said hesitantly. "If you go into Penzance at all, I'd think it a kindness if you'd call on my cousin's wife and perhaps take her a few provisions. *He* won't be there if you go late in the morning, and it's not fair to blame the wife or the children for the man's failings."

After a minute Mrs. Yandle nodded.

"All right, lovey, I'll do it because you ask me. And as you say, the poor woman's not to blame, nor those babies."

Breda was relieved at her compassion. She hadn't dared to tell Mrs. Yandle what she had done last night, knowing she'd have gotten tongue pie from that moment on, nor did she tell her what she had heard. She intended calling on Mr. Flowers before she boarded the ship for Ireland and informing him, but the person she yearned to tell was Richard.

Her heart gave a sudden little lurch. Despite everything that had happened — the disaster at Wheal Breda, the tragedy of the tinners' deaths, the discovery of her cousin and Sam Stone's treachery, Richard's desertion of her, the dire news she had to tell him — over and above all that was the joyous thought that in a few days' time they would be together again.

He wouldn't be expecting her, and she might yet see a spark of love in his eyes that he would be unable to hide. She prayed desperately that it would be so.

Mr. Flowers was very angry with her.

"You should never have gone to such a disreputable place as the Duck and Whistle! You should have informed me of your suspicions, and I would have gone there myself—"

"Do you think you'd have done as well! You're well known in this town and I hardly think you'd have gone unrecognized. Besides, it would have been rather difficult for you to disguise yourself as a young seafaring boy!"

She had never spoken to him so daringly before, but eyeing his ample figure and distinctive whiskers she felt her mouth twitch, and to her relief he began to laugh.

"Perhaps not," he agreed. "And no harm's been done—"

"No harm! I'd say a lot of *good* has been done. I found out the truth, didn't I? All we have to do now is to force the men to admit to what I heard, and Richard's name will be cleared. They can hardly deny it if they swear an oath to tell the truth."

He looked at her a little pityingly.

"My dear, not everyone has your honesty. Oaths sworn before God in a court of law matter little to desperate men. They'll lie until they're black in the face to save their necks, and that's exactly what Amos Keighley and Sam Stone will be doing when this comes out."

"But it *will* come out!" she demanded. "You will bring this up as evidence on my say-so?"

"Of course. But I warn you it may do more harm than good if all Sam Stone's men stick together."

She had to be content with that, and despite the initial sinking of her heart she wouldn't let her hopes be diminished. She left the chambers and made her way to the quay, where there was plenty of activity on the morning ship bound for Ireland, and Breda hurried aboard.

Yandle had taken her baggage on earlier and she was shown now to the tiny cabin where she would spend the next two nights before the ship docked at Rosslare, the southernmost Irish port. She knew from Richard that this was the right area for Grannaby, but she had no idea in which direction she would have to go. She dismissed such trivialities from her mind. She had come this far, and once she arrived in Ireland a hired carriage would take her the rest of the way, no matter how far distant.

As soon as she had settled in her cabin and unpacked her belongings, she went up on deck, in time to see the vessel edge away from the quayside and the adventure begin. The word came into her head before she had time to think. This was something of an adventure, no matter what the reason for the voyage. She had never been out of Cornwall before, and at the end of it there would be Richard. She felt a great uplifting of her spirits as the sea breezes whipped into her cheeks, wild and exhilarating.

Thankfully she discovered she was a reasonable sailor, not upset by the malaise of several other women passengers. She avoided conversation with anyone except for passing the time of day, fearing that someone might recognize her name and know how closely she was connected with the recent mine disaster.

It was easy enough to keep to herself by the simple expedient of wearing black, including a hat with a small veil to cover her eyes, which she had had the fore-sight to do. People naturally assumed that she was a widow, and left her respectfully alone. She needed no one's company. All she needed would be waiting at the house called Grensham at Grannaby . . .

Three days later she stepped off the ship onto Irish soil. By then she had discarded her black garments and looked healthily refreshed from the voyage in a gown and matching bonnet of cornflower blue. She looked about her, deciding that an Irish port was not so different from any Cornish port. The bustle was the same, the searching for relatives or friends was the same, the feeling of loneliness and slight isolation was the same . . . and so was the memory of the last time she had been hustled along a busy quay, when she had met Richard Delacey for the very first time, and unknowingly come face to face with her destiny.

"Would you be wanting transport to anywhere, Ma'am? I've a ve-hicle waiting along the road," a broad Irish voice said right behind her, quaintly accenting the word.

She looked around quickly at the deferential man of indeterminate years. A top hat was perched jauntily on his head and he had a fine bush of white sideboard whiskers on each side of his cheeks that were reminiscent of Mr. Flowers'. The similarity was mildly reassuring.

"I was wondering if someone could take me to Grannaby, to a house called Grensham," she said hesitantly. "I've no idea how far it is, or if you'd know of the place—"

He gave a short laugh. "Sure, and who wouldn't be knowing Grensham at Grannaby, Ma'am! I can take you there in no more than a couple of hours, as long as you're not expecting a ride in a fine carriage. But I've a trusty nag and he'll not fall by the wayside in a hurry."

"Oh, but —" She had assumed he would lead her to a recognized hire stand, and the way he had described his own transport certainly didn't sound any too comfortable, she thought in some alarm. But by now the man had already picked up her baggage and was moving nimbly in and out of the other passengers, and she had no choice but to follow him if she ever wanted to see her belongings again. She fought to keep up with him.

"Are you sure you know the place?" she said, holding on to her hat as people jostled past her.

"Everybody knows Grensham and the Delaceys, Ma'am. And since we're to be acquainted awhile, the name's Davy," he added. At least she didn't feel quite so alarmed now that he had mentioned Richard's family name, since she herself hadn't given him the information.

"Is it a big house then?" She was almost running now, and then stopped dead as she came face to face with an aged horse chewing at something in a tattered nose-bag. Behind him was a small gig that looked as if it had come out of a museum. The leather was creased and torn, the wheels with their peeling paint decidedly less than circular. The man spread his arm proudly to indicate that this was his ve-hicle.

He gave a chuckle. "You must be a stranger to these parts, Ma'am."

"Yes, I am," she began to feel cross. "Look, I really

wanted to hire a proper carriage. Is this the best you can do?"

"You won't find another," he said cheerfully, and apparently taking no offense. "They'll all have been ordered beforehand or taken by the first passengers off the ship. One of 'em might return in a couple of hours, or might not, but if you want to reach Grannaby before nightfall—"

"All right," Breda said. She climbed carefully into the creaking gig while he crammed the baggage onto the rack and squeezed in beside her. It certainly wasn't the way she had intended making her appearance at Grensham, crushed up beside this extraordinary little man, but if it meant getting her to Richard in reasonable time, what did it matter!

It was well over three hours later when she alighted, stiff and aching, from the gig. Several times they'd been forced to stop for Davy to coax the reluctant nag into action, and once he had declared he couldn't go a step further without wetting his throat. And Breda had been obliged to go into the roadside ale house with him or sit in the gig beneath a blazing sun. She chose the former, thankful after all for the cooling cordial the landlady brought to her.

"This little lady's bound for Grensham," her driver commented, and Breda sighed, guessing that in these rural places everyone knew everyone else's business. Just like Cornwall, in fact, as was the entire countryside. She had been surprised to discover the homely familiarity about the patchwork of green fields, the snug white-painted, thatched-roof cottages . . . the landlady looked more interested at Davy's comment.

"Well now, and is it Lord Delacey's new daughter-in-law who's honoring my wee establishment today!"

Lord Delacey . . . !

Richard had never mentioned that his father had a title! She hoped that the utter shock didn't show on her face and gave a small laugh, covering her sudden silence by telling the landlady that she'd taken her by surprise by guessing so quickly who she was.

"Ah well, there's been many a pretty colleen hankering after Master Richard's hand these past few years, dearie, and a few broken hearts among 'em when they heard he was wed at last, I dare say. But here's wishing health and luck to you both."

"And to all here," Davy added, as solemn as a litany.

"Thank you," Breda murmured, wishing she dared ask more about the household that was evidently well thought of, and even more about the young colleens whose hearts Richard had broken!

She knew she had better conceal the sliver of jealousy that ran through her at the words, not wanting to let the woman guess that she knew absolutely nothing about her husband's home or previous way of life. She finished her drink and stood up.

"Can we get on now, please? I'm anxious to reach Grensham as soon as possible."

Davy drained his ale with annoying slowness, relishing every mouthful before he got to his feet. But at last they were back in the rickety vehicle and it was late in the afternoon when the man finally halted the nag. By then, Breda's eyes had been dropping, lulled by the methodical plodding of the animal and wearied by Davy's repertoire of small talk which had eventually all washed over her head.

"There's the place you'll be wanting, Ma'am. That's

254

Grensham," she heard him say reverently now.

Her eyes opened quickly, and then she simply gaped. On a high rise ahead of them was a turreted castle. It might have been small as castles went, but to Breda it was magnificent, surrounded by parks and woodland and beyond it what appeared to be a sea of emerald green turf.

"Beautiful, ain't she?" Davy went on, as caressingly as if the castle was a woman, and totally unaware of her stunned reaction. " 'Tis a fine family that lives there too. Oh, they've had their share of tragedy as you'll well know, but the Delaceys have always been well liked and there's none that begrudge them their fortune, since they work for it. 'Tis said they breed the finest racehorses in the world, let alone in Ireland. Send 'em all over the place, they do, but you'd be knowing all about that, 'o course, Ma'am."

"Yes," she said faintly, knowing nothing about it at all. Why had Richard never *told* her? Letting her go on thinking he was a fortune hunter in marrying the daughter of a Cornish landowner, when he was the heir to all of *this* . . .

Too late, she saw how she could have pumped this guide of hers for information. He'd probably told her plenty already, and she'd closed her mind and ears to all of it while she dozed.

She sat up, suddenly alert. Two horse-riders came thundering across the wide sweep of land ahead of them. A man and a woman, laughing and calling to one another in playful rivalry as they raced their horses. And then the man caught sight of the motionless gig, and of its female occupant. *Richard* . . .

Expertly, he pulled his steed up short and changed

course, to come galloping up beside her, while the woman hesitated a moment and then followed at a canter.

"Breda! By all the saints! I can't believe it's you!"

He slid from the horse's back in one fluid movement, his face a mixture of astonishment and something else . . . she was too filled with emotion at seeing him so unexpectedly to register what it was. It could almost have been delight in his voice, but whatever it was, he was swinging her out of the carriage in his strong arms now, and she was enveloped in his embrace, his mouth seeking hers in a hungry kiss. And for the present she gave up thinking about anything at all.

Her senses swimming, she clung to him.

"Richard," she stammered, "you'll think me a fool for coming here like this, but I had to tell you—"

They both became aware that Davy was listening with interest, and that Richard's woman companion had joined them now, seated superbly on the horse, her dark eyes taking in the little scene with amusement. She was young and very beautiful, her cheeks glowing from the exertion of the ride, and Breda's little dart of jealousy became an instant flame.

"Will you take my wife on up to the castle and see that her baggage is taken inside?" he spoke directly to Davy and then to Breda. "Clare and I will stable the horses and meet you there, my love."

Obviously there was to be no hint that this was not a normal marriage. Not even to Clare, whoever she was—at least, not in public. Breda climbed back into the gig without another word and told Davy to do as Richard said.

256

The sudden joy at being in his arms had left her just as quickly. Instead, she was numb all over, watching the riders gallop toward the west of the castle. In her head all she could hear were the words of the ale house landlady . . . wondering if this Clare was one of the colleens whose heart had been broken when Richard Delacey married. She certainly didn't look broken hearted now, with Richard seemingly still playing the bachelor and clearly enjoying her company, Breda seethed.

"That'll be Miss Clare, your man's cousin," Davy said conversationally. "She often visits his Lordship to cheer him up. Miss Clare and that poor young Miss Maureen that died, were much of an age, so they were."

"She's my husband's cousin?" Breda said stupidly, suddenly thanking God for this garrulous little man, and for a community that seemed to know everybody else's business.

His nag stumbled slightly, and in the few moments that he struggled with the reins, Breda regained her composure. Everyone knew that cousins could be far more than friends, but at least the relationship gave credence to why this Clare was here. And she'd be very foolish to show her feelings to Richard when she'd so far managed to persuade him that she wasn't in love with him.

Besides, they had far more important things to discuss. Whatever their own feelings, they must be overlooked for more immediate worries. The mine disaster, Amos Keighley's and Sam Stone's treachery, and the trial that loomed ahead—they had been temporarily put to the back of her mind, but they couldn't remain

257

there much longer. It was incredible to think that as yet Richard didn't know about any of it, and she truly dreaded telling him.

"Here we are then, Ma'am," Davy said at last, when the gig stopped in the great curving courtyard of the castle. He spoke as unaffectedly as if they were outside any wayside inn, and she felt an odd affection for him. She searched in her reticule for his fare and paid him generously, to which he bowed low, sweeping his top hat in a circle in front of him in a ridiculous show of chivalry.

"I'll see you right inside, Ma'am," he declared, and pulled the bellrope on the huge oak door while he scuttled back for her baggage. A butler opened it directly and looked disapprovingly at the unlikely visitor, and then more civilly at the lady behind him.

Before he could ask their business, Richard had appeared, his riding boots sparking on the cobbled courtyard.

"It's all right, Maloney, you can see to the bags."

"And where will I be putting them, Sir?" the butler asked stiffly.

"In my room, of course. This lady is my wife."

The man's expression changed, and his voice grew warmer.

"Then I beg the lady's pardon, Sir. And may I extend the welcome of the house to you, Ma'am."

"Thank you," Breda said, the blood suddenly singing in her veins at Richard's calm words. They were together now. Suddenly nothing else mattered.

She realized there was no sign of the other woman, and that Davy was climbing back into his vehicle and driving off. The butler had turned to go inside with the baggage, and for a moment they were alone.

"I've missed you," Richard said softly. "I never thought it possible to miss anyone so much. Are you a witch, that you've got under my skin so completely? Or did my dreams reach out to you and bring you here? God knows why you've come, and if I'm still dreaming, then I'd prefer never to wake up—"

"Richard, I've come for a purpose. We must talk seriously," she said, trembling, because she wanted him to go on saying these things to her forever, and couldn't allow it. If he thought she was chasing him like some love starved kitchen maid, the sooner he knew the truth the better.

They stood, not touching, and something in her voice seemed to warn him. He looked down at her steadily, and his eyes assumed the remote expression she couldn't follow. She had fully expected to burst out with the news, but now that she was actually here she seemed to be struck dumb on the subject.

The terror of explaining it and bringing it all out in the open would make it all seem too real. There was the dark sweet longing to delay the moment, while he had seemed truly hers . . . but already she knew she had somehow spoiled things. It was as if he had really believed she had come because she couldn't bear to be without him. And what was more, as if he had wanted to believe it . . . it was heartbreakingly true, of course, but she wouldn't tell him.

Especially not now, when she had seen how he lived and knew what he would inherit, for he would undoubtedly think she was the fortune hunter after all. Even more especially when she would need every penny she could get to save Vivien Hall and its heritage. The destiny that had brought them together now seemed to be doing its best to tear them apart.

"Whatever it is, it can wait until later," he said harshly. "I've a need to be alone with my bride in more auspicious surroundings."

She gulped. "What about the lady—your cousin, I believe? And your father?"

"I see the prattlers have been at work already. Clare has gone home, and my father always takes an afternoon nap and will not appear before dinner. Rest assured that no one will disturb us in our own room, my sweet."

"Richard, I *must* tell you—" she began again weakly, but he was striding ahead of her, and she had no option but to follow him, across the great inner hall and its flagstoned floor, hardly noticing the proudly displayed family tree document in its glass case, or the suits of armor and battle weapons that lined the walls, grim reminders of other days.

The butler was climbing the winding staircase to an upper floor with her baggage, and Richard turned to take her hand and lead her upstairs. His grip was warm and reassuring, and she felt the usual tingle as she felt his fingers link with hers.

She registered that only the magnificent entrance hall of the castle remained in its stark medieval state. The rest of the house, stairs, corridors, the rooms she glimpsed through half open doors, were all beautifully appointed with rich carpets, fine pieces of furniture and porcelain, and every luxury. It was a home that had known vast wealth and prestige, and continued to know it. And she had dared to think of Richard Delacey as a fortune hunter . . .

The butler opened a door at the end of a corridor, and they entered an enormous bedroom, the four-poster bed heavy and ornate, adorned with rich draperies. After inquiring if they needed anything and receiving a negative answer, the man withdrew, and Richard immediately took his wife in his arms.

"Now then, my darling girl," he went on in the same seductive voice she remembered so well of old. "I don't know why you've made this journey, but I refuse to hear any explanations until we've renewed our acquaintance properly. I've no wish to spend time on words, when actions speak far more eloquently. I swear that I've a hunger for you that won't let me wait, Breda, and no man worth his salt would waste moments when his beautiful bride has materialized out of his dreams."

"For a man who doesn't want to waste words, you seem to be doing rather well," Breda said huskily, aware that all the time he was talking he was loosening the fastenings on her gown and her undergarments, and his intention was becoming all too obvious as his mouth teased her own and the familiar flames of passion were instantly ignited between them.

What harm would it do to wait a little longer to shatter his pleasure? the thought whispered inside her. There would be time enough for discussion of what awaited them in Cornwall. So there was time enough now for this . . . she gave up all thought of burdening him with her news for the present and unconsciously wound her arms around him.

"I've dreamed about you too," she murmured, before she could think what she was saying.

He scooped her up in his arms and carried her to the

four-poster bed, smiling down at her with a slightly mocking look on his face as he gazed down at her nakedness. She shivered beneath that look, with a growing heat inside her as he discarded his clothes and lay half covering her. One hand was beneath her shoulders, the other renewed its seeking out of every part of her, as if on a glorious voyage of exploration.

"Then you are not entirely averse to me," he muttered, his mouth on hers, tasting the sweetness of her love-swollen lips.

She tried to give a small laugh, but it caught on a sob and ended up as a strangled sigh.

"I defy any woman to be averse to a man of your expert talents, my darling," she said, attempting to be arch and hardly knowing why. She had come here, knowing he didn't love her, still with the determination to offer him his freedom whenever he wished. She had been driven to come, because of the mine disaster. It was her duty as his wife to warn him . . . and now she knew what a mistake it had been. Because no, she could never be averse to him, never, never, *never* . . .

"If you think of me as such an experienced womanizer, then perhaps this is the treatment you would prefer, my *darling*," he said with exaggerated scorn.

She suddenly gasped as she felt him enter her without any of the sweet preliminaries. It was a crude action, and the hard thrusting movements that followed were equally rough. For a moment Breda could have cried out with the shock of it.

But then, as the onslaught continued, bringing with it its own primitive surging energy, she felt a wildness of abandon she had never known before. He crushed her, and it didn't matter. He bruised her mouth with his, and it didn't matter. He was master and she mistress, man and woman biblically coupled. He forged into her as relentlessly as if they shared the same skin, and when she felt she could hardly bear more of the exquisite sensations, they were both riding furiously to a glorious climax.

She found that she was gasping for breath when it was over, and that Richard had rolled away from her. She felt the trickle of tears on her cheeks. Richard's love-making had been wild, angry . . . and yet more beautiful and giving than anything she could have imagined. There was a time for tender, and a time for wild, she thought, as humbly if she had discovered a new and wondrous truth.

"Forgive me, Breda," she heard Richard say harshly beside her. "No man should treat his wife like a whore."

He stood up and strode across the room, picking up his clothes as he went and disappearing into an adjoining room. The door banged behind him while she lay stunned, disbelieving. A *whore!* Was that how he thought she had received him? Was that how he thought he had treated her? No man could love a woman and demean her so. Hope for them ended. He had merely wanted to make her his conquest and he had succeeded far more than he could have expected. The tears stopped in her utter shock, the misery too great for tears, the harshness of reality taking over.

After some minutes when Richard didn't return, she slid off the bed, and hurriedly dressed herself. She pinned up her hair with trembling hands and tried to compose her face, although the tell-tale effect of tears wouldn't go away quite as easily.

She breathed long and deeply. She had always had a strong streak of stubbornness, and short of rushing straight back to Cornwall, she had a mission here, and it was the one thing that was going to keep her sane. She and Richard had a fight on their hands, and it was one that concerned them both. She couldn't turn tail and run, even if she wanted to.

The door opened, and he came into the room, as decorously dressed as herself now. Before he could say anything, she sat down abruptly on one of the blue velvet-covered chairs near the window, and spoke quietly.

"I've come here for a purpose, and you must hear me out. What I have to tell you is of vital concern to us both, so please listen to me and don't interrupt."

He sat on the chair opposite her, arms folded, his face betraying nothing of his feelings now. He couldn't have the remotest idea of what she was about to say, and she felt a new heartache at being the bearer of news that could break him. Only when she began did his emotions explode.

Chapter Fourteen

He leapt out of the chair, his eyes blazing down at her. She felt real fear, thinking for a moment that he was going to strike her, but then she saw that his anger was not directed at her—except in one respect.

"For the love of God, Breda, why didn't you send for me at once? I'd have come straight back, and you shouldn't have had to bear this alone!"

"It was because I knew you'd come straight back that I delayed letting you know! What good would it have done until we knew what was happening? Besides, there were things to be done. I had to find out what was going on between Sam Stone and my cousin, though you can't imagine how terrified I was, going into that awful Duck and Whistle dressed like one of my own stable-lads. And then there were the funerals to attend—" her voice broke a little, "and the families to see. Then I had to consult with Sam Stone to allocate jobs to the tinners from Wheal Breda among the other mines."

"You're not telling me he's still in your employ?"

"He's temporarily suspended, by mutual agreement," she muttered. "Officially he's done nothing wrong, unless it can be proved otherwise. I didn't know what else to do but suspend him, and it seemed the best course to take for the time being. If I'd sacked him, he'd have called a strike and all the tinners would have been against us then. I still have to pay Sam, of course—"

"Then you're as good as saying he'll have a job back once the court case is over. You're giving him the edge, letting him think he'll win," Richard snapped. "That fills me with great confidence!"

On and on they went, going round in circles and getting nowhere. Each felt a desperate need to be back in Cornwall as soon as possible, to get at the heart of things, and each had secret fears on that score.

"Mr. Flowers is taking on the case, Richard, and I have every trust in him—"

"I'd rather kill the bastards with my own hands," he said furiously. "I'll not have twelve mens' deaths laid at my door when it was the fault of others—"

"Killing Amos and Sam wouldn't solve anything," she replied, terrified at his venom. "They've got to be brought to justice and their wickedness exposed!"

"Tell me one thing. You don't doubt that I took the report to the Stannary Court, do you?" he glowered down at her, his eyes like glittering coals.

"I never doubted it for a moment! Do you think I'd choose to believe Sam Stone over you?"

He stared at her, and she felt the wild color leap into her cheeks at the coldness in his eyes. They had been so close, as intimate as two people could be, in tenderness and in savage passion, and he looked at her now with the eyes of a stranger, all the closeness gone.

"I don't know what to think or who to believe any more. You've never been wholly truthful with me, have you?"

"And have you been truthful with me? You never told me you lived in a castle, did you? Or that your father was titled!"

He shrugged. "I consider all that of little importance compared with what we have to think about now." His voice was clipped and hard and she remained silent, swamped in misery.

"I'm trying to think logically," he went on. "I don't intend to tell my father about all this unless we have to do so at a later date. I see no point in worrying him unnecessarily. We can hardly leave here the minute you've arrived, but I've certainly no inclination for idle social activities. We'll give it three days and then return to Cornwall. I need to see your Mr. Flowers as soon as possible."

She swallowed dryly. "Sam Stone is out for your blood, Richard. He'll never change his story, and I'm so afraid—"

"Well, you and I both know the truth of it, and as long as Flowers does his job, there's no point in anticipating the worst before it happens."

The worst would be a public hanging . . .

"You know they won't let me speak up, don't you? Despite my ownership of the mine, the court won't recognize a woman as a defense witness—"

"We'll cross that bridge when we come to it," he said grimly. "Meanwhile, do you think you're able to put on a different face when you meet your father-in-law? We can't put it off much longer, despite what he'll assume we've been doing up here when he discovers your arrival."

She blushed, knowing he only said it to try and lighten the atmosphere between them. But she knew that what he said made sense. It was best that Lord Delacey was kept in ignorance of the situation in Cornwall for the time being. Breda lifted her chin, and Richard took her hands in his and gave a small nod of approval at the resolution he saw there in her face. They both had a part to play while they remained at Grensham, and each was determined not to let the other down. And despite Richard's harshness, she faced the prospect of the evening ahead with a rush of relief that at least she wasn't alone in her anxiety any more. They would face the future together.

The tall gray-haired man with the distinguished bearing could only have been Richard's father. Breda was welcomed into his family home with all the courtesy of old world charm. Lord Delacey lightly held her shoulders and kissed her on both cheeks as Richard introduced them. The three of them were in the beautiful drawing-room at Grensham now, and pre-dinner drinks of the finest sherry in the thinnest crystal glasses were being served before they went in to dinner.

By then, Breda had ascertained that there was a small army of servants caring for every whim of the Delacey household, and that the castle was run on elegant and autocratic lines. She was thankful she had thought to bring several dinner gowns with her, since both the handsome Delacey men were dressed correctly for dinner in immaculate black, their dazzling white shirts displaying gold neck-pins and cuff-links.

It was a very fine household indeed, and if she herself had not been brought up in a gentleman's house, Breda would have been struck completely dumb. As it was, Lord Delacey did his best to put her at her ease.

"So you were Richard's surprise," he said delightedly, in a mellow accent similar to his son's.

"His surprise? Ah, you mean because he didn't tell you we were married before the event!" She glanced at Richard, briefly admiring the way he managed to hide his earlier fury at her news beneath a genial smile.

"I hope the little surprise was to your liking, Sir," she murmured, hoping the traumatic conversation in the bedroom was not going to surge back and forth in her mind all evening.

"I'm delighted that Richard has made such a good choice," Lord Delacey said smilingly. "I always suspected that he'd simply turn up with a bride one of these days, so I wasn't at all put out by your appearance. The Delacey men have always been an impetuous breed, and he's not the first to present the castle with its future mistress as a *fait accompli*. I know my son and I've sensed a restlessness in him ever since he arrived home, and now I see why. You and he had planned this little visit all the time, despite what he told me about your staying behind with a sick relative."

So that was what he had told his father. Theirs was a relationship based on so many falsehoods, she thought sadly, from gigantic untruths to harmless little white lies.

"I trust she is quite recovered now?" Lord Delacey was saying politely.

"Oh — she's fairly well now, thank you, though I still

worry about her, naturally. I'm afraid we shan't be able to stay here too long—"

"Not stay? But my dear, Grensham is the Delacey family seat. Of course you'll be staying—"

"I'm afraid not, Father," Richard said. "As well as concern for her aunt, Breda is in sole control of the family tin mining business now, so there are many things to be sorted out before we can make our permanent home here. We'll stay for three more days and then we must go back to Cornwall, I'm afraid. We have appointments with her solicitor and various other people to see, but I hope we won't be away for too long."

"So I'm to lose you both again so soon. I'm rather glad you hadn't told me all this earlier, Richard," he commented, and Breda suddenly saw the lonely man that he was with his daughter dead and his son only just returned from distant shores. She understood, but it didn't ease her ragged feelings.

"Oh well, at least you'll be travelling back to Cornwall together this time. I can't say I entirely approve of your travelling all this way alone, Breda my dear. There are always risks for a lovely young woman going abroad unescorted."

"I was quite safe, I assure you, Sir. There were several respectable families on board ship, and I attached myself to one of them," she said quickly.

It was true, at least for a very brief while until she was left respectfully alone in her widow black . . . she wished she hadn't thought of words that could send a cold little shiver down her spine.

Richard gave a short laugh, attempting to join in the general gaiety of the evening and putting his arm loosely around her shoulders in a show of affection for his father's sake.

"Don't underestimate Breda's sense of adventure, Father. I'd say she follows in a good tradition of strong Delacey women. There have also been some rather notorious ones in our history, as I recall."

His small squeeze on her shoulder told Breda that as it turned out, he considered her none too fine a catch either.

Lord Delacey joined in the laughter. "Fortune hunters and social climbers, yes," he agreed. "But from what you've told me about my delightful new daughter-in-law, I think we can discount everything but looking forward in time to a new generation. Let's raise our glasses to that happy event."

Breda drank quickly, and the golden liquid trailed down her throat. He referred to children, of course. A new dynasty for Grensham. It was obviously what he would want, and as soon as possible, to ensure the inheritance and the continuance of the Delaceys. It would be part of the delight he felt at his son's marriage. It was also something she and Richard had never discussed, and was something unlikely to be discussed now. Unless it had already happened, of course.

"I must learn more about these questionable ancestors sometime," she said quickly, covering the moment.

"And I shall take great pleasure in telling you of them," Lord Delacey said. "You shall hear all about the Delacey ladies who grace our family tree, Breda. It will be a fitting introduction to Grensham."

"And the young cousin I saw Richard riding with as I arrived?" she said carefully. "Is she a Delacey too?"

"Clare is my sister's girl," Lord Delacey told her. "Clare Magdalena Fitzallen—quite a mouthful for such a delicate young thing, isn't it? She'll be wanting to come and meet you properly, and perhaps we could arrange a party to introduce Breda to the County. You and Clare could put your heads together on that, I'm sure, my dear."

He spoke fondly of his niece, and again Breda felt that ridiculous spark of jealousy. She had no wish to put her head together with Miss Clare Magdalena Fitzallen's over any matter at all! She bit her lip slightly.

It was foolish indeed to imagine that Richard had never known other women before her, or that he had no other life beyond the one he had already shown her. She knew almost nothing about him, she realized, not for the first time, and yet she had willingly tied her life to his. And not entirely for the mercenary reason he believed . . . She realized suddenly that Lord Delacey clearly expected them to stay for the whole summer, if not forever!

"I'm afraid a party's out of the question, since we'll be leaving so soon," she heard Richard say in answer to his father's comment. "We'll have to leave it until we return, by which time I'm sure my lovely bride will have wheedled a new gown out of me for the occasion."

She forced a slightly hysterical laugh. "Of course! How could I appear in front of your friends for the first time in any old rags?"

Lord Delacey chuckled. "Careful, my love. You're in danger of sounding like one of the dubious lady ancestors I mentioned. I'll show you her portrait sometime. She was nearly as beautiful as yourself, but a scheming little baggage beneath it all."

He spoke with lazy confidence, so approving of his son's choice, and naturally assuming that Breda Vivien Delacey was faultless, and nothing like the person to whom he referred. And she dared not look into Richard's eyes, so afraid she would see nothing but contempt there.

She listened with mounting shock to all they were saying now. Richard was talking freely about making their permanent home here in Ireland, when he'd never mentioned such a thing before! She had simply assumed that he would assume the role of master of Vivien Hall. She saw now that that was a far lesser status than heir to Grensham castle! And Richard was expecting her to relinquish everything that she loved and live here as his wife.

"I suspect that you're a good horsewoman, Breda," Lord Delacey remarked. "Richard must show you the stables first thing tomorrow. I think you'll be pleasantly surprised by our thoroughbreds, reputedly the finest anywhere."

It was said naturally and without false pride, the way someone spoke when owning the best and merely stating the facts.

"That would be very nice," she said with a great effort not to glare at Richard for putting her in this impossible position. And yet it wasn't all his fault. She had put herself here, by her frantic need to be married within the six months of Philip's death, or risk losing Vivien Hall and its assets.

It was a pointless exercise now, she thought dismally. Wheal Breda, the pride and mainstay of Vivien Hall was lost forever, and if she heeded the words of the marriage service, then loving, honoring and obeying her husband undoubtedly meant that she must give up Vivien Hall anyway and move to Ireland.

Not that the luxury of Grensham would be any hardship, of course, but it wasn't home, and it wasn't what she had schemed to do . . . She admitted shamefully now that it *was* what she had done. Schemed to marry Richard Delacey in order to keep Vivien Hall. Her only consolation was that he hadn't exactly fought against it. It had been his desire to marry her in the first place, she remembered . . .

The dinner gong rang, and a maid appeared silently to take the empty sherry glasses from their hands. Lord Delacey offered Breda his arm, and the three of them went to the dining room, where a dazzling array of china and silver awaited them for dinner. If this was the way they dined every evening, Breda thought faintly, as the service and the succulent meal progressed, then so far she hadn't lived at all!

"Do you play the pianoforte, Breda?" Lord Delacey said, when the leisurely dinner was over and they had retired to the drawing-room. "We have a very fine instrument if you'd care to entertain us."

"I do play, of course." It was one of the social skills of every well-bred young lady, and she was thankful now that she had struggled with scales and arpeggios and not given it all up in disgusted impatience when her fingers hadn't reacted the way she wanted them to.

"I've never heard you, Breda," Richard said. "If you look on the music stand you may find some music sheets to your taste."

She looked through them. She didn't want to play at all. She was too tense, all her nerves on edge. She didn't want to be watched attentively by the two Delacey men, one her admiring new father-in-law, the other her coldly angry husband who must be ascribing all his bad fortune to the day he set eyes on Breda Vivien.

But they were waiting for her to begin, and she had little choice but to play the melodies from the music sheets. She wasn't a brilliant performer, but the keys moved lovingly beneath her fingers as she played some of the simpler classical pieces. And then her eyes were suddenly bright with tears as she followed with some of the pretty little ditties of the day. Evenings spent like this with her father and brother flitted poignantly into her mind, and her fingers were briefly poised above the keys.

"I think that's enough, darling, I'm sure you're tired after the journey today," Richard said quickly, seeing the small droop of her shoulders.

"Of course," his father said at once. "How thoughtless of me to keep you here like this. And you young people will want to be together after your parting. I'll bid you both goodnight."

When he reached the door he turned for a moment, smiling at them both. He suddenly looked his age.

"I'm not a man who has a way with fancy words, Breda, but I welcome you here with open arms, and it does my heart good to know that you've made my son so happy."

In the small silence that followed Breda closed the lid of the instrument with a bang. Lord Delacey was a dear sweet man, and if he knew the truth it would surely break his heart.

"We must be better actors than we knew," she said in a brittle voice. "Or did you think I was about to let you down?"

Richard moved across to where she stood, small and defensive and stiff with misery. She didn't know what he intended to do, and then she heard him give a smothered oath and pull her into his arms. His voice was hoarse, and she could sense all the pent-up emotion inside him, but it wasn't anger that he showed her now.

"No, I didn't think you were about to let me down, you seductive little witch! For the last hour I've been forced to watch how you sat so gracefully, and how the silk of your gown caressed your lovely body when I ached to be doing just that. I've listened to your playing, and longed for those slender trailing fingers of yours to be moving sensitively over my skin. I've been filled with such an urgency to hold you like this—"

Oh, my love, the breathless thought sang through her mind forgiving him everything in an instant, no matter how or why the words were dragged out of him. *Your father may not be eloquent with words, but you certainly have the gift, whether they're said only for the moment or forever . . .*

She felt his mouth on hers, kissing her with far more tenderness than he'd done earlier, and she was responding with as much fervor as if this was the night their marriage truly began. Hoping desperately with a tiny corner of her mind that perhaps their combined worry would bring them to a new closeness after all, and that not all was lost after all . . .

He spoke slowly and sensually. "Oh yes, my love, whatever else happens, we still have a passion for one another, don't we? And since you're still my wife no matter what your deviousness had brought us to, I see no reason why we shouldn't enjoy the benefits of our union."

She heard the underlying mockery in his voice and wanted to weep. It had all been a sham then, the sudden display of love, or what she had mistaken for love. Instead it was no more than this other thing, this *passion* that to her swift shame she could never deny whenever he touched her or looked at her or held her . . . nor could she deny that his passion was spectacular. But it wasn't enough. Nothing he could give her would ever be enough, without love.

"You want me to be your wife?" she said huskily. "Even though you don't love me?"

"You wanted me to be your husband, even though you don't love me," he retorted. "Don't let's pretend feelings that don't exist, Breda. Let's just be glad for what we have, for as long as it suits us. And right now, my lovely girl, I'd say we can do with all the mutual comfort the marriage service allows us."

She knew she should refuse him with every bit of pride and dignity she could summon to her aid.

"We married for all the wrong reasons, Richard. In the eyes of God, we sinned—"

His powerful arms crushed hers again, his mouth on hers refusing to let her say any more, and she gave up all thought of sin for the ecstasy of knowing that at least he wanted her. It wasn't the same as loving her, but wanting was the next best thing . . .

"I think we should retire to our room before I make love to you here and now and risk shocking the servants," he went on thickly. "And this time I promise I shan't ravish you, my love. We have all the time in the world."

At least three idyllic days . . . the words were in her thoughts before she could stop them. But now was not the time to remind him of what was to come when they returned to Cornwall. Now was the time for renewing the ties that bound them together, by whatever name society would choose to give it.

Much later, when Breda lay in the after-lethargy of love-making, she told herself it didn't matter. Pride came a very poor second when all her needs were in the hands of this man . . . and she had discovered something else now. While she was in his arms in the intimacy of the marriage-bed there was a perceptible gentling in his manner toward her, even during the times when passion was paramount. She prayed that in time, real love could grow between them, especially when love already existed for one of them. If it wasn't all too late . . .

And all her fine notions about offering him his freedom melted away, for how could she live without him now? She felt a wild deep sob begin in her throat. How could she bear it if the wickedness of Sam Stone and Amos Keighley took him away from her . . . forever?

He turned to her in his half-sleep, his arms folding around her with all the comfort of a warm cloak. He spoke in a softly relaxed tone.

"Worrying about a thing never solved anything, and whatever happens, we'll see it through together, you have my promise on it. Even if they threaten to ruin Vivien Hall, the Delacey resources will save it. I owe that much to Philip, for I valued his friendship highly, and I know how much the place meant to him as well as to you."

She lay with the weak tears running down her cheeks. He still believed she cared more for Vivien Hall than for anything else, and he was so wrong! In that instant, she knew it wouldn't matter if she never saw it again, if it meant losing him. It was just a house, a pile of granite that had prospered on the fortunes of tin. And the greedy mining for more and more tin could take away everything that was most dear to her. Not Vivien Hall or the mines, but *Richard* . . .

"Richard, you don't understand," she began tremulously.

He touched her lips with his finger, stilling her words.

"I do understand, my dear. Try to sleep now, Breda. Everything will look brighter in the morning, and we must at least look refreshed if the charade that we're a normal married couple is to succeed as far as my father is concerned. It won't do for my bride to look haggard every morning."

He turned away from her then, and although he hadn't entirely moved away from her, she felt as if he had abandoned her with those few chilling words. They hadn't been said unkindly, but they isolated her all the same, and told her he would never forget her real purpose in marrying him, no matter how much he forgot himself in the seductive pleasures of the flesh.

She curled up into a ball and tried to take warmth from him, but it was a long time before she slept.

"Would you like to see the horses this morning, Breda?" Richard said casually when they were finishing their breakfast.

"Yes, I would," she answered.

If only to get out of the castle and away from the trusting eyes of his father, for whom they were playing this charade. She couldn't get the word out of her head now, and it shamed her. This should have been such a glorious homecoming for Richard Delacey. Home from a war, and bringing a new bride to his ancestral home . . . instead it was all a sham, and because of her there was a court case hanging over his head. She couldn't blame him if he hated her.

"Are you quite well this morning, Breda?" Lord Delacey inquired. "You look a little pale."

"I'm very well, thank you, Sir. Though I think the travelling is still having its effect on me."

"Ah yes, the travelling. It's a pity that you have to repeat it so soon, but you'll have Richard with you this time," he smiled at her. "I have a favor to ask of you, my dear."

"Anything, if I can," she said, wondering what he could want of her.

"I hope it won't be too difficult. I'm thankful you've never peppered your conversation with Your Lordships, but I'd like you to drop this ridiculous *Sir* nonsense and call me Father. Is it too much to ask? It's a long while since a pretty young lady has called me by that name."

It was the only reference he'd made to Maureen so far, and Breda could see by the pain in his eyes that it hurt him even now to remember her. She spoke softly.

"It would give me pleasure to do so."

280

Richard scraped back his chair from the table. "Then if that's settled, shall we make ourselves ready?" he said briskly, and she wondered if he was none too pleased at this show of affection and familiarity between the other two.

It was as if he felt she had no right to infiltrate herself so smoothly into his family. But she had the right. While she wore his ring on her wedding finger, she had every right.

It was mid-morning by the time they got ready to leave for the thoroughbred stables. Richard seemed in a slightly better humor by then, and she had decided not to ask his opinion of his father's suggestion. For herself, she felt quite elated that Lord Delacey had shown his pleasure in Richard's choice of bride in this way, deliberately believing that this cementing of their relationship in His Lordship's eyes could only be an omen for good. And the Cornish put great trust in omens.

"Shall we walk, or do you prefer to ride? I can arrange for a gig to be brought to the front door."

"I'm quite capable of walking. Nan and I have often walked for hours at a stretch over the Cornish moors," she said. "I'm not a weakling, Richard."

"That you're not," he agreed gravely. "Well then, put on some sturdy footwear, for it's some distance from here, though well within your capabilities. My grandfather, who began the Delacey stud, was very keen to keep the business proceedings well apart from the ambiance of the castle, and it's well screened behind a small wood."

"Your grandfather had good taste. It would be a crime for anything to spoil the beauty of Grensham," she said sincerely.

"It is very beautiful," he acknowledged by the time they had begun their walk and were gazing back at the huge gray stone building in its emerald setting. "I feel a tug at my heart whenever I have to leave it, so I suppose I can understand your feelings for Vivien Hall."

"My feelings are not quite as you imagine," she murmured, "but since we're on the subject, we never really discussed where we would live after our marriage, did we?"

"We did not," he said, his voice hardening again as they resumed their walk toward the sun-dappled greenery of the wood separating Grensham from the stud. "And I see no point in discussing it now until the other business is settled."

"But your father naturally assumes that we'll live here," she persisted, wanting him to say that he wanted it too. That he wanted her with him, where a wife's place should be.

"And you obviously want to be in your beloved Cornwall. Our darker desires have a strange way of dictating our destiny—"

"By that you mean my covetousness, I suppose?"

Bitterly, she realized he never said he'd be willing to stay in Cornwall with her. Would she, if she had all this?

"I think we could argue forever and never find an answer," he said. "Is that what you want? Or shall we put it all behind us for the time being and try to get through these three days as painlessly as possible?"

She knew he was right. The sparks between them were as vibrant as ever, whether they burned with passion or rage. Whatever their relationship was destined to be, Breda knew it would never be mundane. It would be all or nothing.

"We'll continue with the charade," she said dully.

They had entered the wood now, dark and peaceful as a cathedral except for the splinters of sunlight through the whispering branches of the evergreens. The earth was soft and springy beneath their feet, the traces of early mist not quite dispersed from the ground foliage, so that their silent footsteps seemed to be floating along on a hazy sea. The trees seemed to enclose them in a different world, and Breda had the extraordinary sensation of being totally alienated from everything else on earth, except for Richard. And this was followed by an overwhelming longing to remain there.

She felt his arms around her as he turned her into him, and she knew he must see the diamond sparkle of tears on her lashes for the terrible mess their union had created.

"A charade it may be, Breda, but you seem to have forgotten one thing. When I brought you Philip's belongings I told you then that I meant to marry you. We entered into a legal contract, and the honor of Grensham is more important to me than any female whim to break that contract."

She gasped, wriggling out of his arms at once.

"A legal contract? Is that the way you see the sanctity of marriage vows?"

"It's the way I see ours," he said dryly. "You never made any attempt to make me see that you had any other reason for marrying me, my sweet, except for your natural instincts, of course, and no one can be held responsible for those when a hard-headed business deal is at stake."

"I think you're perfectly hateful," she said, her eyes flashing. He suddenly gave a deep chuckle, tucking her arm in his and striding on so that she had no option but to try and match her footsteps to his.

"And I think you're perfectly delightful, whether you're soft in my arms in my bed, or hurling abuse at me in that delicious Cornish voice of yours. But just so that we know exactly where we stand, my love, in the Delacey family a marriage is a marriage for life. And I'm not tempting fate by saying so, so just get that anxious frown off your face and let's go and enjoy the horses."

In other words, he had no intention of letting her go, whatever the outcome of the trial. It was a thought that filled her with unutterable joy, even while she knew he only used her for his own sake.

What kind of man would travel from the far distant shores of the Crimea to court a woman he'd never met, just because he'd been a good friend of her brother? And without even following the procedure of proper courtship, bombarding her with his intentions like the passionate and single-minded man that he was. He had always meant to have her, and fate had given her to him.

Chapter Fifteen

Coming out of the hushed woods into the sunlight again was to enter into summer warmth and activity. In front of them now were the long low buildings of the thoroughbred stables, where a team of men and young boys groomed the burnished horses in the paddocks nearby. Farther away there was a vast exercise course where horses with flying manes and tails, their riders crouched low over their backs, raced against a timing clock held by a trainer. As they approached him, the man turned and gave a delighted smile as he saw Richard, tapping his forelock and then impetuously pumping Richard's hand in welcome.

"Sure, and it does my old eyes good to see you back and healthy, Sir. We'd got word that you were here in the old country again, and I know your father will be feeling fair dandy to have you home, so he will!"

"Thank you, Paddy," Richard said smilingly as more employees came running up to greet him, and to Breda it was clear from their excitement that Richard was held in high esteem. She realized again what a different life he had here, far removed from her original suspicion that he was a fortune hunter! She was sure that the fortunes of Vivien Hall and its tin mines could be swallowed up without notice in the majesty of Grensham.

He introduced her to everyone who greeted him with such obvious affection, and they all bade her a smiling welcome. They behaved less like employees than trusted old friends, she thought with a small surprise, and far more humanly than the aggressive Sam Stone and his cronies or the more subservient tinners.

"How many horses do you have here?" she asked the trainer quickly, willing away any thoughts of Sam Stone or the tinners that would cloud this beautiful day. Richard was right. They could do nothing until they returned to Cornwall, so they might as well try to enjoy these three days of freedom.

"It varies, Ma'am," Paddy said cheerfully, clearly pleased at her interest. "Right now we have nearly eighty, apart from the colts, but we're almost due for the midsummer sale, and then 'twill be the breeding season again, and so it goes on."

He was joined by the stud manager then, and after the introductions and greetings had taken place all over again, the manager spoke respectfully to Richard. "We've a fine set of inquiries for stock this year, Sir, and I anticipate an excellent return. Will you be wanting to see the list today, or will you and your lady leave it for another time?"

"I'll certainly take a look at the list, Shaughnessy, but unfortunately my wife and I won't be here for the sale. We have to return to Cornwall in three days' time on a family matter."

"That's a real shame, Ma'am," the man said to

286

Breda with genuine regret. "You'd have enjoyed the spectacle. Gents from overseas as well as locals come to the Delacey stud for the annual sale, and a colorful affair it is, with the Arabs in their flowing robes and suchlike, jewels sparkling on 'em brighter than if they were womenfolk. His Lordship has a big tent put up to give them every hospitality on the day, and there's a party at the castle for those that are invited to stay as guests, and Miss Clare acts as hostess, though 'o course, if you and Master Richard had been staying, it would have been different —"

"Thank you, Shaughnessy, I think my wife has got the idea by now," Richard laughed as the man enthusiastically warmed to his tale. "Don't ever think of leaving my father's employ, man, or the world would lose a great story teller!"

"Sure, and my words do run away with themselves at times," the manager grinned. "And in my usual hotheaded way I've overlooked adding my congratulations on your marriage, but you'll know I wish you every happiness, Sir and Ma'am. And I confess I was thinking mebbe I could persuade you and your lovely wife to stay on after all, by tempting her a wee bit?"

"You've tempted me a lot," Breda said, laughing at the way he still couldn't resist elaborating on the simplest point. And forcing her thoughts away from that of Clare Fitzallen acting the perfect hostess in the Grensham household. "Unfortunately we are obliged to leave Grensham again at the end of the week."

"Ah well, there'll be other times," the man said complacently. "I'll leave you both to your browsing while I get about my business."

"I'll be in to see those lists before we go back to the

castle, Shaughnessy," Richard called after him. The group around them gradually moved away, and then he turned to Breda, a spark of mischief in his voice. "And now I know how right the gods were to bless you with those beautiful green eyes, my Breda."

"What's that supposed to mean?" she said suspiciously.

He laughed, and she saw how just being here had lifted his spirits. The sun glinted on his dark hair, and a lock had fallen over his forehead. He was still tanned and healthy from his travels overseas. He was surrounded now by those who loved him, and in his own environment he was virile and strong and very dear to her, she thought with a catch in her throat. She felt him squeeze her around the waist.

He was still ready to tease. "Don't they say that green is the color of jealousy? And your sparkling eyes did full credit to this emerald isle a moment ago, my darling. Sure, and the green gems themselves would have envied you," he said, as exaggeratedly as Shaughnessy.

"What nonsense," Breda said heatedly. "Anyway, I don't know what you're talking about—"

"Oh, I think you do, and I find it an interesting thought! But I don't care to be standing about arguing with my bride," he grinned, "especially as the object of her jealousy is fast approaching. You aren't going to let your feelings show too obviously, are you, my sweet?"

She looked up quickly, to where Clare Fitzallen was just dismounting from a horse, her cheeks glowing the way they were yesterday, lithe and supple as the animal she rode. And the flicker of jealousy inside Breda became a flame as the girl approached with outstretched hands. If only Clare had been hostile toward her, it would have been so much easier to dislike her, and whatever she had been in Richard's past. But there was simply nothing to dislike in Clare Fitzallen, nothing at all.

"At last! I was dying to ride over last evening to make your acquaintance, Breda! But Richard said I must stay away until you two love birds had spent some time alone together. And now I see why, and I heartily approve of my cousin's choice. Welcome to the family, dear cousin."

She was vivacious and garrulous, and Breda simply couldn't help warming to her frank manner. She was sure there wasn't an ounce of guile in the girl, which somehow made her own and Richard's past and future relationship more uncomfortable than ever.

Clare linked her arm in Breda's as the three of them walked together toward the paddocks, and then Richard left them together to consult the lists of prospective buyers at the midsummer sale. The two girls leaned on the fence, breathing in the wine-heady air, and Clare was clearly delighted to have Breda's company.

"It's so good to have another female in the family," she prattled on. "You'll know all about poor Maureen, of course? My uncle was devastated when she was seduced by that scoundrel, and I don't think he's ever really gotten over her death. It was one of the worst days of Richard's life when he came back without her and had to tell Uncle Charles what had happened in America."

She gave a deep sigh, and Breda could see this had

been a close-knit family. With her own father and brother gone, she envied Clare her association with the Delaceys so much.

"Do you live near?" she asked.

"Oh yes, just over the hill, though nowhere so near as grand as Grensham, of course. My father's a gentleman farmer, and we have a modest manor house with several cottages for the laborers. Mother's rather into good works at present," she added mischievously, "but they're good sorts, both of them. And what about your family?"

For a moment her tongue seemed to stick to the roof of her mouth, and then she found herself telling this friendly girl about the sadness of the past year, culminating in the way that Richard Delacey had come into her life.

"I'm so sorry, Breda," Clare said softly. "But how wonderful that out of all this, you and Richard found one another. Do you believe in fate?"

Breda gave a small laugh. "You ask a Cornishwoman if she believes in fate? It's like asking if she believes in the sun rising and setting each day!"

"And you're obviously so much in love," Clare sighed happily. "It's so good to see happiness in that grim old castle again. I called to see Uncle Charles before coming to the stud, and already he's a different person since Richard returned home."

"You know we can't stay, of course." Breda didn't look at her as she spoke, concentrating instead on the elegant horses being brought out for their morning exercise.

"Uncle Charles said so, but surely your aunt would recover without your having to go back again? You *are* coming to live at Grensham, of course?"

She could obviously imagine nothing else, and as Breda tried to think of something suitable to say, she realized Richard had rejoined them, his arm around her waist once more, and holding her lightly.

"All in good time, cousin dear. Breda has a few problems to deal with at Vivien Hall, but I've no doubt we'll be in residence long before the end of the year, and then we'll have a huge party and invite every possible beau for Miss Clare Fitzallen. That *is* what you were dying to find out, I take it?"

Clare laughed, and it was easy to see that the rapport between these two went back a long way. Before, she might have been jealous. Now, she felt that in Clare she could find the sister that Maureen Delacey might have been, and she had no doubt that it was the way Lord Delacey looked on this delightfully extroverted girl.

"You know me too well," Clare grinned. "But Breda and I have been getting to know one another as well, and I must say that I totally approve your choice. She's a perfect bride for you, Richard."

"You don't need to assure me of that! I knew you would approve of her as much as Father, who's obviously half in love with her already. I only wish there was time to show her off to the entire county, but there's not."

Breda was beginning to find all this artless discussion of her attributes highly embarrassing, and finally said so, seeing no reason not to be as frank as these two.

"If you've both finished discussing me as if I was a newly acquired thoroughbred, I'd prefer it if we talked about something else!"

"Oh Breda, I do love the way you talk when you're roused," Clare teased. "That lovely accent of yours becomes even more pronounced."

"Does it? How extraordinary," she said. "I mean, that's just what I always think about Richard—"

"Sure and begorrah, but I don't have the smallest hint of an accent, saints preserve us all an' all," he said promptly, as Irish as the Blarney Stone, at which the three of them became suddenly helpless with laughter.

And Breda wished with all her heart that it could always be like this, so carefree and lighthearted, with the summer sunshine blazing down on them, and the beautiful emerald isle living up to its name so gloriously.

All too soon the idyll came to an end. Breda regarded Lord Delacey with very real affection now. She had only known him a short time, but he was already a father figure to her, and she hugged him tightly when the time came to say good-bye.

"I prefer to say God go with you than the finality of good-bye, Breda my dear," he said. "That way I feel sure we shall be together again, and very soon, I hope."

"I hope so too," she whispered. "I hope so very much—Father."

How dearly she would have liked to confide all their approaching troubles in this wise man, Breda thought. But what would be the point in giving him the frustrating anxiety of wondering how his son fared in his trial? A worry shared wouldn't be halved. It would only be multiplied. She and Richard had both agreed on that.

Clare had come to see them leave Grensham, and stood now with her arm linked through Lord Delacey's. Breda's jealousy toward the girl had vanished. Clare was a loving substitute for the daughter Lord Delacey had lost, and if the worst happened, she would be a great comfort for him. She switched her thoughts at once, having already determined never to believe that the worst was remotely possible.

"Come back soon," Clare called gaily to the pair of them.

"We will, I promise," Richard replied. In an undertone to Breda, he said steadily, "and I never break a promise, do I, sweetheart?"

She prayed that he was as strong as he appeared. He was a decent upright man, but she knew only too well that the villains of this world could ruin such a man by lies and deceit and wickedness. She shivered at the thought.

"You never broke one yet," she said steadily. He hadn't done so in their marriage. He had been everything a woman could want in a husband, except for one thing. He still hadn't said he loved her. Technically, he had carried out his vows. Loving, honoring and cherishing her, but he had never said what she so longed to hear. And knowing him as she did now, she knew they wouldn't be said unless they were true.

They left Grensham in far finer style than Breda had arrived. They were taken by a groom in one of the Delacey carriages with a coat of arms emblazoned on either door to the port of Rosslare, to embark on the ship bound for Cornwall. It was early evening when they reached the port, and the ship was due to sail on the tide at seven o'clock.

It would be a different voyage from the lonely and jittery one she had taken to Ireland. Richard led the way to their cabin, and despite knowing what was ahead of them at the end of the short voyage, she found enormous relief in not having to think for herself any more. Richard was with her now, and that changed everything.

The cabin was small and necessarily intimate. There was little space for anything but the two narrow bunks, a chest of drawers that served as a dressing-table, a hanging wall closet and a washing corner. It was serviceable and hardly luxurious, but none of that mattered. Breda was becoming more and more conscious of the confinement in which they now found themselves. Perhaps he was conscious of it too, for he said abruptly that they may as well take some air before they had their evening meal and retired for the night.

They went up on deck, and the swell of the sea below the ship glittered as dark as pewter in the receding harbour lights. The blissful heat of the day had gone, its last lingering warmth diminishing quickly as freshening sea breezes whipped into their faces. Breda pulled her woollen shawl more closely around her.

When would she ever see this hospitable land again? she wondered. Ireland had welcomed her in and given her sanctuary, and she had felt more truly at home, whether in its quaintness or its grandeur, than she had ever expected to feel anywhere other than Cornwall.

"A penny for your thoughts," Richard said quietly, watching her profile. "Or would you prefer not to take the offer? Perhaps you're thinking it was a bad day when you threw in your lot with a Delacey — and if so, I don't want to hear it."

He tried to make a joke of it, but she bit her lip, taking him seriously.

"Perhaps you're thinking it was a bad day when you ever heard the name of Vivien! If you and Philip had never been such friends, so that you inadvertently learned about me, and promised to do what you could for the survival of the mine named after his sister, none of this would have happened!" She caught her breath as the truth of it washed over her. "You'd have been free to go home to Ireland and live your life with one of these pretty colleens whose hearts will be broken now that the dashing Richard Delacey is spoken for—"

She realized how she was babbling on and that other passengers taking a last look at the shores of Ireland were glancing their way. Richard put his arm about her waist and spoke softly in her ear.

"And do you suppose any of these colleens could hold a candle to my beautiful, tempestuous Breda? If they could, I'd have married one of them long ago. No, my darling, my fate was assured from the moment I looked at a certain likeness of a Cornish girl, sketched by her brother, and saw everything I wanted to see in that voluptuous mouth and those seductive eyes."

Her mouth fell open a little. It wasn't what she had expected him to say. Was he saying that he had fallen in love with that likeness? She felt momentarily confused, twisting to stare at him, but it was impossible to see his expression, except for the smile on his lips. She felt his fingers caress the curve of her waist, moving sensuously up and down.

"I knew then, that this was the woman I wanted to

295

tame, the woman I must have," he went on mockingly, spoiling the moment, shattering her brief wild hope.

"And do you always get what you want?" she said jerkily, willing him to continue this seductive little interlude, no matter how it demeaned her as a woman. When he was in this mood, she seemed to lose all sense of pride, she thought weakly, and it was a good thing he never knew it.

"So far. There are a few more things. To be rid of this trial for one. To see justice done, and the bastards who set this whole thing up dealt with in the proper manner."

His mood had changed, and his voice was harsh. Breda sighed, knowing he had gone away from her. She could hardly blame him. The thought of the trial was like a ton weight hanging over his head, and however much he believed in justice, Breda knew he'd seen enough of life to know that justice didn't always prevail. She gave another uncontrollable shiver.

"You're cold. Let's find out what kind of fare this vessel has to offer," he said at once.

They found that it certainly wasn't the best, but it was adequate enough, washed down with hot chocolate or sharp wine.

"I thought to bring some quality wine with me," Richard said. "We'll rid ourselves of this vinegary taste when we return to the cabin."

Breda wasn't sure that she wanted any more. The wine in the dining salon was making her dizzy, combined with the roughness of the sea. The voyage out had been smooth, the sea glassy, but this time it was far choppier. She didn't feel ill, but the combination of the motion and the raw wine wasn't helping her equilibrium at all.

When she murmured as much to Richard, he assured her that the better brew would steady her.

"Can you guarantee that?" she said wryly.

He laughed. "Trust me!"

Wasn't she doing just that? Putting her whole life in his trust? She didn't want her mind to keep revolving around it any more, but whatever she did, her thoughts kept returning to the trial, to Amos Keighley, to Sam Stone . . . and to Mary Keighley too. What must she be thinking now?

And what of the outcome of it all? If — when — Richard was cleared of negligence, then the other two would be damned. And what of Mary and the children then? They would be destitute — except of course, that Breda couldn't let that happen. They were still family, if only distantly by marriage. And families stood by each other in times of trouble . . .

Richard had obviously been thinking of the trial too, but his thoughts had taken a different direction.

"I want you to promise me something, Breda," he said later, when they were undressing in the tiny cabin and trying to find enough space to do so.

"What is it?" she mumbled, her lips feeling decidedly thicker since taking a glass of Richard's finer wine. The taste had certainly been smooth and palatable, but it did nothing to stop the strange spinning of her senses.

"If the worst happens, and you're left alone—"

"Oh, don't say it! It's bad luck!" She cried out at once.

He gave a small smile. "Darling, merely talking about possibilities never made them happen. Forget

297

your old Cornish superstitions and listen to me."

She sat down heavily on her bunk, small and vulnerable in her cotton nightgown, and nodded slowly. Not that she could ever forget her instinctive superstition because it was part of her nature, but at least she would listen.

"If it happens, then you're to get right away. Go to Grensham. My father will protect you and treat you as his daughter. You must know that he already loves you."

But you do not . . .

"And what about my home? Am I to leave it forever? What about the other mines, and the tinners whose livelihood depends on Vivien Hall?" she said through chattering teeth.

"Somehow I imagined you would not have the heart for it any more," he said quietly. "Am I wrong?"

She looked at him across the small cabin, her strong virile husband, and knew that without him, she wouldn't have the heart for anything at all any more. What would it matter where she lived?

"No, you're not wrong," she said, bowing her head so he wouldn't see everything in her eyes. "Sometimes lately I've felt a great urge to sell everything and get right away. I'm no mine owner, Richard. It's not a woman's world, and I never wanted it to be my world. But I feel as if I'd be betraying all that my father worked for if I sold up. You're not the only one with obligations to the past."

"You and I have obligations to the future as well, my darling girl."

She felt the dip of the narrow bunk as he sat beside her, his palm softly circling her breast. She looked up at him sharply, drawing in her breath.

"Do we?" she said faintly.

She would have thought it an impossibility to make love in the narrow bunk, but she was wrong. The next hour was one of exquisite pleasure, her senses drowning in the now familiar preliminaries to love as he aroused her with more erotic sensations than she had ever known. She gave herself freely to him, wanting him with a primitive hunger that matched his own. If she murmured incoherent words of love to him she never knew it. If he heard them, he never commented. They were too fused by passion to heed anything but being part of each other on this steadily steaming ship whose engines throbbed beneath them with a seductive pulsebeat of their own.

It was only much much later when Breda lay still wide awake, and Richard seemed to be sleeping in the bunk barely a yard away, that she wondered about his words. *You and I have obligations to the future as well* . . . There had been a moment when their loving was over when he had pressed gently on her belly, and leaned forward to kiss it. At the time she had thought it a simple, poignant moment.

Now, she wondered if Richard's reference to their obligations to the future meant the secure future of Grensham. A child to inherit the fortunes of that historic castle. It would be perfectly natural for him to desire that. It would be expected that the son of Lord Delacey would produce an heir as soon as possible after his marriage. All great families sought to secure their dynasty.

Had she been a dupe all this time? Had his intentions to marry her through Philip's innocent references to his lovely sister been carefully calculated, seeing her as no more than a suitable mother to his future children? In which case, there had never been any intention in his mind of remaining at Vivien Hall. Unwittingly she had already told him she was half-inclined to sell, but in reality he would never even need to persuade her to do so. As his wife, she'd be expected to live where he chose. It was a wife's duty, and she'd been too blind to see any of it before now . . .

"What's troubling you, my love?" Richard's calm voice broke through her crazed thoughts, and she realized she was breathing so tortuously that her breaths emerged as little gasping sobs in her throat.

His love? In view of her spinning thoughts, the words were an insult.

"Do I mean anything at all to you, Richard?" she said huskily. "In view of all the trouble being heaped on your head now, I should think you rue the day you ever laid eyes on the Vivien family."

He didn't say anything for a moment, and then he spoke softly. "Have you forgotten so soon the words of the wedding service? In sickness and in health, for richer or poorer—"

"And through whatever devious means to an end a wedding was arranged," she said bitterly. "I think it's time we stopped pretending with one another, don't you?"

"I rather thought we had both decided to forget that, but it seems apparent that you can't. You don't have to go on torturing yourself forever, Breda—"

"*Me!* I was referring to the way you practically forced your way into my life! It seems to me you were determined to marry me long before we even met, and my brother's death was a convenient way for you to make my acquaintance—"

She gasped as she felt him shaking her. She hadn't been aware that he had risen from his bunk, but now he sat on the edge of hers, his hands rough on her shoulders.

"Don't ever say that to me again," he said harshly. "Your brother was a good friend and I'll not have his name defiled by a chit of a girl who's unworthy of him."

"Don't tell me about my own brother! I *loved* him."

Her voice caught on a sob, and Richard released her. Gingerly she touched the tender skin that would be bruised from his assault, and bit her trembling lips. Why did everything have to end like this? Minutes ago they had been lovers, and now everything had changed. Now they were more like enemies, when they needed to stay so close in view of what lay ahead of them.

"I'm sorry," she whispered, chagrined at hardly knowing why she humbled herself, or what she was apologizing for, but desperately needing that closeness between them again.

Incredulously, she felt the touch of his lips on her cheek, and his finger smoothed the tangle of her hair. The burning tears stung her eyes, and she was thankful it was too dark for him to see just how his every touch could affect her so.

"We're both under a considerable strain," he said. "The sooner we get this bad business sorted out the better. And then perhaps we can assess what to do with our lives."

The dryness was back in her throat again as he returned to his bunk. In her mind, his words spoke of finality. He had had enough of the wayward Breda Vivien, and wanted to be rid of her. Or he might just continue to consider her as his wife if she managed to do what she now believed he wanted—to conceive a child.

She trembled in the cold bunk. To keep a husband was the worst of all reasons for wanting a child. It was wicked, and it was the way ambitious women plotted and schemed. She turned her face into the coarse pillow and tried not to feel shame at the thought and it was a very long time before she slept, but eventually she did so from sheer exhaustion.

It could hardly be called a dreamless sleep. Hazy images floated in and out of her restless mind like the watery patterns on a color-washed painting. She saw herself standing above the wild Cornish cliffs with the glittering sea far below, and the whispering bracken snatching at her body. She was dressed in a gown of flimsy, floaty fabric, waiting for someone. He seemed to be always just out of reach, and she couldn't see him properly. The edges of his image were blurred, as if they were captured in the frame of a portrait. But she knew instinctively that the man for whom she waited so anxiously was Richard Delacey.

Once her dream self recognized who she awaited, she could see his face above everything else, dark and strong, and loved more than life. He seemed to be searching for her too, but he couldn't see where she was. She called out to him, but her voice was carried away by the breeze that lifted her filmy skirts high about her face and body.

Then the breeze dropped and she was bathed in brilliant sunlight, lethargic and sensual in its sudden warmth. And she was tenderly holding something in her arms. Something that stirred and moved, and opened its eyes to look at her.

The child was tiny and perfect, a replica of Richard in every way except for Breda's startlingly emerald eyes. Watching him waken to wave his tiny fists in the air, she felt as though she could hardly breathe at the wonder of him. Reverently, she touched the tiny mouth and felt the instinctive bite on her finger, and she felt the pull as he tried to suck. And the most enormous swell of feeling ran through her veins and filled her body at this action by so fragile a human being. One that she and Richard had given life to and who was now utterly dependent on them both.

And then the most wondrous moment of all, because Richard had reached her side now, and she was enveloped in his arms. Each was vulnerable alone, but together they were strong against the world . . .

The dream was so vivid that when she awoke with a start, she reached out her arms for something that wasn't there.

"It's morning," Richard's voice said briefly. "I'm going up on deck for a breath of air, and I'll see you later."

In a moment he had left the cabin and she was staring at a blank door. So much for dreams, she thought bitterly, and then ran a shaking hand across her forehead to find it damp. And she knew then that if a child was born of their loving, it would be no result of plotting and scheming — at least not on her part. No matter what Richard's future intentions were, a child would be a gift of God that she would love and cherish.

She heard herself give a tremulous laugh. Was this really Breda Vivien, who a few short weeks ago had never even considered marriage with a man, and was now contemplating motherhood! And with the kind of starry-eyed sentimentality usually written about in dreadful penny magazines directed at young and impressionable servant girls who usually couldn't even read them!

She got up quickly, washed as best she could in the confines of the cabin and dressed herself, remembering to wrap her woollen shawl around her shoulders before she also went up on deck. Sea air could be treacherously cold, even in summer, and the day had hardly begun yet.

By now they would be somewhere in a no-man's-sea, between the Irish coast and the Cornish one. And she felt a great need to be with Richard, to feel the comfort of his body next to hers, and to imagine that this voyage was going on forever, with no ordeal at the end of it. It was a futile wish, of course, but one that she clung to as she made her way among the other early risers taking the air and sought out a familiar lone figure leaning by the ship's rail.

Chapter Sixteen

"Thank the Almighty you've come back!" Mr. Flowers exclaimed with some vehemence, the moment he saw them at his chambers. They had made a point of calling on him before they returned to Vivien Hall to get the most recent news, and the look on the solicitor's face filled Breda with new alarm.

"You knew where I was going, and it's been little more than a week since I left for Ireland, Mr. Flowers—"

"It's been nearer two," he said pickily. "And I was thinking I'd have to send a search party to find your husband if it had gone on much longer."

"What's happened?" Richard said at once, clearly resenting the man's abrupt manner. "Breda's told me everything so far, of course, but there's still plenty of time before the trial for us to discuss the case, surely?"

"There would have been, but owing to bad feeling in the area, the magistrate has decided to bring it forward," Flowers informed them sourly. "Your Pit Captain's been making a fine job of rabble-rousing among the tinners, Breda, with the result that half of them are inclined to come out on strike anyway until the court case is over."

"But that's just what he was trying to prevent. They know they'll get precious little wages if they strike!"

"Things sometimes have a habit of rebounding on first intentions," Flowers told her. "It seems that this is just what's happened after all Sam Stone's hollering and shouting for his rights. Naturally, there's another faction just as determined not to see a strike, but it means the whole of the tinning community is now divided into two camps. Fights are breaking out daily, even property being damaged, until finally the constables had no choice but to inform the court, with the result that the trial's now fixed for two weeks' time."

Breda gasped. "Then if we'd stayed away much longer—"

"That's right. Mr. Delacey would assuredly have been found guilty by default. The Stannary Courts are harsh with their judgments and their penalties, and a man who chooses not to defend himself is presumed to be a coward and inevitably pronounced guilty."

"And you know that I am neither, Sir!" Richard said angrily.

"So you tell me, but it will be a harder job convincing the rest of them," Flowers said.

Breda felt a new stab of alarm. "But you do believe him, don't you, Mr. Flowers? I've told you everything I know, about Richard taking his report personally to the committee, and about my visit to the Duck and Whistle and learning of the treachery of Sam Stone and my cousin. I'll tell them myself if I have to!"

"I need no womens' skirts to hide behind, Breda," she heard Richard say savagely.

"Nor will you be permitted to give evidence," the solicitor reminded her. "A wife's testimony would be seen to be prejudicial in favor of her husband, if indeed a woman was permitted to speak at all during the proceedings, which would be highly irregular."

"Stuff and nonsense!" Breda said, irritated by his fancy words when plain speaking put things so much simpler. "Who is there better to vouch for a husband's character than his wife?"

She stopped, wondering if she had really said that, when she had been so determined from the beginning to suspect Richard's every motive. But never his integrity as an engineer . . . She saw Richard look at her now, and felt herself redden at the sardonic smile on his face and the knowing look in his eyes.

"Your loyalty does you credit, my dear, but I hardly think you've known me long enough for a court to take your testimony into consideration. And the opposition will surely bring that out in court."

He was doing it himself now, she raged, using pompous long words in the manner of the solicitor. Putting her into the role of the little woman at home, who should stick to her embroidery and be quietly kept out of mens' affairs. Not this woman, Breda vowed . . .

"I would advise you to keep out of sight until the day of the trial," Flowers continued. "There's no point in inciting trouble before it's necessary."

"If you think I intend hiding away like a criminal —" Richard began heatedly.

"I'm only giving you the benefit of my advice, Sir. What you choose to do with it is your own affair."

Breda felt her heart sink. There was so little time now. The thought of the coming trial had been cushioned by being still a little time away, but now it was almost here. And if the verdict went against Richard . . . but she wouldn't even think of that.

"Is my cousin still in Penzance?" she asked the solicitor instead. "And his family?"

"He is. And throwing his drunken weight about on every occasion," Flowers said, disgust and disapproval in every pore. "I imagine the poor wife hardly sees him, since he spends days and nights at that disreputable inn on the waterfront."

"I shall go and see her as soon as I can," Breda said at once, hoping to divert the solicitor's thoughts from the fact that Breda Vivien had disgraced herself in his eyes by also frequenting the aforenamed disreputable inn.

"Take every care, Breda," Flowers warned her. "There are those who will not be well disposed to anyone from Vivien Hall at the present time. I don't need to tell you how quickly miners' tempers can be inflamed."

She felt a violent shock at this. Her family had always been well respected and well liked, and it was unbelievable that the solicitor should be warning her in this way now.

"I don't intend to hide behind closed doors either!" she said. "It would only be seen to admitting to the charge if Richard and I did so!"

She saw Flowers shrug, and guessed immediately that that was the way he already saw their departure for Ireland. But Richard had gone before the mine collapsed, and it had been her duty to go after him. The man stood up now to indicate that this interview was at an end. There seemed little more to say. Breda was upset and more worried than she wanted to show, and she longed to be home.

"I shall call on you tomorrow when you're more rested after your journey, Sir," he said directly to Richard. "There are many things we must discuss. Will two o'clock in the afternoon be convenient?"

"Perfectly," Richard said. "I shall be ready for you."

They left the chambers, and Breda felt an odd kind of fear as they climbed into the hired carriage waiting for them outside. After the solicitor's warning, it was as if she sensed danger in every innocent glance of a passerby, as if there were revengeful tinners lurking on every street corner, waiting to rush into the street and accost the travellers, ready to beat them about the head with sticks or stones. As if she expected to see the leering faces of Amos Keighley and Sam Stone counting out the days until the end of the Vivien dynasty, and all that her forbears had worked for.

She felt unable to relax at all until they were well out of the town and the carriage was taking them high onto the moors, to where the distant chimneys of Vivien Hall were already visible on the skyline. Richard had said very little all this time, but now she felt his hand close over hers, and knew he must guess at how painfully fast her heart was beating.

"We'll fight this together, Breda," he said savagely. "We both know the truth of it, and we have God on our side."

"I know," she said huskily.

And irreverently or not, she prayed that on this occasion God would be an especially understanding and forgiving God, in view of all the underhandedness in their commitment to becoming man and wife. Material gain for Breda, pride in perpetuity in Richard, wanting a son to carry on the Delacey name. Both were sins according to God's commandments . . .

She took a shuddering breath. "Richard, whatever happens, I want you to know—"

Whatever she might have said was prevented by a great cacophony of noise. Mens' voices bellowed and screeched and blasphemed, and there was a protesting whinnying from their carriage horses, as the driver whipped them on to quicken their pace. As they galloped across the moors now, Breda peered out through the side of the swaying carriage. Some distance away from them she saw a great body of men converging together. From their clothes and manner, she knew at once that they were tinners, and then she gasped as she recognized the unmistakable burly figure of Sam Stone. He wielded an axe whose blade glinted in the sunlight, and alongside him, egging him on, was the hated shape of her cousin, Amos Keighley.

For a moment she was terrified, thinking they were coming for her and Richard, and she felt his grip on her hand tighten.

"They're not after us, Breda. They have a private battle to conduct amongst themselves."

As she watched, she felt sickened. Sam Stone's axe waved wildly in the air, and the men nearest him scattered before it. Most were armed with sticks from the hedgerow, but a few had more sinister weapons. The tinners in her father's employ had always lived and worked harmoniously, she thought sickly. There had been very few disputes, and never a hint of a strike or outright war. Philip had continued the Vivien tradition of paying a man fair dues for a fair day's work.

Everything here had been good and prosperous until Breda Vivien took control of the business. And indirectly it was all because of her that men had died when Wheal Breda collapsed. She couldn't think rationally any more. She forgot all about the terms of the entailment that had forced her to accept Richard's proposal of marriage when the bragging cousin appeared on the scene. And far from wanting to be here now, she wished herself anywhere in the world but at Vivien Hall. Wildly, she wished desperately that she could be back in the tranquil Irish countryside they had just left, and under the fatherly protection of Lord Delacey.

"It's all right, love. We're well past them now," Richard said, and when her dilated eyes focussed properly again, she saw that they had come over the rise of the moors to the outskirts of the Vivien Hall estate, and the noise from the skirmish had receded behind them.

She leaned back in the carriage, her eyes closed. For a moment she had felt so faint, but she mustn't be weak now. With what lay ahead of them, she had to be as strong as a man. As strong as Richard. She looked at him through her lashes. He too must be going through hell right now, yet he'd never blamed her. It was only Breda herself who was so guilt-ridden at drawing him into all this.

"I'm sorry, Richard," she said, as the carriage clattered through the gateway of the Hall and she breathed a little easier. "I know you'd far rather be at Grensham than here right now, and so would I! It seems to me like the only haven in the world."

As they reached the house, Mrs. Yandle came running out to meet them, tears that were a mixture of joy and anxiety running down her face. Breda jumped down from the carriage and was clasped in her motherly arms.

"Thank goodness you're safe, my lamb," Mrs. Yandle babbled out. "I've been so worried for you, and that Miss Greenwood's been a constant visitor asking after you. And even that poor Mrs. Keighley's been mighty anxious. She's been here a few times when Yandle's gone to fetch her and the babies—I hope that was all right. You did say you wanted me to take her a few provisions, and after I did so I felt that sorry for her and the little 'uns, so I didn't think you'd mind if I fed 'em a meal or two and gave the babies a breath of the open moors—"

She paused for breath, and Breda hugged her ample body.

"You did quite right, Yandie," she said in a choked voice, not wanting to think that if the trial went against them Mary Keighley might well have every right to be here.

There was no doubt in her mind that if it went against Richard, she would be brought down too. And even if she wasn't, she was sure she couldn't face living here any longer. That much was becoming crystal clear to her now. Her heart no longer belonged to Vivien Hall and all that it stood for.

Without Richard she would be lost, and she knew she'd want to crawl away like some wounded animal to be surrounded by all that was his, hoping to draw strength from it. If all went well, she would still want to get away from all the painful memories. And there was only one place: Grensham.

"Shall we get inside?" Richard said now, having paid

off the driver and gathered up the pieces of baggage before a maid came scurrying out to take them from him.

He was already gone from her, Breda thought sadly. He was wrapped up in a world of his own, no doubt planning how he would deal with the coming trial. From now on, she doubted if she would be able to reach him at all, and she certainly couldn't tell him of her momentous decision. On the one hand he would think she was merely humoring him. On the other, he would think she was already seeing in his demise her prospects as the future mistress of Grensham. It was too late now to swear her undying love for him. Too much had gone between for him to believe such a sweet and simple truth.

Nan Greenwood came to the house during the afternoon, as if unerringly knowing that Breda would be back.

"There's nothing fey about my being here, Breda," she said. "I've come over most days hoping for news. I've prayed for you and for Richard, and I've missed you so much."

"I've missed you too," Breda said, uncomfortable at this frankness, and knowing that her own words weren't strictly true.

How could they be, when she had had so much else on her mind! Those girlhood confidences she and Nan used to share seemed a hundred years ago now, as if they had happened to someone else. In that time, she knew she had grown up far and beyond Nan's still-innocent immaturity.

"Did you know your cousin's wife has been here, Breda?" she said next. "Though I'm not sure if I should tell you—"

"It's all right. I already know. And if I didn't, wild horses wouldn't have stopped you from blurting it out, would they?" She grinned, recognizing for a moment the old bantering friendship between them that took no account of Nan's naivete or her own condescending superiority. She felt ashamed of that superiority now, knowing that Nan would always be an unstintingly loyal friend.

"I've spoken to her a few times. She seems quite nice, and I felt sorry for her," Nan said awkwardly. "But I dare say you'll consider I'm being unfair to you in saying so."

"Of course I shan't. I rather liked her too. It's no fault of hers or the children if their father's a charlatan."

Nan's eyes were large and round. *"Is* he?"

Quickly, Breda remembered that Nan knew nothing of her findings at the Duck and Whistle, and that it would be very unwise of her to confide in Nan about that hazardous excursion. She was a dear, but her tongue ran away with her far too often.

"He wants what belongs to me, and in my opinion that makes him less than honest," she amended.

"Oh, I see." Nan decided to steer the conversation away from the unpleasantness of Amos Keighley's claim. "Did you know the oldest boy was quite an artist? He brought up a shell that he'd painted for Mrs. Yandle, and it was a quite delicate scene in blues and greens. As a matter of fact, I thought she'd taken quite a fancy to the boy as well as the young 'uns.

"He showed his shells to me too," Breda said, ignoring her surprise that Harry and Mrs. Yandle should have found any common ground. "He shows a definite artistic talent, and he should have proper tuition for it. I think I shall personally see to it, after — well, afterwards."

It would be something definite to do, she thought determinedly. A tutor for Harry, a nursery teacher for the younger ones. She had the means . . . she *had* the means, she reminded herself with a different emphasis. And hopefully she still did, from the shares her father had left in trust for her in case of emergency. She still hadn't ascertained exactly how much they were worth, and it must be one of the things she should find out from Mr. Flowers.

Because if the trial went the way it should, then it would be Sam Stone and Amos Keighley who took due punishment for the deaths of twelve tinners. And Mary Keighley would be left without a husband and her children without a father. And in those circumstances, Breda was generous-hearted enough to want to do what she could for them.

"I'm thinking of visiting Mary myself at her cottage in a day or so. But let's forget them all today and go for a walk," she said to Nan now.

"All right. It will be quite like old times, won't it?" Nan said gaily, forgetting completely the significant reason why Mary Keighley was in Cornwall at all, in her joy that her old friend was back at Vivien Hall again.

"Almost," Breda murmured, not wanting to dispel the girl's happiness, and wishing she could be carefree enough to share it.

315

Before Breda made her visit to Mary Keighley, Mr. Flowers had spent several hours in consultation with Richard in her father's study, deciding on the best way to present their case. And Breda had requested a private interview with the solicitor before he left the house.

"I need to know just what kind of legacy I have in the shares, Mr. Flowers," she stated. "I still have to deal with the compensations for the families of those who died, and I intend a generous gift for each, so I want to have everything clear in my mind." She took a deep breath. "And besides that, if I should decide to sell Vivien Hall and all the mines, how much would I be worth, including the money from the shares?"

His expression was one of total shock. "Sell Vivien Hall and the mines? My dear girl, do you know what you're saying? It certainly need never come to that!"

"And what if the court finds Richard guilty? I simply refuse to believe in such a possibility, but if the impossible were to happen, what then? Do you think I would want to remain here, even if I wasn't hounded out of the county?"

He looked at her, still blatantly shocked by her bitterness.

"My dear Breda, I think you're simply overreacting! And, if you'll forgive the indelicacy, you've known Mr. Delacey such a short time, while your entire family history is here! To consider selling the family home is nothing short of sacrilege."

She spoke evenly. "I'm the only one left in my family now, Mr. Flowers, and there's nothing left here for me

316

but memories. I don't need a house for those. They'll be with me wherever I go."

He was clearly uncomfortable with such emotional remarks, and cleared his throat noisily.

"And where would you plan to go if you do as you say?"

"To Ireland. To Richard's home."

"Do you think his family will welcome you — if the worst should happen and your husband is found guilty?" He put it very bluntly now, and Breda knew that her face must have gone white as he said what she should have seen all along. Why would Lord Delacey ever want to see her again if Richard's involvement with her became the cause of his public hanging?

She felt suddenly faint, and if she hadn't been sitting down, she certainly would have done so, she thought.

"In that event, I may just have to think again," she said, her voice as heavy as if she were a very old woman.

Mr. Flowers looked at her with more sympathy. "I'm sure you're worrying over nothing. It's my business to see justice done, and to get your husband off, and I have every intention of doing just that," he said briskly. "In a month from now, all this will be no more than a bad dream, and you'll both be starting a new life together, wherever that may be."

He hesitated. "Breda, the thought of your selling Vivien Hall had never occurred to me, and I confess that you took me by surprise. In retrospect, it may be no bad thing. A mining business needs a man at its helm, and as it happens, I do know of a likely purchaser."

"It would have to be someone who would care for the house and keep all the servants on," she said

317

through chattering teeth, hardly knowing what she was saying, except that these were the kind of things her father would have wanted her to say.

"He's a mining man from Devon," Mr. Flowers said. "I can introduce you to him whenever you wish. His name is Graham Hocking, and I'm sure he'd be interested in buying the tin mines as well. I don't mean to push you, but if you're really serious about all this, he might well be your man. He's young, and has a small fortune to spend on what he requires. He's come here seeking an overseer's post, but I know he'd really like to buy into Cornish tin and settle here. I've met him on several occasions recently, and I would personally vouch for him."

It was suddenly going far too fast for her.

"I'm not sure. I'd half intended offering Mary Keighley and the children a home here at Vivien Hall," she said in some confusion, because even that had only been a half-formed idea in her mind.

But there had been something in the way Mrs. Yandle had talked about the children so fondly, and it had made Breda realize what was missing in this great empty house. The sound of childrens' laughter was just what it needed, and it was unlikely now that those children would be hers and Richard's. She was filled with a sense of doom that she couldn't seem to shake off.

"That would be exceedingly generous of you, Breda," Flowers said, not altogether approving, but knowing better than to argue with her when she was in this strange mood. "But I daresay that if Mr. Hocking were to buy the place, you could put in some proviso for your cousin's family to have certain quarters here, if that was your wish. It would all need to be drawn up quite legally, of course."

"Of course." She was beginning to feel quite lightheaded now and wished that he would go. She couldn't cope with any more decisions or discussions today.

"I shall be in Penzance tomorrow, Mr. Flowers. Shall I call on you to see if you have my accounts in order?"

"I would normally need far more time—" he caught her look. "Very well, but please leave it until well into the afternoon. And—about Mr. Hocking? He's staying here at the Crown Hotel for the next few weeks. But you'll want to discuss it all with your husband first, of course."

"No. My husband mustn't know of my plans. He'll think I'm anticipating the worst," she added hastily as his eyebrows rose. "Perhaps I should meet the gentleman and see what I think of him before making any kind of decision."

"I could suggest that he call on you to offer his services as general overseer to your mines. You should have appointed someone long before now, Breda, rather than leave so much power in the hands of Sam Stone."

"I know," she said. "All right. If you can get in touch with him, he can call on me tomorrow morning. I know Richard will be away from the house then."

After he had gone she sat still in a kind of daze. The notion to sell up and to install Mary and her children at Vivien Hall had never been more than fleeting thoughts, and a wish to do something for the hapless family. Now, almost before she knew it, the ideas were

319

taking root — the only thing was that that neither Mary nor the unknown buyer knew anything about them yet. And they were hurdles still to cross.

Neither did Richard know anything of her vague plans, and it was important that he had no idea that she was proposing to leave Cornwall after the trial, whatever the outcome. If things went as they should, it would be to Grensham with him.

Otherwise, Mr. Flowers' dire comment about his family not welcoming her if all went badly had been more of a shock to her than he might have guessed. She simply hadn't considered it.

Was she completely mad? she wondered, passing a trembling hand across her forehead. She was wasting precious time in considering these other peoples' lives when Richard's ordeal should be paramount in her mind . . . but she knew that it was only because his ordeal was so terrifying to her that she allowed her thoughts to be diverted in the way they did.

Graham Hocking was shown into the drawing room during the following morning by a curious Mrs. Yandle, after being assured that Breda would see him. She stood up as he entered, and saw a broad-shouldered man, in his early forties, she guessed, with brown hair and eyes and a rugged complexion, and the kind of warm smile that made her return it as she took his outstretched hand.

"It's very good of you to see me at such short notice, Mrs. Delacey," he said at once, his accent not so different from her own, but with the sightly more countrified Devon roll. "Mr. Flowers will have told you something about me, I trust?"

"Very little," she said, indicating a chair to him, and seating herself where she could see him clearly in the light from the window. "I know that you're a mining man and that you're looking for an overseer's post — am I right so far?"

"Absolutely. I'm also looking for a property to buy." She was glad that he resisted letting his gaze roam around the fine room at that moment. "But I'm perfectly willing to settle for a good position first of all, and not rush into buying anything less than suitable. I'm quite comfortable at the Crown Hotel in Penzance for the time being."

And a man who remained at an hotel couldn't be badly off, Breda thought.

"Perhaps you'd care to see the details of my past dealings? I owned several mines until recently until a bigger concern bought me out with a handsome offer it would have been foolish to refuse. It was then that I decided the time had come for me to move on."

Breda quickly looked through the sheaf of papers he handed her. It all seemed genuine enough, and from the cut of the man's clothes and the way he spoke, he was obviously not a rogue. She prided herself that she knew enough about human nature to deduce that much, overlooking just how wrong she had been about her own husband.

She handed him back the papers, saying that they all seemed highly impressive. "Do you have a family, Mr. Hocking? Forgive my curiosity, but I was told that you're a Devon man, and the far west of Cornwall is a long way from home for you."

"I've been a widower these past seven years," he said

briefly. "My wife died in childbirth. My son too."

"Oh. I'm very sorry." She felt acutely embarrassed at asking the question now. She sought about for something less emotive to say, noting the sudden shadow that crossed the man's face. What happened seven years ago was obviously no more than yesterday as far as he was concerned.

"Then you'd hardly be looking for a property of this size, Sir," she said ambiguously.

The shadow passed, and he gave a small laugh.

"On the contrary, Mrs. Delacey. An estate like this with the flourishing tin-mining business would be ideal. But I had not realized it was for sale—"

"It is not."

They both jumped as the door clicked shut and Richard came into the room, his face hard and set. After a moment's nervous silence, Breda felt her temper begin to rise at his arrogance. Vivien Hall still belonged to her, and she would do with it as she liked.

"Richard, Mr. Hocking has come to apply for the post of overseer," she said coldly. "On the advice of Mr. Flowers, I think it an admirable idea to appoint someone with a background knowledge of mining, and I've no hesitation in offering the position to this gentleman."

Graham Hocking had got to his feet. "I appreciate that, Ma'am, but perhaps after all I should be discussing all this with your husband—"

Breda spoke directly to him, without allowing Richard time to intervene. "Not at all. The mines belong to me. You may know from Mr. Flowers that we have had a recent disaster at Wheal Breda, which was our principal mine, but the landward mines are all as sound as any can be ascertained to be, and producing good quantities of best quality tin."

Hocking looked uncertainly at Richard, whose face was thunderous with anger now, but when he spoke it was with icy calm.

"My wife is quite correct, Sir. Vivien Hall and its mines belong to her, and if she is satisfied with your credentials, then I have nothing to say. As to the estate being for sale, I doubt that you've heard correctly on that matter, since it would take a miracle to pry my wife away from it."

He turned on his heel and left the room as quickly as he had entered it. Graham Hocking spread his hands in apology.

"If I've stirred up a hornet's nest, I'm sorry."

"You haven't. I'm sure you can't have been in Penzance and not known of the circumstances here at present," she said wearily. "I'm still trying to decide what to do, Mr. Hocking, but if I say that the sale of the entire estate is a possibility, I'd take it kindly if you kept the knowledge to yourself for the time being. Are you in any great hurry to buy?"

"Not at all. I've waited seven years to get my own feelings in order, so I can fully appreciate yours, Ma'am," he said with great understanding.

He was quite the nicest man she had met in a long while, Breda thought. Apart from Richard, of course . . . another thought struck her as he prepared to take his leave.

"There's one other matter. If certain circumstances occur," she said, skirting all around the words it would be such bad luck to say out loud, "there is a family living in Penzance for whom I intend to do all I can. My intention is to offer them a home here at Vivien Hall. The lady is my kinswoman, and there are three children. If it came to the point of my selling the estate, it would be on the condition that the family has permanent quarters here for as long as they wished. I realize it's an unusual condition, but I feel it's best to discuss it at the outset."

"There would be no objection on my part," he said readily, and now at last he did look around him, at the comfortably elegant furniture and wall coverings, and out through the long windows to the tree bordered grounds beyond. "This is a house that cries out for the sounds of childrens' voices, and no house is a real home without a woman in it. I'm sure we would be able to live harmoniously enough without getting beneath each others' feet."

How odd, Breda thought, when he had gone. He said almost the same words that had been in her head. Vivien Hall was a house crying out for children, and yet with a primitive certainty she had known they would never be hers. She was just as certain that Graham Hocking was destined to be the next owner of Vivien Hall, and that fate had sent him here. Her father would definitely have approved of him.

There were only two hurdles to overcome in her overall plan. That of breaking down Mary Keighley's pride in being offered charity, and the more immediate one of facing Richard's wrath when she had stated her position here so possessively and undermined his authority as her husband. Neither was a prospect she enjoyed thinking about.

Chapter Seventeen

Dusk had already transformed the brilliance of the summer afternoon into the soft pinky blue of evening before Richard returned to the house. He had obviously been riding hard. His hair was wind blown, and the scent of the moors was still on him. But it was clear from his first words that he was in no better humor than when he'd left.

"Would you prefer it if I slept in another room tonight?" he asked Breda coldly.

She flinched at his tone. "Why on earth should you think such a thing?" she asked in genuine bewilderment.

"I thought perhaps the lady of the house would prefer to send for me when she wanted servicing rather than be forced to accept my unwanted attentions."

She gasped at his crudeness.

"Your attentions were never unwanted," she said shakily. "Nor did I ever consider them forced on me."

"You speak in the past tense, my love," he said, the word conveying no sense of endearment. "Do you already have me condemned and hanged, or is your head completely turned by your new sense of possession, and perhaps the thought of a new admirer?"

For a second she thought it was his head that was turned, and then realized he was referring to Graham Hocking.

"You must be mad if you can even think such a thing," she said flatly. "Mr. Hocking was a most agreeable man, and if you chose to interrupt our discussion and view it in a different way, then it's your misfortune. All I know is that it will be a great relief to me to have him here. I should have gone about finding an overseer long before this, and then I may not have had to put up with Sam Stone's lecherous insinuations!"

She stood with her hands on her hips, her eyes blazing. How dare he come in here and treat her like this, when she was doing all in her power to help him!

"What I saw was my wife ogling another man," he retorted.

"I don't even know the meaning of the word!" she said freezingly. "And if I did I'm sure it would never apply to me, since it seems a particularly unpleasant one—"

He strode across the room and seized her wrists.

"It means eyeing him in a more than friendly way with those amorous green eyes of yours, my sweet one," he snapped. "You may not even be aware that you do it, but every man around you recognizes it, and I won't stand for it."

She glared at him, furious and upset.

"And what gives you the right to tell me how to behave and how to look? Would you want me to hide my face behind a veil like some Eastern woman? Is that what you want?"

For a second she saw the raw anger in his eyes and was momentarily afraid. And then he let go of her wrists, and his hands were holding her face, and after a moment, when she wondered if he was going to wrench her head from her neck, he pressed his mouth to hers. She couldn't have moved if she had wanted to—and she didn't want to. Whatever he did, she loved him, she thought wildly. Even while she acknowledged it, she despised herself for being so weak.

"This is what I want," he said, moving his mouth away from hers a mere fraction. "And this is what gives me the right."

His palm slid to her breast, its peak instinctively aroused by his touch. She felt his other hand reach for hers, to caress the gold band on her third finger.

"And this." Without warning, he lifted her limp hand to his lips and kissed the wedding ring with unexpected tenderness.

"I don't find it easy to apologize," he said roughly. "It's one of my faults you have yet to discover—"

"Really? I wasn't aware that you had any," she said, unable to resist the barb. He gave a slight smile, and the upward curve of his lips was enough to make her heart turn over. She felt a stab of alarm, not realizing until that moment just how strained he looked with all the recent worries, and she would have given anything to be able to lift the tension from his face.

"I probably deserved that," he said. "But what I'm trying to say is that my thoughts run away from me in all directions at the moment, and if I was too headstrong over your new overseer, then I'm sorry."

"Well, yes, I'd say that too headstrong describes it fairly adequately," she said solemnly, but he was no longer smiling, and she saw that the brief intimacy was already vanishing. He moved away to stare out of the darkening window, gone from her physically as well as emotionally.

"You must know that I'm saving all my logical thoughts for the trial, Breda. I don't seem to have room in my head for anything else right now. So please try to understand if I seem remote from you until it's all over. Better that perhaps, than putting up with unreasonable outbursts of anger."

She did understand, more than he knew. She seemed to have acquired a new perception about the things he left unsaid. And if he was trying to tell her in his clumsy way that anxiety about the trial was sapping all his manly feelings, it didn't matter. It could even be why he had suggested sleeping in another room . . . He could be vulnerable too, which only made him more human, and more dear to her. Uncaring whether or not he wanted her to know it, she went to him and put her arms about his waist.

"It's all right, Richard, really it is. And in my heart I just know everything will turn out right."

"Do you? Is this your Cornish intuition telling you so?" he was immediately defensive, his voice mocking, and clearly not prepared to accept any female sympathy. "Perhaps it's also telling Sam Stone the same thing. I presume it works for hard-headed men as well as for impressionable young women, or do women have the monopoly on such things?"

"Perhaps we do. But in answer to the question that started all this, then no, I do not want you to sleep in another room tonight."

If she hoped to provoke him into some bantering reply, she was disappointed. It was as if he hadn't even heard her, and he was already wrapped up in his own world again. She let out her breath in a sad little sigh.

There was clearly no satisfying him. She moved away and left him alone in the drawing-room, staring out at a summer's day that had lost all its brilliance in the blue dark of evening. To Breda it seemed abysmally symbolic.

The fisherman's cottage that the Keighleys were renting for the summer was warm and spicy with the hot smell of baking. Mary Keighley was pathetically pleased to see her. It was early afternoon and the children were down at the beach, so Breda was glad for a time alone with the other woman. Mary looked pale and unhappy, and dark shadows beneath her eyes told their own story.

"You'll take some tea wi' me, won't you, Breda? And a hot scone fresh from the oven."

"That will be lovely," she said. "But first of all, tell me how you've all been faring. Is Harry's health any better for being in Cornwall?"

Mary's eyes brightened. "The lad's so much better I can hardly believe it. I only wish we could stay for good, but I know it would mean things going badly for you and your man before that has a ghost's chance o' happening."

She was red with embarrassment, and turned away to brew the tea, and Breda gave her a quick smile.

"It's all right. I know what Amos has in mind. He thinks that if my husband is convicted, he'll accuse me of complicity and once I'm disgraced he'll try to get me out of Vivien Hall and claim the inheritance. I'm right, aren't I?"

"Aye," Mary said sorrowfully. "I wish I'd known what a wicked bastard he could be before we were wed, for I'd never have done it. 'Twere the worst day's work in my life when I hitched myself to him. I make no apology for saying so, and I hope God won't strike me dead for it."

"I'm sure He won't," Breda murmured. "But Amos won't get rid of me that easily."

She looked thoughtfully at the woman, accepting the strong tea and the hot scone, oozing with butter and strawberry jam, and spoke carefully.

"Can I trust you, Mary?"

"If it's owt to do with ridding myself of yon lad, then my lips are as sealed as if they were sewn together," she said in all seriousness.

"It's not quite that. But I've been thinking hard these past few days, and if I were to sell Vivien Hall, and arrange with the new owner for you and the children to live there in comfort for as long as you wished, what would you say to it?"

For a few minutes Mary didn't speak. Her face flushed even more, her eyes widened and darkened as she took in all that Breda was saying, while her hands twisted her apron in a convulsively nervous movement.

Beyond the cottage, the distant sounds of children's laughter could be heard from the beach, and in the small silence both womens' eyes were drawn to the square of window to where the three Keighley children played on the sand at the waters' edge.

"It would be so good for them," Breda went on.

330

"Harry would benefit so much, and it would be my pleasure to arrange art lessons for him, and a tutor for the little ones—"

"No!" Mary's voice was sharp and brittle. "I don't know why you're saying these things to taunt me, but you owe us nothing, lass, and I'll not accept charity from you!"

"*Charity!* It's not charity to offer a home to my relatives—"

"I'm nothing to you! But for an accident of marriage, you'd never even have heard of me. I'm no kin of yours."

"But the children are. If Amos is a cousin of a sort, then his children are also my cousins. You can't deny that, and if you won't let me do this for you, then let me do it for them."

"Why should you? Is this your conscience speaking, because you married your man in order to keep control of your grand home, when in the normal way it might have come to Amos? Oh aye, we know all about that, don't forget!"

Breda's face was white as she faced this unexpected anger. Mary was almost beautiful in her outraged dignity, she thought, the usual pallor gone, and her blue eyes flashing.

"That sounds very much to me as if deep down you allied yourself with Amos's wishes after all!"

"Mebbe I did at the time. It all seemed like a grand and impossible dream when he saw the piece in the newspaper. Can't you understand that? A chance for us to better ourselves at last. That was all he cared about, but it meant more than that to me. It meant our Harry could always breathe clean air in his lungs if we came south to live."

"And that's just what I'm offering you," Breda snapped.

Mary ignored that for the moment.

"Why would you want to sell, anyway, when you were so desperate to hold on to what was yours? Or is your husband not so keen to be a bought man after all?"

Breda shrugged, sensing that the insult was made more out of wounded pride than spite. Mary Keighley had far more pride than Breda had bargained for. She gave a wry smile.

"My husband's home in Ireland is far grander than mine! His father is Lord Delacey, and all that I own could be swallowed up in his property and be hardly noticed," she said frankly. "You ask why I want to sell Vivien Hall. I have two reasons. One is that a wife's place is with her husband, and for Richard that means going back to Ireland. And since I love him, I'd rather be there with him than here in Cornwall without him."

"And what's the other reason?" Mary said when she paused.

"Perhaps I'd never really thought about it until this moment," Breda said slowly. "But I suppose in the back of my mind there was the idea that if Vivien Hall no longer belonged to my family, then Amos could never get his hands on it. If it legally belonged to someone else, the new owner would assuredly fight tooth and nail to keep it and Amos would have no claim. There's nothing in the entailment to stop me selling what's still mine."

"But what would you be gaining, if it no longer belonged to the Vivien family?"

"It would still do so in a way, if you and the children lived there. I've no grudge against any of you, and it would be fitting for Vivien descendants to live there, even if they didn't actually own it."

Mary didn't speak for a long time. She sat down slowly, and Breda could see that while she still resisted the idea of charity, it wasn't quite so unpalatable to her now.

"And what of this new owner? Do you have anyone in mind? I understand the trial is only two weeks away. Forgive me, Breda, but if you wanted to be rid of the property before any—any verdict, you would need to find a purchaser immediately, and it couldn't be done!"

"I've already done it," she said. "At least, I only have to see my solicitor and the gentleman concerned and I'm sure it can all be settled before the trial begins. It's watertight, Mary. You and the children will have a permanent home at Vivien Hall. The prospective purchaser has already agreed to a proviso in the contract to that effect."

Mary's sudden flare of hope died just as quickly. "And what of Amos? He's still my husband, and he'd demand to live there with us. It's no use. I'd never be rid of him, and your sacrifice would have been all for nothing." She began to cry softly.

Breda took her cold hands in hers and spoke intently. "I don't intend to let my husband hang, Mary. There are others who must be brought to justice for the deaths of those poor tinners, and I mean to see that they do. I can't say any more now, but please trust me."

Mary blew her nose, sniffing back the tears with a watery smile. "You're a good lass, Breda, and aye, I do

333

trust you."

"And you'll say nothing of what I've told you here today? It's vitally important that Amos has no idea of what I'm doing," she said urgently.

"I've told you. It's our secret, and none will hear it from my lips, but we'd best hush up about it now. The children will be back soon."

"Let's go down to the beach and find them," Breda said at once, hoping to cheer away the gloom from her face. "It's a long while since I've made sand pies and searched for shells."

Later, she had two more calls to make. One was to the Crown Hotel, where she sought out Graham Hocking and took afternoon tea with him in the grand salon overlooking the sea. He looked pleasantly surprised at this visit from a lady. She came straight to the point.

"How serious were you about buying Vivien Hall, Mr. Hocking?"

He put down his cup and looked at her steadily.

"Completely serious. The more I've thought about it since coming to see you, the more I know it's exactly what I've been looking for."

"And how quickly would you be prepared to sign the contract? I have my reasons for wanting to sell immediately if possible."

He spoke quietly. "Mrs. Delacey, I think I should tell you that I'm well aware of all the circumstances through Mr. Flowers, and I understand more than you suppose. I certainly want to buy, but please be very sure that you want to sell before you dispose of your birthright."

334

Her eyes filled with sudden tears. "How kind you are. Not many people would have put it in quite those words. It reassures me that you will care for the house. But you haven't even seen it properly yet."

"That's of no consequence, since I've no wife to point out its deficiencies." He smiled to take the sting out of the words. "Besides, I've been assured by Mr. Flowers that it's sound, and that's good enough. The position is perfect, and I've already taken the liberty of inspecting the mines."

"Then you haven't been idle."

"I have not," he smiled. "And what of the lady you mentioned? Is she willing to throw in her lot with me?"

He spoke teasingly, but the wildest idea came into Breda's head at his words. An idea too romantic and preposterous to even put into serious thought, but for a Cornish woman with a vivid imagination and a strong belief in destiny, it was a possibility that held all the promise of a delightful future. Mary Keighley and Graham Hocking . . . neither had yet seen the other, but Breda had seen them both and knew that they were simply made for one another . . .

"I've just been to see her," she nodded. "And I'm certain she'll be very happy to agree to it. She resisted the idea at first, but I know her love for her children will overcome all her pride in the end."

"Then I suggest we get down to business whenever you wish, Mrs. Delacey."

She took a deep breath, no longer thinking about what she was doing. All she wanted was to get it over and done with.

"Would you think me too impulsive if I suggested seeing Mr. Flowers this afternoon? Now that I've made the decision, I'd like to get it done as quickly as possible. And since you know of my husband's impending court case, you must guess that it would give me peace of mind to have the sale completed before then."

She hoped desperately that he didn't suspect her of rushing him into this in order to let him deal with any further claim from Amos Keighley, should the trial go against them. It was just what she *was* doing, she thought guiltily, but she had no doubt that Graham Hocking and Mr. Flowers together were formidable enough to ward off any such claim.

"Mrs. Delacey, as I said, I'm fully aware of all the circumstances, including the time element, so there's no need to feel embarrassed. And I still want to buy your property," he added with a smile. "So let's not waste any more time."

"There's just one more point," she said awkwardly. "I need to make the sale legal as quickly as possible, but I don't wish to move out until the outcome of the trial has been decided. Am I being totally unreasonable in asking this favor of you?"

"Totally," he said, and then he laughed. "And perhaps I'm totally bewitched by those dazzlingly persuasive eyes of yours to be agreeing to it, but you have my word."

And in the midst of her joy, Breda was more than thankful that Richard hadn't been around to hear the compliment.

It was only a short distance to the solicitor's chambers, and if Mr. Flowers was taken aback at the deputation now being shown into his office, it was nothing to his shock at hearing that these two had practically settled everything between them already. It was not his practice to conduct business so hurriedly, but neither was he normally faced by two such determined characters as these. They were a match for each other, he thought fleetingly, if Breda hadn't already got herself married . . .

"You expect me to draw up a bill of sale here and now for the entire property and assets of Vivien Hall?" he repeated, too used to the peculiar requests of some of his clients to show too much surprise. "With the proviso that Mary Keighley and her children should occupy quarters in it for as long as they so desire? Is that correct?"

"That's correct," Breda said.

"Perfectly correct," Hocking replied.

Flowers leaned back in his chair. "My dear Sir, you should at least inspect the house before you offer to buy!"

Graham Hocking looked at Breda. "Have you lived in it happily all your life?"

"I have."

"And has this Mrs. Keighley and her children seen the house and appeared to like it?"

"Of course," Breda smiled, seeing the way his thoughts were going. He looked at the solicitor.

"Would you doubt the integrity of two such charming and intelligent ladies? No true gentleman would dare! Please proceed with the bill of sale, Mr. Flowers."

It was more than two hours later when Breda was on

her way back to Vivien Hall, beginning at last to feel stunned by all that she had accomplished this day. Other people shared the secret now. She prayed that she could rely on them all, because the last thing she wanted was for news of her decision to leak out before she was ready to tell it herself. She was certain of Mary's silence, and that of the two men. And Mr. Flowers had assured them of the highest integrity of his two assistants who had witnessed the signing of the triple document, one copy each for Breda and Graham Hocking, and the last for Flowers himself to keep in his vault.

There only remained her own decision as to whether or not to tell Richard. She already knew it was too big an undertaking to be kept from him, but she couldn't guess how he would take the fact that she had done it without his prior knowledge. She had felt so determined that morning, and now that it was all done, she was beginning to feel a growing alarm at not telling him. She was sure he'd have done his best to prevent it, knowing what Vivien Hall had always meant to her, and his objections were just what she'd managed to avoid.

Come to that, as well as selling the house from under him, she wasn't even certain he would still want her as his wife once the trial was over. He had his pride too, and if things went badly and she was pushed to stand up and defend him, he might be so humiliated it may even turn him against her. Breda found herself frowning at the thought. Pride was assumed to be such a show of strength, when in effect it could be such a fragile thing, and not even the strongest of men was proof against it.

She still hadn't found the answer by the time she reached the top of the moor. The house and grounds were spread out before her, bathed in sunshine. Vivien Hall had never looked more beautiful as it did then, when in theory it no longer belonged to her. She felt the most enormous tug at her heart as a blaze of sunlight was suddenly reflected from the windows. At that moment, she was almost disbelieving of what she had done, in willingly giving up all this. And all for love of Richard.

She swallowed hard, trying to tell herself it was just a house. A collection of stone and wood . . . but a house that had been a home for so long, and filled with so much love. Unshed tears shuddered behind her eyes, remembering the halcyon days spent with her father and brother. Carefree, childish days that had seemed never ending and always sunny, because they had always been so happy. She hardened her heart against the wistful memories and tried to think positively.

Childish days would return again to this house, only this time it would be the sounds of the Keighley children's laughter that filled the empty rooms, and Mary's children who would chase around the lawns and shrubberies and go skidding down the sandy cliffs to the tiny coves below. Maybe one day in their shared pleasure of the children, Graham Hocking and Mary Keighley would be laughing into each others' eyes and see the laughter change to something else . . .

But Breda Vivien wouldn't be here to see if her unwitting matchmaking ever came to fruition. She would be far away in Ireland. The dreaming stopped abruptly, because who knew just where her future lay?

She certainly didn't, not yet.

It was a long while later when Richard came striding into the house. She didn't know where he went these days, but he chose to spend as much time away from her as possible. It was only at night, when the soft darkness enclosed them, that the bitterness between them seemed to dissolve, and his arms reached out for her. For all that he'd told her coldly he intended to move into another bedroom, he hadn't done so after all. And the passion still existed between them.

She knew that he used her — at least, that was how it appeared to her. He wanted her for his pleasure, but for nothing else. And she, because she loved him so much, and ached for a word of tenderness from him now and then, she gave herself up to pleasure, and simply let herself be used.

The look he gave her now was dark and forbidding, and she suddenly felt unnerved as he threw down his gloves on a side table. He sprawled out in one of the armchairs, caring nothing that his boots were dirty and marking the carpet.

"And how have you enjoyed your day today, my love?" He oozed sarcasm.

"It was pleasant enough. I went to Penzance to visit Mary Keighley and the children — "

"Ah yes, the cousin's wife makes a convenient alibi."

Breda stared at him. What devilment was this! Richard was so unpredictable these days, and understandably so, but she couldn't read the dark expression in his eyes now. She ran her tongue around her dry lips.

"I assure you Mary is no alibi! I told you a few days

ago that I intended to see her. Whatever wickedness Amos has done is no fault of hers, and I'm sorry for her."

"And who else did you see?"

She felt her nerves begin to jump. "What do you mean?"

"I mean your little tete-a-tete with a certain gentleman at the Crown Hotel," he said, his voice suddenly hard. "Do you think it's quite decent for my wife to be seeing another man before they've even got the noose around my neck?"

Her temper boiled over. She leapt up from her chair, her body as tense as a spring.

"You're a blind fool if you think I have eyes for anyone else but you!" She despised herself for letting him see everything that she felt for him, when he cared so little for her, but incredulously, he never seemed to notice.

"I know why you married me, and I know what I saw today. You're not the only one who went to Penzance today, my dear, only I went to try and extract the truth out of your charming cousin at that hovel where he works. All to no avail, of course. The bastard will lie through his teeth until they rot!"

"You were in Penzance today?" she said faintly.

"I was," he said grimly. "And I witnessed a very touching scene outside the Crown Hotel. No one could miss the way your paramour held your arm to assist you across the street."

"And you base your suspicions on that! Since you were spying on me, didn't you also see that I was in danger of being trampled by a horse as I stepped into the street without looking, and that Mr. Hocking pulled me back in time? Or do you prefer your own interpretation of what happened?"

"I was not spying on you, as you so delicately put it."

"What else do you call it? Anyway, your suspicions are quite unfounded. Mr. Hocking means nothing to me. Good heavens, I hardly know the man."

"But you know him well enough to allow him to escort you to your solicitor's chambers, and to spend a considerable time there together. For whatever purpose, I can't yet fathom. But when you came out you shook hands very warmly before you parted, and both looked extremely satisfied with yourselves."

Breda couldn't believe she was hearing correctly.

"You *were* spying, and it's unworthy of you, Richard," she said tremblingly. "How dare you follow me and hang about in the shadows like the seediest kind of private detective."

"It was certainly not my intention to follow you," his voice was still as cold as ice, "but when I saw you with that other fellow, I felt a distinct need to know what was happening. Like you, my dear, I like to keep control of what is mine."

"I suppose it's me you're referring to in that ungallant way. Can't you see that you're as covetous as anyone? Anyway, I didn't think you cared for me at all, except for when we're between the sheets at night."

She bit her lip, furious at being goaded into saying something so sordid. He stood up and moved swiftly toward her. Arrogantly he pulled her into his arms.

"You're bought and paid for, sweetheart, and never forget that. And I'm ordering you to have nothing more to do with this Hocking fellow, do you hear me?"

"I should think the whole house can hear you! And I

342

shall see whomever I please, whenever I please. You entered into our marriage contract fully aware of the terms, but nobody owns me!"

She was appalled that this was happening. They should be so close, with all that lay ahead of them, and instead of that they were glaring at each other with hate in their eyes. Suddenly she couldn't bear it. If everything between them was gone, then she had sold her birthright for nothing. But even that was of less importance than the feeling that she had lost Richard. She gave a soft little moan, and melted against him. The words tumbled out of her, and she hardly knew what she was saying.

"Richard, can't we stop tormenting each other like this? You've completely misunderstood my motives for seeing Graham Hocking today. He means nothing to me, and I promise you I didn't call on him for any personal reason. I did it for us."

"What the hell are you talking about?" he said, but she could see her passionate outburst had affected him. She looked up into his eyes, and knew she had to tell him.

"I will tell you exactly why I saw Mr. Hocking today, and why we both went to see Mr. Flowers," she said huskily. "But since I'm finding it so hard to say the words, perhaps this will explain everything."

She twisted away from him and went to the small bureau where she had locked away the precious bill of sale. Her hands trembled as she took out the bulky document and handed it silently to Richard. He scanned it quickly, and she saw his expression change. She pressed her hand on his arm.

"Don't you see that I had to do it? Whatever happens, Vivien Hall will never belong to Amos Keighley, Richard. It's legally sold, and is no longer in the possession of the Vivien family. And after the trial—"

"And after the trial, where will you belong, Breda?"

"I'm your wife. A wife's place is with her husband." She was nervous again. He wasn't reacting as she had expected. Why wasn't he grateful? If he was, he had too much masculine pride to show it. If he wasn't, it meant he simply didn't care where she went. She swallowed.

"Are you sure you didn't sell the place because you'd rather it went to anyone rather than the cousin? Was it all done out of spite?"

"I don't know how you can say that, knowing how much I've always loved it," she said, very near to tears now. "It's my home, Richard, and it's been in my family for generations. It would take a very strong reason for anyone to sell what was so precious to them. And if you haven't worked out what that reason is yet, then you're more stupid than I thought."

She had her pride too, and she didn't want to see any dawning realization in his face. She walked out of the room with her chin held high, and only when she reached the sanctuary of their bedroom did she collapse on the bed and let the tears flow.

Chapter Eighteen

Some time later Breda heard the door click open and shut, but she didn't move. She didn't want to face Richard's knowing eyes right now. She heard him move across the room, and moments later he had gathered her up in his arms. After a few resisting seconds, she clung to him mutely, uncaring whether she humbled herself or not. She was in his arms, where she had every right to be.

"All this time and I never knew," he said softly against her hair. "I thought your sole intention in marrying me was for the sake of Vivien Hall."

"So it was," she mumbled, still trying to hold on to her pride.

He tipped up her chin and she had no option but to meet his eyes. But it was only for a moment before she lowered hers.

"Do you deny that you love me?" he demanded.

She gave a short laugh. "Would you believe me if I denied it now? You've gained the advantage over me now, haven't you? I'm far weaker than you imagined the strong willed sister of Philip Vivien to be!"

"I don't think of our marriage as a battleground, Breda," he said, his voice thick with amusement. Her eyes flashed.

"Don't you? It appears to have been little else for most of the time."

"I seemed to recall certain times when we haven't exactly been enemies," he said, curving a finger around her cheek and kissing away the tears. Oh yes, he could always resort to passion, and she would always surrender, but it was the last thing she wanted right now. It would simply humiliate her more if she thought he was doing it merely to please her, and to satisfy his natural lust.

"Please don't do this," she said in a low voice as his hand moved lower to caress her breast. With a huge effort she resisted the swiftly surging pleasure at his touch. Her body betrayed her while her mind screamed out that she wanted to be left alone . . .

"Darling, why don't we stop all this pretense?" Richard said, moving his mouth against hers in a way that fired all her senses. "You must know that I—"

"No." she said sharply. "If you say you love me now, Richard, I'll never forgive you."

He began to laugh until he saw that she was desperately serious. "Why the devil not?"

"Because I won't believe you. I know it isn't true, and that at certain moments you'll say anything if you think it's what I want to hear."

His eyes narrowed. "So that's what you think, is it?"

"It's what I know." She felt a deep sorrow at the certainty. There had been many moments of passion when he'd said he wanted her and needed her. He had been tempestuous in his loving, and his endearments had made her blood flow faster. But he had never said he loved her.

Even in moments of wildest passion, he had never brought himself to say it. A charlatan would have said it glibly, but she truly believed that he would never say it unless he really meant it. And if she had forced him into it now, it would mean less than nothing.

"You seem to forget that I asked you to marry me long before I knew of the bloody entailment on Vivien Hall."

She shivered at his anger. They seemed to have a such a knack of arousing anger in one another—as swiftly as they could arouse passion.

"I don't forget, but I always thought it was done as a kindness to my brother. You thought of me as the poor unfortunate sister with no man to look after her, then when you saw me—"

He stood up and looked down at her. There was no longer any anger in his voice. There was no expression in it at all, and it suddenly frightened her.

"So you really think I'm the kind of man who'd marry a woman out of pity and nothing else. Dear God, woman, haven't you been listening to me at all these past months?"

He didn't wait for any reply but banged out of the room. Breda heard him shouting for Yandle to get his horse rubbed down, and guessed that the animal had been left standing outside while Richard stormed into the house. When she was alone, she wilted. It would have been so easy to let him profess his love for her, and in many ways she could have kicked herself for not letting him go on.

She felt her mouth tremble. She had always thought

herself so strong, and now she knew just how vulnerable she was. But she just wouldn't believe that Richard had loved her all this time. His proposal of marriage had been so brash, so arrogant, and she had repulsed him so vehemently. She was sure he'd seen her as the challenge of his life, and had pursued her quite relentlessly.

It was possible of course, that he had grown to love her . . . but she dismissed the idea flat. How could he love her, after learning of her devious plans to find a husband! If he had used her, then how much more had she used him!

Her head throbbed with the way they had managed to destroy each others' lives, and at the way they had drawn friends and families into the deception. Guiltily, she knew how she would have shamed her father if he knew the way she had tried to save Vivien Hall in such an underhanded way.

She pushed such uncomfortable thoughts out of her mind. It did no good to dwell on the past. There were far more important matters to deal with in the immediate future, and their personal affairs must be put aside until after the trial. Resolutely, Breda went to the washbowl on the nightstand and splashed cold water over her face until she looked reasonably presentable, and then she went to find Richard.

He was in the stables, and she saw how his capable hands soothed his horse, clearly still agitated from too hard a ride that afternoon. She pushed away the image of how many times those same hands had caressed her and brought her to the peak of passion so exquisitely.

"I think we should call a truce," she said.

"That's fine by me." To her relief, he didn't pretend

to misunderstand her.

"We need to present a united front and not to be at loggerheads all the time," stubbornly she felt the need to be exact, since he seemed disinclined to add anything more.

"I've said I agree. What more do you want?"

He wasn't helping, she fumed. He was perfectly calm now, his feelings under control, and she almost preferred it when he was angry. At least there was more reaction than she was getting from him now. Surely he must realize her irritation . . . after a few minutes of silence he looked at her thoughtfully.

"I've been thinking about your sacrifice," he said.

"My what?" she stared at him.

Richard shrugged. "Call it what you like, but for whatever reason, you've sacrificed your home. And in a few weeks' time, one way or another you'll have to decide where you're going to live."

She felt her heart begin to pound. "I thought that decision had already been made," she said thickly. She was his wife after all, and a wife lived with her husband.

"I think it's best to wait until after the trial to make the final choice. I know there are a lot of expenses to be met for the families of the miners, and I see from your document of sale that you're to make provision for Mary Keighley and her children. It's very generous of you, but your money won't stretch endlessly."

"Yes it will. At least, it will stretch farther than you might think. The money from the shares my father invested have realized a very high sum. And Mr. Hocking has paid handsomely for the house and mines. I shan't be a pauper."

She didn't want this conversation. She wasn't a businesswoman, and had left it to Mr. Flowers to deal with her affairs. She was assured that she would be able to see to everything. But Richard's words sounded too much like a warning for comfort.

"If you decide to buy an establishment of your own," he went on with sudden male arrogance, "I shall provide it. And should the trial go against us, I shall write to my father directing him to arrange it, the letter to be sent to him only if it becomes necessary."

He delicately refrained from putting it more bluntly, but Breda flinched, stunned by what he was saying.

"There's no need for you to do that."

"I intend to do it all the same. Whatever you gain from the sale of the estate will remain yours. You deserve that much, my dear. You've fought so hard to retain it."

The little irony didn't escape her, even though he was still being very calm. He wanted nothing to do with any benefit from her sale. Amos Keighley would never get Vivien Hall, but Richard didn't want it either. She felt utterly humiliated.

"Can we leave any discussion about the future until we know what's to happen?" she said, her mouth tight. "In any case I refuse to think about it so negatively. I'm convinced everything will be all right."

"I suppose this is your Cornish intuition again," he said with a faint smile. "I fail to see that it's done you any favors so far."

He turned to remove the blanket from the horse's back as one of the young lads came into the stable to give it a rub down. And Breda thought numbly that he was probably right. For all the good her intuition had done her about Richard Delacey, she might as well have trusted a crystal ball.

After their agreement to the so-called truce, they were obliged to think a little more seriously about the future, at least in one respect. They called in Mrs. Yandle and her husband that evening, and told them quietly about the sale of the estate.

Uncharacteristically, Mrs. Yandle burst into noisy tears, and Yandle cleared his throat several times.

"I can't believe it's come to this, Miss Breda! Your dear father 'ould turn in his grave—"

"My father's not here any more, Yandie, and I had to do what I thought was best," she said steadily.

"But where will you go?"

Yandle put an awkward hand on her arm. "Don't take on so, my dear. It's not our place to question Miss Breda, and you seem to forget she's a married lady now. 'Tis only natural she'll be going to her husband's home in Ireland."

He tactfully refrained from adding that presumably this is what would happen after the trial, whether her husband came away from it alive or dead. Breda felt her throat tighten, unable to reply for a moment, and then Richard took over. She felt his hand close over hers.

"That's right, Yandle. But since you've both been such faithful friends of the family, my wife wanted you to know our intentions right away. But this news is to go no farther than these four walls for the present and we're entrusting you both with it."

"We understand, and you don't need to ask for our

silence, Sir," Mrs. Yandle said at once, and he gave a brief nod.

"I know that. We also want you to know that you need have no worries over your positions here. Also, the gentleman who has bought Vivien Hall has agreed to Mrs. Keighley and her three children occupying a wing of the house for as long as they wish."

Mrs. Yandle's small cry of pleasure was suddenly dampened.

"What of the husband, Sir? Miss Breda's cousin?"

Her opinion of Amos was all too clear, and when Richard said shortly that there was no question of him ever living at Vivien Hall, her relief was obvious.

"Then you can rely on me and Yandle to give every service to the new owner, and especially to the little family. Not that we won't truly mourn your leaving, Miss Breda," she added. " 'Twill be a sad day for us all."

Breda ran to her and put her arms around her ample figure. "And for me too, Yandie," she whispered. "But it's done now and there's no changing it."

She felt the housekeeper pat her back comfortingly.

"I suppose we should have seen it coming, my lamb. 'Tis a man's place to provide a home for his wife, and once your little business is over, you'll both be able to settle down to a happier life together."

Mrs. Yandle had steadfastly refused to consider the possibility of anything but complete vindication for Richard, and a severe punishment being meted out to Sam Stone and whoever else was responsible for the atrocity at Wheal Breda. Breda felt a lump in her throat now at the housekeeper's blind faith in justice, and the assumption that once the trial was over, Breda's future would be secure with the man she loved.

"You won't be losing me forever," she said huskily to Mrs. Yandle. "I promise I'll come back and see you one day—"

And for all any of them knew, she might well not be as far away as Ireland. Mrs. Yandle gave her a resolute smile.

"I should hope you would. I dare say you'll be wanting to see those children again sometime, and me and Yandle will want to be seeing your own healthy babies when the time comes."

And at that, Breda dare not look at Richard, knowing that such a dream was becoming ever more distant.

Richard agreed to Yandle driving them both to the courtroom in Penzance. He would have preferred to take the reins himself, but without actually saying so, Breda managed to let him see the sense of it, just in case he should be detained and she had to return home alone. She couldn't have put the suggestion into words. While it still remained unsaid, it was still no more than a horrendous possibility and not a very real threat.

Despite the warmth of the day, Breda felt chilled right through to her bones. She still couldn't really believe that today was happening. It was all a hideous nightmare, and soon she would wake up and find none of it had ever happened . . .

She heard the boisterous sounds of shouting away to their left, and when she turned her head sharply, it was to see a steadily moving convoy of miners walking toward Penzance. In for the kill, she thought sickly, intending to see justice done. And if this was a nightmare, then she was living through every ghastly minute of it.

"It's only to be expected that they'd turn up," Richard commented, hearing her indrawn breath. "Flowers told me he anticipated a good crowd."

"You make it sound like a carnival," she said bitterly. "How can you be so calm?"

"Is there any point in being otherwise? I've put my trust in your solicitor. I've told him everything and I believe him to be a fair man. He'll put my case to the best of his ability, and I'll be allowed to have my say, don't worry. They won't get away with it so easily, Breda."

She shivered. It was still three against one. Sam Stone and her cousin Amos, and the committee man who had been so easily bribed to ignore Richard's report on Wheal Breda.

"I intend to have my say as well," she said.

"I doubt that you'll be given a chance. Women aren't supposed to be reliable witnesses, especially when they have a vested interest in the defendant." He tried to make a joke of it, but it fell very flat as far as Breda was concerned.

"All the same, the mine was my responsibility, and ultimately I'm to blame for not seeing that the work was carried out," she said through dry lips.

He answered furiously. "I don't want to hear you mention that again. We don't need to give them any more ammunition to fire at us, Breda. One charge is enough, and that's the one we'll deal with."

"And you don't think they'll act more leniently toward a woman?" she had to ask, and was rewarded with his icy stare.

"I've already told you I've no intention of hiding behind a woman's skirts. This is mens' business."

He was hopeless, she thought, finding some solace in anger during this traumatic journey. She might have been able to sway the judges using womens' wiles. It wasn't unknown for even the strictest of them to be persuaded by a woman's tears, and although she'd never believed herself capable of resorting to such ploys, she knew now that she'd do anything to save Richard from the gallows.

By the time they reached Penzance, it seemed as if the whole town and surrounding districts had turned out for the occasion. The courthouse was on one side of a large square, and the area was already filled with people milling about, laughing and chattering as if this was some great festive occasion. Street sellers had begun to capitalize on the crowds, and stalls had been hastily erected to sell snacks and drinks and fruit to assuage all appetites during the hungry hours of the trial.

Breda began to feel lightheaded. She wanted to weep, seeing how it was all being viewed as a kind of peep-show, instead of a trial for a man's life — an innocent man's life.

She alighted from the carriage with trembling legs, and Richard hustled her through the curious onlookers to the ante-room where Mr. Flowers would be waiting for them. There were a few boos as they pushed their way through, together with a few cheers and shouts of good luck. It seemed that Richard had his supporters as well as those who had condemned him already.

"I'm glad you're here in good time," Mr. Flowers greeted them. "I have a few things to go over with you, Mr. Delacey. Breda, I suggest you go straight to the visitors' gallery. I've reserved a seat at the front for you. You'll be directly above the proceedings, so you won't miss anything."

She was shocked. "But I want to be near Richard. I don't want to be pushed up in the gallery as if this is of no importance to me. I want to speak up—"

Flowers spoke testily. "My dear, I've had a consultation with Judge Wilson, and as I suspected, he won't allow it. He's quite adamant, and if you persist in trying to speak, you'll only jeopardize the case. My advice is to observe and remain silent."

"I fear you've given my wife a difficult piece of advice to follow," Richard said, seemingly the least tense of the three. "She rarely remains silent when she's got a cause to fight."

"She had better do so in this case," Flowers said dourly. "Or I won't be responsible for the outcome if Judge Wilson gets his feathers ruffled. I give you fair warning, Breda, he's not the most amicable of men, and with your Pit Captain and cousin's testimonies combined, we've got a tough enough fight on our hands without you complicating things."

She felt totally rebuffed. She had no option but to do as she was told and take her place in the front seat of the public gallery. It was already filling up with people jostling for seats, but she had a perfect view of the entire proceedings.

Her first impression was of a gloomy interior, already becoming close and stuffy as the people crowded inside. Below her was the bench on which the three judges and other officials would sit. There was the dock, in which Richard was seated now, with Mr. Flowers leaning toward him, a sheaf of papers in his hands. On the far side were the leering faces of Sam Stone and her cousin Amos Keighley, glancing her way now and then, and looking supremely confident.

Some of Sam's cronies and fellow workers were also in the main body of the courtroom, presumably to be called upon to give evidence. She saw the man Penrose look her way and avert his eyes quickly, and guessed that he'd be pulled two ways now. Penrose had worked for the Vivien family for many years and knew them to be fair bosses. So perhaps Breda's presence here would remind him of that fact and it would be to their advantage, she thought, with a small sliver of hope, though hardly knowing why.

She had a sudden savage desire to shout at Amos that she had already thwarted his plans to own Vivien Hall. It would never belong to him now, any more than it now belonged to her. But she contented herself with merely looking back at them unblinkingly, and it was the two of them who eventually muttered to each other and looked away.

The trial began with a long intonation from the barrister for the Stannary Committee, pompously describing the dangerous nature of tin mines gouged out beneath the sea with their labyrinth of tunnels, and deploring the greed of landowners who put men at risk by enticing them to swelter in the dark depths for the miserable metal without thought for the safety of the men. Breda disliked him on sight, with his long nose

357

and pinched nostrils, and the affected little habit he had of clearing his throat after every few laborious sentences.

"Your name is Richard Delacey, presently residing at Vivien Hall?" he finally asked. Richard said that he was.

"Then, Richard Delacey, you are accused of inadvertently causing the deaths of twelve tin miners in the mine known as Wheal Breda, by reason of neglecting to inform the Stannary Committee of the dangerous condition of the said mine. How do you plead?"

"Not guilty," Richard said in a strong voice, at which there was an immediate uproar among the spectators, while the judge hammered vainly for silence.

"He's as guilty as hell," Sam Stone roared out as the noise dwindled away. The judge rounded on him at once.

"You, Sir, will be silent unless you are called. If not, I will have no option but to request you to leave the court immediately. This is not a sideshow. Please remember that a man's life is at stake here."

Breda couldn't tell whether the judge's remark was advantageous to their cause or not. The first barrister sat down and Mr. Flowers stood up and prepared to question Richard. She leaned forward, noting that Richard never as much as glanced her way. It was something she noted all the rest of that interminable day. He seemed completely contained within himself. He answered with authority, but as the proceedings continued it was obvious to Breda that it was not going well.

Richard said all that was required of him. When he was questioned by the Stannary Barrister he steadfastly refused to deny that he had submitted his report.

"How can this be, Sir?" the barrister asked with withering scorn. "Do you expect the court to believe your word against that of every man on the committee, a body that's long been known for its integrity and honesty?"

"I do," Richard said. "And my word is as honest as any man's."

"Perhaps you would care to point out this mythical committee member to whom you say you handed your report," the barrister went on smoothly.

"If I could see him in this court I would do so," Richard said unflinchingly. "But we both know that he is not here. I understand he has gone abroad on urgent business matters of his own, which seems remarkably timely, if I may say so."

"You may not," the judge told him. "It's not your place to offer comments of that sort, Mr. Delacey. Confine yourself to the answers required of you, if you please."

Breda felt sick, listening to them all. It seemed to her that Richard had been tried and found guilty long ago and all this was only a formality. Mr. Flowers gave Richard every possible assistance in showing himself to be an upright engineer who had nothing to gain by withholding the dangerous condition of Wheal Breda, but every time the other barrister undermined him with skillful words and phrases.

Eventually Sam Stone was asked to give his evidence, and Breda held her breath as the scurrilous accusations rang out.

"I had my doubts about his engineering ability the minute I saw him," he sneered. "What do Irish engineers know about tin mining?"

"Just the facts, Mr. Stone," the barrister reminded him, seeing that the judge was about to intervene.

"Well, he said there was seepage, but every tinner knows there ain't nothing new about seepage. Show me a mine under the sea where there ain't seepage and I'll show you a miracle!"

"But the props and ladders?" the barrister prompted him.

"Me and my men used 'em every day on every shift, and we thought they were as solid as rocks. It weren't no act of God that brought 'em down," he said piously. "It were that man's neglect, and my men want to see justice done!"

He pointed a dramatic finger at Richard as he spoke, and immediately there was a fresh uproar in the courtroom and the public gallery all around Breda, with most of the hecklers bellowing for Richard's blood.

She saw Mr. Flowers move forward to question Sam Stone.

"Do you deny that you were in a certain Penzance hostelry with Mr. Amos Keighley and several Wheal Breda tinners one night? Do you deny that you bragged about how you had slashed at the pit props to weaken them, so that a slight landfall could discredit Mr. Delacey in the event that he hadn't put in a report recommending urgent repairs?"

Breda held her breath at Mr. Flowers's sudden staccato questioning. She saw the judge look up more intently, and Sam Stone's eyes narrowed.

"I'm often to be found in some hostelry," he snapped. "And any man who says I was bragging about slashing pit props is a bloody liar—"

"And what if a woman says it!" Without warning, Breda heard herself shout out the words. She was on her feet, her eyes blazing down at the hated man below.

"Madam, please be quiet," the judge ordered at once. "I'll have no female intervention in this court—"

"Sir, my name is Mrs. Richard Delacey, and my father was Justin Vivien of Vivien Hall and the owner of the Vivien tin mines—"

"I don't care if you're the Queen of Sheba, Madam," he thundered back at her, and then glowered at Mr. Flowers. "And you, Sir, I suggest you advise this woman to keep quiet, since it can only jeopardize your client's case. We will adjourn for fifteen minutes."

He swept out of the courtroom attended by his scurrying assistants, and there was a buzz of noise all around Breda from people who hadn't realized who she was. There was also a mixture of sympathetic glances and catcalls from those who did. She saw Mr. Flowers wave her to the anteroom at the entrance of the courtroom, and when she got there she faced him and Richard. Red-faced, she felt her mouth tremble at their furious faces.

"I was only trying to help!"

"I've already told you to keep quiet, Breda," Flowers said sharply. "The more you rile the judge, the less chance Mr. Delacey has of winning his case."

"Why don't you go home?" Richard said. "There's nothing you can do here."

"Are you mad?" she asked him, hardly believing she had heard him aright. "How could I rest, not knowing what was happening here?"

She ached to put her arms around him and kiss away

all the worry in his face, but he was so remote, so far away from her, caught up in a man's world where he didn't even want her help. She felt choked.

"Then do as Mr. Flowers tells you. This is hard enough for me without worrying about an outburst from you every so often. I don't need a wife to defend me."

"You don't need a wife at all," she said, and for a moment there were only the two of them staring at each other, hurt and bitter, neither knowing how to reach the other.

Mr. Flowers turned to her briskly. "I think the judge will stop proceedings for today very soon," he said. "He rarely wants it to go on much longer than this and he'll want to weigh up the evidence so far."

Breda turned her anger on him.

"When are you going to bring out all the things I told you I overheard at the inn! Sam Stone hardly flinched when you tackled him about slashing at the pit props. Why don't you force Amos to admit that they arranged the so-called accident, and that Sam was meant to delay the new shift long enough to get the men out? Why don't you make him admit that he was drunk and didn't do it? It was his neglect, not Richard's that caused those men to drown. I *told* you all that, so why don't you use it?"

"I'd be grateful if you would leave the legal business to me, Breda. There's a time for being cautious and a time for shocking them with new evidence. If it happens too soon, it can ruin everything. It's far better to let them think they've almost won and be off their guard before we throw everything we've got at them. I've written down every detail of the conversation you overheard, so rest assured I haven't forgotten it."

She had to control her frustration at this, knowing she would have blurted out everything at once and admitting that he knew his business better than she did. They heard a bell ring for recall to the courtroom in five minutes and as they made to leave, Richard caught hold of her hands.

"Do as he says, my love."

She nodded, feeling her throat thicken. She was so weak, to be so affected by a soft word from him. But she simply couldn't help it. She loved him, and seemed to have always loved him, and she desperately wanted to tell him so.

"Richard—"

"Will you please go on ahead, Mr. Delacey, while I have a few private words with Breda?" she heard Flowers say, and the moment was gone.

Numbly, she waited to hear whatever new admonishment the barrister was about to give her. If he was about to forbid her to attend the hearing at all, then he reckoned without her, she thought grittily.

"How much do you want to help your husband?" he began quietly, and she gave a cracked laugh.

"I hardly think you need to ask me such a thing! Richard is the most important thing in my life, and I'd give anything to see Sam Stone and Amos Keighley brought to justice for what they've done to him. I won't leave, so don't ask it of me! Even though I don't know how I can bear to sit there and listen to everything going so badly. It *is* going badly, isn't it?" Her voice shook as she asked the question.

"There's a good deal of weighty evidence against us," he said stolidly.

"But it's all lies! You know it is! Do you think Philip would have trusted Richard so completely if he hadn't been an honorable man? You knew my brother—"

"Your brother's not here to testify to your husband's character, my dear," he reminded her, "and the court will act on what it sees, not on hearsay."

"Does that include the things I heard at the inn? Are you trying to tell me no one will believe my evidence?"

"Not entirely," he said carefully. "But this is what I want to discuss with you."

Chapter Nineteen

When they returned to Vivien Hall at the end of the first day, Richard spoke aggressively. Far from looking beaten by the damning false evidence of Sam Stone and Amos Keighley, followed by that of the committee official, he wore the look of a man who had come to a definite decision and didn't intend being opposed.

"Breda, you're to stay away from the remainder of the trial," he ordered. "You're doing me no good at all by being there, and every time you make an outburst, you make things worse. And I'm warning you, I won't be disobeyed in this even if I have to lock you in the bedroom—"

"All right! I agree with you!" she said quickly. Too quickly, because she saw his eyes narrow at once.

"I mean what I say. And no amount of wheedling will make me change my mind. I'd be a bloody fool if I thought things weren't going atrociously, despite what Flowers says, and I've no wish for my wife to witness my humiliation."

"You speak as if we've already lost!" she muttered.

"No. I speak as a realist," he said grimly. "Now I

need to be alone for a while, so I'll be in your father's study until it's time for dinner."

He made no attempt to touch her, or comfort her. It was just as if he couldn't see how deeply his pain was affecting her too. He couldn't see, or he didn't care. But how could she blame him, when those evil men had so stoutly sworn together that no report had been submitted to the Stannary Committee, and when Mr. Flowers had challenged them on the so-called discussion at the Duck and Whistle, they had violently denied everything?

Now it seemed that Richard simply didn't want her in any way. In any true marriage, a man needed his wife's support . . . but theirs was anything but a true marriage, Breda thought bitterly, and he was too proud to want her pity, or admit how much he needed her.

As if to prove her completely wrong, he turned to her that night in the darkness of their bedroom. Needing her then, perhaps, more basically than wanting her mere presence amidst the harshness of those who had already condemned him.

He reached out for her in the night, and as always she responded without a second thought, as the sweet familiarity of his touch invaded her half-sleeping senses. She felt the slight roughness of his hand as it palmed her breast, and then her body's tingling reaction as he gently squeezed and fondled her. She held her breath, wanting him so much, but knowing how unpredictable his moods were of late, hardly daring to speak or move in case she broke the spell of these fragile moments.

She felt his mouth seek out her breast and then the

sensual tonguing of her aroused nipple. First one, and then the other . . . the swift heat of passion spread through her body like fire as she held him close. Her eyes were half closed as the exquisitely pleasurable sensations began to burst within her as his hands and mouth explored every part of her, and the preliminaries to loving went on . . .

And then, just as she sensed that neither of them could delay their joining a moment longer, she heard him give a harsh laugh, and he pushed her away from him.

"So much for wishing, my darling," he said, with savage mockery. "It seems that even my body betrays me, and such pleasures must wait for another time. Always supposing that my accusers allow me many more nights on this earth, of course."

She lay dumbly beside him as he turned away from her. Somehow she knew instinctively that there was no place for sympathy or understanding in his mind at that moment. He would only feel even more humiliated and emasculated if she tried to tell him it didn't matter and that one night's failure didn't mean the end of anything. To a man like Richard, any kind of failure mattered, and when it was a question of his very manhood betraying him, it was an assault on everything that he was.

He was gone from the bedroom when she awoke the next morning, and with unsteady hands she pulled the bell rope for her washing water to be brought upstairs. Instead, the maid brought her breakfast in bed, saying it was on her husband's orders.

"I'm not ill," Breda said crossly, struggling to sit up, and the remembered misery of last night filling her at once. "And I'd prefer to have my breakfast downstairs with Mr. Delacey, so just bring me my washing water as usual."

"He's gone, Madam."

Breda felt her heart lurch.

"What do you mean, he's gone?"

The girl raised her shoulders expressively. "He left over an hour ago for Penzance and said you weren't to be disturbed on any account until you rang, since you were very tired."

So Richard had gone to the courthouse without her. Breda looked quickly at her little clock and saw that the day had already begun. Her curtains hadn't been drawn back and the bedroom was still in semi-darkness so she had been quite unaware of the time. He had done this deliberately. And today was so vitally important . . . she flung back the bedclothes and snapped at the gaping girl.

"Take the breakfast away and never mind about fresh water. I'll use what's in the jug from yesterday. And send Mrs. Yandle to me at once."

The maid backed out of the room hastily at this unusual display of temper from her mistress. Moments later Mrs. Yandle appeared, her eyes widening as Breda gave her swift and explicit instructions in a tone that warned anyone to question her.

"Are you sure you know what you're about, lovey?" she couldn't resist asking all the same. "Mr. Delacey was very firm in saying you wouldn't be going to the trial today."

"I know exactly what I'm about, Yandie," she said

determinedly. "And even Richard wouldn't have a snowball in Hades' chance of stopping me now."

By the end of the morning the noise in the court-room was becoming deafening. Anyone crowding in for the kill was convinced that the case against Richard Delacey for negligence was as good as proven, and the judge had difficulty in making himself heard above the din as he hammered for silence.

"I shall clear this court if there's any further disturbance," he thundered. "Now then, Mr. Flowers, you say you have a last minute witness to prove your statements regarding the characters of Mr. Samuel Stone and Amos Keighley. I fail to see how this can have any bearing on the case."

"But it does, Sir. It concerns the night at the Duck and Whistle Inn when I suggested to them that they discussed the weakening of the pit props at Wheal Breda and Sam Stone's intention to get the men out in time before any real danger occurred. Also, the accusation that if Stone hadn't been drunk at the time, he would have attended to his task, which was arranged between himself and Amos Keighley. My client upholds the fact that because of all the circumstances it's these two, and not himself, who should be on trial here for murder."

Judge Wilson had to bellow for silence again at the uproar this produced, and this time the guffaws from Sam and Amos were among the loudest. Only Penrose, one time tinner from Wheal Breda, looked uneasily at the other two and then down at his own shuffling feet.

"I want to call on a young man who was present in the inn on that evening and is prepared to swear to everything in the statement I gave you," Flowers said loudly, at which the heckling began to dwindle away. Richard Delacey looked sharply at the barrister, having heard nothing of this new development, while Sam and Amos whispered quickly together.

"Very well," said the judge.

Flowers walked to the side of the courtroom and beckoned to a slight figure waiting in the anteroom alongside. A figure wearing cheap clothes, a cap pulled well down over his face and a scarf around his throat and the lower half of his face. Flowers gave him a brief smile and faced the judge.

"Sir, I intend to prove that Sam Stone and Amos Keighley conspired to incriminate an innocent man for their own gain, namely that of obtaining Vivien Hall by foul means, the details of which have already been explained to you. As it happens, that is a fact totally denied to Mr. Amos Keighley now, since Vivien Hall has been legally sold by Mrs. Breda Vivien Delacey—"

"What!" Amos Keighley was on his feet now, his face purple with rage. "The bitch can't do that. I've every right to the place once she's out of the way, and I'll swear that she knew just what her husband was about in not sending in his report—"

"Once the terms of the entailment had been fully executed, Mrs. Delacey was legally allowed to sell at any time," Flowers said calmly. "I can assure you that you have absolutely no claim on the property now."

Impatiently, Richard began to wonder why he was taking this line of discussion, though the sight of Sam and Amos fighting verbally and noisily between themselves gave him a grim pleasure. Before the judge could also intervene and question Flowers on what appeared to be a diversion, Flowers spoke rapidly to the young boy standing awkwardly in the dock.

"I would like you to tell this court exactly what you overheard on the night in question. You've already told me about the two men gloating over their plot to discredit both Mr. and Mrs. Delacey and that you can identify the tinners who were present at the Duck and Whistle, but I'd like you to tell it in your own words, so that justice can be done."

There was a small silence, and then Sam Stone's voice bellowed out, though noticeably hoarser than usual.

"The little runt can't play your game, you bastard, because he's one of they Frenchies and don't understand a word of English."

Flowers looked at him with interest.

"Can you explain to the court just how you know these facts, Sir, when you deny that you ever met Mr. Keighley at the Duck and Whistle?"

Amos swore viciously as Sam fell silent with fury at being trapped so neatly. "All right, so we were there that night! But we know the lad was French and couldn't speak any English, so don't try that trickery with us!"

"And what if he's not French? What if that was trickery too?"

Out of the corner of her eye, Breda saw Penrose's face go a sickly color.

"Sam, we only had the serving-girl's word for it," he burst out hoarsely. "It could all have been a trick —"

"Shut up, you bloody fool," Sam shouted back.

371

The judge hammered on the table for silence, and told Flowers to continue. The barrister looked directly at his witness.

"Will you tell everyone what you heard?" he said gently.

Breda spoke in a husky voice that was nothing like her own. In any case, it was muffled by the scarf around her face, but it was still clear enough to be heard. She hardly needed to try and disguise her voice, because it was hoarse with fear at all that was happening. If all went well, their enemies would condemn themselves. If it didn't . . .

She pointed directly at Sam and Amos, visibly stunned now by the enormity of how the tables were being turned on them. She heard them gasp as she began to speak in a Cornish accent.

"Those two men discussed how they had plotted against Mr. Delacey, and how Sam Stone had neglected to get the men out of Wheal Breda in time to stop them from drowning. They're the ones responsible for the deaths of twelve men—"

She had to pause while the deafening courtroom noise broke out again, and she saw how Richard's knuckles were white as he clenched his hands together. The others may not recognize her yet, but he would know exactly who this surprise witness was now, and he'd be hating this deception, just as he had hated the thought of her going to the inn in the first place. But these were desperate times, and in such times desperate measures must be taken. She looked away from him and plunged on.

"There were several tinners present, and they too could testify if they were brave enough. If they had any consideration for the Vivien family who always treated them fairly they would do so—"

"You young swine. You tricked us, pretending to be a Frenchie!" Sam shouted, beside himself now. "Who's paying you for these lies?"

"They're not lies."

A new voice was heard among the rest. Penrose's voice was heavy with shame, but loud enough for him to be pushed and shoved by those nearest him for him to be questioned properly.

"Will you testify to everything that my witness has said?"

"Everything," Penrose said bitterly. "Including the fact that Sam Stone bribed the committee man to keep back Mr. Delacey's report. What the boy says is all true, and I hope the other tinners who heard it have guts enough to swear to it. The Viviens always did right by us, and 'tis up to us not to see a good man hanged for the likes of Sam Stone."

"You stupid bastard!" Sam and Amos were still raging, but gradually one after another tinner who'd been at the inn that night stood up and vouched for what Penrose was saying, until it was obvious who were the guilty ones.

"And what of the report that Mr. Delacey supposedly sent to the Stannary Committee?" Flowers went on relentlessly to Penrose. "Do you know anything of that?"

"Aye. I know that Sam Stone persuaded him to delay presenting it, since he was so sure there was no danger at Wheal Breda."

"I'll kill you for this, you swine," Sam yelled out, but it was obvious by now that opinion in the court had turned heavily against him.

Judge Wilson held up his hand for silence. "It seems clear that we have the wrong man in custody, but thankfully a great wrong has been avoided by the evidence of this young witness, despite his rather dramatic last-minute appearance. Mr. Delacey, you are free to leave this court. In view of the gravity of what has transpired, Stone and Keighley will be detained behind bars until a new trial begins. The question of the accomplices will be dealt with separately."

"Aye, it's just as well you're keeping us behind bars," Sam shrieked out, gone completely berserk now and having to be held back by officials as he lashed out at anyone standing near. "If you weren't, I'd kill that little bastard who did for us."

He was standing quite close to Breda now, and very slowly, she unwound the scarf from her neck and chin. Not taking her eyes off him for a moment, she removed the stable boy's cap and shook out her long dark hair. She didn't say a word, but the contempt in her green eyes said it all.

She heard the shocked gasps run around the courtroom as people realized the identity of the surprise witness, and saw how the faces of Sam and Amos blanched with shock and fury.

"*You!*" Amos spluttered.

"Yes, cousin, it's me. How do you like knowing that I was that miserable little French boy supposedly unable to understand a word you were saying that night?"

She said the words, but she couldn't even glory in her moment of triumph. She felt too sickened at knowing how closely they had averted what would have been a certain death sentence for Richard. She closed her eyes, not wanting to look at the two men any longer as they were taken away, and then she heard Penrose's halting voice nearby.

"I'm sorry, Ma'am. None of it was my idea, and if I could turn back the clock I'd do it in a minute—"

"It's too late for turning back clocks, man," Richard said harshly. "We're thankful you spoke up when you did, but you'll still have to face certain charges, so you'd better look to yourself and your family and never mind us now."

Breda was beginning to shake. Now that the tension of this terrible trial was over, what she had done was just starting to sink in. She stood mutely while people milled around, congratulating them both, shaking her hand and then Richard's . . . and all she wanted was to be away from here and alone with him.

Finally, Mr. Flowers bundled them away from the crowds and into the ante-room where Breda's own clothes were folded tidily behind a screen. She had got her wish to be alone with Richard, but instead of folding her into his arms, he took her by the shoulders and shook her hard.

"I ought to break your neck," he said harshly.

"Oh, don't think I didn't know how you'd hate my playacting!" she burst out. "But don't you see, it was the only way! They would never have admitted anything without suddenly realizing they'd been overheard in the Duck and Whistle, and you'd be on your way to a hanging by now. Were you so ashamed of seeing your wife dressed like a boy that you can't even credit me with saving your life? Or is it the fact of a woman coming to your rescue that your male pride can't stomach?" she finished bitterly.

For a moment he didn't say anything, and then he snatched her to him so fast the breath was almost knocked out of her.

"For God's sake get out of those ridiculous garments and be yourself again," he said roughly. "I've no wish to be pointed out for embracing a young boy!"

"You do intend to embrace me again, then?" she said, her voice cracked.

"I'll give it some thought," he said with a kind of grim humor, "but not right now. Change your clothes and let's get away from here. I've seen enough of this place."

It was almost too much to hope that everything was going to be wonderful from then on, Breda thought. The reason for their marriage and all its repercussions still weighed heavily on both of them, overshadowing now the fact that Richard's innocence in the Wheal Breda affair was widely publicized and the right villains about to be brought to justice. Breda knew Mary Keighley wouldn't grieve too much at her husband's hanging. But the three children were about to lose a father, and Breda ached at the thought of their coming sadness. She said as much to Richard.

"They're young," he said, after a week when they seemed to do nothing but answer the door to wellwishers. "They'll get over it, and it won't be so hard for them to start again in their new surroundings."

Breda couldn't fail to notice the emptiness in his voice. All that week since the trial ended, he had seemed very far away from her, just when she had hoped they could begin a new phase in their lives. His

376

words reminded her of the appointment they had that afternoon. She glanced at the grandfather clock in the corner of the drawing room.

"Graham Hocking will be expecting us at the Crown Hotel soon. I'm glad I sold Vivien Hall to him, Richard. I wouldn't want to stay here now," she said slowly, only just realizing the full truth of it.

"Sometimes I wish I'd never seen the place," he said savagely, shocking her into silence for a moment.

She could hardly blame him. If he'd never met Philip Vivien, and through him, seen Breda's sketchy likeness; if he'd never promised to bring Philip's belongings home and made the inspection of Wheal Breda; if Breda herself hadn't agreed to marry him for less than honest reasons of her own . . . there were so many ifs, she thought dispiritedly. So many reasons why he must hate her, and although initially he'd teased and taunted her with every intention of marrying her, she guessed he must be regretting the day he ever set eyes on her now.

She spoke in a shaky voice. "We don't have to continue with this farce of a marriage. Once Graham Hocking has settled on a date to move in here, I shall go to Helston to stay with my aunt and uncle for the time being until I decide what to do. You can arrange to finish the marriage any way you like."

He didn't answer for few minutes and when he did he didn't look at her.

"My father will think it highly questionable if I return to Ireland without you for a second time. He's getting old, and it will be enough of a shock when I tell him all that's happened here these past weeks, without worrying about the state of our marriage," he said shortly. "Once the date with Hocking is settled, we will leave for Grensham. You will accompany me and behave like a wife. Is that clear?"

Breda stared at him. He was a stranger she didn't know. She bowed her head, knowing she had no real choice. She could run away, but he would find her. And what was the point of it all? Without him she was nothing anyway. She hated herself for her weakness, but she seemed to have no will of her own any more.

"It's perfectly clear," she mumbled.

Even at the Crown Hotel in Penzance there were people who nodded and smiled at them both, as if the Delaceys had suddenly become heroes in the community. It was so ironic to have people so happy for them, thought Breda, when the two of them were less happy than they had ever been in their lives. They had ridden into the town on horseback, both deciding they needed the exercise and the caress of the moor land breezes blowing through their senses. Graham Hocking greeted them with obvious pleasure.

"My dear Mrs. Delacey, I'm so pleased for you both," he said simply. "And you Sir, must be mightily relieved at the outcome of it all, and endlessly grateful to this clever wife of yours."

"Oh yes, I have a very clever wife," Richard said, and Breda wished to heaven that Hocking hadn't used those particular words. But he evidently didn't hear the sarcasm in Richard's voice that she did, and set about ordering tea for them all.

"By the by, I've been to see Mrs. Keighley," he remarked, "and assured her that the arrangement is quite legal and her future home is assured. She's a fine woman, and the three children will undoubtedly benefit from a more settled environment than they had previously. I gather the father was not the most sensitive of men. Mrs. Keighley tells me he frequently beat them and that they always cowered when he appeared."

"Really?" Breda said. "It seems she confided in you more than she did in me then, Mr. Hocking."

"I'm sorry! I assumed you knew, or I would never have been so indiscreet as to repeat it," he said hastily.

"It's no matter now," Richard put in. "Shall we get down to the matter we've come here for? Namely, to decide when you want us out of Vivien Hall, and I suggest the sooner the better for all concerned."

Breda blushed at his brusqueness, but it seemed she was the only one to notice it. She knew she was becoming overly sensitive to every nuance in his voice lately, but as the two men began to talk together, her mind wandered a little. So Graham Hocking had been to see Mary and thought her a fine woman. And he was obviously taken with the children. Perhaps in time, events would turn out as she had fancifully surmised after all . . .

"Shall I leave you to discuss the details while I go to see Mary?" she said suddenly. "Whatever date you decide on will suit us, Mr. Hocking, and I know my husband is anxious to return to Ireland. I shan't be gone long."

"Take as long as you like. We'll have plenty to talk about until you come back," Richard said, as if he cared little whether she went or stayed.

Breda bit her lip as she left the hotel, her eyes starting to sting at the way everything had gone so wrong.

The one good thing—the one *tremendously* good thing—was that he hadn't been found guilty at the trial. She had lost her home, but she already knew that it no longer mattered where she lived if she didn't have Richard. It would be a bitter mockery to go to Grensham and act the happy bride, but if he insisted that she did it for a while, if only for his father's peace of mind, then she would do it.

She reached the cottage near the beach, and found Mary hanging out the childrens' clothes on the washing line. There would be maids to do that for her at Vivien Hall. Mary's life too, was about to undergo a vast change. She turned as soon as she heard her name called, and Breda saw how pale she was. She felt suddenly nervous, knowing that Mary must be blaming her for her husband's fall from grace. It was all due to Breda Vivien after all. Everything was . . .

Mary walked across to her quickly, and took her hands in her own. "I'm right glad to see you, Breda. I wanted to come to the house, but I felt it was best to wait a while, for fear it might have looked as if I was—well, you know, looking over where I was going to live." She stopped abruptly, a tinge of color coming into her face.

"It's all right, you don't have to feel awkward with me, Mary. I've just left Richard with Graham Hocking to sort things out—"

"He came to see me. He I a good man, Breda." The color went deeper, and she turned away. "But come into the cottage and have a bite."

"I don't want anything, thank you, I just came to see that you're all right. I'm so sorry—about Amos, Mary. Oh, you'll think that's a stupid thing for me to say in the circumstances, but I'm sure you'll be feeling — well, because of the children — "

It was simply impossible to find the right words, and Breda gave up trying. Mary patted her hand as they went indoors.

"Don't try explaining. The children know what's happened, and Harry understands even if the little 'uns don't. What's done can't be undone, and they'll learn to accept that. And I know I got on my high horse when you first offered us a home and a tutor for Harry, but now I'm more grateful to you than I can ever say, Breda. I know we'll be all right."

She would, too. Even though she had gone through a bad time explaining everything to the children, already she looked different. And to Breda's imaginative mind, the idea of her and Graham Hocking getting together one day wasn't such an impossibility after all . . .

"I may not manage to see you again before we leave for Ireland, but I'll write to you, Mary," she said. "I don't want to lose all my links with Cornwall, and you must call on my friend Nan as well. I'm sure you and she could become friends. And you can give me news of the children and Mrs. Yandle."

"I'd like that. You know how I wish you well, Breda. Write and tell me when there's a babby on the way too."

Breda smiled, her eyes suddenly too bright, and said that she must be going. She hugged Mary quickly. There was no sign of the children, but she was glad of that. Right now she couldn't bear to see them. She was just beginning to realize that Mary Keighley already had so much . . .

By the time she reached the Crown Hotel, Richard was waiting for her outside. He told her that he and Graham Hocking had fixed on a week from today for him to move into Vivien Hall.

"Does it give you enough time?" he asked. "I assumed that you'd want it all done as soon as possible now."

"It'll do," she said listlessly, hardly caring where she went any more. As for how soon—the sooner she left her past behind the better, even if she had no idea of her real future.

Once they had ridden through the town and were up on the moors, she spurred her animal on to a gallop, partly because she was suddenly finding it difficult to breathe, and partly so that Richard wouldn't see the bitter tears that stung her eyes.

If they hadn't been so blurred, she might have seen the rotted stump ahead, and swerved the horse in time. As it was, he stumbled and almost fell, and Breda shot over his back onto the turf, to land with a crack on her head. She was completely winded, but still conscious for a few dazed moments. And then, just as she heard Richard's anguished cry and felt him holding her tight, the world seemed to slide away.

When she awoke she realized at once that she was in her own bed, but her head still hurt with a dull ache and she didn't open her eyes more than a fraction. She seemed to be in some kind of vice . . . with a little shock she discovered that the vice-like grip was Richard's arms. Through her half-closed lids she saw that it was dark outside, so she must have been here for some time. A fire had been lit in the fireplace for her comfort. Someone had undressed her, and Richard's breath was warm on her skin as his head lay across her breasts. He was muttering raggedly, as if the words were torn from him, and constantly repeated like a litany.

"Dear God, don't let her die before I have a chance to tell her how much I love her. Neither of us has been totally honest in our relationship, but give us a second chance. At least I wasn't dishonest in promising to love and cherish her, even if she never knew it. Give me another chance to make her know that I love her more than life—"

Breda struggled to open her eyes, her hand tremulously reaching out to stroke the thick dark hair as Richard's head jerked upward at her movement.

"Richard—" she whispered.

"Thank God," he said hoarsely. "I was so afraid—"

"I heard. You were afraid you'd never have the chance to tell me you loved me." She trembled as she spoke, wondering if she really had heard him say it, or if she'd still been dreaming.

For a second his eyes sparkled, and she felt her mouth shake. Was he going to deny it even now? Pride was such a foolish thing to keep them apart, and hers no longer mattered.

"I'm never going to go away from you, Richard. Not if you love me as much as I love you."

He gave a strangled groan. "Love you? I've loved you far longer than you know. You were always mine, Breda, but when we met, you were even more beautiful than I'd imagined, and the only way I could hide my feelings was to be brash and arrogant. You had every right to hate me—"

"But I never did. And it's not hate that I feel for you

now, Richard. You know that I love you and I always want to be with you—"

She was caught up in his arms again, her spirit soaring to meet him on a emotional tide.

"We've wasted so much time, my darling," he said huskily.

"But we needn't waste any more," she said, and then blushed at her brazenness, suddenly shy for the first time with him as the firelight shone in her eyes, making her meaning clear.

"You had quite a crack on your head, love, and the doctor said you shouldn't have too much excitement," he said, his relief at her quick recovery making him tease, even while she felt the certain evidence of his arousal.

"I'm sure my head will survive, but I'm not sure that I will if you persist in treating me like porcelain. You could, of course, be gentle with me," she said, teasing him back.

And then all the teasing was over, as Richard held his wife in his arms and proceeded to show her that love that was sensual and gentle could be just as spectacular as when it was wild and tempestuous. And despite all that had gone before, Breda felt immeasurably blessed, knowing she had everything she had ever wanted. She had always believed in destiny, and he was hers.